SCARBOUND

CASTLES OF THE EYRIE
BOOK TWO

EVIE MARCEAU

CHAPTER I

**A DRESS FOR AN ENGAGEMENT . . . maiden roses .
. . like a prisoner . . . beating wings**

The day of Bryn Lindane's engagement party was the most miserable of her life.

She'd tossed and turned all night in the small bed tucked away in Barendur Hold's mage chambers, dreaming of terrible things: sea monsters rising from the deep, lambs slaughtered by wolves in the castle's livestock pens, faceless ghosts hovering in her room's corners. But of all the disturbing images her sleeping mind had conjured, none was worse than the alarming reality that she faced: Rangar Barendur, the prince who had saved her life and was bound to her heart and soul, had been sent off to war as a pretense so he couldn't object to Bryn marrying his brother.

She woke shivering in the small room.

Rangar's broken heart will be the real nightmare when he returns and finds me married to Trei, she thought.

Ever since she'd become the crown heir to the Mir throne—and thus had a target painted on her back—the Barendur family who had taken her in had sworn to protect her. Their kingdom, the Baersladen, couldn't be more different from the Mirien, where she'd been raised. Her childhood homeland was sunshine and far-reaching fields. Rangar's was storm and sea. Hers was manners, education, and science. His was rough living and magic. Even their castles were complete opposites. Castle Mir was all refinement and opulence, and Barendur Hold was a squat monolith where most of the castle's residents, servants, and livestock slept together on the floor during the coldest winter months.

It had taken some getting used to, but Bryn had grown comfortable with the communal living style in Barendur Hold, even begun to admire it. Still, she was more than happy to have the privacy of her own room, small as it was. She craved the space to think, and now she had plenty to occupy her mind.

Tossing back her bedcovers, she reached for a shawl to wrap around her shoulders. Now that the first hints of winter were approaching, she could never seem to get warm. Growing up in the Mirien where the weather was always mild and snow was a rare sight hadn't prepared her for the extreme conditions in the Outlands. She feared the worst of winter.

Then again, there was a chance she wouldn't even *be* in the Baersladen come winter. There was a throne in the Mirien waiting for her—though she wasn't prepared to sit on it.

Someone knocked on her door.

She snapped out of her brooding reveries and hugged the shawl closer around her body. "Come in."

The door opened for Mage Marna, the kingdom's head mage and Rangar's aunt. Behind her was an older woman Bryn recognized as Helna, the seamstress who had altered Saraj's gown to fit Bryn on the night of the Harvest Gathering.

"Lady Bryn," Mage Marna said, folding her hands together. "I'm sorry to wake you, but we have much to do to prepare for your upcoming nuptials. Helna has come to take your measurements for your wedding gown."

The color drained from Bryn's face.

As a girl, she'd never given much thought to what her wedding gown might one day look like. Of course, she'd assumed she'd marry a duke, as her sister had, or perhaps a baron or count, and that her royal wedding would be a formal three-day affair amid the manicured gardens of Castle Mir as was the custom.

Instead, she was practically eloping at knifepoint.

She dug the heel of her hand against the heartache that was blooming in her chest. Her poor heart had felt like a beaten and battered little bird ever since she'd been confronted with the impossible choice of love or duty, her happiness or her kingdom's safety. A voice in her head urged her to reject the wedding dress—to reject *the whole thing*. It was Rangar who had her heart, not Trei! For as noble and dashing as the eldest prince was, she had no desire to marry him. To sleep at his side every night, to bear his children. The thought alone made her blanche. But the harsh truth was, she didn't have a choice. The Barendur family wasn't forcing her into this marriage—her own sense of responsibility was. The only way to save her kingdom was to unite the Baersladen and the Mirien through political marriage.

"The dress. Y..yes." Bryn tried to hide how her hands were shaking as she stood and shrugged off the shawl.

Helna approached with a warm smile, though her eyes shone with pity. Everyone in the kingdom knew of Rangar and Bryn's romance—it had been the topic of gossip for months. So it was no surprise that the common folk were as shocked as Bryn to hear it wouldn't be *Rangar's* ring on her finger any longer, but Trei's.

"There, there, my lady," Helna said kindly. "We'll get you a beautiful dress. You'll be a gorgeous bride."

Bryn couldn't muster even a pretend smile. The last thing she cared about was a dress when her heart was being torn in two!

As the dressmaker began to take her measurements with a length of string, Bryn turned to Mage

Marna and asked apprehensively, "Has a formal announcement been made yet about the wedding?"

Mage Marna continued to fold her hands tightly, and Bryn realized she was just as tense and uncertain about this change of plans as Bryn was.

The mage gave a tight nod. "Yes, word went out at first light. A wreath of maiden roses was hung in the village square—that is how we publicly declare royal marriages. We would usually send out messengers to all the villages of the Baersladen with word of the nuptials and an invitation for all who can to attend, but in this case, we've decided to keep the affair small. Only those here at the Hold and in the portside village will attend. After the wedding, we'll send out messengers to announce the . . . good news."

Mage Marna didn't specifically mention why they were waiting to send out messengers until after the wedding, but Bryn knew. They didn't want to risk word of it reaching Rangar, who was fighting at the border of the Baersladen. He would move mountains to ride back and stop the wedding if he heard.

"Of course," Bryn echoed hollowly.

Helna finished taking measurements and squeezed Bryn's shoulder. "I'll be back tomorrow for a fitting."

As soon as the seamstress left, Mage Marna paced the length of Bryn's small room. "The ceremony will be held tomorrow just before sunset. We've requested that the castle tradespeople stop all other work and focus on constructing a wooden stage in the village square. The kitchen workers will bake all night to prepare for the feast that will follow the ceremony. And lessons have been suspended today and tomorrow for all children so they can go into the fields and gather maiden roses for decorations."

Bryn gazed down at Rangar's ring on her finger, knowing she'd soon have to take it off. *Even though I'm not ready to. I'll never be ready to.*

She said quietly, "I don't see the point in making it a grand affair. If I must go through with this wedding, can't Trei and I simply be married by a vicar in the courtyard with the family as witnesses?"

A shadow crossed over Mage Marna's face. Her lips pressed together tightly before she admitted, "There is much unease in the Eyrie; it won't do if you look miserable as our two kingdoms unite, or worse, if you and Trei marry in secret as though it's a scandal. That is why we are doing what we can to portray this as a joyous occasion to convince our two populaces to accept and celebrate the change. While I have sympathy for your situation, you still must present yourself as a happy bride. Do you understand?"

Bryn ran a hand over her face, trying to ease the ache that was beginning at her temples. "I do. I don't like it, but I do."

She expected the mage to leave, but instead, Mage Marna went to the narrow bedroom window and looked out over the ocean. When she spoke again, her voice had lowered.

"I know you have your own difficult feelings about this marriage, but I think we should consider what will happen when Rangar returns. My nephew has always been prone to a rageful temper." The mage knit her fingers together, troubled. "King Aleth has already vowed that if Rangar attempts to invalidate the marriage or . . . or engages in any form of adultery that could jeopardize the marriage's legitimacy, Rangar will be thrown in the dungeon until his temper cools. It would be best if you keep your distance from him when he does return. Don't speak with him, especially not in private."

Bryn felt a flush of indignation at the mage's words. "If you're implying that I might be unfaithful to Trei, I take offense at that."

"I know my nephew," Mage Marna said, finally facing her. "Rangar can be forceful when he doesn't get his way. I only want to prepare you."

The firm set of the mage's mouth softened, and she gently touched Bryn's face. "You have a good heart, Lady Bryn. I doubt your parents would have made the sacrifice you are making. Giving up love takes courage. You will be an effective ruler for your people."

Her hand fell away from Bryn's cheek, but instead of leaving, she touched the small hexmark on Bryn's ear.

Dropping her voice, the mage added, "You also show promise as an apprentice. I know the Mir people abhor magic, but you have the potential to be a new type of ruler. You could usher in an era where magic is accepted alongside science in your kingdom." She let her hand fall from Bryn's ear. "Something to think about."

Bryn's eyes widened. It was a bold—even treasonous—suggestion.

After they were finished, Bryn got some bread from the kitchen as a meager breakfast, avoiding all the excited questions that the servants peppered her with about the wedding, and tried to escape the gossip and curious looks by leaving Barendur Hold. She'd planned on taking a walk to clear her head, but she was surprised when the gate guards stopped her.

"Sorry, my lady. We can't let you through."

"I just want to go to the pastures," she said, motioning to the hills beyond the castle. "Only for a few moments of fresh air."

One of the guards shook his head forcefully. "King Aleth's orders. You're to remain within Barendur Hold until after the wedding. No exceptions. It's for your own safety."

Bryn balked. It was true that Captain Carr, the current usurper of the Mir throne, had likely sent spies and perhaps even assassins after her, so she couldn't deny that Aleth's order made sense. She *shouldn't* be leaving the safety of the castle. But it was hard not to feel like a hostage.

Back inside, the castle walls began to close in on her. Everyone she passed wanted to congratulate her on the upcoming marriage, their eyes gleaming with unspoken curiosity.

They know I'm in love with Rangar, she thought to

herself. *They're wondering if I'll go through with this…and what will happen when Rangar returns.*

Finally, desperate for fresh air and privacy, she climbed the tower stairs and stepped out onto the castle's flat roof. A pair of sentries sat around the beacon fire in the far corner, but they barely glanced her way as she hurried to the opposite corner, where she'd long ago discovered an abandoned pigeon house. It was the closest thing she'd had to a private space before Mage Marna had given her a room in the mage chambers.

Within the crumbling walls of the old pigeon shed, she wrapped her shawl tight and gazed out at the vast ocean.

The expansive water was broken only by some distant, uninhabited islands and a few fishing vessels. She forced herself to draw in slow, steady breaths to calm her racing heart. The ocean had always been a calming presence, and it didn't fail her now. Though storm clouds on the horizon threatened rain, staring out at the endless stretch of water eased the thorniest of her fears.

I am the crown heir and must do what is right for my kingdom, she reminded herself. *I must marry Trei. Hard as it will be, I must forget about Rangar.*

But how? How to deny the love she felt? A love that twisted her up inside and left her breathless? That was easier said than done. Even now, her heart ached for Rangar, as did the base of her belly whenever she thought of his touch. His kisses made her feel light-headed, the stuff written about in fairy tales, stirring sensations she'd never felt . . .

A sudden flapping of wings tore her from her thoughts. A huge bird—far too large to be a pigeon—glided down from the sky, sharp talons outstretched. Bryn shrieked and ducked, covering her head with her hands. She instantly feared this was some trick of Captain Carr, a bird trained to pluck out her eyes . . .

But the bird landed gracefully on one of the old pigeon roosts and stilled. When Bryn got up the nerve to peek through her fingers at it, she was surprised.

"Zephyr?" she said, stiffening with recognition.

The falcon cocked its head at her. Zephyr was never apart from Saraj for very long, and Bryn was just starting to worry if something had happened to the falconer when she heard footsteps outside the pigeon shed.

"Bryn." It was Saraj's unmistakable voice. "Come out of there. We need to talk."

Bryn cringed. Her heartbeat began to pick up again. Sweat dampened her palms. Saraj was the closest thing she had to a friend in the Baersladen. The falconer had been kind to her, letting her borrow clothes and giving her sisterly advice.

And now I'm betraying her.

Steeling her nerves, Bryn opened the door and faced the woman whose lover she was about to marry.

CHAPTER 2

THE ROOFTOP VISIT . . . shared pain . . . forget about the past . . . first a chance, then trust . . . sneaky Val

A bolt of apprehension shot through Bryn from the base of her skull to the tips of her toes as she opened the shed door to face Saraj.

The head falconer was dressed in her usual forest-green gown with the long slits up the sides and trousers underneath to facilitate the movement she needed for her work. Her long dark brown hair was pulled back in a loose braid, letting strands blow around her face. She folded her arms tightly across her chest.

"Saraj," Bryn said, wringing her hands. "I cannot tell you how sorry I am about—"

"Stop." Saraj's face was firm as a stone, but Bryn saw a wealth of emotion glistening in her eyes: anger and hurt swirling together. "I don't wish to hear it."

Saraj tore her eyes away from Bryn and looked out to sea. For a long time, she said nothing, then finally took a deep breath. "I am not angry with you, Bryn. I know this marriage was not your idea nor your wish. People in your and Trei's positions are expected to do what is best for their kingdoms, including forming advantageous alliances through marriage." Her chin tipped high but then her strength gave way and her face twisted with anguish. A moment passed before she was able to gain control of herself again. "But by the gods, it's unfair. It's such a mess, Bryn. Rangar and you. Trei and me . . . " She shook her head, unable to continue.

As relieved as Bryn felt that Saraj hadn't come to accuse her of trying to steal Trei, the relief was short-lived. This was a woman whose heart was broken just as badly as Bryn's. Bryn felt tears in her own eyes and stepped forward hesitantly, wanting to comfort Saraj but unsure if Saraj would accept it.

Saraj sucked in a breath, apprehensive, but then wrapped her arms around Bryn.

The two women held each other fiercely, feeling one another shaking in their arms. Bryn wiped away tears, pressing her face into Saraj's shoulder. Saraj hugged her tightly and then finally let go. Though she had managed to keep tears at bay, her eyes were red.

"I feel deeply guilty for my anger," Saraj admitted. "I know this is what's necessary for the kingdoms. Tens of thousands of people's security and livelihoods are at stake, so what does my heart matter? But Bryn, it's crushing. When Trei told me the news this morning, I thought I would suffocate from rage."

"I understand how you feel," Bryn whispered. And she did—she knew the weight of that same crushing anguish. Resting her hand on her friend's arm, she said, "Saraj, I assure you, I have no romantic feelings toward Trei. I would never wish to take him from you."

Saraj nodded, wiping her nose. "I know. Believe me, Trei and I talked circles around each other this morning. At one point, I threatened to have my falcon gouge out his manly parts. But as much as I hate it, I don't know what to do but accept it." She sighed and leaned back against the shed's stone wall as she murmured, "Duty comes before love."

But then her eyes flashed to Bryn, uncertain, and she added, "Right?"

Bryn swallowed. This was the ultimate question that had been going through her own head ever since the night before when King Aleth had broken the news that the only way to ensure safety for both their kingdoms was for her to marry Trei.

Duty or love, love or duty.

She'd debated it all night until her mind had turned to mush. She felt torn between the two ideals, just as she felt torn between the Mirien and the Baersladen. One was the home of her birth, the other her adopted home. She owed a massive recompense to the Mir people after her parents' cruel reign, and she couldn't turn her back on them now that she was the crown heir, yet her heart wasn't in the Mirien.

It was here, with Rangar.

"Right," Bryn echoed, though both women only stared at each other, far from convinced.

Saraj wiped her nose again and straightened, nervously smoothing her clothes. "King Aleth assures me that in time, all our feelings will fade. That we'll forget there was a time when Trei and I were together, and you and Rangar. 'Youthful dalliances.'" She paused, then shook her head. "I can't imagine that's true, but I want you to know that I'll never hold it against you that you'll marry Trei and give him heirs. If possible, I'd still like for us to be friends."

Bryn felt her heart falter at the falconer's words; it was one of the most magnanimous things anyone had ever said to her. Tightening her hold on Saraj's arm, she said, "Saraj, you're the closest thing I have to a sister here, and it would break my heart all over if I lost Rangar *and* you."

Saraj gave her a sad smile then whistled to Zephyr, who hopped onto her shoulder.

Saraj reached out to wipe away Bryn's tears gently, as a sister would do. "Let us try our hardest to forget about the past. Tomorrow, you wed, and life will be different for all of us."

All day, Bryn mulled over Saraj's words. *Duty comes before love.*

It was what she'd been raised to believe and had indeed been true for her family members. Her mother had wed her father as part of a political arrangement. Her sister, Elysander, had been betrothed from birth to Duke Dryden in Dresel, and while Elysander seemed pleased with the match, she certainly wasn't in love with the man. Likewise, Bryn's brother, Mars, had never formed any true romantic attachments before his death, knowing he'd one day have to marry for political reasons.

So why should I feel sorry for myself? Bryn asked herself. *What is being asked of me is no different from any other royal.*

Yet her assurances felt stale. She couldn't imagine going through life without Rangar by her side. And the worst of all was knowing that he *would* be close. Every day, she'd have to see him around the castle knowing full well that she was in love with him...yet bedding with his brother.

Saints.

She tried again to go to the village square to watch the stage being built, but the guards once more stopped her, not even letting her cross the moat bridge. So, she watched from the bridge as children carried buckets full of freshly picked maiden roses and wound them into bouquets with ribbon. They waved at her excitedly, beaming to think they were helping prepare for a royal wedding. Despite her sorrow, she forced a smile and waved back.

The children don't know any better. They think this is a happy occasion.

"Lady Bryn." A deep voice from behind her made her jump.

She turned to find Alain, one of the Mir refugees, standing on the other side of the bridge.

Instantly, alarm bells went off in her head, and she glanced around to make sure the soldiers were close by. She'd never had any specific reason to be wary of Alain, but Valenden had warned her that Captain Carr's spies had infiltrated the refugee group. Any of them could be a traitor.

"Alain, hello to you," she said, forcing a smile while keeping her distance.

He wore a troubled look. Bryn hadn't known Alain well when she'd lived in the Mirien. Mam Delice had told her that he was a farrier who helped organize the uprising against her family. So, he was primed to dislike her. Since he'd arrived in the Baersladen, he had only ever treated her with suspicion.

He motioned to the decorations going up in the village square and said gruffly, "I heard there's to be a wedding between you and Prince Trei. Is it true?"

Still wary, Bryn nodded. In a voice she hoped sounded confident, she said, "Yes, it's true. Tomorrow evening."

Alain seemed to consider this information for

some time, and then, to Bryn's surprise, he removed his cap. It was a gesture of respect he'd never given her before. She stared at him in shock.

"When I heard whisperings of the wedding," he said, "I didn't believe them. If you'll excuse me for being so bold, we all know about the nights you spent with Prince Rangar. They say by marrying Trei instead, you'll consolidate the two kingdoms and bring new leadership to the Mirien; that Prince Trei will rule more fairly, as they do here." He paused. "I never thought I'd see the day when a member of the Lindane family made a sacrifice for the good of the Mir people."

Bryn blinked, not sure what to make of Alain's words. He was boldly insulting her family's legacy, yet with good reason. Her parents and Mars *had* done terrible things to the Mir common folk. With Trei on the throne, life would vastly improve for her people.

"It's my duty," she said, keeping her head high.

Duty over love...

Alain still stared at her like he couldn't quite believe she would do such a thing.

She sighed. "I know my parents' rule was tyrannical. At least, I know that *now*. I didn't at the time, and that was my failing. I was young, but not so young that I shouldn't have seen the suffering beyond the walls of Castle Mir. I hope you believe me when I say that coming here has changed my idea of what leadership means and that I fully intend to be a superior ruler to the Mir people than my parents ever were. That is why

I'm marrying Trei, to make that a reality. Or at least to attempt to do so."

Alain still appeared a touch suspicious, but he replaced his cap and gave her a more appraising look that, for the first time, bordered on respectful. "If that is truly the case, Lady Bryn, I would be pleased to see you and Prince Trei on the Mir thrones."

It wasn't exactly a resounding endorsement, but it was leaps and bounds above how she'd previously been treated by her people. In fact, just a few months ago, Alain might have strung her up in the gallows with the rest of her family.

"I will do right by my people," she assured him in a confident voice that surprised even herself.

"Aye, I just think you might." He gave her one more look and once he turned and left, she let out a tight breath. A strange feeling swelled in her chest that she recognized as pride. After being lumped in with her despotic parents for so long, her people were finally willing to give her a chance. That was all she could ask of them—a chance. She'd have to prove herself to earn their full devotion.

I can't disappoint them now.

She returned to watching the wedding decorations going up with a mix of emotions, though her mind continued to sweep back to Rangar. He was stationed at the border, probably sleeping in the open woods, eating gruel, fully believing that soon he'd return to Barendur Hold and they'd be married and finally share a wedding bed . . .

She pressed a hand to an ache in her rib cage. It crushed her to think of the lie she was living.

Rubbing the ache in her side, she was about to return to her room in the mage chambers when she spotted Valenden on the far side of the village square. He was near the docks, speaking to a messenger on horseback.

A messenger? she thought with a twinge of suspicion. *Who would he be sending a message to?*

Valenden handed the woman a letter and after a short exchange, the woman spurred her horse into a gallop, kicking up dust that made the villagers in the square cover their mouths and cough.

Valenden glanced from side to side furtively. Bryn frowned.

He's up to no good.

His gaze suddenly snagged on Bryn's. He went still, his face revealing nothing, and held her gaze for a long time before turning sharply and heading out toward the woods.

Bryn had half a mind to chase after him and demand to know what he was scheming but then thought better of it. She'd already crossed too many boundaries with Valenden; it was time to forget about both younger brothers and focus on her betrothed.

Besides, the guards would stop her from leaving the castle grounds, anyway.

Taking a deep breath, she went to find her future husband.

CHAPTER 3

A DELECTABLE TASTE . . . a private talk . . . golden chains . . . giggling gossip . . . amplified magic

The third floor of Barendur Hold comprised the council chambers, the library, and numerous workrooms where servants performed their daily duties.

After searching for some time, Bryn finally found Trei in a corner room that was stuffed to the gills with bolts of fabric, spinning wheels, and worn clothes piled in heaps to be turned into scraps for braided rugs.

Four soldiers flanked the door, which was a substantial clue that her betrothed was inside. No one else in the castle required so much security. When she approached, they parted to allow her entrance.

Trei stood naked from the waist up, his hexmark scars on prominent display, between two wooden dressing dummies while Helna stretched measuring string across his chest. The dummies bore portions of the half-finished suit she was preparing for him.

Bryn stopped short in the door, instantly flushed to see Trei's state of undress. It wasn't the first time she'd seen Trei partially unclothed since modesty was far less important in the Baersladen than it was in the Mirien. It was common to see soldiers training shirtless or fishers in only breeches as they pulled in their hauls. But Trei was more formal than his brothers. He almost always wore clean, well-mended clothes unlike Rangar or Valenden, who'd wear yesterday's shirt off the ground without a second thought.

Her eyes widened. "Oh!" She pressed a hand to her chest as she averted her eyes. "I'll return later."

Trei looked unashamed as he gave a genuine shrug. "Stay, Lady Bryn." And then, as though sensing what had made her flustered, he added, "If you'll forgive my current state."

Bryn's fingers fiddled nervously with the upper button of her blouse as her eyes slid back to Trei's bare chest against her better intentions.

This is my future husband. As of tomorrow night, they'd be wed. And with it would come all the expectations of their wedding night. They'd be required to consummate the marriage and immediately begin attempting to sire an heir.

Her mind filled with blush-inducing images of

what that wedding night would hold. What would it feel like to kiss Trei? Would it be like Rangar's kiss? Or would Trei have his own way?

Her hand fell away from her blouse as she instantly felt guilty for her thoughts.

Rangar had her heart and always would. Even if her political position required her to marry Trei, she couldn't change her feelings. Should she attempt to seek no pleasure from her wedding night with Trei? Keep their love-making formal and cold out of respect to Rangar?

She realized both Trei and Helna were staring at her. She quickly cleared her throat. "I spoke with Saraj."

A serious look clouded Trei's face. Helna paused her measurements and turned away, busying herself with one of the garments on the dressing dummies.

Trei glanced at the guards. "Leave us. I'd like a moment with my betrothed."

The guards silently filed out of the room, and without having to be asked, Helna gathered up some fabric scraps and followed them.

Trei closed the door behind them and turned to Bryn. She felt herself draw in a sharp breath.

"Saraj might be heartbroken for now," Trei said in his gravelly voice as he straightened a wrinkle on the suit hanging on the dressing dummy. "But her heart will mend."

Though his words were spoken confidently, Bryn

could read in his eyes how deeply pained he was by having to break his engagement to Saraj. He might have been trained in all the right things to say, but it didn't mean that he believed them. He loved Saraj with his whole heart and had for years; the entire kingdom knew it.

Bryn looked down at her folded hands. "She came to speak to me. She spoke of how duty comes before love. It is obviously a difficult situation for all of us. I wanted to talk to you to see if you were . . . .all right."

Trei's hand stilled on the fabric. He faced Bryn with slight confusion in his eyes. "Me?"

He was her future husband, wasn't he? "Yes."

He ran a hand through his hair, mussing it distractedly, and then finally let his hand fall. "You're the only person who asked how I feel about this. Besides Saraj, of course."

Bryn's heart went out to him. As firstborn, Trei had borne the burden of the throne on his shoulders since birth, a responsibility Rangar and Valenden had never felt. Like her, they'd been free to live their lives as they had seen fit. But Trei had dedicated himself to ruling the kingdom one day, and he'd made sacrifices so selflessly that everyone had taken him for granted.

"Well," she said, blushing, "I truly want to know."

Still looking off-kilter, Trei thought a moment. "I've always understood my duty as heir to the Baer throne. I had indeed hoped Saraj could be my queen, but perhaps it wasn't reasonable of me to believe I could have a match that was both politically advantageous *and* romantic. I shouldn't have let myself hope." He straightened suddenly as though he'd misspoke. "Please, don't think that I am not pleased by our union—"

"It's all right, Trei," Bryn said softly. "You don't have to pretend with me. Please don't feel obliged to act like you're happy about this. I know you're in love with Saraj. You never need to worry about offending me or making me feel better about that for the sake of propriety. I think if we're going to truly be wed and spend our lives with one another, we must dismiss formality. You love Saraj. I love Rangar. Yet you and I are also friendly . . . let us start from there."

He crossed his arms over his bare chest, looking at her with an odd expression, and then nodded. "We start as friends."

Friends who are going to make love tomorrow night. Bryn couldn't help but think the scandalous thought and quickly turned away before her face betrayed the thoughts in her head.

She bobbed her head, not meeting his eyes for fear of blushing all over again. "Good. I suppose, then, I'll see you . . . tomorrow."

At our wedding.

As she started for the door, he called, "Wait, Bryn."

When she turned back around, he took something out of his pocket. It was a delicate gold chain necklace.

He explained with some hesitation, "This

belonged to my mother before she passed away. I had meant to give it to you tomorrow, but perhaps now is better, outside of all the formality. I thought you might put the ring Rangar gave you on it and keep it around your neck. I know this is hard for you. I don't want you to feel like you must deny what you felt for him."

Bryn's hand instantly went to the ring around her finger, the one Rangar had given her as an engagement ring with the imprinted maiden rose petal. She still hadn't been able to bring herself to take it off even though she was betrothed to another.

Now, taking a deep breath, she twisted the ring off her finger and strung it on the delicate chain, then fastened it around her neck. It hung just below her dress collar, nestled between her breasts, low enough for only her and Trei to know it was there.

She touched the ring gently. "Thank you, Trei."

Slowly, he took her hand in his as though testing out the feel of it. A flush of warmth spread up Bryn's arm. He ran his thumb over her palm as he said, "My father, my aunt . . . they know I'll do my duty. And yet you came to see if I was all right." His thumb paused in the center of her palm as his green eyes considered her. "I can see why Rangar fell in love with you."

Feeling suddenly shy, Bryn nodded. She opened the door to let Helna return, who gave her a curious look. The older woman's eyes instantly went to the visible portion of the chain around her neck, but Helna said nothing.

Mind spinning from their talk, Bryn escaped to the kitchen, hoping that the perpetual bustle there would ease the emotions tangled in her chest. As she entered the smokey kitchen, she touched Rangar's ring between her breasts, relieved to have it close.

The kitchen was crowded with villagers who'd come to help prepare for the wedding feast. Sweaty-faced girls stirred pots of boiling stew while boys turned a spit over the massive fireplace. The air smelled richly of roasting meats and sweet, honeyed fruits.

Bryn relaxed slightly, distracted by the activity. She spotted a friendly face and grinned. "Roxin!"

The stout kitchen maid looked up from a table laden with baskets full of figs and smiled back. "Lady Bryn! By the gods, I'm going to have to say Queen Bryn soon, eh? Why aren't you upstairs getting pampered and fitted for a gown instead of down here with the likes of us?"

"I thought I could lend a hand," Bryn said, hoping it wasn't obvious how desperately she needed a distraction.

Roxin guffawed. "A future queen plucking chick-ens? Well, why not? Or better yet, you can help with the brandy. See these figs? Take that paring knife there, cut off the stems, and then throw them in the iron pot." Roxin tossed her an apron.

A few maids moved aside to make room for Bryn at the big worktable. She put on her apron and started preparing the figs, all too aware of the younger girls staring wide-eyed and slack-jawed at her. She tried to ignore their attention, but it was useless.

"You're going to marry Prince Trei!" one of them cried in wonder.

Bryn forced a smile that she hoped looked happy. "That's right." A pain stabbed her in the belly, thinking of how wrong it felt.

"He's very handsome," another girl said, and they all started giggling.

Roxin chided them and waved them away with a dishrag, then called over a few sturdier chefs to help with the heavy iron pot. "Lady Bryn, best you take a step back now, too. Time for us to finish the brandy."

At first, Bryn felt confused. She saw no fruit press or distillery equipment, but then she recalled that Roxin had a unique hexmark that allowed her to ferment fruit with magic. Bryn went to stand by the kitchen's narrow window as a dozen of the kitchen maids joined Roxin around the table. They joined hands and bowed their heads. Then, in a low whisper, they began reciting a spell. The iron pot full of fresh figs began to rumble slightly. A sickly-sweet smell filled the air. Bryn stared in wonder as the fruits started to break down into syrup. One of the girls poured in a pot of boiling water while another stirred. The women continued to chant as Roxin touched her hexmark and traced the hex shape in the air. Finally, the women lowered their hands and stopped chanting.

Roxin stepped forward with a ladle. She dipped it

into the iron pot, blew on the syrup to cool it, and took a sip. She grinned widely in triumph. "Try it."

Bryn carefully accepted the ladle and took a small sip. The brew was scalding, hot but the flavor was delicious and complex, and it instantly warmed her stomach.

"That's incredible," she breathed.

Roxin smiled proudly as she motioned for the girls to bottle and chill the brandy in the cold storage rooms. "I'm the only one with the hex to ferment fruits, but the others all have amplifier hexes—it's something most of us get on our eighteenth birthday when we become adult members of the Baersladen."

"An amplifier spell?"

Roxin nodded. "When we work together, we can achieve feats far greater than as an individual."

Bryn had previously had no idea that spells could be amplified if casters worked together. All her life, she'd been told that magic was backward and essentially useless, capable of only parlor tricks like sparking a flame without a match. Now, she truly understood what a lie that had been. Not only could a single caster do more than spark a flame, but united, they could achieve amazing things.

No wonder my parents discouraged magic, Bryn thought with a prickle of anger. *If the Mir common folk knew how powerful they could be working together, they could have overthrown my parents much sooner.*

Bryn remained in the kitchen helping until Mage Marna came to find her, telling her it was time to familiarize herself with Baer marriage tradition. For the remainder of the evening, she sat in the library, flanked by protective guards, reading dusty old books to learn about the intricacies of the impending cere-mony that would bind her to a good man, a kind prince . . . but not the man she loved.

CHAPTER 4

**WEDDING DAY . . . stormy skies . . . dark dreams . .
. a waiting crowd . . . a difficult question**

All that night, Bryn dreamed of Rangar.

They were together in Barendur Hold's barn in an empty stall filled with fresh, soft straw, drinking a bottle of Roxin's sweet fig brandy and laughing until growls outside silenced them. Wolves stalked the barn's main section. Rangar laid her back in the straw and pressed a finger to her lips to keep her silent. He protected her body by lying on top of her, hiding them under his bearskin cloak until the wolves passed. But he hadn't let her up once the danger was gone. Instead, his body remained pressed against the length of hers. He'd kissed her brandy-soaked lips and removed her clothing stitch by stitch until she had only the straw and his bearskin cloak as covering. Then, growling from desire, he'd worshipped her body with hands and lips and eyes until she'd felt herself crash apart with a thunderous sound.

Jolting awake, Bryn woke from the dream to find it *was* thundering outside.

Clouds had rolled in overnight, and heavy rain now drowned Barendur Hold. Looking out the window, she saw that the courtyard had transformed into a mud pit. The wedding decorations in the village square that the townspeople had worked so hard on were soaked. The sky was gray and stormy, matching her heart's mood.

Today I marry Trei Barendur.

Her body started shaking. She fished the necklace out of her blouse and squeezed Rangar's ring in her fist as she wondered for the millionth time if there was any other way.

Rangar was probably out there now, dozens of miles away, caught in this same storm. She could picture him hunched in his bearskin cloak against the drenching rain, soaked through and through, miserable. Maybe he'd dreamed of her, too, and reassured himself it was only a matter of time before he was back in Barendur Hold with Bryn to warm him.

Tears flowed down her face as she buried her face in her pillow and sobbed. Eventually, once her body was thoroughly worn out, she sat up and wiped her eyes.

Enough now, she told herself. *No more tears.*

It wasn't long before Calista, one of the mage apprentices, knocked on her door. "Lady Bryn? It's time to get dressed."

Bryn managed to clean herself up and emerge from her room with dry eyes, but Calista gave Bryn's red-rimmed eyes one look and grimaced. "Lady Bryn, you can't show up to your wedding preparations looking like you've just sobbed out a gallon of tears."

Calista took her hand and led her into the mage storerooms where she dug around in the containers of herbs and potions and came back with a glass jar. She poured a small amount of oil onto a rag and then delicately dabbed the solution around Bryn's eyes.

"This contains a natural balm to relieve red eyes. There, now blink a few times." She stood back, nodding. "You look better already."

"Thank you, Calista," Bryn whispered, trying not to cry again.

Calista squeezed her shoulder. "Mage Marna sent guards to escort you to the bathhouse. I'll be asking the gods to grant us clearer skies later today."

Bryn nodded. The guards led her down to the bathhouse on Barendur Hold's lower floor. The bathhouse was usually full of residents but was now empty except for a few female attendants who swooped in on Bryn as soon as she entered.

The attendants stripped Bryn of every stitch, lathered her up in foaming soap, and then scoured her with harsh cloths that left her skin bright red. They slathered her with scented oils to leave her skin and hair luxuriously soft. One woman trimmed her nails with a fine pair of scissors while another began weaving a complicated braid that took the better part of two hours to complete.

By the time her pampering was finished, Bryn's scalp ached from having her hair pulled into such tight knots. An attendant gave her a hand mirror, and Bryn was taken aback: she hadn't seen her own reflection in weeks other than blurry glimpses in pools of water.

"Oh—that braid is beautiful."

They'd given her a traditionally Baer hairstyle, and though her hair was vividly blond, she almost looked more Baer than Mir. It struck her that she *was* about to become a Baer citizen, at least through marriage. Though she was the crown heir to the Mir throne, once she wed Trei, she would be his bride. She would join *his* family, not the other way around.

After the bathhouse, the guards led her upstairs to the seamstress's room where Helna did the final fittings for her gown. It was a gorgeous garment, but nothing like what Bryn was used to. In the Mirien, brides wore white lace to their weddings. She'd never attended or seen a Baer wedding, and she hadn't thought to ask about the details. This gown was made of velvet so dark grey it was nearly black and accented with small obsidian gems.

Helna beamed at her. "What a beautiful bride you make, Lady Bryn. Trei won't be able to take his eyes off you." The smile faltered on the older woman's face. She sighed deeply. "If Rangar were here . . ."

But she quickly shut her mouth and turned away, knowing she'd said too much.

Bryn pretended she hadn't heard, though she knew everyone in the castle was gossiping about the same thing: The Mir princess marrying the wrong brother. King Aleth and Mage Marna had been careful to keep the wedding announcement brief so that gossip wouldn't have time to spread to Rangar on the borderlands, but all the castle residents and villagers knew. Though they were all smiles and words of congratulations to her face, Bryn suspected all anyone could talk about was what a terrible mess it would be when Rangar returned.

Wiping her hands of chalk, Helna glanced out the window and frowned at the sky. "Wish this rain would stop, but it won't be the first time a bride marries in a storm. Ah, look at that—people are already starting to arrive."

Bryn peered out the window at the village square beyond. A few dozen villagers huddled together under makeshift tents that had been erected, or hunkered beneath their cloaks. The sky was too grey for her to see the sun, but judging by the pinkish cast to the clouds, she guessed it was almost sunset.

A knock on the door made her spin sharply. To her surprise, Valenden stood in the doorway.

His eyes raked down her body in the wedding gown then took their time making their way back up to her face. He gave a low whistle before saying, "It's time. The rest of my family is already gathered in the great hall. They sent me to fetch you. Because of the weather, they don't want to start the ceremony until the last possible moment."

"Of course," she said in a hollow voice.

Valenden continued to evaluate her, his gaze now fixing on her elegantly braided blond hair. His jaw tightened.

She cocked her head at him. "What is it, Val?"

His eyes flickered to Helna, who was cleaning up scraps near her worktable. He stepped closer to Bryn and lowered his voice so the seamstress wouldn't overhear. "I'm thinking that this wedding is the worst idea my father ever had."

Alarm shot through Bryn as she hissed back, "There's no other way. It isn't your father's fault. He only suggested this course of action—he isn't forcing me into this."

When Valenden remained silent, she grew warm and insisted, "You think I *want* to break Rangar's heart? What am I supposed to do? It's either protect his heart or save my entire kingdom."

"He saved your life."

"And I saved his, thanks to your little poisoning prank! Rangar and I are even when it comes to that. We're both bound to the *fralen* bond." She paused, resting her hands on her hips, feeling heat blooming in her cheeks. "Why are you so loyal to Rangar now when you certainly weren't that night in the woods?"

She looked at him pointedly.

Valenden dragged his head back and forth as he

raked his nails through his hair. He looked like he was on the verge of telling her again that it was wrong to marry Trei, but then he clamped his jaw shut and said, "I'll take you downstairs."

The guards escorted them to the great hall, which had been lit by extra candles to give it a magical glow. The giant doors were thrown open to the drawbridge spanning the moat. Rain fell in a heavy sheet outside, dousing Bryn's mood.

Mage Marna waited at the door with more guards. When she saw Bryn, she shook out a woolen cloak and gently set it over Bryn's hair and gown.

"The weather doesn't want to cooperate, but unfortunately, we dare not postpone. Tradition decrees you be married at sunset beneath the open sky. We'll keep the ceremony short, then bring the celebrations inside for the feast."

Bryn's stomach was doing flips. Squinting through the rain, she saw several cloaked figures on the stage. She recognized King Aleth's hulking shoulders and Trei's imposing height. Searching the crowd, she finally spotted Saraj in the second row, cloak pulled up over her head against the rain. She also took note of a small group of people off to the side and was surprised to recognize the Mir refugee group. It was no shock to see Mam Delice there, but she also recognized Alain.

My people are watching—I must be brave.

"Are you ready?" Mage Marna asked.

Bryn couldn't help but throw Valenden one more

look, almost daring—*wanting*—him to talk her out of it, but he refused to look at her.

Instead, she only gave a small nod. *Think of the Mirien.*

Mage Marna held out her arm to escort Bryn. Bryn took it shakily, feeling like someone else was in control of her body. As they stepped out of the shelter of the great hall into the rain, her whole body went numb. Her feet carried her through the mud as though she was half asleep.

Surely this isn't me *marrying Prince Trei of the Baersladen. This must be a dream.*

But the pounding rain made it all too real. Even with the cloak hooding her, dampness ruined her intricate hairstyle. Helna's gorgeous dress was already streaked in mud along the hem.

As though dazed, Bryn clutched Mage Marna's arm as they crossed to the stage and mounted the few steps.

Each of the men present acknowledged her with a nod: King Aleth, his thick beard hiding half his face; the vicar, a tall man in a black cassock; and Trei.

Mage Marna led her to stand beside Trei, and as soon as she was in her position, the gathered crowd gave a cheer and yelled a traditional call three times that made Bryn's heart thunder.

Her chest felt too restricted in the dress with the fabric soaked and sticking to her skin. She forced herself to take steady breaths.

My wedding day. To someone else!

Had her mother felt like this at her wedding? Had Elysander? Was Bryn just the latest in a long line of heartbroken royal women?

As much as she wanted to squeeze Rangar's ring around her neck, she forced herself not to. There would be no bigger sign of disrespect toward Trei. For his part, Trei looked every bit the dashing prince. The suit Helna had made for him fit his broad shoulders perfectly, though his rain cloak hid much of it.

"We shall begin," the vicar prompted.

Bryn's mind was elsewhere, not here on this stage at her own wedding. As the vicar went through the ritual that she'd been taught the previous day, her mind felt only numb.

She was afraid to look at Trei. Afraid that all she would see was not the person she wanted.

This is supposed to be Rangar *at my side.*

When it was finally time to agree to the marriage, Bryn looked Trei's his eyes for the first time since the ceremony began and was surprised.

Trei wasn't Rangar, it was true, but he was hardly a rogue. Trei was her friend and someone she trusted, who had risked his life for her just as the rest of his family had. At the vicar's question, Trei swore himself to her, and then the vicar turned the question on Bryn, and the entire crowd went still, awaiting her answer.

"Bryn Lindane of the Mirien, do you bind yourself with Trei Barendur, Prince of the Baersladen?"

Bryn opened her mouth, unsure what she would say.

CHAPTER 5

**A FEAST INTERRUPTED . . . vows . . . shelter from
the rain . . . a first dance . . . Legend**

Standing on the stage in the pouring rain, Bryn looked out at the Mir refugees in the crowd who had come to see if their new crown heir would follow through on her promise to make amends for the crimes of her family.

Swallowing, she said in a voice she hoped wouldn't shake, "I do."

It was like a knife to her chest, a pain she'd never known.

"You may begin the marriage with a kiss," the vicar prompted.

Trei's green eyes fell on hers, and she saw the anguish in them. This was hard for him, too. The love of his life, Saraj, was watching in the crowd, heartbroken. Yet he was doing what he had to for his people.

So would she.

When Trei touched her chin gently, she tipped it up. His face lowered to hers. She closed her eyes as their lips touched beneath the pounding rain. The kiss wasn't as unpleasant as she feared. There was a sweetness to it, a promise of something. Friendship, maybe. Over time, it could be something more.

It was small, but there *was* a spark.

The gathered crowd started cheering, throwing their hoods back to shout the good news to the sky. Bryn stared at them in shock. They didn't seem to have picked up on any of her or Trei's reluctance. Their beloved prince had married, a joyous feast would follow, and soon, the two kingdoms would be joined and all the Mirien's bounty would be open to them. It was a new era for the Eyrie.

I'm married. It happened.

That awful pain stabbed her again. Trei glanced at her, reached out, and gave her hand a slight squeeze.

On her other side, King Aleth rested a heavy hand on her shoulder. She flinched, still feeling more like this was a hanging instead of a wedding.

"Welcome to the Barendur family," the king said. "This is indeed a joyous occasion. Let us celebrate with brandy and music!"

Joyous was not the word that came to mind to Bryn. The ache in her heart had spread to her head, and it throbbed painfully. The crowd looked anxious to get into the dry warmth of the great hall. King Aleth stepped off the stage, which signaled the start of the wedding feast, and the villagers rushed toward the castle entrance.

Despite her cloak, the rain poured down Bryn's face and seeped beneath her clothes, chilling her down to her bare skin. She gave an involuntary shiver and felt Trei move his hand to the small of her back. "Let's get you inside, out of this weather."

He led the way down the steps and over the muddy ground until they were at last within the walls with a roof over their head. The great hall had been beautifully transformed for the festive occasion in stark contrast to the sullen, rain-drenched ceremony. Warm fires roared at either end of the hall, and candles flickered on each of the tables laden with bouquets of maiden roses and bountiful baskets of pastries and cheeses. Musicians struck up a rousing *velta*, and now that the villagers had shed their mud-stained cloaks and were warming up with the fires and pitchers of fig brandy passed around, the ache in her head eased slightly.

"Goodness, look at you!" Helna cried. Along with Mam Delice and a team of bathhouse maids, the seamstress swept up to Bryn and attacked her damp hair and gown with towels. After a few whispers of magic and some good old-fashion scrubbing, Bryn looked less like a drowned cat and more like a proper bride.

"There now," Mam Delice said, patting her hand.

"You enjoy your party, Lady Bryn." The old woman gave Trei, waiting at her side, an approving look. "King and Queen of the Mirien."

"Oh, we won't be officially coronated until we're in Castle Mir, with my parents' crowns," Bryn clarified quickly. Technically, she and Trei would remain a prince and princess until then. And given that Captain Carr unjustly held control of Castle Mir, there was no telling how soon such a coronation would be possible.

Mam Delice waved away Bryn's clarification. "You're as good as a queen now to me. And Prince Trei, I've heard nothing but praise for you in my time here. If anyone can right the wrongs in the Mirien, it will be the two of you together."

"Thank you for your blessing." Trei took the old woman's hand. "I am honored."

While he spoke with the cook, Bryn couldn't take her eyes off him. *Her husband.* Mam Delice's observations were right: Trei was the kind of king who could lead a broken land to peace. As he escorted Bryn onto the dais where a special table had been set up for them, she looked out at Mir refugees dancing arm-in-arm with Baer villagers, laughing and sharing brandy. It was the first time she'd seen the two groups interact peacefully.

Maybe all of this is worth it, she thought. *Our marriage is already bringing our people together.*

But her heart objected to her head.

Bryn found that once she had some food in her belly, she began to feel calmer. The kitchen had outdone themselves, drizzling Mir honey over the bread and fruits in a touching tribute to her homeland. Everywhere she turned, someone was pressing a pitcher of fig brandy on her, and she soon found her headache had settled into a dizzy blur.

Leaning close to Trei, she whispered, "I don't see Saraj in the crowd."

He bristled for an instant, then cleared his throat. "As an official within the Baer court, she was expected to attend the wedding ceremony, but not the feast. She . . . said she wanted to be with her birds."

Bryn swallowed, feeling awash with guilt. "I suppose I can't blame her."

Trei rested his hand over hers and gave a small smile, though the pain in it was clear to see. Bryn smiled back, filled with sadness for all of them—Trei, Saraj, Rangar, herself—but perhaps also a tiny drop of hope.

At one point, Roxin appeared by her side with a special bottle of apple liquor, giving her a wink. "Watch it now; this is the *strong* stuff. It's gotten many a nervous virgin bride through their wedding night." Mischief danced in Roxin's eyes. "That is, assuming you *are* a virgin, and you and Rangar never . . . "

"Of course not," Bryn gasped, swiping the bottle as heat rose to her cheeks. It was the first time anyone had dared to mention Rangar all day. In fact, it felt as though the entire kingdom had intentionally gone out of their way to pretend the youngest Baer prince didn't exist.

Roxin smirked like she didn't believe Bryn. "Well, between you and me, Trei looks like he'll part your legs and make you forget all about Ra—"

"Shh!" Bryn hissed. She was starting to breathe hard now, and she just wanted all talk of Rangar to cease. "Thank you. For the drink."

Roxin gave her another wink.

The feast grew raucous as the night continued. The musicians played feverishly, prompting the dancers to whirl in spins and sashays. Laughter prevailed as the attendees fell deeper into their cups. Tentatively, Bryn told herself to view this party as a fresh beginning. The rainstorm outside was her past, brooding and tragic. This feast symbolized hope for her people—and perhaps for her.

"May I have a dance?" Trei asked.

She swallowed, knowing she could hardly refuse. *We're supposed to appear happy, not broken-hearted.*

"Of . . . of course."

He took her hand and led her into the crowd, which parted to make room for them. The musicians switched to a slower tune. King Aleth pounded on the table and raised his chalice at the head table. "To the future King and Queen of the Mirien and the Baersladen!"

The crowd cheered deafeningly. All eyes turned to them expectantly, anxious to watch the first dance between the newlyweds. Bryn hesitated before lifting a shaking hand onto Trei's shoulder.

A crash sounded nearby, and several people

shrieked. At first, Bryn ignored the commotion at the other side of the hall near the gate—just some overzealous partiers, she assumed. But the musicians abruptly stopped playing.

What's happening? Brandy slowed her mind. She turned in confusion toward the commotion, only to suck in a gasp and press a hand to her mouth.

Saints!

A mud-streaked horse and rider had crashed through the gate into the great hall. The rider, dressed in a soaking wet dark cloak with the hood pulled high overhead, spurred his horse into the crowd of dancers, who shrieked and backed away.

Trei's hand tightened protectively around Bryn's back. "Damn the Saints," he muttered, the first time Bryn had heard Trei say a black word.

"Who is it?" She asked, though her throat was bone dry. A terrible premonition was spreading like poison through her body.

"I cannot see the rider, but the horse is Legend," Trei said stiffly.

Legend. The name of Rangar's mare. Bryn hadn't recognized the horse at first because Legend was dark brown, not black, but now Bryn realized that mud had darkened the mare's hair.

She nearly doubled over. *This can't be happening!*

The rider dismounted with a heavy thud as the dancers scattered back to give him room. He turned in a slow circle until he faced Trei and Bryn and then stalked forward while he lifted a hand to draw back his hood.

Dark hair soaked from rain. Fresh battle scars over the old ones.

Rangar Barendur had returned.

Bryn felt herself gaping as though she was looking at a ghost. Covered in rain and mud, Rangar looked like a beast. The scowl on his face portended dark things. She found herself unable to move as he stalked toward her, though his brown eyes were fixed on Trei, not her. Rangar's expressions were always hard to read, and even now, his face bore no overt malice, though there was something in the way he moved that called to mind a lumbering bear ready to strike.

Fleeting thoughts came and went in her mind: *How did he find out about the wedding? Who could get a message to him so quickly?*

The entire great hall fell into a terrified hush. Out of the corner of her eye, Bryn saw King Aleth quickly signal to the soldiers stationed around the hall, who rested their hands on their blades.

As rain still dripped down his face over the old scars, Rangar stopped a pace in front of the married couple.

Trei's hand remained around Bryn's back, and Rangar's eyes shifted to it.

"Brother . . . " Trei started but didn't seem to know how to finish.

A tense moment hung in the air before it broke

sharply as Rangar lunged at Trei with a growl, fist swinging and murder in his eyes.

CHAPTER 6

RANGAR'S RETURN . . . battle of brothers . . . wounded hearts . . . wounded bodies . . . Val's secret exposed

Bryn screamed.

Rangar had lunged at Trei like a beast dripping mud, blind with fury. He'd trained his whole life as a soldier—he knew how to fight. His fist was on a collision path with Trei's jaw, but Trei had also spent time in the Baer army and managed to pivot away in time so that instead of shattering his jaw, Rangar's blow glanced off his shoulder. If Trei had let go of Bryn, he could have dodged the blow entirely. Instead, he'd moved in front of Bryn, protecting his new bride.

Trei straightened and clutched his shoulder. The

joint seemed at an odd angle as though it was dislocated, but Trei hid the pain well.

"Rangar," he said tightly. "You're supposed to be on the border, defending the kingdom."

Rangar growled as he paced in a tight circle. "Was this your plan, Trei?" He pointed an accusing finger dripping with rainwater toward the dais where their father sat. "Or was it *his*?"

"Father knew you would react like this—"

"What? Like *this*?" Rangar pulled back his arm to throw another punch. The crowd gasped. Trei parried, but his formal attire restricted his movements, and the blow glanced across the side of his head. Trei fell to one knee.

At a signal from King Aleth, soldiers began to close in.

Bryn threw herself on Rangar, clutching his shoulder to hold him back. "Rangar, stop! He's your brother!"

Rangar had been posed to strike Trei again but stopped when Bryn touched him.

For the first time since he'd broken down the gate, he looked at her. His face was shadowed with emotion. There was anger there, but not as much as she'd expected to see. Instead, it was *hurt* that haunted his eyes.

Her own heart faltered, and her lips parted. "Rangar—"

"Did they threaten you?" He cut off her words as he raked his dripping hair back. "Did they force you to do this, Bryn?" His voice broke, turning tender—his rage was aimed at his family, not her. But she could hear the real question he was dancing around: Had she willingly bound herself to his brother?

She reached out a beseeching hand as though trying to tame a beast. The crowd pressed in close, and she had to lower her voice to keep from being overheard. "Rangar, you don't understand. Neither of us had a choice… It's what had to happen for the safety of both kingdoms. It's a political arrangement, that's all. Nothing more." She dropped her voice even lower. "I swear to you that I do not love Trei."

This feast was supposed to appear a joyous occasion whether she felt that way or not, but Bryn couldn't keep up appearances forever—not when Rangar looked at her with such simmering anguish.

"So it's true. You agreed to this." He stared at her like he was looking at a stranger, his eyes full of suffering, yet his body still primed for a fight. "Bryn—"

Trei pushed to his feet, inserting himself between Bryn and Rangar. A line of blood trickled from his temple where Rangar's ring had sliced the skin.

"Step back," Trei snapped. "If you raise a hand to her—"

Rangar's eyes blackened as he whirled on his brother. "You think I'd hurt *her*?" Fury sprang back into his voice. "My Saved? The woman I've loved for years? I'd sooner rip my heart out than lay a finger on her in violence." He threw a hard look between them. "But I suppose the two of you beat me to that."

Ragnar lunged at Trei again, stopped only by the town's blacksmith and one of the fishermen, who held him back.

King Aleth clapped sharply. "Enough! Guards."

The soldiers who had moved closer now rushed in. It all happened so fast. Bryn's head was still sluggish from brandy, trying hard to catch up.

Rangar fought with the strength of a bear, making four grown men struggle to hold him. "You are no brother of mine!" he spat at his brother. "I'll end you for this, Trei Barendur!"

"Get him out of here," King Aleth growled, growing red-faced. "Lock him in the tower!"

As they started to pull Rangar away, Bryn pressed her hand against her mouth, speechless. She took a hesitant step forward. "Rangar, wait—"

As the soldiers dragged him off, Rangar met her eyes, but there was nothing to say. She could only gape. *It was true. What Rangar fears is true.* She'd betrayed him, and she'd known this moment would come sooner or later. She hadn't expected it to happen *at her wedding*. He could have stopped the ceremony before it happened if he'd arrived just an hour before. But it was too late now. She and Trei were married in the eyes of the Saints and Gods alike.

Breathing hard, Bryn debated running after him and begging King Aleth to let them speak for a few minutes. *Appearances be damned.* She couldn't let Rangar disappear without trying to explain how heartbroken she was as well, how much she still loved him.

But then, she felt a presence at her side. "Let them take him," Valenden hissed quietly. "He needs to cool off. He's nothing but rage now."

She felt her breathing starting to come too fast. Panic was setting in.

Trei grabbed her chin and tipped it up to meet his. "Bryn? Bryn, are you all right?"

She blinked, dazed, her heart thundering. "I . . . Rangar . . . " She swallowed, then looked closer at the man she'd just married. The man who'd taken a punch to protect her, who she'd ignored so she could make Rangar feel better. "Trei, you're bleeding!"

"It's fine." Trei ignored the line of blood at the side of his temple. He cupped her cheek. "I'm sorry, Bryn. For all of this. Rangar shouldn't have been back so soon . . . someone must have gotten a message to him on the border. I fear it's ruined your wedding day."

In a low voice, she breathed, "Saints, Trei, I don't care about the day. I care about . . . " She paused, warring over how to keep the peace between both brothers. "You *and* Rangar."

Distracted, Trei glanced over his shoulder toward the dais. "I must speak with my father. Val, can you . . . "

"I've got her," Valenden said.

Trei nodded and disappeared from Bryn's side. Slowly, she became aware that the entire congregation of the great hall was staring at her. Their faces were full of shock except for a few kitchen maids, who were already whispering gossip.

Bryn swallowed hard.

This is very bad.

Valenden announced sharply to the onlookers, "What are you all staring at, eh? A royal wedding and a fight between brothers not enough entertainment for you?" He motioned to the musicians. "You there. Give them something to dance to. And you." He signaled to a pair of kitchen maids. "Bring up more brandy from the kitchen."

The musicians hesitated but took back up their instruments. The villagers didn't immediately begin dancing again but then turned away from Bryn and spoke to one another in lower voices.

Gossiping . . . they are all gossiping about me. Yet how could she blame them after she and Trei and Rangar had given them such a show?

She felt the sting of impending tears and pressed a hand to her face. Valenden wrapped a hand around her back and led her through the crowd to the edge of the hall, and from there, to the covered walkways that flanked the courtyard.

Once they were outside of the overly warm great hall and into the cool night air, Bryn felt better. She sucked in a few long breaths to calm herself. Then, she leaned against the railing of the breezeway, resting her forehead on the cool stone.

All she could picture was Rangar atop his horse. Dripping rain. And then his eyes so full of fury and pain. He must have ridden at breakneck speed all day and night to make it back as quickly as he had.

She said breathlessly, "How . . . how did he even hear? How did he *know*?"

She'd only been informed of the marriage plan two days ago. How was it possible for a messenger to make it to the border to give Rangar the message in time? Unless perhaps it was a homing pigeon, except there weren't any more of those. Another type of bird, perhaps . . . .

"Saraj," she said. "It must have been Saraj! She sent a falcon."

"It wasn't Saraj," Valenden muttered darkly.

When Valenden remained oddly quiet, Bryn suddenly whirled on him. "What do you know, Val?"

He scrunched up his nose, and Bryn gaped at him. "*You* did this?"

He winced.

She sank back against the railing as her mind spun. "That rider I saw you with in the square a few days ago . . . it was a messenger, wasn't it? *You* sent the message to Rangar about the wedding."

He looked away and didn't deny it.

She rested her hands on her hips accusingly. "Why would you do such a thing?" she demanded. "Is this about . . . what happened between you and me?"

Valenden scoffed. "Don't flatter yourself that much, princess. I didn't tell Rangar you were to wed Trei because I wanted you for myself. It was because, believe it or not, I care about my brother. That one night between you and I was nothing—just me being a drunken cad. Rangar worked it out with his fists at the time, and it's done between us. But *this*, Bryn." He shook his head. "Marrying Trei is not nothing. It isn't a drunken night. Rangar deserved to know what was happening. My father and aunt were wrong to have sent him away."

"But Val, you saw how he reacted. He looked like he was going to *kill* Trei!"

"He deserved to know, Bryn."

She felt a shiver and wondered if he was right. Everything felt like such a mess. Did she regret marrying Trei? She thought of the Mir refugees' faces at the ceremony, how hopeful they had been. She hadn't had a choice, had she? Tens of thousands of people's safety hinged on this marriage. But maybe it was true that Rangar should have been informed from the beginning, his feelings listened to and given consideration. Perhaps it had been cruel to have kept it from him until it was too late for him to stop it...

She started sobbing as the weight of what she'd done hit her. *Saints, it's all my fault.*

Valenden let out a curse, then a sigh, then gathered her up in his arms and rested his sharp chin on the top of her head. "There, there, now."

She sniffled as she pressed her face into his chest. "Aren't you going to tell me duty comes before love? Everyone else has."

Valenden barked a laugh. "You know I do precisely the opposite of what everyone else does."

Bryn felt herself melting into his arms, relieved to have a friend. As much as she wanted to be furious at Valenden for sending the messenger to warn Rangar, she couldn't find anger in her heart. Rangar would have found out as soon as he'd returned, anyway. He'd ruined her wedding feast, but she had never cared about the festivities. The gown, decorations, and food hadn't mattered in the slightest—all she'd cared about had been the look on her people's faces when they'd realized their kingdom would soon be in benevolent hands.

She murmured, "I need to see Rangar."

Valenden stroked her back gently. "Not a good idea. Not tonight. Let his temper cool. Besides, there's no way my father and aunt would allow it. You're married to Trei. Even in the Baersladen, where decorum matters little, a married woman can't speak alone to a former lover."

Bryn drew back, peering up at Valenden. "I *have* to speak to him, Val."

Valenden scrubbed a hand over his face and then sighed. "Fine, fine. I'll see what I can do. They put him in the jail cell in the tower, and I happen to know one of the tower guards has a weakness for *statua* herb."

She wiped her eyes and breathed, "Thank you."

But Valenden looked troubled. "You still have a wedding night ahead of you."

The blood drained from her face. Rangar's arrival had stricken those thoughts from her mind. She'd been worried enough *before* his arrival about what it would be like to make love with Rangar's brother . . . and now she had to do so while Rangar was under the same roof, cursing both her and Trei with every bone in his body.

Valenden reached into his pocket and came back with a flask that he passed to Bryn. "Drink this. All of it."

She took it gratefully and drained it to the dregs. Then, shaking, set off to find her new husband.

CHAPTER 7

WEDDING NIGHT . . . marriage rules . . . the man in the tower . . . broken hearts . . . hexmark magic

"I would suggest that we wait," Trei said as he stood alone with Bryn in the second-floor bedroom designated as their newlywed suite, "Except you know the traditions as well as I do. Our two kingdoms do not differ in that respect."

They could still hear the rising and falling notes of the wedding feast music coming from the great hall. Bryn faced her new husband from the far side of the bed, terrified to come closer.

She *did* know the tradition. Her mother had neglected to teach her many things, but she knew that royal marriages were consummated on the wedding night.

Feeling dizzy from brandy, she looked toward the ceiling with a curse on her lips. Rangar knew the tradition, too. If he weren't locked in the tower cell at that moment, he'd be down here now, banging on the door, ready to punch Trei again if he so much as looked at Bryn's bare shoulder.

She sank onto the bed with legs that had turned to jelly. "I don't know if I can do this, Trei. Not after Rangar . . . That look on his face . . . " She buried her face in her hands.

Trei knelt by her side. "If I could spare you any hurt, you know I would."

She muttered, "It was awful, Trei. He was so pained. *I* did that to him."

"We both did." Trei reached up to stroke her hair but winced at the movement and grabbed his shoulder.

Bryn gasped. "Your shoulder! I've been so worried about Rangar; I forgot you were wounded. Are you okay?"

He nodded as he dropped his hand from his shoulder, but his face remained pinched. "I'm fine. While you were with Valenden, my aunt healed the worst of the wounds. It will be fine tomorrow."

Regardless, Bryn scolded herself for not having expressed concern for Trei sooner. He was her husband of one evening, and she'd already failed him!

She swallowed and asked in a whisper, "Do you think he would have . . . seriously hurt you?" She couldn't stop thinking about Rangar's threat to end Trei for what he'd done.

Trei massaged the bridge of his nose, looking weary. "You're asking if he'd kill me? No. I know my brother. He might throw some punches and wish me dead, but he doesn't have such wrath in him. In any case, it doesn't matter. We should banish Rangar and . . . and anyone else...from our minds tonight."

She paused. "Saraj, you mean."

Trei lifted a tight shoulder. "Yes." Then he touched her cheek. "*You* are my bride, Bryn. That is all that matters."

It most definitely wasn't all that mattered, but Trei had a way of speaking with such confidence that the tension in the room broke like soap bubbles stretched too thin.

"Your gown lost its battle with the mud," Trei observed, motioning to the sodden hem that not even magic had entirely rid of stains. "Shall I . . . help you out of it?"

The blood drained from Bryn's face. *He is my husband. This is what husbands and wives do.*

"Ah, um, yes," she said in a weak voice as her pounding heart protested. "Please."

She turned her back to him so he could start to undo the long row of buttons. She stared at a crack in the bedroom wall, trying hard not to wonder what Rangar was doing at that moment. The tower cell was better than the dungeon, but not by much. She could picture him pacing a circular path again and again, raging as he imagined everything his brother and his betrothed were doing a few floors below.

Trei reached the lowest button at the base of her spine. His fingers grazed her skin, and she felt a shiver run up her back. Her heart might not be with Trei, but he was a handsome man—it could be worse. *Better than that bastard baron from Ruma.* Slowly, Trei pushed the fabric off one of her shoulders, revealing bare skin covered by a thin chemise strap.

His large hand cupped her small shoulder. "You're beautiful, Bryn."

With her back to him, he couldn't see the pain that crossed her face, but she felt it contort her features. She bit her lip so hard it stung, and then she forced herself to turn around. "Here. Let me help you . . . with your shirt."

With shaking fingers, she started to undo the buttons at his throat. She was close enough to smell candle smoke on him from the feast as well as fig brandy, though he hadn't drunk more than a few sips all night. *She* was the tipsy one, not him, and she suddenly wished she had remained sober as her mother had always told her. *A princess keeps her wits about her.* Then again, how could she have gotten through the night without ample glasses of brandy?

"It was a . . . lovely ceremony," she whispered in an attempt to break the tension. Her hands reached the last button on his shirt, and she smoothed the fabric back off his shoulders. She swallowed hard. The lantern light reflected off the hexmarks scarring the hard planes of his abdomen. She'd seen him shirtless before and knew he was powerfully built, but it was another thing entirely to be mere inches from his body, knowing that he would soon be pressing her to the sheets.

Trei said gruffly, "No, it wasn't."

She looked up in surprise to find him giving a wry half-smile. He continued, "That was the most depressing wedding I've ever seen. We were nearly drowned. It felt like the gods were torturing us."

She was so relieved to hear someone admit the truth that she burst out laughing. She pressed a hand to her mouth. "Oh, thank goodness. I was so tired of pretending it wasn't the most miserable affair of my life."

His smile revealed a small dimple on one cheek she hadn't noticed before. "I felt like my horse when he's at pasture during a storm."

She leaned in, shaking her head. "*I* felt like a mouse who fell in a bucket of dishwater."

"Like a fisher after three weeks at sea, soaked to the bone."

"Like a pot of marigolds, overwatered and wilted."

They both started laughing out loud. Bryn hugged her belly as her whole body shook with laughter. It felt marvelous to let go of the tension that had filled the entire day. She'd been afraid that life with Trei would be all formality, but now she saw another side to him.

Wiping his eyes, he pushed up on one elbow, still chuckling. His shirt had slid back over his shoulders, revealing his large frame and smooth skin marred by hexmarks and a few battle scars. He shrugged the rest of the way out of his shirt and tossed it aside.

Bryn reached out a curious hand and ran her finger down his left arm, tracing the various hexmarks.

"So many," she whispered. "If you have this many hexmarks, why don't you use magic as often as your brothers?"

He watched her finger tracing the marks on his forearm and said, "I don't have as much cause to. They're out in the field more than I am."

Regardless, he certainly had achieved as many marks as either Valenden or Rangar. She got lost in examining all the intricate symbols on him, wondering what spells they commanded. He had the finding and purge marks, as she did, amid dozens more. A thrill stirred in her to think of all the magical possibilities Trei could bring to the Mir people.

She was so captivated by his hexmarks, tracing them up to his shoulder, that she hadn't realized their faces were only inches apart.

"Bryn." His voice had deepened. He cupped her jaw, dragging his thumb over her cheek. "I meant what I said. You're beautiful."

Her heart leaped as she understood the time had come. The energy in the room shifted. Their friendly laughter evaporated, and now it was just the two of them with their wedding clothes unbuttoned, sitting on the newlywed bed.

When he lowered his mouth to hers, she found

herself as ready as anyone could be in her position. She'd been mentally preparing for this moment. She'd expected the kiss to feel like duty—*close your eyes or stare at the ceiling*, her mother had once told her—but it didn't feel like that. As hard as she wanted to find fault with him, she genuinely liked Trei. Good looks, an honorable bearing, keenly intelligent but quick to laugh—Trei's only fault was that he wasn't his brother.

Don't think about Rangar. She scolded herself as Trei deepened the kiss. His lips brushed hers in a testing caress. His hand slid over her shoulder, pushing the remaining fabric of her wedding dress down to her waist.

She kissed him back just as experimentally. The sensations running through her body weren't the wild passion she felt with Rangar, but they weren't entirely unwelcome, either. Her heartbeat kicked up when he ran his thumb over her chemise's strap. Uncertainly, she touched the back of his neck, weaving her fingers in the hair at his nape. He responded by anchoring his hand on her hip and bunching the fabric in his fist.

So different from Rangar, she thought, *and yet they're brothers. There's still an echo of Rangar in Trei. Saints, and Valenden, too.*

Trei broke the kiss long enough to gather her dress around her waist and tug it down over her legs. She lifted her hips to help him and wiggled out of it until she was left in her chemise. It was white cotton but thin enough to be somewhat transparent, and when Trei's gaze fell on her, she felt herself trembling.

"By the gods," he muttered.

He returned to the bed but, instead of sitting beside her, gripped her shoulder to guide her back until she was lying on the sheets. Holding himself above her with one arm, he took a moment to look over her face as though memorizing her.

Then, he lowered himself for another kiss. This one felt different. Instantly, Bryn felt a bolt of energy shoot through her. She had on her chemise, he had on his trousers. Nothing else. Only a few garments separated them. It suddenly felt very real, and a flood of mixed emotions came with it.

Rangar, she thought as Trei tasted her lips with a quick stroke of his tongue. *I want Rangar.*

She commanded her hands to touch Trei's chest, exploring his rigid muscles. A part of her thought only of Rangar and his pain, but there was another part of her, one made pliable with brandy, that responded in the way any woman would with a man like Trei. He tasted like Mir honey, and she deepened the kiss for another taste.

Trei cradled her head as he kissed her, his fingers working to undo her braids until he could wrap his fingers around her hair and pull just hard enough to tip her head back to trail his lips down her neck.

She clutched onto his shoulders, digging her short fingernails into his skin to get ahead of the intense sensations she was feeling. He suddenly ground his hips against hers, and she sucked in a breath as her whole body quivered.

He knows what he's doing. She felt some relief that she was with a man who was both skilled and gentle for her first time, but the thought was immediately eclipsed. *Rangar was supposed to be my first!*

Trei pulled away as he fumbled with the belt around his trousers. Without the warmth of his body, Bryn felt a sudden chill. She started shivering from the cold and uncertainty. In another few moments, Trei was going to do what men did with their wives. Claim her in every way as his.

But I'm not his.

Rangar had saved her from wolves when she was eight years old, then again on the night of the Castle Mir uprising. He believed through the *fralen* bond that it was his duty to watch over her, and he had, even at great risk to his own life. He'd even poisoned himself in an attempt to have *her* save *his* life so that they would be even—equally each other's Saved and Saviors.

Which meant she was Rangar's Savior now. She'd never truly believed in the *fralen* bond, always uncomfortable with the idea that someone could own another's soul, but she couldn't deny that a powerful bond existed between them. In a way, *Rangar* was her duty just as much as this marriage was.

"Trei, stop!" She gasped and sat up, crossing a hand over her chest. Her face twisted as tears threatened. "I'm so sorry. I can't do it. I wanted to, I tried to, but I can't stop thinking about him . . ."

Surprise passed over Trei's face like a mottled patch of shade. As soon as her tears appeared, he let go of his belt and dragged her into his arms, holding her on his lap.

"Shh, Bryn, it's all right." He stroked her back. "I just . . ." He gave a deep sigh. "Thank the gods."

She looked up at him in surprise to find that his face was just as strained as hers.

"I'm sorry, too," he said. "I was going to try, but I couldn't get my mind off Saraj," he confessed. "She's all I've thought about today. Ever since my father suggested this plan, I know it's been torturing her. And me." He pulled Bryn closer and pressed his forehead against hers.

Relief filled her that she wasn't alone in this. For as calm and confident as Trei had seemed, it had only been an act. He'd been just as conflicted over making love to a woman that wasn't Saraj.

"What are we going to do, Trei?" she whispered.

"I don't know." He stroked her back softly. "They'll know if the marriage isn't consummated."

"How could they possibly know?" she asked.

Eventually, it would stir suspicion if she didn't fall pregnant within a few months, but that felt like a lifetime away, more than enough time to figure out a better solution.

"Your people don't have magic as we do," he said and indicated a hexmark halfway up his bicep that looked like a series of sun symbols. "This lets us see auras. They're a sort of hazy colored light surrounding a person. It's helpful to know if someone is being deceptive."

"You mean they'll know if we're lying?" she finished.

He nodded. "Few people have this hexmark, but my aunt is one. She'd take one look at us and know."

"Couldn't we convince her to keep it secret?"

"I don't know. I don't think she'd keep it secret forever, not when others could see the deceptive aura, too." He paused, dragging a hand over his jaw. "We don't have to make a public appearance until the Wedding Tour when we ride to the villages of the Baersladen so the common folk can meet their new queen. That isn't for a week. That buys us a bit more time. I'll speak with my aunt and ask her to remain quiet until then."

Bryn buried her face in his chest and nodded.

A few more days before losing her virginity to Trei wasn't a perfect solution, but at least it would give her time to talk to Rangar first. She'd never forgive herself if she let Trei bed her while Rangar was just overhead, prowling around the tower, imagining all the ways she'd betrayed him.

"So, then, what do we do now?" she asked.

He ran a hand down the length of her hair. "Now, princess, we get some sleep."

Her whole body sagged with exhaustion. She hadn't realized how strung out she'd been until this moment of relief, knowing that the consummation didn't have to happen that night.

She flopped onto the bed without bothering to pull on the lace nightgown Helna had made for her. Trei slipped between the sheets next to her. She found herself scooting close to him, letting him wrap a hand around her small frame.

They fell asleep like that, in each other's arms but each dreaming of someone else.

CHAPTER 8

A NEW TRADITION . . . colored auras . . . Wedding Tour plans . . . forbidden to be alone . . . secrets in the steam

Knock, knock.

In the morning, a kitchen maid brought in a tray of scones and pine leaf tea, blushing to find the future king and queen still in bed and half-naked.

"Oh! I'll leave this . . . here." The maid set the tray on the foot of the bed and scampered off, already giggling behind her hand.

"Great." Bryn moaned as she sat up, rubbing her eyes. "I suppose we should prepare ourselves for gossip to sweep through the castle like the plague."

The sheet fell off Trei's bare chest as he sat up and

swiped a scone. "Let the servants talk. It's better for us if everyone in the castle is gossiping about our supposed passionate night of lovemaking than speculating it might never have happened."

Warmth bloomed on Bryn's cheeks when she remembered the night before. The marriage hadn't been consummated, which was a relief, but she could feel the shadow of Trei's kisses all over her lips. All they'd accomplished was pushing the deed off for a few days.

She glanced at Trei and felt a flush of guilt. She stuffed a scone into her mouth to bury the emotions.

Someone knocked on the door, but before Trei could ask who it was, Mage Marna swept in.

Bryn nearly choked on her scone to see the white-haired woman looking over them with a searching gaze.

"You've slept in," Mage Marna observed dryly.

Trei gave a casual shrug, not meeting his aunt's eyes. "Hardly surprising for newlyweds, is it?"

The mage narrowed her eyes. Her gaze closely inspected the tangled sheets, Trei's shirt tossed on the floor, Bryn's bruised lips—but then she let out a scathing scoff.

"You didn't consummate the marriage."

Trei slid a wary look to Bryn and muttered, "I told you she'd be able to tell."

Mage Marna tipped her head up toward the ceiling in exasperation. "You know tradition's requirements, Trei. As do you, Bryn—"

"Calm down, Aunt." Trei scrubbed a hand over his face. Bryn had rarely heard anyone speak to Mage Marna without fear in their voice, and she was surprised at Trei's tone. "We both understand what's expected of us. But you must realize you gave us two days to come to terms with turning our lives upside down. There is . . . collateral damage to consider."

"Duty comes before love," the mage said evenly. "Saraj and Rangar know that as well as everyone else."

"We'll consummate the marriage before the Wedding Tour," Trei assured her, then glanced at Bryn. "Just give us a few days to get used to one another."

Mage Marna's lips pinched. "The tradition is archaic, I will grant you both that, but we're all bound by it. If I can see it in your auras, then so will others. I'm not the only one in the kingdom with the aura hex; there are others, especially in the outer villages you'll visit on the Wedding Tour. If they discover the marriage isn't valid, it threatens the stability of both kingdoms and our hopes to unite them."

Trei said tightly, "We understand."

Bryn felt a shiver of apprehension and sipped deeply on her tea to calm her nerves.

Mage Marna let out another long breath. "I didn't come here to discuss *that*, in any case. Aleth and I were up all night discussing what's to be done with Rangar."

A tense silence fell over the room. Bryn pulled the sheets higher over her chest. She couldn't help but glance at the ceiling, where somewhere overhead,

Rangar had probably paced all night and was pacing still.

"Valenden was the one who sent a messenger to warn Rangar," Mage Marna informed them. "He confessed when Aleth threatened to throw him in the tower with his brother."

Trei glanced at Bryn, and Bryn felt overcome with the sense that Trei had already known this information, just as she had. They'd both kept it secret to protect Valenden.

"Valenden will be punished accordingly," Mage Marna continued. "Interfering with state business is no small crime." She sighed. "But Rangar's punishment is our greater concern."

"Rangar didn't commit any crimes," Bryn said quietly. "You lied to him, and he discovered the lie. That's it."

"He assaulted the future king," the mage challenged.

Bryn glanced at the bruises on Trei's temple and shoulder that had darkened overnight. She couldn't very well defend Rangar when he had assaulted her husband, who was half-naked in bed with her.

"It was nothing," Trei scoffed, waving off any concern. "He was angry. The soldiers stopped him before he got in another swing."

"He threatened to kill you," Mage Marna insisted.

"He's threatened to kill me over far less," Trei muttered. "On our fishing trip last summer, he said he'd slit my throat if I finished the last of the ale."

Mage Marna went to the window, looking out over the stormy sea. The rain hadn't lessened from the day before, casting everything in mottled shades of gray. "You're defending him because you love him, but we all know he will be trouble. This time, it's serious."

Bryn felt a flutter of fear in her chest and piped up, "But he isn't a *prisoner*. He's your nephew! You can't leave him locked in the tower forever."

Mage Marna turned from the window. "Yes. That is true. Aleth and I came to the same agreement." She gave a wary pause before adding, "We're going to release Rangar this morning, but with the caveat that he cannot be in a room alone with either of you. Trei, his temper could get the better of him, and he could very well assault you again. And Bryn, though I doubt he would ever harm you, there are . . . other things . . . he could attempt in a private room that would be just as detrimental to the kingdoms."

Bryn's eyes widened. She understood perfectly well. They were afraid Rangar would attempt to seduce her into leaving Trei, perhaps even running away with him. Even a passionate embrace with the future queen would be grounds for treason.

Mage Marna stated, "Soldiers will accompany you wherever you go, Bryn, to ensure Rangar keeps his hands to himself."

Bryn groaned inwardly. Mage Marna hadn't suggested that Bryn might also commit adultery with Rangar, which was a small kindness, but Bryn certainly felt she was as much on trial here as Rangar.

As much as she wanted to object more, it was useless. "I understand."

Mage Marna squeezed her hands together against the cold. "Good. Now, I'll speak to Calista and Ren. They're the only ones with the aura hex in the castle. It would be wise for you two to get dressed. Now that riders have been sent out with the, ahem, *good news*, there is a long receiving line forming in the great hall. Villagers who want to meet their future king and queen. I suspect the line will only grow as the day continues."

Bryn and Trei sat at the great hall's head table for several excruciating hours, handing out maiden roses to the long line of common folk who had traveled to meet them and bless their union. She was heartened to see every one of the Mir refugees at the head of the line, giving her Mir blessings and expressing their anxious excitement to discuss the future of their kingdom.

By the time late afternoon came, and Bryn's legs had gone numb from sitting, a stir came from the direction of the courtyard. She sat straighter, searching the long line until she saw a familiar figure stride in.

Her stomach plummeted.

She leaned close to Trei and whispered, "Rangar is here."

Rangar was flanked by two of the most enormous soldiers Bryn had ever seen. They were absolute hulks of men, the only ones strong enough to restrain Rangar if necessary. From Rangar's tense posture, it was clear the soldiers had been a requirement of his release from the tower cell.

As soon as the common folk spotted Rangar, they quickly moved aside, willing to give up their place in line either out of respect for the prince or a salacious desire to witness the drama that was about to ensue.

Rangar slowly sauntered up to the head table. The soldiers stopped behind him and rested hands on their swords in a warning.

Bryn felt the breath leave her lungs.

He said nothing at first. Instead, he took his time looking over the baskets full of maiden roses with a guarded expression. A memory flooded Bryn of Rangar taking her to see the roses and assuring her that she would adapt to the harsh land just like them.

"Rangar." Trei nodded slowly, cautiously. "I assume you've come to pay your respects." His tone was stiff, and the message was clear: now, in public, was not the time to get into another skirmish.

Bryn felt terribly torn: Part of her wanted to disappear into her chair and escape Rangar's pained, wrathful look. But another part was desperate to be close to him again. She curled her hands around her chair arm and squeezed tightly. Her heart felt like it was about to burst out of her chest.

"Not exactly the words I had in mind, brother,"

Rangar replied through a clenched jaw. "But seeing as these soldiers are prepared to separate my head from my body if I don't behave, I suppose I can't tell you what I *really* want to say."

Bryn couldn't stand the animosity between the two brothers. She leaned forward, looking up at Rangar through her lashes, and whispered fiercely, "Rangar, please. We didn't have a choice."

His eyes snapped to hers. She jolted upright. When he'd arrived at the wedding feast the day before, he'd barely been able to bring himself to look at her. He'd focused all his rage on Trei instead. But he wasn't avoiding her gaze now. Now, she saw his raw pain and realized he hadn't been ignoring her out of spite; he was terrified that she might have done this willingly.

"King Aleth and Mage Marna explained the succession rules to us," she said slowly, keeping her voice low in an attempt to keep gossip to a minimum. "Both kingdoms would suffer greatly unless the crown heirs were united. Trei and I . . . neither of us wanted this. We didn't want to hurt you—"

"Stop, Bryn." Rangar's jaw was squeezed tightly. His hands curled into fists by his side. "I don't want your pity."

"It isn't pity—"

"*Stop.*" His jaw worked as though he had more to say, but the soldiers were right behind him as well as hundreds of listening ears eager for rumors. He leaned across the table and muttered lowly, "This isn't even remotely close to being over. So don't get too comfortable in your new roles as husband and wife."

"Is that a threat?" Trei asked testily.

The soldiers adjusted their stance, preparing to intercede.

Rangar gave a mirthless laugh. In a louder voice meant to be overheard, he said condescendingly, "Congratulations to the both of you."

He turned and strode away, the soldiers following.

Bryn realized she'd been holding her breath. She let it out in a rush as she slumped back in the chair.

Trei rested a hand on her arm. "Are you all right?"

"I think . . . I might be finished for the day." The receiving line still had hundreds of villagers, but there was no way she'd be able to get to them all that day anyway.

"Of course." Trei signaled to the guards that Mage Marna had assigned to Bryn. They escorted her to the hall, where she finally had a moment of privacy and leaned against the wall to catch her breath.

This isn't even remotely close to being over.

What did Rangar mean by that? The marriage was a done deal. True, it wasn't official until it was consummated, but Rangar didn't have the aura hex. He had no way of knowing it wasn't valid yet. What could he possibly do to get her back now, short of slaughtering Trei and leaving her a widow able to remarry? Which, of course, Rangar would never do, not even with his temper.

She spent some time pacing the endless halls,

wishing the rain would let up so that she could go outside and breathe fresh air. She hated having the soldiers shadow her at all times. She felt like she would lose her mind until she turned a corner and ran smack into Valenden.

"Oh! Val." She swallowed. "I heard you earned Mage Marna's ire."

Valenden was dressed in his usual rumpled clothes, though his hair looked especially tousled. He shrugged. "She assigned me latrine duty for a week. Could have been worse. Actually, I've been looking for you. My aunt arranged for a bridal bath, some tradition for the night after the wedding . . . I don't know how these womanly things work." He briefly glanced at the guards. "It's ready for you in the women's bathhouse."

Bryn cocked her head, confused. She'd never heard of such a tradition, and Mage Marna wasn't known for pampering. But Valenden had an oddly insistent look in his eye, so she slowly nodded. "Right . . . Mage Marna mentioned something about that this morning."

"Come, I'll walk with you." He gave a mocking bow to the guards. "And *you*, of course."

Valenden led the way through the castle to the bottom level, where the men's and women's bathhouses branched off. Steam pumped out steadily through the curtain that served as a doorway. Valenden swept back the curtain and coughed at the burst of steam. "Your guards will wait for you here, of course. To protect the modesty of the future queen."

This was clearly news to the guards, but they glanced between one another and nodded before flanking the doorway.

As Bryn entered the bathhouse, she didn't miss Valenden's small wink.

The stone chamber was filled with steam that made everything cloudy. The ceiling dripped with condensation. The boilers must be working at full strength because she'd never seen the air so thick. The bathhouse appeared empty for this supposed new ceremony, without even an attendant with a robe and towels.

"Hello?" she called hesitantly.

Then, she heard the footsteps. They were the heavy tread of a boot, not the graceful steps of the barefoot attendants.

Rangar Barendur emerged from the steam, dressed in his black riding clothes and boots.

"Rangar!" Bryn pressed a hand over her mouth.

Now she understood this invented ceremony—which Mage Marna certain didn't know about—and Valenden's wink. Somehow, Rangar had slipped his own guards just as she had, perhaps also with Valenden's help. "The soldiers . . . "

"Don't worry about them." He came out of the steam with all the coiled tension of a beast ready to pounce, and she found herself taking a tentative step back. She'd seen his wrath toward Trei. Rangar had always suffered from an inability to control his temper, and she feared it was now aimed at her. He wouldn't raise a hand against her, but harsh words could sting just as much.

She gasped, "I swear, when they sent you away, I didn't know—"

She held out a beseeching hand. He grabbed her wrist and pulled her toward him. She squeaked to feel his arm suddenly around her waist as he pressed her back up against the damp wall and, taking only a moment to brush his thumb across her cheek, devoured her lips with his own.

CHAPTER 9

A FORBIDDEN MEETING . . . grounds for treason . . . interrupted at the worst moment . . . hands to himself

So much for the sanctity of marriage.

Rangar kissed her—his brother's wife—like a famished creature. His hands cupped her jaw, his body pinned her to the glistening bathhouse wall, his lips moved insistently. Bursts of steam from the boilers rose around them, causing them to break out in sweat.

The kiss had happened so fast that Bryn could barely react. She'd been terrified that Rangar would assault her with accusations, so this ardent embrace was not what she'd been expecting. She broke the kiss, her breath coming fast. Steam was already plastering her hair to her face as she cast a quick glance in the direction of the curtain doorway.

"Rangar, the guards!" she whispered. "They're right on the other side of that curtain!"

"Then you'd better keep your moans quiet," he growled before moving back in for a kiss.

But she rested a hand on his chest, holding him off. "By the Saints, wait! This is . . . " She swallowed. *It's treason and adultery...and I'm not sure if I care if it is.* She blinked a few times. "We need to talk."

His eyes were fixed on her lips like he wanted to snatch another kiss, but he held himself back. Resting one hand on the wall behind her, he leaned in and said, "Now that it is just the two of us, tell me the truth. Did anyone force you into the marriage?"

She swallowed, feeling the creep of dread run up her extremities. She'd been afraid of this conversation ever since King Aleth had first told her about the plan to marry Trei. "Not by physical force, no." As soon as Rangar's face darkened, she quickly added, "But it was a political necessity. There was no other way to unite our kingdoms. You aren't the crown heir, so if I'd married you, you wouldn't be king of both the Mirien *and* the Baersladen."

His face went stony, and she touched her palm to his scarred cheek. "Rangar, listen. The wedding was the last thing I wanted. I didn't know that's why they had sent you away to the borderlands. They cornered me after you'd left and explained the situation. Trei and I were both terribly upset about it but ultimately didn't see any option but to put duty before love."

His eyes narrowed. "You and Trei. A happy couple already, is that it?" A shadow crossed his face as he leaned in and dropped his voice dangerously. "Did you like it when he fucked you last night in your newlywed bed?"

She gasped, then grew angry and slammed a fist against his chest. "For your information, we *didn't* consummate the marriage yet out of respect for you and Saraj."

Rangar narrowed his eyes and seemed to consider this for some time, but his temper didn't cool. He barked, "You said *yet*."

She knit her fingers together anxiously. "Well, I mean, I don't see what choice I have eventually . . . "

"What choice other than to ride my brother like a stallion?"

"Rangar!" She clapped a hand over her mouth, aware that the guards were close. She dropped her voice to a whisper. "Don't speak like that."

He raised his other hand to the wall, caging her between his arms. "Bryn, you have no idea what I've felt these past few days. When Valenden's messenger told me about the wedding, I didn't think you would go through with it. I rode day and night to save you, knowing you had to have been forced into it." He looked away, wounded. "Only to arrive too late. And to learn that you weren't forced at all."

She gripped his arm, shaking him. "Rangar, please.

You're torturing me! I can't put what's between us above my entire kingdom, despite however much I want you."

A formidable look sprang into his eyes. "And how much is that?"

She was very aware of the fact that his body was practically flush against hers. She could feel the rigidity of his muscles and suspected that it extended to the manly part between his legs. If she only shifted her hips forward, she'd feel his desire. She sucked in a breath at the thought. Her heart began to thump in her chest.

"We can't," she whispered. "I'm married. It's wrong." Still, her skin was begging for his touch, and she couldn't keep herself from arching her back, grazing his chest with her own.

He lowered his lips to her ear and muttered, "It was wrong of my family to wed you to my brother, knowing it would destroy me. I don't care a damn about propriety, Bryn."

"If they catch us, they could lock us both up for treason."

"It's worth the dungeon to be with you."

Before she could protest, he captured her lips again. Her first instinct was to struggle, but the surge of need that rose in her at the touch of their lips made her body go still. A fluttery sensation spread from her lips to the base of her belly, and she felt herself shivering from want. The sweat dripping down her temples only made her more flushed.

She squirmed against the wall, brushing her hips against his, and felt the stiffness there that told her how badly his own need was.

As he devoured her lips, all thoughts of propriety left her mind. While he'd been away, she'd been able to fool herself into believing they could both move on with enough time, but now she realized what they had wouldn't die that easily.

As he melded his body to her curves, he dropped a hand to the small of her back. He moved it low until he could cup her bottom, then pulled her tightly against his hips.

She gasped, tossing her head back.

"He'll never make you feel like this," Rangar growled in her ear. "Like your body is on fire."

Yes. She knew that now. She'd experienced some pleasant feelings with Trei, even a brief spark when he'd kissed her, but nothing like this.

Rangar's hand began to bunch up her skirt to her thigh. He stroked her bare leg, leaving her trembling in urgency. She felt her nipples harden under her blouse and leaned forward to graze them against his chest, moaning at the brush of contact.

"No man will ever give you pleasure as I do." He grabbed her by the back of her neck, pulling her close so he could tease her ear with his teeth. His other hand, plunged under her skirt, trailed to the thin undergarments that were already soaked with her desire. "I don't want him to have you."

"He's my husband," she panted.

He pushed her back hard against the wall, panting now himself. "Then let me have you first."

Her eyes widened. What he was proposing was adultery, a serious crime. Even in the eyes of her saints and his gods, there was little worse than being unfaithful to a wedded partner. Before she'd married Trei, she would have willingly let Rangar make love to her. It was *him* who had wanted to wait until marriage. But now, she was bound by an oath.

"We can't."

"No one has to know."

Flushed, she whispered, "Mage Marna can see my aura. She can tell that kind of thing."

"So tell her Trei was the one who fucked you senseless. She'll be pleased." His hand grew more insistent between her legs as his thumb pressed on the outside of her undergarments. She found herself falling speechless. The sensations that his touch was stirring in her were impossible to ignore. A tingle spread throughout her lower half, making her hips squirm.

She closed her eyes, leaning her head back against the damp wall. He dipped a finger between the hem of her undergarments and her skin, stroking her core. She let out a cry, and he pressed a hand against her mouth.

"Shh." He jerked his head in the direction of the guards.

With his hand still pressed over her mouth, she nodded. He licked his lips, a fevered look in his eye. He started moving his hand again, filling her with starbursts of need.

"Undo my trousers," he ordered.

She found herself unbuckling his belt as though her hands weren't her own. She knew this was wrong. She'd made a vow to another man. A good man. His brother! But Trei could never fill her with pleasure as Rangar could.

As his hand moved faster over her tight, wet core, he leaned in to replace his hand over her mouth with his lips.

Then, suddenly, they heard footsteps and a sharp intake of breath.

Bryn froze. Rangar stilled, his hands still plunged under her skirt. Slowly, terrified, Bryn turned her head.

Mage Marna stood in the bathhouse with the curtained doorway open, the soldiers behind her. Their eyes were wide as they took in the scandalous scene—not even trained soldiers could hide their shock.

Instantly, the mage turned to the soldiers. She made a quick hand gesture in the air and muttered a spell. "You didn't see *anything*."

The two soldiers blinked as though slightly dazed.

"Didn't see anything," they repeated.

Mage Marna whirled back on Bryn and Rangar. Bryn quickly moved her hands away from Rangar's belt, and he pulled his hand out from under her skirt.

His aunt grabbed his shoulder, giving him a good shake.

"Are you *mad*? Don't you see what you're doing? Are you trying to tear the Eyrie apart?"

He stepped back from Bryn, but there was no remorse in his eyes. He gave a harsh laugh. "What did you expect from me?"

"I expected you to grow up and be a man. To put your duty above your cock. But I see you're still just some lustful boy who can't keep his hands to himself." She lifted her chin. "Well, then, I suppose I'll have to make you."

Bryn pressed her hands to her mouth. "Mage Marna, please, we weren't going to—"

The mage signaled to the guards sharply. "Take Lady Bryn back to Trei. Speak nothing of this to anyone."

Flushed with guilt, Bryn didn't move. She wasn't about to leave Rangar to face his aunt on his own. He might be strong, but her magic was far more powerful than his muscles.

Bryn pleaded, "No, I'm just as guilty as him."

Mage Marna gave her a stern look. "*You* arranged this rendezvous? Somehow, I doubt that."

Bryn swallowed, feeling sweat run down her temples.

Rangar jerked his chin toward the guards. "Go, Bryn. It's all right. I can handle my aunt."

Uncertain, Bryn asked the mage, "What will you do to him?"

"I won't hurt him," Mage Marna said with a bit less rancor. "I won't throw him in the dungeon. *Yet.* I'll just make sure he keeps his hands to himself from now on."

Bryn blanched, but she felt a soldier press a heavy hand on her shoulder. Rangar nodded to her, his face unreadable, and she had no choice but to leave him with his aunt.

CHAPTER 10

A PUNISHING SPELL . . . erased memories . . . marriage regrets . . . plans to take back a kingdom

Mage Marna's spell on the guards appeared to have successfully erased their memories because, after about ten paces from the bathhouse, they began to speak to Bryn of pleasantries about the wedding feast. As unnerving as it was to hear them prattle as though they hadn't just seen her with Rangar's hands all over her, she was also grateful. If the whole castle knew about her and Rangar's indiscretion, the alliance between their kingdoms would be in jeopardy.

The guards led her to the room designated as the newlywed chamber, where she found Trei reading a book with a platter of untouched food on the table. He closed the book when she entered.

"Bryn. Are you feeling better?"

She had told herself she'd be the model of discretion. She had promised herself she wouldn't draw Trei into trouble that wasn't of his making. Yet she immediately sank onto the bed and started shaking.

Eyes widening, Trei set aside the book and wrapped a hand around her back. "What happened?"

There were a million reasons she shouldn't say anything about what had happened in the bathhouse, but Trei had a forgiving heart, and she knew he wouldn't judge her. Their romance might be a facade, but their friendship was true.

"I spoke with Rangar," she whispered.

Alarmed, Trei immediately looked toward the door, then back to her. "Alone?"

She nodded as she pressed a hand against her mouth. She muttered between her fingers, "He's hurting greatly."

Best not to mention the *other* things that had happened—or almost happened—between them. Trei might be her friend and a confidante, but his grace only extended so far. "Your aunt found us speaking together. The guards must have overheard us talking and fetched her."

Trei sighed as he rubbed his tired eyes. "That's going to be a problem. My father thinks Rangar simply needs to find someone new to warm his bed to take his mind off you. He's already sent scouts to find village girls who might catch Rangar's eye. Ones with fair hair in particular . . . It won't work, of course. Rangar's been in love with you for years. He intended to spend the rest of his life with you."

"The *fralen* bond," Bryn said in a distant voice. "I never believed in it, but . . . I don't know . . . I *do* feel something different with him. Like we are bound together in some way. I don't think I can deny it much longer."

Trei rested his hand on hers. "Perhaps, but you and I have a bond as well." His finger moved along her finger to stop on her wedding ring.

Bryn swallowed. "I know."

"Do you regret marrying me?"

She hesitated before saying honestly, "I believe it was the right thing to do for my people. They've suffered so much at my family's hands; I didn't have any more choice than you did."

Trei picked up the book he'd been reading and opened it to a dense-looking chapter. "I've been researching the Mirien's coronation tradition. We can't formally take control until we wear the actual crowns of the king and queen, and Captain Carr holds possession of Castle Mir. He isn't going to want to give those up."

She slid over the book, reading through the passages. "So, how do we get the crowns?"

He lowered his voice. "I believe we can use the Wedding Tour to our advantage. My father will share more details, but we must turn the Mir populace against Captain Carr."

She frowned down at the book. "That sounds dangerous."

Trei laughed but not mockingly. At her questioning look, he said, "Bryn, we're the rulers of two of the strongest kingdoms in the Eyrie. Of course, it's dangerous. We'll be facing danger every day for the rest of our lives."

She studied him for a long while. "How can you live like that? Knowing that every day there might be an assassin waiting to slit your throat?"

Trei closed the book, drawing her hand into his. "Because I see how beautiful life is. How full of hope. Because I won't let fear stop me from bringing that beauty to others."

There was such sincerity in his words that she found herself leaning into him as he wrapped her arms around her. She closed her eyes, heart galloping, and tried not to think of messes, dangers, and forbidden kisses among the steam.

Bryn didn't see Rangar for the next several days.

Every night, she and Trei slept in bed together, putting off the consummation they both knew was inevitable. She spent her days sitting long hours in the wedding receiving line, handing out maiden roses and blessings with as much enthusiasm as she could muster, or working with the castle's staff to plan the upcoming Wedding Tour. It would be two weeks on the road of wearing a new gown every day. In preparation for the tour, thousands of scones were baked with the maiden rose emblem pressed in them and drizzled with Mir honey. When she wasn't participating in the post-wedding traditions, she was in the council chambers with King Aleth, Mage Marna, Trei, and Valenden, discussing strategies for taking back the Mir crowns with as little bloodshed as possible.

Mage Marna turned to Bryn. "It would be good for you to speak with the refugees. Ensure they know of your plans to rule benevolently."

Valenden scoffed at the suggestion before Bryn could answer. "Let's not forget that Captain Carr has spies among that group of refugees. Spies who may very well make an attempt on Bryn's life. And you want her to chit chat with them?"

"I'll accompany her," Trei offered.

"No. That won't do." King Aleth shook his head. "Bryn is Mir. It has to come directly from her. *She* must have earned their trust, not a foreign prince."

"He's right," Bryn agreed. "I'll speak with their leader." As soon as it looked like Trei and Valenden were both about to object again, she raised a calming hand. "I'll be sure to take my guards."

That seemed to appease the brothers. When the meeting was dismissed, Valenden walked with her, insisting on accompanying her into the village square. Before they left the castle, she found herself peeking into every room and then once outside, down every lane.

"Something tells me you aren't looking for a misplaced hat," Valenden observed.

She stopped, glanced at the guards trailing ten paces behind them, and whispered, "Where is Rangar? I haven't seen him in days."

Valenden matched her tone. "Our father sent him out with a team of woodsmen to camp for a few days in the forest to help fell some trees. Barendur Hold needs a large store of firewood for winter."

"Oh." Her relief at Rangar's safety was met with disappointment. "Well, I'm glad Mage Marna didn't murder him."

"No," Valenden said slowly, "But she *did* ensure he won't touch you again."

Bryn spun on him. "What do you mean?"

Valenden kicked a clod of dirt as he glanced over his shoulder at the distant guards. "Since posting guards on the both of you didn't work, and Rangar doesn't care about the law, she used magic. She placed a spell on him so that if he physically lays as much as one finger on you, it will leave black marks wherever he touches. Your lips, your face, your arms, *other places*. Marks that can't be washed off with any amount of soap or scrubbing."

Bryn gaped. "A spell can do that?"

Valenden nodded. "If he touches you, everyone will know. He'll literally leave fingerprints behind.

She's assured him that if she sees those marks on you, he'll go straight to the dungeon for treason."

Bryn grumbled, "Lords and ladies . . . what a mess."

"If I was you, I'd do my best to stay away from Rangar. Don't tempt him because only he will suffer. They won't throw *you* in the dungeon. They need you too much."

They fell silent as they neared the dock. Alain and a handful of the Mir refugees had begun to help bring in the fish off the boats, and Alain was now practically buried under still-writhing fish and sea creatures laid out on the shore.

"Princess Bryn." Alain nodded before motioning to the fish. "This might not be the best place for a lady."

"I can assure you, I've seen worse," she said, trying not to wince at the smell. "I was hoping to speak with you about a strategy for a return to the Mirien."

Alain eyed her carefully as he pulled off his thick work gloves. If she was being honest, Alain had always frightened her a little. He was a large man with a thick beard that threatened to swallow his entire face. He picked up a still-flopping fish with his bare hands and slit its throat, tossing it back onto the pile.

Bryn flinched. An image of her father slumped on his throne, throat slashed, entered her mind. She'd never discovered the murderer's identity, but it was likely to have been one of the uprising leaders. *Someone like Alain—if not Alain himself.*

She forced her chin high as she explained their

plan. "But it will only work if we are confident the Mir populace will embrace Trei and me as legitimate rulers. The Barendur army can stand against Captain Carr's small forces, but not the entire populace."

Alain leaned on a shovel, stroking his beard. "So you want me to ride into the Mirien at your side and vouch for you, is that it?"

She gave a single nod and spoke plainly. "Yes."

Alain glanced at the other Mir refugees working on the docks and said, "I'll need to discuss this with the others. Have you already spoken with Mam Delice?"

"I don't need to. She's known my intentions as long as she's known me."

Valenden added, "We'll need to know if we have your support or not by the end of the week. Lady Bryn and my brother are leaving for their Wedding Tour, and when they return, it will be time to move on Captain Carr."

"You'll have my answer before then," Alain vowed.

They parted ways with Alain's promise to speak with the others. Bryn felt hopeful but not entirely convinced. As she and Valenden walked along the shore, listening to the waves, she asked, "Do you think there's a chance Alain is the spy?"

Valenden made a doubting face. "If he is, it's almost too obvious. The primary leader of the uprising. A beast of a man." He shook his head. "I don't think it's him."

She sighed. "That narrows it down to . . . everyone

else." With nearly forty refugees, it was too many for the Baer forces to keep an eye on.

They walked the rest of the way in silence. It felt like a small break from the storm she knew was coming. Taking back her kingdom was going to be the hardest thing she'd ever done. And all the while, she'd have to do it without Rangar by her side.

Valenden's warning echoed in her ears.

If he touches you, everyone will know.

CHAPTER 11

FINGERPRINTS . . . damn the mage . . . "don't think about him" . . . a change of clothes

The night before the Wedding Tour came all too soon, and with it, the final night of celebration in the great hall. All Bryn could think about throughout the feast was what would come later that night. She and Trei had put off consummating the marriage as long as they could, but Mage Marna knew the truth, and she'd warned them that they couldn't keep pretending once they left Barendur Hold. Anyone with the aura hex would see them and immediately know the marriage wasn't valid.

Rangar had returned from his trek into the forest to fell trees for firewood. *King Aleth must feel confident he won't be so foolish as to touch me again*, she thought. She forced herself to look anywhere but where he stood with other soldiers by the far fireplace, but she was all too aware of how his eyes bore into her from across the room.

"Lady Bryn," the dressmaker said. "It's time to change into your evening gown."

Another ceremony, another gown. Bryn excused herself, her eyes trailing over the great hall, surprised to find that Rangar had vanished—he'd probably stepped outside to get drunk with the soldiers. Well, better he made trouble out there than inside the castle. Her guards followed her to the dressmaker's chamber, where she shut the door and closed her eyes, letting out a long breath, relieved for a few moments of solitude.

Her evening dress hung on a wooden dress form. It was the most delicate gown of all, made of loose lace. It would be the final dress she'd wear that night when going to bed with Trei. It was here, the night they had to finally consummate the marriage . . .

"Lords and ladies," she muttered.

"How about a prince?"

She spun as her heart shot to her throat. In the single candle's light, Rangar emerged from behind the curtains. She pressed a hand to her chest.

"Rangar!" she said in a low hiss, glancing at the door. The guards were just on the other side. "What are you doing here?"

"What do you think?"

She knew that look in his eyes. She whispered, "Rangar, don't."

He stopped an inch from her. She could feel the heat from his body. Smell the candle wax on him, and the mead. He leaned in so that his lips rested a breath from her ear. She could feel desire rolling off him like heat from a flame.

"Bryn . . ."

She flinched away, afraid of Mage Marna's spell. "They'll throw you in the dungeon," she whispered in warning, "if you lay a hand on me. It's treason."

His gaze fell to her lips. "I won't touch you."

She narrowed her eyes. "I'm quite sure *lips* will leave the same black mark as fingers."

"I won't leave any marks," he insisted, keeping his voice low. "I swear it."

But he didn't move away. He leaned closer, backing her up against the wall. His chest grazed her own, but there was the safety of clothing between them to protect them from Mage Marna's spell.

"This is trouble," she whispered. "The dressmaker could come in at any moment. She might keep it a secret, but the guards outside won't." The truth was, though, that Bryn wanted this too. She craved feeling every inch of him against her, his hands once more pressed against her scars and his lips pressed to her own.

But we can't. It's impossible.

Rangar fumbled in his cloak for a moment. She

wasn't certain what he was doing until he produced a pair of leather gloves that he hastily pulled on.

She rolled her eyes slightly. "I don't know if that counts—"

"We aren't breaking any rules," he promised in a rushed voice. "No touch. No flesh to flesh. That's what the spell forbids." He ensnared her bare wrist with his gloved hand. She sucked in a breath, waiting for the telltale black marks to show, but they didn't.

A satisfied smile cut across Rangar's face. He pressed her back harder against the wall, his knee between her legs.

She shook her head at the same time that she was parting her lips. He gripped her hair, tugging her head back. His other hand kneaded against her dress where her scars rested. His touch was hard, as though he had something to prove.

"You see?" he breathed in her ear, careful to keep his lips from touching her skin. "It's allowed. It doesn't leave marks."

She panted, "I don't think this is what the mage had in mind."

"Damn the mage."

His fist tightened in her hair, and she tipped her head back further. Her neck was bare, and she could feel how badly he wanted to run his lips along her throbbing pulse, but instead, he moved his hand to her backside. Before she realized what was happening, he picked her up and set her on the worktable next to them, pushing aside reams of fabric and thread, which fell to the floor.

"We should stop," she whispered, though she didn't want him to.

"I can control myself," he said in that husky voice. "I won't touch you. I swear it. But I need to feel you. I need to be with you, Bryn."

His hands bunched the fabric around her waist. She was half afraid he would rip her dress's seams open, but instead, he lowered his gloved hand to her boot, running it up her bare ankle. She felt the slick warmth of his glove and tipped her head back, lips parted. His gloved fingers caressed her bare calf. They traced the underside of her knee far up her skirt. He was breathing hard. So was she. His gaze was on her face, then focused on her lips, as his hand worked under her skirt. He dragged his hand past her knee to the sensitive area inside her thigh. She bucked on instinct.

"Shhh," he said, his eyes dilated and dark. "Close your eyes. Spread your legs."

Her cheeks burned. She started to protest, but his hand against her inside thigh was impossible to resist, and she knew it was wrong—knew they were skating dangerously close to treason—but it felt so unfathomably right that she couldn't bring herself to stop. She arched her back. Opened her legs another inch. A soft growl came from his throat as he leaned in, pressing his lips to her clothed shoulder. His gloved finger ran to the edge of her undergarments, dragging back and forth over the fabric. Bryn felt on fire. She'd always stopped him before when they'd come close to impropriety, and he'd always done as she'd asked. But tonight, she couldn't bring herself to tell him to stop.

"I can't . . . " She didn't even know what she was trying to say. "I don't . . . "

His shallow breaths came fast as he ran the leather glove over her undergarments. Then, without warning, he slipped a finger under them, breaching her core. She cried out softly, and the sound seemed to drive him wild. His other hand cupped her shoulder as though to keep himself at a distance—to protect him from his instincts.

She closed her eyes again, leaning back against the wall. When she didn't stop him, Rangar pressed his finger deeper into her, where no man had ever touched her. She gasped, and he growled. Sweat beaded on his forehead. His lips were dangerously close to her own.

"Don't kiss me," she warned.

"I don't care," he said in a growlsome voice. "I don't care if they see my mark on you. I don't care if they hang me for it. I need to touch you, Bryn."

His hand worked against her core, and she latched onto his shoulder, twisting her hands in his shirt's fabric, moving her hips as her body instinctively told her to do. He leaned closer, pressing his groin against her leg.

He moaned near her ear, "He can't touch you like this. I'll kill him. I will."

"Shh. Don't think about him."

"He gets to touch you. He gets to have you. To take you to his bed tonight." His hand moved faster. Bryn knew this was very much against the spirit of Mage Marna's hexmark. What they were doing was dangerously close to treason, gloves or not. It might not leave a black mark on her, but what if someone opened the door and caught them?

"Rangar, we should stop."

"Don't say that unless you mean it. Tell me to stop, and I will. But I don't give a damn what we should or shouldn't do, only what you want. Do you want me to stop?"

"*No.*"

She sucked in a breath as his hand moved faster. Saints, had he done this before? Of course, he had. The world wasn't fair—men didn't have to remain chaste as women did. But she couldn't imagine he'd had that look on his face for anyone but her. That look that was so feverish, so drunk on the smell of her, so intent on making her feel exactly what he wanted her to feel.

She let out another gasp, and he whispered in her ear, "Give yourself over to it, Bryn. To me. Do you think Trei can make you feel this way? I want you to remember, when he takes you to bed tonight, that *I* was the one who made you feel like this."

She could barely process his words. His hand on her shoulder was hard, his fingers pressing into her skin. He was so dangerously close to kissing her but held himself back. She knew she would hate herself in the morning. This was a sin, even if he didn't leave a mark. But she couldn't bring herself to stop. The pressure was building at the base of her abdomen, and all she wanted was to feel more of him. It was *him* she wanted. *Him* she loved as much as the air itself. Damn it all, she was ready to rip that glove off him and press every inch of her bare flesh into his hands.

Then her pleasure crested and crashed over her, and she cried out and grabbed him around the shoulders, breathing hard, just aware enough to ensure she didn't touch his bare skin. His hand stopped and traced down her leg, then he ground his hips harder against her with a groan.

"Bryn, close your eyes."

"What?"

"Close your eyes," he said, panting. "Until I tell you."

She did. She heard the fumble of his clothes and another groan, and it was clear enough what he was doing, though she'd never been close to a man when he'd done it. He kept one hand on her waist, his fingers digging into her, the other hand giving himself the same pleasure he'd given her. She felt him shudder and then breath heavily, and then heard more adjusting of clothing.

"Look at me." He pressed his hand to her face, and her eyes snapped open at the touch, alarmed, but she relaxed when she saw he was still wearing gloves.

His eyes were hooded, feverish. "Bryn, remember. *I* made you feel like that. I did."

Her body was still shuddering. What they'd done

was wrong, and yet she couldn't even process how incredible he'd made her feel.

"You have no idea how much I want to kiss you," he muttered.

"Don't," she breathed.

"You might have married my brother, but I'll never stop loving you, Bryn Lindane. One way or another, we'll be together."

She tilted her face up at him, wanting to believe him, wanting it all to be true. He cupped her cheek one final time with his gloved hand. Then, he climbed out the window, disappearing around the parapet.

Alone, shivering, she sank to the floor. Her whole body trembled from the aftershocks of his touch. What they'd done had been so very wrong, and yet she couldn't bring herself to regret it. Not in the least.

She wasn't sure how long she sat there on the floor until the dressmaker knocked gently on the door, peeking in, then startled to find her still wearing her afternoon dress.

"Are you well, my lady?" she asked.

Bryn shakily pushed to her feet. "Um . . . just a dizzy spell."

Helna gave her an odd look but extended a hand to help her to her feet. The old seamstress began to undo the buttons at the side of her dress and help her change into the new one.

"You're just nervous about the travel tomorrow," Helna reassured her. "The Wedding Tour is a grand affair. You'll get to see the entire Baersladen, but I imagine it will lack the comforts you're used to. Better enjoy one final night on a proper bed with that handsome prince of yours."

Helna winked, and Bryn felt awful, knowing Helna meant Trei, not Rangar.

Once she was in the lacy evening dress, her hair freshly combed, Bryn had no choice but to return to the feast, sit at Trei's side, and know that in a few hours, she was going to lose her virginity to him after having completely lost her heart, once again, to Rangar.

CHAPTER 12

A SHOCKING DISCOVERY . . . a knife, returned . . . a prince asleep . . . all eyes on one brother

The feast was another interminable affair, this time meant to wish the newlyweds well before they departed for the Wedding Tour in the morning. The castle's staff had worked hard over the previous week to prepare for the voyage: Not only had they cooked this going-away feast but they'd already packed and readied three carriages for the journey: one for Trei and Bryn, one for the soldiers who would be protecting them, and one for the servants and a few flower girls who'd accompany them.

Bryn knew she should feel grateful for all the hard work that had gone into celebrating her marriage, but the truth was, she was devastated. After her rendezvous with Rangar in the dressmaker's room, Rangar had made a brief appearance at the feast to toast the couple well on their journey, his dark eyes boring into her soul the entire time. But it was just as upsetting to see Saraj, who Bryn hadn't spoken to since the wedding day, sitting by the far hearth with Aya and some other falconers. Saraj's face looked sallow with dark rings around her eyes as though she hadn't slept for days. Bryn's heart broke to see her friend so transformed by grief.

I'm not the only one suffering, Bryn thought sullenly.

Trei must have also been deeply pained to see Saraj because he soon leaned toward Bryn and muttered, "I'm going to retire early. I want to get plenty of sleep before the voyage tomorrow." He hesitated. "I'll . . . see you shortly."

"Of course." They were a miserable pair, Trei and her, she thought. Both lovesick over someone else. She tried to act grateful during the remainder of the evening as royalty and soldiers and peasants alike approached the dais to greet her. At one point, Mage Marna raised a glass to her with a grave look, and Bryn swallowed hard. She understood what the older woman was trying to say. *No more waiting.* Bryn couldn't start the Wedding Tour as a virgin.

But she found it impossible to get up the nerve to join Trei upstairs in the newlywed chamber. She sipped more and more wine, growing increasingly anxious as the evening stretched on. Earlier that evening, Rangar had let her know exactly what true passion felt like. After what had happened between them, how could she be with someone else?

She threw glances toward Saraj, wishing she could join her friend and that there wasn't an awful tension between them now. Her problems were types of things she'd like friends or sisters to talk to about, but she couldn't confide in Saraj about sleeping with her former lover. And her sister, Elysander, was far away in Dresel, probably playing the part of the duchess perfectly—everything Elysander did was perfection.

By the time the musicians stopped, Bryn realized she was more than a little tipsy.

Ah, well, if I'm to lose my virginity to my lover's brother, I might as well be drunk.

After the event ended, she climbed the tower stairs trailed by her guards, who took care that she didn't stumble back down the winding stairs. Her thoughts turned again to her sister. What had Elysander's wedding night been like? Since birth, Elysander had been betrothed to the Duke of Dresel and had successfully married him—granted, with a major uprising and fleeing for her life involved. But Elysander was a maven of courtly manners. Come her wedding night, she probably hadn't grieved and thought about another man. She'd doubtlessly charmed her husband with tender caresses and seductive whispers.

"Oh, Elysander," Bryn muttered aloud. "I could use your guidance."

She suddenly longed for her sister again and, more

so, a chance to get to know Elysander in their new roles. They'd never had a chance to mourn their parents together, and now they'd lost Mars, too. It was only the two of them, and Bryn wondered if their paths would ever cross again. Dresel was a long way away, far south of the Mirien.

She reached the door to the newlywed chambers and turned to the soldiers. "This is far enough. Thank you."

"We'll be stationed just down the hall," the elder of the guard said.

Bryn gave a tipsy nod and then slipped into the newlywed room. The light was out, and the curtains at the window were drawn. She'd never realized how pitch-black the room was with the drapes closed. There was an odd scent of citrus in the room—something Trei must have eaten at the feast.

"Trei?" she whispered. "Are you awake?"

There was no answer, and this presented a conundrum. It was their final chance to consummate the marriage, and as far as Bryn could tell, her husband had fallen asleep. She bit her lip and felt in the dark for the bed posters. What was she supposed to do, shake him awake? Climb on top of him?

"Trei, wake up," she said louder. She reached the bed and patted it until she found his foot beneath the covers. She gave it a good shake.

But Trei didn't stir, and she felt her way to the window, where she grasped the curtains. She pulled them back. Moonlight streamed in, surprisingly bright. She blinked a few times as she turned toward the bed.

She saw Trei.

She saw *blood*.

For the second time in her life, she saw a waterfall of red pouring from the throat of a man she cared deeply about.

Bryn screamed until she was hoarse. The guards stormed into the room with their swords drawn. Their eyes weren't accustomed to the low light, and they posed in fight stances, preparing for a battle.

"Trei!" Bryn gasped between sobs. "It's Trei!"

One of the guards quickly lit a lantern. Once they got a look at Trei's body in the bed with blood soaking into the sheets, they fell silent.

It was clear as moonlight: *Trei Barendur was dead.*

"Gods save us," one of them muttered.

The other raised his sword as he checked the corners of the room and anywhere someone might be hiding. "Lady Bryn, did you see anyone?"

She shook her head, only then realizing that she might have been in grave danger if the murderer had still been in the room when she'd come in. "No, no, he was here alone."

She couldn't think straight. Couldn't process what was happening. Could only stare at the floor...

Not Trei. Please, not Trei.

One of the soldiers shouted down the hallway for reinforcements. The other tried to question her further, but she found her mind spinning at his probing barrage.

Yes, the room had been dark when she came in. No, she hadn't heard anyone else. Yes, she'd known he had gone to bed early.

Finally, she forced herself to look directly at the body.

He hadn't been dead long, judging by the color of his skin. Whoever had slit his throat must have done so and left only moments before she'd entered. One of the soldiers draped Trei's fatal wound with a cloth, but it didn't reach far enough to cover his face. She reached out a shaking hand and closed Trei's eyes. It was the only thing she could think of to do.

"Oh, Trei," she whispered. "I'm so sorry."

She started sobbing. Trei might not have been her husband of choice, but he *was* her husband. Moreover, he was an honorable prince and someone she'd considered a friend. They had grieved together, confided in one another, and made plans to rule two entire kingdoms side-by-side.

Yet someone had wanted him dead.

She sank onto the edge of the bed and pulled back the sheet to stroke Trei's still-warm hand. But something clattered to the floor, and she jumped up. The soldiers heard the clatter and came in, looking around for the source of the sound.

All eyes went to a knife that had fallen when she'd moved the sheet.

Bryn picked up the knife on instinct. The blade was coated in Trei's blood. Once she tore her eyes away from the blade and saw the hilt, her eyes went wide.

She dropped the knife again with a gasp.

One of the soldiers picked it up. "Lady Bryn? Do you recognize this knife?"

Of course she recognized it, though she hadn't seen it in some months. It was *her* knife. Or rather, Rangar's knife, which he had given her on their journey from the Mirien to the Baersladen. She'd lost it during her first days in Barendur Hold when she'd left it with her clothes in the bathhouse, and the servants had taken away the whole bundle. Try as she could, she hadn't been able to find the knife again. It had been missing ever since then.

One of the other soldiers went stiff. "That knife belongs to Prince Rangar," he said gravely, recognizing the hexmarks on the hilt.

The other soldiers fell silent, and Bryn suddenly realized what they were all thinking.

"No," she said in a rush. "I mean, yes. The knife was once Rangar's, but not anymore. He gave it to me, and then I lost it . . ."

But her explanation fell on uninterested ears. The soldiers snapped into attention, ignoring her as though they'd already made up their minds. Footsteps outside hurried toward the bedroom. In the next moment, Valenden came barreling in, stopping short at the sight of Trei.

"By the gods," he muttered in shock.

Bryn went to throw her arms around him. "Val, someone killed him!"

Valenden looked stricken. He dragged a hand through his hair, shaking his head. "Trei . . ." Then his gaze snapped back to Bryn. "Who killed him? Who did this?"

One of the soldiers cleared his throat and held out Rangar's knife, and Valenden's eyes went wide.

"No," he practically growled. "Rangar? No, he would never. They're brothers!"

More footsteps came striding down the hall, and Bryn felt numb to see King Aleth and Mage Marna hurrying to the scene. The king's face was white, and Mage Marna had a hand pressed to her chest. When they took one look at Trei, the king let out a howl. Mage Marna fell back against the door jam and muttered a prayer in a language Bryn didn't know.

"What happened?" King Aleth snapped at the soldiers. "You were supposed to be guarding him!"

"We didn't leave our post," one volunteered bravely. "We've been at the door since Prince Trei retired—no one else came in or exited. The murderer must have entered through the window. This was in the bed."

He showed King Aleth the knife.

Silence again filled the room until Valenden snapped, "There is no way Rangar did this!"

"That's his knife," Mage Marna whispered.

"But he gave it to me, and I lost it," Bryn implored. "It's been missing for months. Anyone could have had it."

"Begging your pardon, Mage Marna," the elder soldier said to the older woman. "Prince Rangar himself might have found it shortly after it went missing and kept it hidden until now."

Mage Marna ran a shaky hand down her chest. "Rangar said he was going to kill Trei . . . "

Bryn tore away from Valenden, throwing her arms in the air. "You can't be serious! Rangar would *never* hurt Trei!"

The mage's eyes snapped to hers. "When Valenden kissed you, Rangar broke his nose. And Trei *married* you. A graver punishment for a graver transgression."

"Rangar loved Trei," Bryn insisted, growing more panicked. "Yes, he was displeased with our marriage, of course, but he loves his family fiercely and would only ever want to help them. Go. Ask him. He'll tell you the truth that he is innocent!"

Everyone looked to the king, who had sunk onto the edge of the bed, stroking his dead son's hair like he was a child again. In a hollow voice, King Aleth said, "She's right. Find Rangar. We must question him—but put him in chains first."

Bryn spun on them, ready to argue, but Valenden beat her to it.

"I agree with Bryn. Rangar would never do this."

Mage Marna clasped her hands together to keep

them steady. "Valenden, I know you love Rangar as well. But the fact is, this is his knife, and he recently threatened Trei with murder. He's also one of the only people familiar enough with the castle to know how to get past the guards to get into this room through the window."

Bryn felt a frantic thrashing in her chest like a bird that couldn't get free. *They can't be serious. They can't actually think Rangar did this!*

Mage Marna took one look at Bryn and signaled to Valenden. "Take her out of her. Somewhere safe."

Bryn tried to protest, but Valenden pulled her out of the room, arms wrapped tightly around her, as he whispered fiercely in her ear, "I know that Rangar didn't do this as well as you do, but it doesn't look good for him. We need to figure out how to prove his innocence or..."

"Or what?" she breathed.

Valenden looked pale. "Or he could hang."

CHAPTER 13

THE FALCONER'S VISIT . . . the dungeon . . . doubts and fears . . . cancelled plans . . . more of Valenden's tricks

That night was one of the worst nights in Bryn's life. Her husband was murdered. Her lover was accused of the crime. Soldiers were tearing through Barendur Hold even now, searching for Rangar.

Finally, Valenden came pacing into the mage chambers with a curse. He snarled, "They found him."

Bryn looked up from her tea, which one of the apprentices had made for her but she hadn't touched. "Where?"

"He was out drinking on the docks with some sailors."

"There," she said triumphantly. "The sailors can vouch for him, yes? That he was with them when Trei was murdered?"

But Valenden's face remained stony. "He'd only been with them a few minutes, apparently. Before that, he claims he went for a walk along the coastal forest. Naturally, no one believes him." He paused. "They put him in the dungeon."

"The dungeon!"

She wished she could vouch for him to prove that he'd been elsewhere when the murder happened. If she had to confess to their dalliance in the dressmaker's room earlier that evening, she would, but the truth was, it wouldn't help. That had happened when Trei was still alive and at the feast. Telling everyone they'd been together then would accomplish nothing.

Valenden sat next to her on the bench, taking her hand. "No one wants it to be true that Rangar murdered his brother, so they'll do a proper investigation. They won't condemn him without discovering the truth." He squeezed her hand tightly. "They'll prove it wasn't him."

Bryn buried her head in her arms on the table. Her heart felt battered and bruised. She'd been searching for that knife for so long, afraid it had fallen into unscrupulous hands. It was such a recognizable knife hilt that she'd been shocked that no one had returned it to her or Rangar—unless they *had* returned it to Rangar, and he hadn't told her.

For a second, doubts crept into her head.

He did threaten to kill Trei . . .

And he said clear as day he'd find some way for us to be together...

As soon as she had those thoughts, she banished them.

No. Rangar isn't a killer. Not like this.

"Saraj!" she said suddenly as a fresh wave of panic washed over her. "Has anyone told Saraj?"

Valenden looked grim. "I'm sure word has spread to her by now."

"Oh, that poor woman." Bryn felt ill again to think of how Saraj must be feeling.

Valenden eventually convinced her to go to bed in an effort to save her strength, though she tossed and turned all night, not even bothering to change out of the blood-stained dress. She wasn't sure if she'd slept at all or simply blacked out from worry, but as morning light came through the window of her small chamber, she heard an older woman's voice speaking with the guards outside.

Bryn stumbled out of her room and into the mage workroom, where Mage Marna was speaking with the soldiers. Her voice was hoarse as she gasped, "Rangar?"

"Is in custody," the mage said carefully. "He is safe. He denies the crime vehemently."

Bryn clutched her hands together, squeezing the ring on the chain around her neck. "I must speak with him."

"I don't think that's wise, Bryn."

"Please," she begged. "He's behind bars; what harm could either of us do?"

Mage Marna hesitated before warning in a quieter voice, "Bryn, you must take extra care now. These are perilous times. We examined the scene of Trei's death and found signs of a struggle." The older woman took a deep breath. "He wasn't asleep when the murderer cut his throat."

Bryn stopped short, feeling a terrible chill. "What?"

"He fought against his attacker," the mage continued. "There were cuts and bruises beneath his clothes. The lamp wick was cold, implying the attack happened in the dark. Presumably, the murderer was waiting for him to return to the chamber. By all we can tell, Trei fought well. But the murderer had the advantage of surprise."

"Oh, Trei," Bryn said, pressing a hand to her mouth.

The Wedding Tour, of course, was canceled.

Once word spread of Trei's passing, the entire castle sank into mourning. A dark shadow fell over the faces of all the residents who had loved their eldest prince dearly. Most of them had either watched him grow up or grown up alongside him, singing fishing shanties together, letting him settle their disputes, dancing with him at the gatherings. King Aleth had sent riders out only a few days before to the outer villages to proclaim the good news about the marriage, and now he was forced to send another team of messengers with the terrible news that their prince would not be coming to visit them after all.

Bryn remained cloistered in the mage chambers for her private mourning. Fortunately, Calista and Ren gave her all the space she needed. It was one of the few places within the castle where servants didn't enter, and Bryn reveled in the privacy. Even the guards remained stationed at the outer door.

"Where is she? Where is Lady Bryn?" A tearful voice suddenly called from the hallway, though the soldiers stopped the person before entering.

Bryn came out of her room only to stop stiffly when she saw Saraj being held back by a guard. Tears stained the falconer's face. Saraj had looked sallow and miserable for days, and now she looked even more like a hollowed out shell of a person.

When Saraj caught sight of Bryn, she clenched her jaw. "I must speak with you."

Apprehensive, Bryn nodded for the guards to let Saraj in, though they checked her first for any possible hidden weapons. As soon as Saraj was in the main workroom, the two women regarded each other for some time, and a million different thoughts tumbled through Bryn's mind. Had Saraj come to berate her? To accuse her of not watching out for Trei?

But then Saraj let out a sob and threw her arms around Bryn. "Gods, Bryn. He's gone."

Bryn clutched Saraj with all her strength. She hadn't realized until that point how badly she'd needed a friend. With Trei gone and Rangar in the dungeon, Valenden was the closest thing she had to a friend, but after their tumultuous history, she'd always felt the need to keep herself at a distance.

The two women held one another while letting the tears come, and once their grief had finally worn them out, they sank onto the bench. Ren appeared from the back room with two cups of fortifying mint tea, which he silently set on the table for them and retreated again.

After some time, Saraj finally spoke. "You were the one who found him. I'd like to hear exactly what happened."

Bryn explained about coming home from the feast, finding the room dark, and then the gruesome discovery. As much as she wanted to leave out the part about Rangar's knife, she had to tell Saraj everything.

"I know it wasn't Rangar," Bryn insisted. "You must believe me. Even in the throes of his worst temper, he would never kill Trei."

Saraj sipped her tea, then set it down with shaking hands and said, "The castle is torn: half the residents believe Rangar did it, and the other half swear he wouldn't. It didn't help that he publicly threatened Trei."

Bryn let out an exasperated sigh. "Everyone thinks Rangar has the most obvious motivation, but they're ignoring the fact that we're at the brink of war with

Captain Carr's spies in our midst. When I married Trei, it took the target off my back and put it on his."

Saraj's eyes flashed. "You think a Mir spy killed him?"

Bryn nodded. "I've heard the guards outside whispering about it, too, so I know that King Aleth and Mage Marna also suspect it as a possibility. But they refuse to let Rangar out of the dungeon unless they're certain."

"How will they prove the murder was a spy unless the spy is caught?"

"That's exactly the problem," Bryn said, anxiously toying with the handle of her mug. "What if they don't catch him? Will Rangar stay locked up forever?"

Saraj glanced at the doorway where the soldiers were standing, and then the opposite direction toward the inner mage chambers, where Ren had disappeared to. She lowered her voice to a whisper and said, "Have you spoken with Rangar?"

"They won't let me see him."

"Has Val?"

"Yes, he's gone to the dungeon to speak with Rangar a few times. He says Rangar denies the murder, of course. That he was shocked and heartbroken to learn the news." Bryn set down her mug, suddenly feeling sick to her stomach to think of Rangar alone in the dungeon. It was a portion of the castle she'd never visited, so she couldn't speak to the conditions, but it didn't take much imagination to picture it as a windowless, dank, uncomfortable place.

Rangar was there alone mourning the passing of a brother.

She felt the urge to cry but wiped her nose, pulling herself together, and said, "He claims he hadn't seen that knife since he gave it to me before we even came to the Baersladen. He doesn't know where it's been all this time."

Saraj let out a long breath, looking worn through.

Bryn confessed, "Perhaps it doesn't matter now, but Trei and I . . . Well, we never consummated the marriage. We were both in love with someone else." She reached out to take the falconer's hand. "He loved you so much. He played the part of a dutiful husband, but I assure you that he was a wreck behind closed doors. It tore him apart to have lost you."

She thought Saraj might cry again, but instead, Saraj only stared down at her tea and eventually whispered, "Thank you, Bryn. For telling me."

During such turbulent times, Bryn tried to keep in mind her kingdom's wellbeing. She had married Trei to ensure a peaceful rule, and now that plan was dashed. She was back to being the crown heir of a kingdom currently usurped by Captain Carr, who would stop at nothing—murder, forced marriage, war —to stay in charge.

She spent long hours in the castle library going through the books that detailed succession rules among the Eyrie kingdoms, reading about old treaties until her eyes grew bleary. She hadn't realized that she'd fallen asleep on one of the open books until Valenden shook her awake.

She awoke with a start, but Valenden clamped a hand over her mouth and whispered, "Shh. Pretend to still be asleep and don't open your eyes until I say so."

Questions filled her mind. Valenden was obviously up to one of his schemes, but he was one of the few people in the castle she trusted with her life, so she closed her eyes and laid her head back down.

Valenden pulled out her chair and gathered her in his arms, one hand under her knees and the other supporting her back. Her heart thundered. *What in the Saints' names is he doing?*

He carried her to the door and said to the guards, "Lady Bryn fell asleep while reading. She's exhausting herself by going through these old books. I'm going to carry her back to the mage chambers."

"We have orders to stay with her."

"By all means," Valenden said indifferently.

As Valenden carried her upstairs, Bryn fought the urge to open her eyes and ask him what he thought he was doing. But she heard the guards' footsteps right behind them and did all she could do—pretend to remain asleep and wonder what the hell Valenden was up to this time.

CHAPTER 14

THE PRISONER . . . eyes closed, princess . . . a helpful spell . . . the secret door . . . stairs to the dark

As Valenden carried Bryn down the hallways with her eyes closed as she pretended to sleep, she tried to mentally map out where he was taking her. It wasn't until she smelled the mixed scent of herbs that she realized they were headed toward the mage storerooms.

"Calista?" Valenden called. Bryn heard someone—presumably Calista—set down clinking glass bottles.

"What mischief are you up to now, Val?" Calista whispered.

"I'm ready for any *help* you can give us," Valenden muttered.

Calista's voice lowered knowingly. "Right."

Bryn wanted more than anything to open her eyes and find out what was going on. To her surprise, she heard Calista murmur the words of a spell and, in the next moment, Valenden unceremoniously dropped her onto the bench.

Bryn's eyes snapped open as she massaged her sore bottom. "*Ow.*"

"You can open your eyes," he smirked.

"Yes, I figured." After scowling at him, Bryn took in the room and jolted. The two soldiers who were supposed to be guarding her were now slumped against the wall, fast asleep. So *that* had been Calista's spell.

"We must hurry," Valenden said, nodding toward the soldiers. "Calista's spell will only keep them asleep for about half an hour." He turned to the apprentice. "You have the bags?"

Calista opened a cabinet and took out two canvas rucksacks, which she passed to Valenden. He nodded his gratitude and then took Bryn by the upper arm. "Come, we must not delay."

"I don't even know where we're going!"

"That's probably for the better," he muttered.

Instead of heading down the main tower stairs, Valenden took Bryn down a narrow corridor that ended in the second-floor latrines. She held her breath against the smell. He went to the window and peered outside, then waved her over. "You first."

"Excuse me?"

"This portion of the outer wall was constructed with handholds to serve as a makeshift ladder in case there was ever a fire and people needed an alternate way out of the Hold. The handholds lead down to the courtyard." At her worried look, he added, "It's perfectly safe. My brothers and I climbed down it a million times as children."

Bryn rolled her eyes but hitched up her skirt and threw a leg out the window. Valenden held her steady as she moved her feet along the outer wall until she found the handholds that he'd spoken of. Carefully, she descended. The makeshift stone ladder must have been constructed centuries ago because the stone had been worn slick by rain and wind. She found herself nearly slipping a few times and catching herself at the last moment. Her heartbeat galloped, but she finally managed to make it to the ground.

Valenden dropped down into the courtyard rosebushes next to her, the two bags slung over his shoulder. "There, that wasn't so bad, was it?"

"I thought I was going to fall to my death!"

He scoffed and took her hand, leading her into the shadows. "Now, not another word until we get there."

She knew better than to ask where *there* was. It was clear that he was trying to avoid being detected by any guards or castle staff. At the courtyard's corner, he pushed open a wooden door that looked like it might be a closet for gardening supplies, but to her surprise, led to another set of stairs. The staircase was very dark with only a faint glow coming from somewhere deep.

After winding down the twisting stairs and into a narrow stone passageway, Valenden held up a hand. "Wait here."

He moved into the flickering lamplight up ahead. She heard him exchange low words with someone, then the clink of coins changing hands. He returned with a grave look as he took her hand. "Hurry. We don't have much time. This is the only guard I can buy off, and his shift ends in ten minutes."

He pulled her into a dank underground chamber lit only by a few weak lanterns. *A dungeon.* Puddles of groundwater made the stone floor glisten, and she heard more cave-like dripping water throughout the rooms. The bedrock had been hewn into small, windowless cells, each secured by iron bars. She glanced in each cell as Valenden pulled her forward; a skeletal man with a thick beard rested against the bars of one with a wooden bowl at his feet. Most of the others were empty.

Valenden stopped at the last cell. "I'll come back for you in five minutes, so speak fast."

A figure who'd been sitting on the cell's floor pushed to his feet and approached the bars. Bryn's apprehension surrendered to relief as Rangar's face moved into the light.

She grabbed the bars. "*Rangar.*"

"Bryn. You're okay?" He reached through the bars toward her face, but she pulled back on instinct, thinking about Mage Marna's spell.

He said, "Do not worry. The spell that forbade me

from touching you was tied to your marriage, and that's over now."

Putting her trust in him hesitantly, she leaned forward and let him graze his fingers over her bare arm, relieved to find no black marks cropping up. She melted into his touch.

Her eyes scoured the deplorable cell; it was nothing but damp rock, a single blanket, and a bucket to use as a latrine. Her throat constricted to think of him here: it was even worse than she'd imagined.

His eyes were large and full of pain as he turned her chin to meet his gaze. "Bryn, I'm not a murderer. I would never do that to Trei—"

"I know," she reassured him, finding his hand through the bars and clasping it. "I never believed you were guilty. The knife . . . "

"I haven't seen that knife since I gave it to you in the forest months ago. I suspect it got into the hands of Captain Carr's spies. He must have threatened or bribed one of the bathhouse girls who found it. They used it to frame me."

Bryn's chest felt tight. "When I married Trei, I didn't think about the risk to him..."

"Trei...Trei always knew the risks." Rangar's voice broke when he said his brother's name. He swallowed. "Listen, there are things you don't know." He squeezed her hand, using his other thumb to tip her chin up to look him directly in the eye. "Did my aunt tell you there were combative wounds on Trei's body?"

She gave a slight nod.

"Valenden spoke to the undertaker who examined him. The first wounds were low on Trei's chest. Not at *his* neck height, but at *yours*."

Bryn's eyes went wide. "You think Trei wasn't the target?"

He nodded solemnly. "I think the spy was hiding in your room in the dark, thinking you'd be the first one back, as you usually are. They didn't expect Trei to return early, so they weren't prepared when he defended himself. Then they slit his throat and laid him in bed, then left my knife to frame me."

"But if your father and aunt know that I was the target, not Trei, then they should believe that you didn't do this!"

"There isn't enough evidence Trei *was* the target," Rangar said. "They can't release me without proof."

"They can't hold you without proof either!"

He shook his head. "My knife with Trei's blood on it, my threat against him . . . that *is* proof according to many."

She pressed her face against the bars, the cool iron soothing her hot skin. "We have to get you out of here."

"No. We have to get *you* out of here. I don't trust the guards will keep you safe—look how easily Val and Calista were able to incapacitate them. There's a good chance Captain Carr's spy—or spies—killed Trei but meant to kill you. You must leave Barendur Hold. It isn't safe."

She stared at him, speechless. Finally, she whispered, "Where would I go?"

She was crown heir to the Mir kingdom, but as far as she knew, her people still planned on stringing her up on the gallows as soon as she returned.

"Val and I have been working on a plan," Rangar said in a low rush. The lantern light reflected off his face, highlighting the scars, reminding her of just how many times he'd risked himself for her. "The Hytooth royal family in the Wollin is sympathetic to us. We've been in communication with them ever since the siege on Castle Mir. They refused to swear loyalty to your brother before his death, and they refuse to negotiate with Captain Carr now. Val will sneak you out of Barendur Hold and get you to the Wollin. Eventually, when I can, I'll meet you there."

"How?" she marveled, clutching the iron bars.

He reached through to stroke her cheek. "I'll always find a way back to you, Bryn."

She leaned into his hand, closing her eyes. Trying to put the terrible conditions of the dungeon out of mind and focus on the two of them. In a terrible twist of fate, they were free to be together again. She never would have wished for Trei's death, and yet, the truth was she was a widow now. Bound by no marriage vows. It wasn't being wed to another man that separated them now—it was iron bars.

"I'm supposed to look out for *you* now, remember?" she whispered. "I saved your life from that poison, so your soul is mine to protect. And yet you're the one always helping me even while you're behind bars."

He pressed his forehead against hers, stroking her cheek. "You don't even believe in the *fralen* bond."

"I believe in owing something to one another. I believe that our pasts do bind us."

He smirked softly. "You don't owe me anything, but I'll take a kiss if you'll give it freely."

All she had to do was tip up her chin to touch her lips to his. Her hands coiled around the bars as he wrapped a hand around her waist, pulling her as close as they could manage. The kiss was softer than that turbulent tussle in the closet but no less affectionate. Bryn suddenly felt starved for Rangar. This boy whose heart she'd stomped all over, who was saving her life in return. She pressed herself closer, frustrated by the stiff bars.

"Promise me you won't marry again," he said gruffly before tipping her chin up for another kiss.

"I promise," she whispered, coiling her fingers around the bars. "No one. Never anyone else but you."

She rested a hand on his chest and could feel his heart pounding. She bunched his dirty shirt, filled with an urge to hold on, to never let him go.

A low whistle sounded from the far side of the dungeon, and Rangar broke the kiss. "That's Val. You should go before the guards switch shifts."

Her eyes widened. "I can't just leave you here!" She grabbed his collar with both hands, clutching tightly.

He placed his hands over hers and eased them off his body, shaking his head. "You can't be found here. You must go. Now."

A war was waging in her mind. How could she possibly leave him in a *dungeon*? Rangar had never done anything wrong. She'd been the one to betray him by marrying his brother. He was certainly no murderer, no criminal . . .

She felt tears in her eyes. "I'm afraid I'll never see you again."

He stroked her hair softly through the bars. "Princess, you'll see me again. We're soulbound. We have something almost no one is lucky enough to have. There is magic in the world, so you need to believe. We'll be together again."

Their lips met again for a kiss. Bryn poured everything she had into it, wanting Rangar to feel every ounce of her love, her concern, her protectiveness over him.

Footsteps sounded, and she felt Valenden's hand on her shoulder. "Bryn. *Now*. The soldiers are returning."

She didn't want to let go of the bars. She stared at Rangar one final time, memorizing everything about him, promising herself she would believe as he urged.

"Take her, Val," Rangar said sharply.

And she had no choice but to flee down the dungeon hall with Valenden, hiding in a shadowy alcove as the new soldiers arrived for their shift, and then dash up the stairs, through an exit out of the courtyard to which Valenden had the key, and race out into the dark forest.

CHAPTER 15

AWAY TO THE WOODS . . . a third ring . . . a short rest . . . dreams and revelations . . . the lemon

It was a damp night with a nasty chill in the air. Clouds had rolled in over the moon, casting the night world in deep shadows. Valenden seemed to know the path through the forest by heart, which gave Bryn a small measure of confidence.

She followed him blindly, trying not to think about everything she was leaving behind. Every belonging she had to her name, her prospects as a mage apprentice, the promise of being queen to both the Mirien and the Baersladen. And of course, the greatest loss of all—leaving Rangar behind.

"Stop," Valenden said, motioning for her to sit on a

fallen log. "We need to take a break. Catch our breaths."

Bryn sank onto the log, hugging her arms tightly to keep from shivering.

Valenden dug through one of his rucksacks and took out a wool blanket that he wrapped around her shoulders. "I'm sorry this little voyage of ours had to be on such short notice. I spent all the coin I had on hand to bribe the guards, and Rangar didn't want you to remain in that castle a day longer knowing an assassin might be after you."

She hugged the blanket close. "What about your family? What will they think happened to you and me?"

"Rangar will tell them the truth in a few days once we've put some distance between ourselves and the castle. My family will understand. They've always known how dangerous it was to have you in our midst, especially since your brother died and you became the heir. You haven't sat in on all our council meetings—it was always a possibility thrown around that one of us might need to be prepared to hide out with you for a while." A shadow crossed his face. "Of course, we all assumed it would be Rangar."

As Bryn finally caught her breath, her head felt a little clearer. "We're going to the Wollin?"

Valenden nodded as he paced, glancing distract-edly among the trees. "Yes, we think their royal family will be sympathetic."

"How far of a journey is it?" She'd seen maps of the

kingdoms of the Eyrie, but it was difficult to judge inches on a piece of paper against the reality of mountain ranges, vast forests, and winding paths. The Wollin was a long and narrow coastal kingdom bordered by the Baersladen to the north, the Mirien to the east, and Ruma to the south. She knew little else about the kingdom other than having met the Wollin queen a few times, a very elderly woman who didn't always seem to be in control of her rational mind.

"About two weeks on foot."

"Two weeks!" Bryn gaped. "How are we supposed to eat?"

"I *borrowed* a few valuables from the castle that I can barter when we need coins. The greater concern is keeping you hidden. There aren't many fair-haired girls your age in this part of the Eyrie, and everyone will soon hear rumors that the Mir princess is on the run."

"I can cover my hair with a scarf . . . "

"I have something better. Roxin gave me this." He handed her a small jar. She untwisted the cap and sniffed it, recoiling.

"It smells rancid."

"It's charcoal mixed with flax seed and castor oil. Roxin prepared it for you at my request. She said to comb it through your hair and reapply every morning to give it a darker shade."

Bryn made a face as she dipped her hand in the mixture and began to work it through her loose hair. Once it was coated, she wiped her hands on a rag.

He extended her his hand. "We need to keep moving. Once the spies discover you've left, they'll be coming after us."

They began hurrying through the dark forest again. Bryn wasn't the same clumsy girl she'd been several months ago when she'd fled Castle Mir with the Barendur family. All her time hiking in the mountains to tend to the lambs had strengthened her legs and made her sure-footed on uneven ground, but she was still grateful for Valenden's presence. She knew the forest was filled with bears and wolves, and she wouldn't want to be out alone.

They hiked for several hours in what Bryn deduced was a southern direction, judging by the placement of the stars. It was comforting to focus on her steps over vines and roots since it kept her mind off the more troubling issues at hand. She was a princess with no kingdom. All her plans had been shattered when she'd discovered Trei murdered. Now, once word got out about his death, all the kingdoms of the Eyrie would be plunged into even more tension and suspicion than before.

Eventually, a small structure loomed in a clearing ahead. Valenden led her toward the sagging old place, which was a step above a shed but couldn't quite be called a cabin. It had a roof and walls on three sides but was open on the other one.

He dropped his bags on the dirt floor, massaging his aching shoulder. "We'll sleep here for a few hours until morning."

"What is this place?" she asked.

"Deer hunters use it," he explained. "A campsite. At least it's a roof over our heads and a break from the wind. Go sit, I'll fetch us some water. There's a stream nearby."

She curled up in the corner of the lean-to with her blanket wrapped tightly around her, listening to the forest sounds until he returned with a full flask. She drank down the water gratefully. He made a campfire, then began unpacking the bags. He pulled out an apple and a hunk of cheese wrapped in wax paper and divided the meager rations between them.

"Take off your ring," he ordered.

She stared down at the ring that Trei had given her, which glittered with sapphires and diamonds. Valenden was right, of course. It was far too valuable to flash out in the open while she was on the run. She twisted it off her finger and strung it on the same chain around her neck that also held Rangar's ring.

Valenden continued to unpack his rucksack. She was surprised to see him pull out several women's gowns that looked like the practical work dresses the kitchen maids wore beneath their aprons.

Then, he opened a box and handed her a simple silver ring.

"Now, put that on," he said, handing her the box.

It looked very much like the type of plain wedding bands that married villagers wore. "What's this for?"

He gave her one of the usual wry Valenden smiles

that said he was up to no good. "What, isn't it as fine as the two rings my brothers gave you?"

She leveled him a hard look.

He returned to unpacking the bags again as he explained, "An unmarried man and woman can't very well travel together without attracting attention, especially standing out as much as you do. You and I are going to pose as newlyweds. We were married in Moranton up north, and I'm bringing you home to my family in the Wollin."

"Newlyweds, Val? Really?" She felt a squeeze of heartache. She'd been a *real* newlywed until the night before when she'd so cruelly become a widow.

"It's either that or have everyone assume you're my harlot."

"Just say I'm your sister!"

"We look nothing alike, darling, and you speak Baer with an accent. People would be suspicious as soon as you opened your mouth."

He took another ring out of the box and slid it on his own finger. "This was Rangar's idea, by the way."

"*Rangar* suggested we pose as newlyweds? After he broke your nose when you kissed me?"

"Oh, he made sure to threaten me with plenty more broken bones if I try to kiss you again. But he also knew I was the only one who could get you out of the Baersladen safely."

She hugged her knees tightly with a frown. "Why *are* you helping, Val?"

He frowned back at her. "What do you mean?"

"You and I aren't soulbound like I am with Rangar. You don't owe me anything."

He rested his hands on his hips and looked up at the cloudy night sky. Finally, he sighed. "I suppose I grew bored with being a cad and thought I'd try out this hero thing for a while."

She rolled her eyes and tossed her apple core at him, but the truth was, Valenden was risking his life for her. He'd sacrificed just as much as she had—and lost perhaps even more.

She said sincerely, "Thank you, Val."

He settled next to her, holding up his hand beside hers to admire their matching rings. "No thanks necessary, darling wife. Just don't hog the blanket."

He tugged teasingly on the wool blanket, and she wrapped it around the two of them, and then fell into a restless sleep. She dreamed she was back at an orange grove she'd visited as a little girl in the south of the Wollin. Citrus only grew in the southern kingdoms, and she'd loved the season when cartloads of oranges and lemons and grapefruit would roll into Castle Mir. For weeks, every meal would be laced with lemon rind, citrus juices, candied orange peel.

She woke sometime later with a start, the smell of lemon rind strong in her memory. Gasping, she shook Valenden awake beside her. "Val, Val, wake up!"

His eyes snapped open as one hand reached instinctively for the blade by his side. She was reminded that when he wasn't drunk, he was actually a highly skilled fighter. But when he realized that they weren't being attacked, he relaxed.

"Dammit, Bryn, I'd finally just fallen asleep . . ."

She pounced on him, grabbing his shoulders. "Val, it's the lemon rind!"

He gave her a look that said he worried she'd lost her mind. "What are you talking about? You woke me to talk about lemons?"

"I smelled it in the newlywed chamber the night Trei was murdered. I didn't think much of it at the time because the kitchen had been featuring Mir delicacies in all the meals as a tribute to my homeland. Mir honey, Mir cheeses . . ."

He nodded, rubbing his eyes. "I'm aware."

"I assumed they'd included preserved lemon rind in a dish that Trei had eaten, and that's why I smelled it. But they didn't. It just occurred to me. There was no lemon or any citrus in the meal."

"And?" he said groggily.

She sat up on her knees, staring into the fire crackling outside of the shelter. "Alain's son. The one who's been helping with the fishermen on the docks. Mam Delice told me once that he keeps his flask filled with lemon liqueur."

Valenden stopped rubbing his eyes, letting his hand fall.

"Alain's son is the spy," she breathed. "He's the one who killed Trei."

CHAPTER 16

DISGUISES . . . a new look . . . stories from the past . . . rest at last . . . a very small bed for two people

Valenden sat up straighter at the bold accusation. "Are you certain, Bryn?"

She squeezed her hands together tightly. "Have you ever smelled lemon in the Baersladen? I certainly haven't. The assassin *had* to be Alain's son. I don't know if his father is also a spy—maybe his son was acting on his own. Alain certainly seemed willing to work with Trei and me as regents, but maybe his son didn't. I think his name is Broderick."

Valenden stroked his chin. "There isn't much we can do about it now. My family will need to know this information as soon as possible, but if we return now, we risk getting caught by Broderick and whoever else he might be working with. I'll send a messenger as soon as we reach a town."

They tried to return to sleep, but Bryn's mind was too occupied. She started practicing her spells to distract herself. Valenden watched, unable to sleep either, and eventually sighed.

"Your wording is fine," he said, "but your hand gestures need practice. You look like you're finger-painting with mud. The spirit of the hex needs to come through in how you move your hands."

She tried again, and he said, "A little better. Look, we have two weeks together on the road. I'll help you practice if you like."

"Will you really?" Her eyes lit up.

"We have to do *something* to pass the time, and Rangar made it clear we can't do my preferred activity."

He watched her perform the finding spell hand gesture and critiqued her form until morning, when he looked at the rising sun and tossed her the bag. "Time to keep moving. Pick out a dress, wifey."

She sifted through the dresses inside until she found a plain dark blue one that looked her size. She started to undo her buttons, then frowned.

"Turn your back, Val."

He had stripped to his waist, running a damp cloth over his chest before they set out again, and now he scoffed at her. "You think I haven't seen a naked woman before?"

"I think you've probably seen hundreds," she retorted. "But you aren't going to see *this* one."

He cackled as he turned his back. She found herself sneaking looks at the hexmarks on his shoulders, curious about them. But then he pulled on his shirt and, once they were dressed and packed, they set out to hike again.

After several hours, they emerged from the woods onto a dirt road that looked like it was used fairly frequently. Valenden consulted the sun for directions. "If we head that way, we'll reach the village of Timmon by noon. If I can pawn some of the silver candlesticks I took, we might be able to afford a pair of horses."

They set out down the road. At one point a carriage passed, and Bryn began to panic, instantly afraid her darkened hair and simple dress wasn't enough of a disguise and they'd recognize her. But Valenden told her to keep her head down, and the carriage rolled on by with nothing more than a wave to them.

Once they finally reached Timmon, she found it to be little more than an outpost village at a crossroads. Other than a few clustered houses, there was only a single storefront that served as a restaurant, tavern, and trading post.

Valenden adjusted his bag and started for the door while Bryn hung back, nervous.

"I'll do the talking," he reassured her. "It's better if they don't hear your accent. Just pretend for once in your life to be a meek, obedient wife."

She shot daggers at him. He took her hand and led her inside, where a lanky young man sat behind a counter with several shelves of staples behind him. There were two tables for patrons to eat at, both empty now.

Bryn pretended to inspect some rope for sale while Valenden went up to negotiate a price for the candlesticks.

As she browsed the goods, she found herself far more interested than she'd expected. Her whole life had been spent behind castle walls until Rangar had saved her from the siege. She'd gotten a brief sampling of life camping out under the stars, but then it had been back within the walls of Barendur Hold. She'd never experienced the life of a commoner. She'd never been in a *store*. She marveled at the buckets of iron nails for sale for a penny each; the sacks of flour and wheat; the jars of hard candies, bolts of fabric and thread; various tools.

My parents should have shown me all this. How could I ever rule people when I don't know what their lives are like?

Valenden finished his bartering and bid the shop boy farewell, taking her hand and leading her outside.

"He bought the candlesticks for a decent amount of coin, but this village has no horses for sale. He said there's a public carriage that will come by tomorrow bound for Garriston, but I think it's too risky to travel in close proximity to others."

"So it's more walking?"

"More walking."

Bryn found that she didn't mind the walk. It was fascinating to see glimpses of daily village life. The road from Timmon to Othwall was dotted with humble cottages and farms, and she enjoyed watching the people go about their lives. Previously, she'd always been sequestered in a royal carriage, and everyone had politely stopped and waved. Now, no one bid them the slightest interest, and she found it refreshing.

"Tell me about when you three were boys," Bryn asked to pass the time. "What trouble did you get up to?"

Valenden kicked a rock. "Ho, we could walk for months and still not get through all the trouble we got into. Trei, being the eldest, never wanted to see Rangar and me misbehaving, but he was quite fond of pranks himself. He used to leave rotting fish in our sheets to make us think we'd caught some reeking disease. Once, he poured out my flask of mead and replaced it with castor oil. I spit it all out on a girl I liked."

Bryn chuckled, enjoying hearing this other side of Trei, though it also filled her with sorrow. "Tell me more."

"Well, there was a time when Rangar and I wanted the same horse, an unbroken stallion. My father said whoever could tame it could keep it. Little did I know, Rangar had rubbed crushed chili pepper in its nostrils when it was my turn to break it. I ended up snapping my collarbone when it threw me."

"No!" Bryn said.

Valenden nodded. "And then Rangar rubbed soothing lotion on the horse's nose and climbed on top like it was tame as a lamb. He had that horse for years, used to flaunt it in front of me."

She grinned.

Valenden glanced back at her slyly. "I already told you about the time we snuck away from our meeting with one of the forest princes to go to the Mirien for the Harvest Gathering. Our father never found out about that little escapade. He would have skinned us raw. But it was hardly the only time we went somewhere we weren't supposed to. I recall a time we were supposed to be on a training expedition with the former captain of the Baer army, but we bribed him and spent a few days on the docks in Wentwest." He grinned at the memory. "Trei spent all his money on dice games. I ended up besotted by some boy who turned out to be a thief and stole everything I had, even my clothes. But Rangar chased him down and not only got my clothes back but took the boy's as well."

Bryn dragged her head back and forth in wonder. "Your childhood was . . . very different from mine. I wasn't allowed to leave the castle unless I was with my parents. Though when we were young, I remember playing hide-and-seek in Castle Mir's secret passages with my siblings. That was as adventurous as we ever got." She sighed. "My brother and sister and I grew apart as we got older. Mars was always very protective of me, but he was seldom around. Always off training with the army or studying."

"And your sister?"

"Elysander thought I was too much of a daydreamer. She tried to get me interested in dancing and singing, but it never caught my fancy. She lost interest in me eventually and spent more time with other court girls."

They continued swapping stories of their youth as they made their way past other villages, and then Valenden helped Bryn practice the purge spell hand gestures until she felt confident she captured the urgent spirit of the spell in her movements.

"Back in Castle Mir," she recalled, "I asked Rangar about getting the hex to spark a fire. He said it was too advanced."

"Bah, it isn't in the slightest. He only said that because he needed you to learn the purge spell instead so you could save his life. I can give it to you—I'm no mage, but it's only a small cut on the shoulder blade, and I've done it before. Some of my fellow soldiers and I gave it to each other during training as part of a hazing. Mage Marna was furious—she likes for her and her apprentices to be the only ones carving hexmarks. Anyway, the wording isn't complicated, though you do have to take care with the pronunciation. It sounds similar to the spell for making someone sneeze."

Her eyes lit up. "Yes, please, Val."

"Tonight, then."

By the time the sun was setting, they finally reached Othwall. Valenden went to ask about horses and got a lead on two, though the farmer wouldn't be able to meet with them until the morning.

"There's an inn a few blocks that way," Valenden said, hefting his bag. "We'll spend the night there."

Bryn wrung her hands and kept her head low as they entered the inn, a two-story building with a tavern attached. An elderly woman came out to greet them, her eyes immediately going to the wedding rings on their finger. As soon as she noted they were married and not a single man and woman scandalously traveling together, she smiled warmly.

"How can I help you two lovebirds?"

Valenden must have also noted how fixated she was on their marital status, so he grabbed Bryn's hand. "My wife and I need a room for tonight."

The innkeeper beamed as she dug around for a key. "So young! Oh, I love new love."

Valenden threw Bryn a devilish smirk. "Yes, we married just three days ago in Moranton. I'm bringing my bride home to the Wollin. We'd like the most private room you have . . . " He wiggled his eyebrows suggestively. "You understand . . . only three days married."

The woman turned slightly pink, and Bryn felt certain she herself was blushing, too. But the innkeeper merely chuckled and handed Valenden a key. "Upstairs, the last room on the right. It's our nicest, and it's furthest from the other guests." She pressed her lips together coyly. "Sleep well tonight . . . if you sleep at all."

Bryn thought she might combust and burn alive from embarrassment, but Valenden wrapped an arm around her back, pressing a kiss to her temple. Though she was shrieking inside, she pinned a stiff smile on her face.

As soon as they were settled in the room, which was barely larger than a closet with a tiny bed, Bryn smacked Valenden on the shoulder. "You didn't have to ham it up *that* much."

"We had to be convincing!"

"'Your most private room'?" she challenged.

"Yes, so that the other patrons don't overhear us talking about how you're the secret heir to two of the Eyrie's wealthiest kingdoms." He rolled his eyes. "You should thank me."

She scoffed again, but she was too tired to argue. "Well, you can make it up to me by fetching some water so I can wash off this dirt from the road."

Now it was Valenden's turn to roll his eyes. Of the three brothers, he was the least likely to step in and help someone in need, especially if it meant participating in hard work. But he didn't complain as he grabbed the empty water jug and carried it downstairs.

Alone in the guest room, Bryn sank onto the small bed. She took a few deep breaths now that she had a moment alone with her thoughts.

It was still hard—nearly impossible—to accept the

fact that Trei was dead. He'd given up so much for her, a nobleman to the core. Especially when *she* had been the target, not him.

And now Rangar rotted in a dungeon, and Valenden was practically a fugitive.

She hugged her arms, feeling like she'd brought a curse on all three Barendur brothers.

Valenden returned carrying the heavy pitcher, which he poured into a ceramic basin. Steam rose off it, and Bryn sat up straighter, interested. "A hot bath?" It was more than she could have dreamed of.

Valenden grinned. "The inn's well water was freezing, but the innkeeper heated it up for us. Said something about cold showers not being good for romance."

He tossed a towel to her that the innkeeper must have given him.

"Well, turn around, at least," she said, catching the towel. "Our newlywed charade stops behind closed doors."

"If you want me to give you the spark hexmark, I'm going to have to see you naked."

"Only my back," she countered. "And that's different."

He looked like he wanted to make a clever retort, but then thought better of it and turned his back as she'd asked.

Keeping an eye on him, Bryn started to peel off her clothes. She hesitated to remove her chemise and be completely naked in the same room as Valenden. But the truth was, she hadn't washed the chemise in days, and the grueling walk had left it soiled and sweaty. So off it came, too, as she shyly glanced at Valenden's back.

He was a cad, that was for certain, but he was also her friend.

Saints help her—she had actually come to *trust* him.

CHAPTER 17

ON THE ROAD . . . plans for the Wollin . . . coffee and scones . . . rumors of royalty . . . squirrels

In the inn's guest room, Bryn began to splash water over her body, reveling in the warm, scented-soap water. Scouring her skin with the towel, she threw quick looks at Valenden's back.

"What do you know of the Hytooth family in the Wollin?" she asked.

Valenden's shoulder rose and fell. "We spent a summer in the Wollin once as boys. I think I was around twelve. Father wanted us to learn to swim and sail, and the seawater there is far warmer than it is in the Baersladen. The king and queen were elderly even then. Now they must be ancient. They have no children of their own but ample nieces and nephews, all with those bright red Hytooth curls." He ran a hand through his hair thoughtfully, then chuckled. "I kissed at *least* three of them."

"You were twelve!" Bryn exclaimed as she ran the damp towel under her arms.

Still with his back to her, Valenden sighed contentedly. "And?"

She looked at the ceiling and let out a breath. "And you believe the Hytooths will help us?"

"Assuming the queen is still sharp-witted," he answered. "Her mind's been fading for years. Her husband, the king, is apparently in good health but was never that clever to begin with. It's always been Queen Amelia making the decisions under his name."

Bryn considered this as she finished her makeshift bath. The Wollin rulers were their only chance to find allies. The forest kingdoms of Vil-Kevi and Vil-Rossengard were friendly but kept to themselves. Captain Carr currently controlled the Mirien. Baron Marmose had influence in Ruma, and he certainly wouldn't side with her unless it was to become king himself. She knew little of Zaradona, but they had always been excellent trading partners with her parents, so their loyalties to a new regime were unlikely.

She finished the bath, hung her chemise to dry, and pulled on her dress but hesitated before buttoning the front. "Is now a good time for the hexmark?"

He glanced back over his shoulder. "Lay face-down on the bed."

Her heart thumped as she did as he asked. She

wasn't sure if she felt more of a thrill or apprehension —after all, only mages were supposed to carve hexmarks. But Valenden's movements looked well practiced as he sterilized his knife blade over the lantern flame and then splayed his fingers on her back.

"Here." He dug his index finger into a spot beneath her left ribcage. "This is where the spark hexmark goes. You already have a freckle there. See, it's fate."

She tried to roll her eyes, but it didn't work well with her face pressed to the blanket.

"Now, don't scream, or the innkeeper will get really excited about what's going on up here in the newlywed room."

Before she could offer a retort, he made a few quick slices on her back, then clamped a damp cloth on the wound.

She sat up, twisting around to try to see the hexmark on her back. "That's it?"

"I told you I knew what I was doing. Now, listen carefully."

He told her the words of the spell and taught her the hand gesture, though she'd seen Rangar and the other Baer people perform it enough to already know it by heart. Within a few minutes, she'd successfully summoned a spark in the palm of her hand.

Valenden grinned. "Fate, as I told you. Now I'm going to bathe while the water is still at least slightly warm."

She looked up from the flickering flame in her palm. "I promise I won't look."

He winked as he began unbuttoning his shirt. "Darling, *I* never asked you not to look."

She groaned and went to the window, placing her back to him as he shamelessly stripped. While she continued to practice sparking a flame in her palm, she said, "So you think you can get a message to Barendur Hold about Broderick?"

"In the morning," he said from behind her. "I'll ask around. The villages of the Baersladen have a messenger system, so it shouldn't be a problem. The only issue will be maintaining confidentiality. I can't very well confess I'm the famous Prince Valenden with a royal missive."

Bryn summoned a flame again, then closed her palm to douse it. "Don't you have a hex for that? To influence someone's actions?"

"Why, Bryn, you're getting devious with all these hexes. I like it."

Her vision shifted, and she realized that instead of looking through the window she could also look *at* the window, which faintly reflected Valenden's naked body behind her. Eyes widening to glimpse his bare backside, she quickly turned to face the wall instead.

He finished his bath and dressed, then flopped into bed with a groan. "My aching feet. There isn't some Mir tradition of giving foot massages to your husband, is there? Even a pretend husband?"

She sat on the foot of the bed, rolling her eyes, but reconsidered. He *had* saved her life. She tossed back the covers, grabbing one of his feet. "Oh, fine. A few minutes."

He sat up on his elbows, face scrunched. "Really?"

"Really."

He leaned back on the pillows while she tugged off his sock and began kneading his feet. *At least he's freshly bathed,* she reckoned. Foot massages were *not* a Mir tradition and not something she'd usually deign to do, but she was also very aware of the fact that Valenden was risking his life for her. There were assassins after her who wouldn't hesitate to kill Valenden. He might be infuriating, but beneath his posturing, he was doing one of the kindest things for her anyone ever had. Not to mention one of the bravest.

She supposed it earned a few foot rubs.

Leaning back on the pillows, he grew serious. "If they find Rangar guilty of Trei's murder, they'll hang him."

She stilled for a moment before returning to rubbing his feet. She'd suspected as much, though she hadn't wanted to think about it. "They'll prove his innocence. I know they will."

She gave Valenden a sad smile over her shoulder. Rangar might be her lover, but he was Valenden's brother. Valenden feared for Rangar's fate perhaps even more than she did, especially after having lost Trei.

"I know how hard it is to lose a sibling," she said quietly, her mind on Mars. Grief swelled in her, but she forced it down, channeled it into her hand movements. "I'm grateful for the years I did have with Mars."

"You actually liked Prince Mars, didn't you?"

"Of course."

"I mean, and let me think how to put this delicately, you truly loved him, didn't you? Not just because he was family, but because of who he was. Even after his actions after the siege."

Bryn tried not to take offense at Valenden's words because she knew he didn't mean any. He was merely speaking the truth. Everyone in the Eyrie had heard of Mars's failings as a benevolent heir to the throne.

"I will always love my brother," she said, eyes filling with tears for the few good memories they'd had as children. "I understand he wasn't fit to rule, but I will never believe he acted out of malice or greed. He was simply taught to be the way he was. If only he had a second chance at life, I think he could have been a great king."

Valenden didn't answer, and when she glanced at him over his shoulder, she found him snoring.

She scoffed and tugged his socks back on, then tucked his feet in the bed and pulled up the covers to his chin.

She laid in the tiny bed beside him, and all night, thought about what a tragedy both of their brothers' short lives had been.

~

When Bryn awoke in the morning, the other side of the bed was empty.

She sat up in alarm, overcome by flashbacks of stumbling into the *other* newlywed bedroom only to smell the reek of death. But Valenden's boots were gone, which meant he must have left willingly. She got dressed and went downstairs, where the innkeeper perked up, giving her a wiggle of her eyebrows.

"*Comfortable* night?"

Bryn was growing rapidly tired of all the insinuations about her and Valenden's supposed romance. "Yes, fine," she said, waving in the air. "Where is my . . . husband?"

"He left about an hour ago. Said he had some errands to run in town and that you should get breakfast." She motioned to the tearoom through the door. "My sister is the cook. Best scones you've ever tasted. Mir honey in honor of our new queen."

Bryn froze on the spot. It suddenly occurred to her that she'd forgotten to reapply Roxin's charcoal paste to her hair that morning. A quick glance into the reflective windowpane reassured her that her hair was still a dull shade of brown.

The innkeeper sighed. "Such a shame about Prince Trei."

Bryn knew she was treading on dangerous ground. They couldn't afford for rumors to spread that she and Valenden weren't the commoners they said they were. But she hesitantly asked, "What do they say about his death?"

The innkeeper's eyes widened with a glint of gossip. Dropping her voice, she intimated, "They say Prince Rangar's knife was found at the scene. Apparently, Princess Bryn has been so distraught by the whole incident that she hasn't left her room at all. She locked herself up with the mages." The innkeeper shook her head before adding in a whisper, "You know, there are rumors Princess Bryn was involved with Rangar first. She was his Saved, and you know how it goes . . . those soulbonds sometimes turn romantic. They say Rangar killed his brother out of jealousy."

Bryn turned away quickly before her face betrayed her pain. She should have expected rumors to have traveled this far already, but it still stung. Somehow, she would have to not only save her neck and Rangar's, but clear his name throughout the Eyrie, too.

"Right," she muttered. "I'll take that scone now."

After she'd sipped coffee and eaten her fill in the tearoom, Valenden sauntered back in, placing a messy kiss on her cheek for show. She fought the urge to wipe it away.

"And where have you been?" she asked.

"Taking care of that *errand* we discussed," he said, and she knew he must mean the letter to Barendur Hold. "I took your advice. That trick you suggested. A letter is already on its way north."

It eased her worries to know that soon, King Aleth would know of Broderick's treachery. Of course, her proof that he was Trei's murderer was circumstantial, but she hoped it would cast enough doubt that they would free Rangar.

"Were you able to find horses?" she asked.

He smiled smugly as he sipped his coffee. "In fact, I did. A strong gelding for me, an old nag for you."

"Val— Vayne!" she quickly corrected herself, using the name they'd agree he'd go by.

He raised a shoulder. "What? You barely ride. I thought you'd prefer a slow, gentle nag."

She rested her chin on her hands, wrinkling her nose. "Oh. Hmm. Yes. I suppose you're right. I'm just so used to assuming everything with you is a trick."

"Believe it or not, there are times when I make myself useful."

Her shoulders softened. He was right. She hated to think of where she'd be if Valenden hadn't agreed to get her out of the Baersladen.

He finished his breakfast and tossed a few coins on the table, then stood. "We should get moving. Even on horseback, it's still days to the Wollin."

They packed their meager bag and paid for the lodging, while Bryn cringed at the innkeeper's further insinuations about their passionate night together, and then Valenden led her outside to show her the horses he'd bought.

His was a heavyset black gelding; probably a farmer's plow horse. Hers was a mousy-brown mare with a sway back and knobby knees, but the mare had such gentle, soft eyes, and didn't flinch with Bryn clambered gracelessly on top, that Bryn felt an immediate affection for the animal.

They set out from Othwall on another dusty, interminable road. Though Valenden complained about the distance, Bryn continued to enjoy the trek. It eased her bruised heart to watch the rolling hills go by, the high mountains far in the distance, to observe farmers going about their business. There was nothing at all remarkable about the villages and homesteads they passed, but it was all new to Bryn, and she soaked everything up.

Besides, it was a great time for another session practicing her hexes.

By late afternoon, they had left farmland behind and entered another forest. The road was pleasantly shaded by towering oak trees and squirrels darting around overhead, chittering down at them. They'd fallen into a companionable silence, and Bryn found herself lulled by the mare's steady gait. She wondered if the Hytooth family in the Wollin would be as welcoming as Valenden claimed. She hoped so. She needed a blessing after so much heartache and tragedy.

Besides, she'd always wanted to see Hytooth Palace, the sprawling seaside castle known for its smooth, sand-colored turrets and swaying palm trees. She'd come to love the stormy cliffs of the Baersladen, but the beaches there were rocky, inhospitable places. It was rumored that the Wollin beaches were full of soft sand as far as they could see, with crabs and shellfish practically crawling out of the sea straight into nets. Her stomach rumbled to think of food more like what she'd grown up with instead of raw venison and strong mead. Not that she wasn't grateful for Barendur Hold's kitchens, but there was only so much venison a person could eat . . .

She was deep in her head, and they were deep in the forest, when a strange whistle cut through the air. It was followed by a chittering sound that was much too loud to have been a squirrel.

She squinted up at the branches overhead, frowning. "Val . . ."

"Shh," he hissed, drawing his short sword.

The look on his face snapped her out of her reverie. Instantly, her body tensed. Her mare sensed the change and stopped, refusing to budge.

More chittering came, sounding like it was coming from that big oak . . . No, the copse of laurel . . . No, from behind them now . . .

"Blast!" Valenden cursed, wheeling his gelding around, circling Bryn's mare protectively. He raised his sword.

"Valenden, what is it?"

"This road is known for banditry," he said, keeping his eyes on the trees. "And I don't think we're about to be attacked by squirrels."

CHAPTER 18

BANDITS ON THE ROAD . . . the woman in black . . . chances of escape . . . the rainbow forest

The bandits might not have been squirrels, but they swooped out of the trees just like them. Materializing out of leafy cover, dozens of figures dropped gracefully onto the road.

Bryn's heart shot to her throat as she twisted in her saddle to try to follow their movements. The black-clad figures blocked the road ahead of and behind them. More figures appeared from deeper within the forest, cutting off the possibility of leaving the road and taking their chances in the woods.

At first, all the bandits appeared identical. They each were dressed in black trousers, black boots, black or gray shirts, and they all wore bandanas around their heads with eyeholes cut out. They had an arsenal of knives and swords strapped around their waists.

"Ho," one of them called, a gray-haired man who'd been the first to drop down to block their path. He raised a hand as though in a mockery of greeting. "Ho, there, travelers. May we have a word?"

"Have a word," Valenden muttered low enough for only Bryn to hear. "More like have our heads."

"Let us pass," Valenden said louder to their leader. "We are newlyweds on our way home to Wollin. I'm a goatherd and have spent all my coin fetching my bride. We have nothing for you to steal."

Their leader flashed a cruel grin. "You think us bandits? No, friend, we are nothing of the sort. In fact, we protect this road *from* bandits. You are in the territory of the Forest King. We wish to provide you with safe passage, especially on such a joyous occasion as your recent wedding!" He gave a more appraising smile in Bryn's direction. "And *what* a bride . . ."

Valenden grabbed the reins of Bryn's mare on the off chance that the horse might bolt amid the danger. "Do you leer at my wife, sir?"

The bandit leader held up his hands. "Not I. But the point stands that we are protectors of travelers on this road. You are free to pass, of course. Though we do struggle to make ends meet out here away from our families, looking out for travelers such as yourselves. Could you but spare a few coins, we'd be grateful."

Valenden groaned and reached into his shirt, coming out with a small sack of coins. "Here. For the *good defenders* of the road." He tossed the sack to the leader, who caught it easily in one hand.

Bryn sucked in a breath, hoping that would be the extent of their extortion.

Valenden said tensely, "Now if you'll move aside . . ."

"Ah, well," their leader drawled. "You see, I have this bum leg of mine." He lifted his pant leg to reveal deeply scarred skin and twisted bone as though he'd broken it long ago and it hadn't healed properly. He stepped forward on a limp that Bryn didn't think was part of the charade. "What we *really* need to do our jobs well is a pair of horses."

Valenden went dangerously quiet. Bryn could feel him seething. In a low voice, he whispered to Bryn, "We cannot allow them to take the horses and all our coin."

"So what do we do?" she whispered.

The leader cleared his throat. "Save the romantic chitchat for the bedroom, my friends. Unless you want to speak louder, that is," he said with a winking leer. "My men haven't heard such talk in quite some time."

Valenden's back stiffened. Bryn appraised the bandits, hoping to glean some advantage. The leader had seemed burly at first, but he clearly had a limp. The others had also all struck her at first glimpse as fit men in their prime, but now that she looked closer, she was surprised to find that at least half appeared to be women, though their baggy clothes and bandana face coverings made it hard to know for certain. One clearly female bandit had a rifle, but rifles were notoriously unreliable. She'd have to have exceptionally good aim to shoot them while they were galloping away on horseback.

"We make a run for it," Valenden said quietly, Bryn's mare's reins tight in his hand. "You hold on to the saddle as tightly as you can. I'll do the rest. We must hope this old mare has some life left in her."

While they were speaking, Bryn became aware that one of the bandits, the woman holding the rifle, was moving determinedly toward the leader. The woman kept her back mostly to Bryn as she whispered something low to the leader.

He asked a few questions that Bryn couldn't hear, and the two of them discussed quietly.

"Now!" Valenden said.

He spurred his horse into action. The startled beast took off, bunching its muscles. Bryn's horse was slower on the uptake, kicking into a gallop with more reluctance. Valenden tugged on the reins hard, trying to navigate the mare.

Bryn grabbed the base of the mare's mane with all her strength, squeezing her legs and praying she could hold on. The horses lurched forward awkwardly, one fast and one slow, tethered together by the reins.

The instant Valenden had spurred on the horses, the bandits swarmed them with knives and swords raised. But Valenden had a good start and was just about to tear past the bandit leader when the woman speaking with him raised the rifle skyward and fired.

Even though the rifle wasn't aimed at them, the crack of the rifle made her horse rear up, spooked. Before she knew it, Bryn tumbled off the back of the horse, fingers slipping out of the mane.

She fell hard on her backside, wincing as pain shot through her hip. She'd broken the fall with her ankle and now worried she might have broken or sprained a bone.

"Gods," Valenden cursed under his breath. He pulled his horse around in a tight circle back to where Bryn lay. Her horse spooked again and tried to bolt, but one of the bandits grabbed its reins.

Valenden placed his horse between Bryn and the bandits and drew his sword.

For a moment, tension crackled in the air.

Valenden wasn't as highly trained a soldier as Trei or Rangar, but Bryn had seen him practice and knew he was more than capable of fighting. There were lithe muscles beneath those clothes of his and a body that could snap into action if needed.

Still, it was Valenden against over a dozen bandits —the odds weren't in their favor.

Raising his sword, Valenden said, "There must be something else you want. We're quite resourceful. Whatever you want, we can get it for you if you let us go."

The gray-haired bandit leader ran a hand over his chin, appraising them.

"Sorry, friend," he said, "but what we want is your *wife*."

Bryn and Valenden had no choice but to let themselves be captured. Though Valenden had been ready to fight off a dozen bandits to protect her, Bryn had yelled for him to lower his sword and dismount before he got himself killed.

Once the bandits saw how she'd twisted her ankle in the fall, they allowed her back on her horse, while the female bandit rode on Valenden's gelding, leading her mare by the reins. The masked woman threw back glances at Bryn every once in a while. Even with the black mask and her hair tucked up, there was something familiar about the elegant way the woman held herself.

They had bound Valenden's hands and taken away his sword, so he had to walk next to Bryn's horse, tethered by a rope. He tossed his hair back and cursed every few steps, struggling to walk with the rope threatening to pull him off balance.

"What do you think they want with me?" Bryn whispered down to him.

He gave her a long look that didn't inspire much confidence. "If our hosts were all men, I'd fear more for your safety. But I can't imagine a group of bandits that is half female would allow a woman to be harmed; then again, I've learned there is much I don't understand about women."

The bandits soon broke from the road onto a trail that Bryn would never have even noticed. They moved gracefully through the underbrush, making almost no noise. It was a beautiful forest; not even Bryn's fears could distract her from that fact. The forest in Vil-Kevi had been monstrous and nearly sentient; the woods in the northern part of the Baersladen were sparse and shrubby wind-twisted pines. But the forest here, near the border with the Wollin, was more like Saint's Forest back home. There were deciduous trees with broad leaves, changing color now into vibrant yellows and reds and oranges. The fallen leaves crumpled under her horse's hooves. She'd never seen such a rainbow of colors before.

After about an hour through the woods, the leader slowed to a stop, then raised his hand to signal for the others to halt as well. Bryn's heart kicked up. Her eyes searched the trees, looking for any sign of danger.

The bandit leader gave a sharp whistle. It echoed through the underbrush, and in another second, a whistle answered from deeper in the forest.

There are more of them.

Bryn looked to Valenden for direction and found his body tense, his attention keenly centered on a place ahead and to their right.

"Look," he whispered, jerking his chin.

She stared at the trees, shaking her head. "What? I don't see anything."

"Look harder."

She tried to pick out shapes among the trees; to her surprise, her eyes snagged on a rope ladder that was the same color as a tree trunk. She followed it upward, where she found a dark shadow amid the trees. She wouldn't have thought twice about it, but now she looked closer and noticed how despite the leaves cleverly concealing it, it appeared to be a structure.

The leader whistled three times now, and many whistles answered from throughout the forest.

Bryn gasped to find themselves suddenly surrounded. More bandits suddenly dropped down from other structures hidden in the trees.

The lead bandit, who had called himself the Forest King, faced them with a grin. "Welcome to our village, friends. Now, let's see how much coin you have on you." He motioned to his associates. "Separate them and search them."

Bryn gasped as two bandits cut through Valenden's tether then dragged him away.

CHAPTER 19

**THE TREE COTTAGE . . . the Forest King unmasked
. . . a determined princess . . . a shocking reveal**

Bryn was left alone with the Forest King.

He appraised her keenly with a wolfish grin still on his face. "Get her down from that horse."

Two men pulled her down from her mare. She searched the woods for any sign of Valenden, but they had forced him up a ladder into one of their treehouse structures, and he was hidden now by leaves as surely as if the forest had swallowed him.

"Val!" she called out.

The Forest King signaled to one of his men, who silenced her with a hand over her mouth. The king took a menacing step closer, resting a hand on Valenden's sword that he'd holstered at his side. "It's only you and me now, princess."

Bryn's heart thumped in her chest, warning her of the danger.

How does he know who I am?

Reading the surprise in her eyes, he laughed darkly. "Didn't think we'd see past your disguise?"

With the bandit's hand over her mouth, she couldn't answer. But now she looked around more urgently for Valenden. The fact that the bandits knew she was the crown princess placed both of them in far more danger than if they'd simply been captured travelers.

The Forest King strode closer, dragging his gaze up and down her body. "Lucky break, I'd say. Here we were hoping to commandeer a pair of horses, and instead we find a runaway princess. *Far* more valuable. In fact, I'd say you're the most valuable prize to be had in these parts."

He motioned toward the treehouse where they'd taken Valenden. "And who is your companion, princess? I doubt he is your husband, Prince Trei of the Baersladen, as I hear he's dead." He leaned in close enough to whisper in her ear, "Whoever he is, I hope he isn't your new sweetheart because those close to your family have a way of suffering terribly, don't they?"

Bryn narrowed her eyes.

To her surprise, a voice behind the Forest King

spoke in Mir, "That's enough, Jon. There's no need to torture her."

It was the female bandit with the rifle.

To Bryn's surprise, the Forest King obeyed the woman. He straightened, folding his arms across his chest, and answered back in flawless but accented Mir, "Oh, I'm only having a bit of fun."

The woman came forward, taking her time appraising Bryn. There had been something familiar about the way the woman spoke: Mir was a common language, and they weren't far from the border, so it wasn't entirely surprising to hear it spoken. What had struck Bryn more was how confident the woman's tone was—and how readily the Forest King had listened to her.

"Let her speak," the woman said, waving away the bandit's hand.

As soon as the bandit had released his hold on Bryn's mouth, she gasped, "One woman to another, I ask you. Don't listen to this Forest King or whatever this rogue calls himself. Let my companion and I go free, and we'll make it worth your betrayal of your leader."

The masked female bandit and the Forest King exchanged a long look. Then the woman turned to Bryn and cocked her head as she asked in an even more familiar voice, "What has you thinking *he* is the Forest King?"

Confused, Bryn looked uncertainly between the bandits. *He never actually called himself the Forest King,* she realized. *He only said we were in the Forest King's realm.*

In fact, the man with the limp had never called himself their leader at all. He'd done most of the speaking, so it had been natural to assume that was the case, but now Bryn noticed how all the bandits, even the one called Jon, deferred to the woman with the rifle.

"*You're* the Forest King," Bryn said to her in surprise.

The woman nodded in grim satisfaction beneath her black bandana. "Yes, and you are going to tell us exactly what brings a banished Mir princess into these woods."

The bandits forced Bryn up a rope ladder into one of the treehouse structures. Despite her apprehension, she couldn't help but be amazed at the engineering marvel that was the tree structures. This one was the size of a small cottage, built between the tree's massive branches, almost entirely hidden from the ground by the tree's leaves. A thatched roof overhead had an opening to let out the smoke coming from a stone-lined fire pit that was lit now with a pot in the coals steadily bubbling.

A series of rope bridges spanned from tree to tree, connecting different platforms and treehouses like this one. From what Bryn could tell, there were at least three full-sized tree cottages and a half dozen other platforms where bandits napped, kept watch, or played dice games.

"Where have you put my companion?" Bryn asked.

"Your *husband* is there," Jon said, pointing to a treehouse connected by a rope bridge. "He's safe for the time being. That said, his continued safety is up to you."

He folded his arms, glancing at the Forest King, who had remained quiet until then.

"Now," Jon said, "Tell us how a Mir princess who was stolen away from her home by a violent Baer prince now finds herself a newlywed peasant."

Bryn felt a flush of indignation. "Rangar isn't *violent*. And he didn't steal me away."

Right now, Rangar was rotting in a dungeon because of her, and he certainly didn't deserve the reputation he had apparently acquired throughout the kingdoms as a kidnapper.

Jon and the Forest King exchanged another look before the woman nodded for him to continue questioning.

"If that is so, you'll need to explain how you escaped the siege on Castle Mir."

Bryn folded her arms, feeling protective of Rangar and his reputation. These criminals did not know what Rangar and his family had done for her.

She said, "On the night of the siege, Prince Rangar warned me of the impending attack. He and his brothers helped me escape. They took me to the Baersladen for my protection. I went voluntarily. They risked everything to help me. Valenden—your prisoner there in the next tree cottage—is Rangar's brother."

Jon raised his eyebrows. "You married the brother of the man who supposedly kidnapped you? After you first married the late Prince Trei?"

Her heart faltered as she thought of Trei. Exasperated, she said, "Valenden and I aren't married. We're only posing as newlyweds for safe passage."

This prompted another unspoken exchange between the two bandits, and the Forest King nodded again.

Jon continued the interrogation. "Why would you leave your home voluntarily with princes who you didn't know?"

Tipping her chin to face him, she said in a steely voice, "Because I believed what Rangar said about my parents. That they were tyrants. I never knew the truth before then, which was my own failing. Now that I know, I've sworn I'll never let the Mir people suffer again. I married Trei Barendur to give them an honorable king. I fled to avoid assassins sent by Captain Carr. I will sit on my rightful throne, and I'll prove I'm not the despots my parents were."

Her speech seemed to have taken the bandits by surprise. She'd always had the reputation as the daydreaming youngest princess with her head in the clouds. But stating her case in front of these dangerous criminals made her feel powerful, and she took pride in what she'd said. They could threaten or torture her, but she wouldn't ever run away again.

Jon turned to the Forest King and said in Mir, "Well? Heard everything you needed to?"

Bryn felt as though she was missing something between the two of them. She had expected them to laugh in her face or threaten her, but they had simply listened calmly.

"Yes," the Forest King said and then faced Bryn. "And I think you mean *our* parents."

Bryn hesitated, confused. Before she could ask what the Forest King meant, the woman untied her black bandana and let it fall to the floor.

A familiar face looked back at her.

Bryn pressed a shocked hand to her mouth. *"Elysander?"*

Her sister looked like an entirely different person than the pampered young woman Bryn had last seen months ago. Elysander had always been a vision of feminine grace with every hair in place, dressed in beautifully tailored gowns, her face carefully dusted with rust like their mother's.

Now, she wore no rust or powder on her face. Her blond hair was pulled back in a simple knot at her nape that could be tucked into her cloth mask. Her clothes were baggy enough that she could easily be mistaken at a distance for a man.

But it was the defiant look in Elysander's eyes now that truly set her apart from who she'd been before.

Elysander took a step forward. "Bryn," she said in a softer voice, the voice Bryn knew. "Sister."

Bryn found herself stumbling forward, head spinning, as she embraced a sister she hadn't thought ever to see again, a sister who—if it was even possible—had been harboring even more secrets than Bryn herself.

CHAPTER 20

THE FOREST KING . . . black bandanas . . . royal hobbies . . . favors from criminals

"Forgive me for all this artifice," Elysander said, motioning to her black bandana mask around her neck. "I had to know if we could trust you."

Bryn found herself staring at her sister in shock. Bryn and Elysander had been close in early childhood, playing hide-and-seek around the castle and stealing tarts from the kitchen, but over the last decade, they'd grown apart. Elysander had been trundled off to science classes, taught how to dance and entertain, all the traits she would need as the future duke's wife. And to Bryn's young eyes, Elysander had readily embraced the expectations placed upon her. She'd appeared to adore dancing and dresses, education and etiquette.

But now Bryn wondered if she perhaps hadn't known her sister at all.

"You joined a group of *bandits*?" Bryn cried.

Elysander raised an eyebrow. "Who said anything about joining? I thought it was clear I *formed* the group."

Bryn pressed a hand to her head. An ache had begun there, spurred by her confusion over seeing her prim sister dressed in men's trousers with her golden locks hidden in a messy knot.

Elysander rested a hand on Bryn's shoulder, and suddenly the older sister she'd always known was back. "Bryn, there is much you don't know."

"Lord and ladies," Bryn muttered darkly. "You *think*?"

"Mars and I knew about what was happening in the Mirien since we were around your age. He found out from a small group of soldiers who were trying to turn him against our parents. He didn't believe the soldiers at first until they showed him proof of our parents' crimes. A few years ago, he confided the truth to me. He'd been gathering information and meeting with informants who painted a very different picture of what was happening in our kingdom than we'd been led to believe. Captain Carr was feeding Mars a lot of the information—but I swear, neither Mars nor I knew about the uprising. We would have warned you if we had. Carr kept that to himself, hoping our whole family would be slaughtered and he could usurp the throne."

Bryn's mouth had gone dry. "Why didn't you tell me?"

"You were our little sister," Elysander confessed with sympathy. "We intended to tell you one day, but you were always different from the rest of the family, Bryn. You had such tenderness to you, and you saw the best in everyone. We didn't want to shatter that sweetness."

"It wasn't sweetness," Bryn said in a hardened voice. "It was naivety. There was nothing kind or innocent about it; I was kept in the dark, told everything was fine in the kingdom, so I believed it. I was never taught to think for myself. I made a lot of mistakes, yes. But you and Mars should have told me the truth."

"You're right. I see that now. It was our error." Elysander's hand squeezed her shoulder.

Bryn wasn't sure what to make of the situation. She was grieving Trei, worried about Rangar—and now Valenden, too. She had an entire kingdom's future resting on her shoulders. And now she'd discovered her sister was cavorting around as a bandit.

"And *this?*" Bryn said, motioning to her sister's masculine clothes. "I thought you escaped to Dresel and married Duke Dryden."

"I did," Elysander said, then gave a little half-smile. "That's Jon."

Bryn turned in disbelief to the older man who still wore his mask. Grinning, he took it off. Bryn had met

Duke Dryden when she was much younger but hadn't seen him in five or six years and would never have recognized him now. He hadn't had a limp when she'd known him before.

The duke wrapped his arm around Elysander's waist.

"Dresel is a peaceful kingdom," he explained. "And I'm a lesser duke. It isn't a highly important title, so I have few responsibilities there and no family or relatives to look after. I was bored in my younger years, dabbled in activities that could be considered . . . less than lawful."

"Banditry, you mean. Even as a duke, you were a criminal."

He shrugged guiltily.

Elysander explained, "I escaped the siege on Castle Mir with the help of loyal soldiers who knew Mars and I weren't sympathetic to our parents' rule. They took me to an inn, where Jon had sent some of his men to find me."

"Some of his bandits, you mean."

Elysander took a deep breath. "It wasn't the ideal way to learn my betrothed spent half his time as a criminal, true, but at least that fact saved my life. It took a while for me to get used to the idea of marrying a fugitive, fully knowing how much he'd robbed from other royal families."

"Elysander has an open mind," Jon said, looking at Bryn's sister fondly. "And for that, I was very grateful. I hadn't intended for her to find out about my side activities, but given the siege, it was the only way to get her safely to Dresel. At first, she tried to convince me to stop robbing travelers; over time, she instead convinced me to let women into the ranks and work toward liberating the Mir people instead of stealing. Then, with my blessing, she took over completely as leader."

Everything they said made Bryn's head spin. While she had been searching for lost lambs and learning magic in the Baersladen, she'd imagined that Elysander had been hiding out in her duke's mansion sipping expensive tea. Yet her sister had been using *crime* to help their people.

"But these lands are still technically in the Baersladen," Bryn pointed out. "What brought you so far north of Dresel and the Mirien?"

Elysander said, "You did. We heard rumors that you'd fled Barendur Hold. We've been looking for you." She touched Bryn's hair. "I didn't expect that you'd dye your hair. It took us a while to track you down, as we were looking for a blonde."

"It was Val's idea," Bryn said, examining her dark locks. "Prince Valenden, I mean."

"That's the other thing. We didn't know if he was an ally or enemy. We wanted to question you both first before revealing our identity."

"Valenden is many things," Bryn said. "But he's not an enemy. I'd trust him with my life."

Elysander gave her sister a sly look. "And this newlywed charade . . . is it truly just for show? He's a handsome man, though his reputation for drink and debauchery has reached us even in Dresel."

Bryn scoffed. She thought back to her kiss with Valenden on the night of the Harvest Gathering and what a mistake it had been. "Val is only a friend," she insisted. "It's his brother who . . . " She trailed off, not sure how to finish. "I'm not talking about Trei."

"You mean the younger prince. Rangar Barendur." Elysander's eyes flashed. "Yes, I remember what happened with the wolf attack. He claimed you all those years ago. The *fralen* bond."

Bryn didn't have the energy to explain everything that had happened since then, how she'd grown from fearing Rangar to loving him with her entire soul.

She said quietly, "He's currently locked in a dungeon, and I'm afraid it's my fault." She turned toward Duke Dryden. "Is there any way your bandits could help him?"

Duke Dryden stroked his chin. "So now I have *both* the Lindane sisters asking for favors?"

Elysander nudged her husband in the ribs. "Jon."

He relented. "How far is Barendur Hold from here?"

"On horseback?" Bryn did a quick calculation. "Maybe three days' ride. Twice that on foot."

Duke Dryden looked off toward the distant mountains. "I'll send a few men to quietly look into the situation and see what is possible. That is all I can promise at the moment."

"Thank you, Jon," Elysander said, gently touching

his wrist. Bryn was surprised to see this display of true affection between the two of them. Elysander and Duke Dryden had been betrothed since Elysander was born and the duke had been fifteen years old. It was a considerable age difference even now that Elysander was twenty-one and the duke thirty-six. His hair was graying at the temples, and his limp made him appear much older than he was. Yet he was an undeniably attractive man, with light brown skin and dark features and an impish smile that contrasted with his age.

"I'll leave you two," he said. "I suspect you have much to catch up on. Dinner should be ready soon—I can smell the wild grouse roasting."

He descended the ladder, favoring his good leg.

Bryn did smell roasting meat in the air, and her stomach growled. She turned to her sister, knitting her fingers together. "Will you release Val from wherever you're keeping him?"

"Yes, if you vouch that he is trustworthy."

"He might steal a few hearts, but that's all."

Elysander gave her a quizzical look. "What exactly happened with you and the three Barendur brothers?" She held out her fingers, counting off. "You fell in love with Rangar, fled with Val, yet married Trei?"

Mention of Trei dampened Bryn's spirits again. She thought of saying goodbye to Saraj and wondered how the falconer was faring.

She sighed. "That essentially sums it up."

Elysander shook her head, marveling. "And here I

feared you were locked in some tower, ravaged by a wild prince, forced to wash his clothes."

"My life in Barendur Hold was far from a nightmare." Bryn felt a pang of longing to be back in the Hold, listening to the storm outside and the waves crashing. "I assure you, I wasn't some helpless prisoner. You have had your adventure . . . " She touched her arm beneath her sleeve where the finding spell hexmark was carved. "So have I."

Elysander studied her face as though seeing Bryn no longer as her little sister but as a grown woman.

She wrapped an arm around Bryn's shoulders and said more jovially, "Come, let's fetch that scandalous prince of yours and have something to eat. Our lives are very different when we're on the road as opposed to home in Dryden Hall, but no less festive."

They descended from the tree cottage to find a camp had been set up on the forest floor. A few men chopped vegetables and roasted grouse while others passed around flagons of ale. One of the female bandits began explaining the mechanics of their forest village to Bryn, which was only used in summer and fall when there was ample leaf cover and disassembled for winter and spring.

Bryn's stomach was growling when someone suddenly sidled up beside her, swiping at her mug of ale.

"I'll take a sip of that if you'd be so good, darling wife."

Valenden looked no worse the wear for his brief

incarceration, though he had a few leaves tangled in his hair. He took a deep drink of Bryn's ale before handing back the empty mug. "I hear your sister is the one who has us in all this trouble."

Bryn looked down at the drained mug and rolled her eyes. "We're lucky Elysander found us and not real bandits."

"These *are* real bandits, sweetheart. Your sister and her husband are rogues."

"Only sometimes," Bryn objected. "For most of the year, they're the highly regarded duke and duchess of Dryden Hall."

"Right." Valenden scanned the camp. "Now, I need more ale."

While he went to hunt up another drink, some of the bandits brought out instruments and began playing a Dresel song. Several of the female bandits had taken their hair down and were flirting with the men, dancing and swapping stories. Bryn noticed a few couples pairing off and sneaking into the treetop platforms.

She warmed herself by the fire, deeply grateful to have her sister back in her life and to know that Elysander was not only well but loved. She leaned her head on Valenden's shoulder as her thoughts turned to Rangar.

If only she could share this good food and drink with Rangar. If only it were *Rangar* she was leaning against, not his brother.

But she told herself that tonight it was enough

that she and Valenden were safe and reunited with her sister. Tomorrow, she would face harder choices. Tomorrow, she would persevere.

Tonight, she would drink ale and laugh with her sister.

CHAPTER 21

**FORK IN THE ROAD . . . a team of riders . . . a toast
to Mars . . . hangmen and coffins . . . the brass key**

The following day, Duke Dryden sent a team of riders on Valenden and Bryn's horses north to see what they could discover about Rangar's situation; in the meantime, Elysander invited them to stay at the forest encampment until they received word back.

Bryn was relieved to be off the road and didn't mind the knots in her neck from sleeping on a platform fifteen feet in the air. She was fascinated to watch her sister in action as the Forest King.

Now, Bryn understood what Elysander had actually been doing all those years when it seemed she was training to be the perfect princess and daughter. Elysander had been showing one picture to their parents: a dutiful, beautiful, loyal daughter. But in reality, she'd been learning everything she could about the real situation in the Mirien. Studying hard to understand where their parents had failed and how she might one day do better. She'd perfected the role of a royal lady to please Duke Dryden because it had been her only chance of escaping the Mirien with her head attached to her shoulders.

It had been sheer luck that she actually *loved* her betrothed.

Living this double life—Forest King and duchess— was easy for Elysander, Bryn realized, because she'd already been living a double life for years.

Over the next few days, Bryn was able to have long talks with her sister, marveling as she got to know this new side of Elysander, but there was one thing Bryn still wondered about. She broached the subject one night over ale.

"Something's been bothering me, sister. If Mars knew about our parents' poor leadership, then why did he follow in their footsteps when he took over the crown? He increased taxes and the armed presence in the villages."

Elysander set her drink in her lap, looking troubled. "That same question has haunted me, too. It wasn't what I expected of him. All I can guess is that Captain Carr must have been feeding him lies." She sighed. "I don't know. It doesn't fit with the brother I knew, who could be quick-tempered and prideful but wasn't a tyrant."

It comforted Bryn that someone else had seen her brother for the good person she remembered. In the Baersladen, everyone had been quick to condemn Mars, and she could hardly blame them: her brother's actions had clearly indicated tyranny.

But they hadn't known him as she had.

"I suppose it doesn't matter anymore," Elysander said mournfully. "We'll never know what was going through his head."

Bryn felt the familiar pain of his loss. There had been too much death these past few months. Her heart felt broken and mended over and over, and she wasn't sure how much more breaking it could take.

Bryn raised her drink. "To Mars."

"To Mars."

They poured out a small amount of ale on the dirt and then drank deeply. Then, Elysander shifted, resting her elbow on one knee. "So what will you do now as crown heir?"

Bryn took her time in answering. "Well, the plan was for Trei to rule. I wish you'd known him—he was beloved by everyone in his kingdom. He was wise, kind. He would have been the ruler the Mirien needed. Since he's gone..." Her voice broke and she had to pause. "I don't know what will happen now. Valenden hopes the Hytooths in the Wollin will help me uphold my claim to the Mir throne." She took another long sip of her drink before confessing, "I love my kingdom, but we both know I'm not prepared to be queen. Won't you take the crown?"

Elysander barked a laugh. "Me? A bandit?" She turned serious. "No, Bryn, I wouldn't even if the laws allowed it, which they don't. I'm already married. My claim to the throne was relinquished when I wed. Jon and I are trying to help the Mir people by, ah, *redistributing* wealth to the common folk, but that's as far as I wish to be involved. Perhaps months ago, I would have considered taking the throne. But not after the siege."

Bryn cocked her head, curious. Memories flooded her of that awful night when the castle filled with smoke. She had climbed from her window into Elysander's room only to find blood everywhere and her sister gone. "What happened to you that night?"

Elysander's face turned grim. "The soldiers outside our rooms that night weren't soldiers. They were Mir commoners wearing the armor of soldiers they'd killed. They dragged me out of my room at knifepoint. I tried to get away, but one stabbed me." She pulled back her shirt collar to reveal a scar on her shoulder. "They took me to gallows they had set up in the front of the castle. Hundreds of our people had come to watch. Mother was there . . . "

Bryn sucked in a breath.

Elysander continued in a barely audible breath. "They put a noose around my neck. Father was already dead, slaughtered on his throne. You and Mars were both missing, and I prayed you'd made it out of the castle alive. They were out for our blood, Bryn—the common folk. They hated us even more than I'd imagined. They hung Mother first."

She paused, holding in a sob, and once she had calmed down, said steadily, "Then they strung me up. But some of the soldiers were the ones who'd been telling me about the unrest in the country. They knew I was sympathetic to their cause, but the common folk wouldn't have believed them— not in that moment. They were blinded by vengeance. So, the soldiers cut me down just before I suffocated, had me pretend to be dead, and smuggled me out in a coffin next to our mother's corpse."

Elysander ran a hand around her neck as though remembering the burn of the rope.

Bryn could barely speak. "Oh, Elysander. I had no idea."

Her sister stared into the dirt. "Yes. So while I do not fault the Mir people for what they did, I could never find it in my heart to rule them after that—after seeing the hatred for our family in their eyes. So now Jon and I do what we can, wearing masks, so no one knows the person giving them money is the same one who they spit on while watching her twitch at the gallows."

Now it made sense that Elysander had so readily accepted her husband's double life in crime; a mask to her identity had to be welcome after what had happened to her. Bryn was surprised Elysander even bothered to help the Mir people at all. Many people would have simply fled to a peaceful life in Dresel, lived in luxury, and not given a thought to the past.

Elysander dug into her trouser pockets and pulled out a key on a golden chain. "You should take this."

"What is it?" Bryn accepted the small brass key.

"It works on the gates within the secret passages of Castle Mir. Mars and I were each given keys by the soldiers who remained loyal to us. I'm never going back there, but you might, so it could come in handy one day."

Bryn draped the necklace around her neck, where the key lay beside her wedding rings from Rangar and Trei.

"Thank you," she said quietly.

Elysander reached out to clutch her hand. "No one will think less of you if you give up the throne, Bryn. It will be extremely dangerous to try to take it back from Captain Carr."

Bryn squeezed the key. "I can't let a usurper rule our people."

Worry passed over Elysander's features. "I fear for your safety, Bryn. Can the remaining Barendur princes really keep you safe?"

"Valenden and Rangar have always helped me, but my safety is ultimately my own responsibility."

Elysander blinked, surprised. "I never thought I'd see my baby sister turn into such a spitfire." She paused. "Maybe you do have it in you to rule after all."

A silence fell over them as Bryn considered her sister's words. Like everyone else, she'd always assumed she wasn't capable of ruling. But her body had grown strong in the Baresladen mountains, and she'd learned from the Barendur family what true leadership meant. She'd seen how a kingdom could function fairly.

Could she one day sit on the throne? Did she want to?

As the music played in the background, Bryn and Elysander switched to other subjects. Elysander told her lighter tales of life in Dresel when she was acting as a duchess, not a renegade. Bryn hoped that she'd one day make it to the southern kingdom and see Dresel's sunny hills that bled into the sands of the Great Desert.

The sound of hooves caught their attention. The bandits stopped their music and merrymaking to turn toward the approaching riders. Valenden climbed down from a treetop platform where he'd been bathing, stripped naked to the waist, utterly shame-less about showing so much skin.

Duke Dryden climbed out of one of the treetop shelters to meet with the riders. After a few moments, he came over to Bryn and Elysander.

"You too, wild prince," he called to Valenden, using the nickname they'd given him.

Bryn stood, anxious. "The riders have news of Rangar?"

As Bryn, Elysander, and Valenden gathered around the fire, Duke Dryden said with a grim expression, "Aye. The good news is that my bandits were able to break the young prince out of Barendur Hold's dungeon."

Bryn pressed a hand to her chest, not expecting this happy news. "Rangar is *free*?" She looked to Valenden, who looked just as tentatively hopeful.

"It's more complicated than that, I'm afraid," the duke continued. "My men freed him and were riding south on their way here when they were intercepted by a spy in the Baersladen loyal to Captain Carr."

"Broderick," Bryn muttered. "I'd swear on my mother's name it was Broderick."

"I don't know, but he had Mir soldiers with him. They let my men go—not that anyone could hold my bandits for long anyway—but took Rangar prisoner."

Bryn covered her mouth with her hand. "Rangar was taken? Where?"

Duke Dryden said heavily, "To Castle Mir."

CHAPTER 22

A CHANGE IN STRATEGY . . . one dungeon to another . . . political marriages . . . no more disguises

This new information changed everything.

Bryn and Valenden spoke with the bandits who had liberated Rangar, who explained what had happened in further detail. They gave the abductor's description, and Bryn nodded tightly.

"Yes, that's Broderick, all right."

As night fell, the rest of the camp went to sleep except the sentries. Bryn, Valenden, Elysander, and Duke Dryden sat around the fire, speaking in low voices.

"We can still continue to the Wollin," Valenden suggested. "The Hytooths will still shelter you, Bryn, and support your rightful claim to the Mir throne."

Bryn toyed nervously with Rangar's ring strung around her neck. "The Wollin is five days on horseback from here. It's in the opposite direction from Castle Mir. We'd only be moving further away from Rangar and any chance of helping him."

"I'm not sure I know how you could help him, anyway," Elysander said quietly. "Captain Carr will have put him in Castle Mir's dungeon, and there is much more security there than at Barendur Hold. Not even our bandits could get you in."

Bryn argued, "I can't just hide out in the Wollin while Rangar is imprisoned by Captain Carr! It was a good plan when we thought we had time to build an army, but that would take months. Rangar's life is in danger with every passing day."

"But if you go to Castle Mir to help him," Elysander countered, "Captain Carr will capture you, too. He might kill you and Rangar both! And you, too, Valenden!"

They debated more possibilities, and Bryn was grateful for the duke's advice both as a royal court member and a criminal—he knew the ins and outs of all levels of society. At last, he said, "What does Captain Carr want more than anything?"

"A rightful claim to the Mir throne," Elysander answered.

Duke Dryden nodded, stroking his short beard. "And what is the easiest way for him to get that?"

All eyes shifted to Bryn.

Valenden was the one to voice what they were all thinking. "To marry the crown heir. Bryn. But the crown heir must marry a man with royal blood. A prince or, at the least, a duke or count."

Bryn clenched her jaw tightly before admitting, "Captain Carr is a distant cousin of our father's. The connection is weak, but he does technically have royal blood."

"Exactly," the duke said. "So, what if you go to Castle Mir not as an enemy, Lady Bryn? Don't arrive with an army and a vendetta. Show up claiming to be exactly what everyone there already thinks you are: a captive. Insist that you *were* kidnapped by the Barendurs, managed to escape, and returned at great hardship to your homeland. If you can convince Captain Carr that you aren't his enemy, he'll have no reason to kill you. Not when marrying you is a much simpler way to achieve his goal. In fact, your safety would quickly become his priority."

"I would *never* marry that man, not even for a political advantage." Bryn felt a wave of revulsion. Captain Carr was old enough to be her father, and she hadn't forgotten the vile things he'd told his soldiers he wanted to do to her and Elysander.

"I'd never *let* you marry that man," Valenden interjected. "But I see the wisdom in Duke Dryden's plan. It wouldn't be hard to drag out a betrothal over weeks or months. Claim you need time to heal from your vicious captivity at my hands."

Bryn shot him a look, and he smirked.

"But even if I can get into Castle Mir, how can I free Rangar from the castle dungeon if not even your bandits could get him out?" she asked.

They discussed it more at length, and Valenden offered, "I'll return to the Baersladen for help. Banditry might not break him out, but magic could."

Elysander looked at Bryn with wide eyes. "Magic? Bryn, are you all right with that?"

Bryn's hand drifted to her ear, feeling for the hexmark scar carved there. "Magic isn't what we were made to believe, Elysander. The southern kingdoms abhor it, but the northern kingdoms embrace it. Vil-Kevi, Vil-Rossengard, and the Baersladen most of all. I've . . . embraced it myself. In fact, I had hoped to train as a mage."

Elysander shared a doubting look with her husband. "We've always been told that magic is dangerous."

"We were also told magic was useless," Bryn countered. "The equivalent of cheap tricks. So which is it, useless or dangerous? The truth is, Elysander, it's more powerful than anything you could imagine. And it's freely available and taught in the Baersladen. That's one reason why the Baer people thrive even in a harsh environment. They can be independent. They don't rely so much on their crown because they can do more for themselves."

Elysander didn't seem to know what to make of this, but she didn't roll her eyes and argue the way Bryn would have expected her to do months ago. She only said, "So you walk right up to Castle Mir and say you've escaped and returned home? Captain Carr will see straight through that."

"Not necessarily," Bryn said. "Everyone's always overlooked me. Said I was the naive one, the sweet one. I can use that to my advantage. Play-act as an innocent."

Valenden considered this but ultimately shook his head. "It isn't enough. Not on its own. We need a public spectacle, something to corroborate your story." Running a hand through his hair, he said, "We'll go to Ardmoor. It's a trading town, so there are people from all the Eyrie kingdoms there. There will be Mir soldiers loyal to Captain Carr. We'll change your hair back to blond, then stage an escape in a public space so that everyone sees you running from me. You'll go straight to the Mir soldiers and beg for their help."

Bryn was instantly aware of the danger this would put Valenden into. "But what if they capture you? You could be hung for kidnapping a crown heir!"

"We'll have to make sure they don't catch me," Valenden said, lifting a shoulder.

"My men can help with that," the duke offered.

Valenden gave him a grateful nod. "Then I'll return to the Baersladen to get help, and you'll be taken to

Castle Mir. Convince Captain Carr you're loyal to him, even willing to marry him. While you're there, find out all you can on Rangar's whereabouts. Use the finding hex. When I return with reinforcements, we'll free him with magic. Once he's free, Rangar will be able to help us overthrow Captain Carr. He's a captain of the Baer army himself—he knows how to organize a siege."

Bryn paced by the fire, looking up at the moonlight. Where was Rangar now? In a jail wagon on his way to Castle Mir? Gazing up through bars at the same stars overhead?

She squeezed his ring around her neck, feeling an intense longing to see him. Trei's ring brushed her fingers, too, and it left her with a deep sense of loss.

Now Valenden would be at risk, too.

She had torn apart the Barendur brothers—she couldn't let it be for nothing.

"All right," she said. "Let's do it."

It was a tearful goodbye between Bryn and her sister.

Elysander remained at the treetop encampment with most of the bandits, who intended to continue west now that Bryn had been found, robbing a few more wealthy households before putting away the camp for the winter and returning to Dresel.

With her meager supplies packed on her mare, Bryn gave her sister a tight embrace. Elysander had lost weight after the siege and was more angular than she'd ever been. It reminded Bryn that she'd never really known her sister. Elysander had only done what she had to in order to survive. And now that she'd shed that role, Elysander was free to be whoever she wanted.

Bryn hoped she might someday have that same freedom. To dress as she liked, sleep where she liked, with *who* she liked.

"I hope this prince of yours is worth it," Elysander whispered in her ear.

Bryn's heart clenched as she pictured Rangar as she'd last seen him: handsome even with the scars, even with the shadows of the dungeon cast over him, his eyes on fire.

"He is."

Elysander pulled back, running her hand over Bryn's still-dark locks. "You must bring him to Dresel one day." She gave a small, sad smile, but then winked. "Send us an invitation to the wedding."

As a small group of bandits packed to prepare for the journey to Ardmoor, Valenden gave Bryn an appraising look.

"What?" she asked.

"We'll need your hair blond again for this to work. Hold still. I'm a little rusty with the bathing spell—it doesn't get a lot of use in my life."

She rolled her eyes. "I bet it doesn't."

He touched the hexmark on his arm and then made the same motion in the air while speaking the spell. Bryn watched her locks down to her chest lighten until all traces of Roxin's brown salve had turned to dust and crumbled to the ground. She felt relieved to look like herself again, yet also more self-conscious. Some of the bandits threw her curious looks. Other than Elysander, who wore her blonde hair tied back and covered with a bandana, they weren't used to seeing long, fair hair.

As soon as they entered Ardmoor, everyone would start to speculate about who she was. She had to be ready.

Valenden held out his hand. "I suppose I should ask for my ring back. It was fun while it lasted to play at being newlyweds. Too bad we never found ourselves obligated to prove it to anyone . . . in the bedroom."

"Yes, a real *tragedy*," Bryn said. "And I think I'll keep the ring. One never knows when one will need to sell it for quick coin."

Valenden snorted.

"I like this one," Elysander said, motioning to Valenden. "If you ever feel like setting aside your title for a few weeks, Wild Prince, you're welcome to join our group of bandits."

"Thanks," Valenden said, "but I'm afraid my princely head is too accustomed to feather pillows than roots."

Bryn rolled her eyes. Valenden had spent plenty of nights in the woods, uncomplaining—he was being self-deprecating again.

"I suppose that's it, then," she said at last. "We're ready."

Valenden helped her mount her horse, then mounted his own.

Duke Dryden rested a hand on Bryn's horse's neck, stroking it gently. "My bandits will make it to Ardmoor before you and take their places in the town square, disguised of course. But when you're ready, so will they be. They'll give you a signal."

"I can't thank you enough for your help," Bryn said. "And for all you've done for Elysander."

"Believe me, my lady, *I'm* the fortunate one."

Bidding farewell to the bandits, Bryn and Valenden made their way on the forest trail back to the main road. Her nerves began to creep back. She was going to walk straight into the den of her enemy, pretending to be on his side. Acting as though she was still that naive girl from months ago instead of a hardened heir dedicated to taking him down.

Captain Carr had wanted to rape her, to kill her . . . She would find it very hard to spare him the gallows once they'd wrestled the castle from him. And why should she? Maybe a public execution would be her first order of business as queen.

Eventually, the smooth beats of her horse's steps eased her anger, and her thoughts turned to Rangar. Her heart kicked up at the idea of being under the same roof as him again. She had located him once before with the finding spell, and she would again. Somehow, she'd bribe the castle guards and visit him in the dungeon. He would be free to touch her without leaving black marks . . .

Valenden looked up at the midday sky. "We'll be there by sunset. It won't be easy to hide your identity once we're there. In a trading town like Ardmoor, there are too many people from all over the Eyrie who will know of the Mir princess who was taken to the Baersladen. We'll have to stage our little play soon."

"All right, but Val, there's one more thing I want to ask of you."

He gave her a curious look. "Yes?"

"Teach me to ride? I know we only have a few hours, but I want to learn all I can."

He tossed a grin over his shoulder. "Well, for one, you don't need to cling to that poor horse's mane like she's going to buck you off. That mare is ancient. She couldn't buck off a turtle."

Guilty, Bryn eased her grip on the horse's mane.

Valenden halted his horse until hers caught up, and then he gave a quick appraisal of her form. "There are different riding styles. We don't use saddles or stirrups in the Baersladen. I find them cumbersome, making it harder to communicate with the horse. But saddles like these . . . " he patted his leather saddle. "Make riding easy. Now, sit up straighter. Hold the reins in one hand, so your other is free if you need it."

She did as he suggested, and he gave a satisfied nod.

"Now," he said. "All there is to do is not fall off."

And he leaned over to smack his hand on her

horse's hindquarters. Bryn shrieked as the mare took off at a gallop, immediately regretting asking for lessons.

"Val!" she yelled back.

Valenden laughed darkly as he rode after her, easing her horse into a smooth canter, and after another few hours, she felt more at ease in the saddle.

Almost ready to face what was soon to come.

CHAPTER 23

THE ARDMOOR CHARADE . . . crossroads . . . dice and drink . . . rumors of a runaway princess . . . the escape

Ardmoor was like nothing Bryn had ever seen.

The town was located in a valley at the borderlands of the Baersladen to the north, the Wollin to the west, the forest kingdoms to the east, and the Mirien to the south. Equidistant from the ocean, forests, and farmlands, it was the perfect meeting ground for trade. Fish and salt blocks came from the ocean, timber and pelts from the forests, and crops from the farmlands. The town had a festive air with open-air booths hawking all manners of goods along the road leading to the grand market in the town's center. Since Ardmoor drew people from all over the Eyrie kingdoms, it was a mishmash of languages, clothing styles, and shades of hair and complexions.

"Take care here," Valenden cautioned, riding up beside Bryn and taking her horse's reins. "Ardmoor is a dangerous place. Many transient people, thieves, and addicts. Stay close to me."

Bryn had feared she'd be instantly identified because of her hair, but she spotted a few other blondes in the crowd, probably come up from the Mirien or descendants of Mir people. Still, she got intensely curious looks from nearly everyone they passed.

As much as Valenden and Bryn had disguised themselves as common folk, the people in Ardmoor had a keen eye for regal bearing. They seemed to pick out Bryn's posture as not one of a washerwoman bent over a tub all day. And Valenden's sword at his side couldn't be mistaken for anything other than belonging to someone of importance.

As fascinating as it was to take in all the sights and smells and sounds of Ardmoor, Bryn soon noticed that beneath the flashy exterior, there were beggar children in the streets and stray, mangy dogs everywhere. There were ample buildings whose painted advertisements seemed to suggest a traveler would find loose women, dice, and ale inside.

As they neared the Grand Market with its fluttering pennant flags of all colors of the rainbow, a thin man stepped out and blocked Valenden's horse.

Valenden rested a hand on his sword. "Can I help you, sir?"

The man kept his eyes on Bryn's hair as he asked, "Coming from the Mirien?"

"Our business is our own," Valenden responded.

The man expertly took in the details of their clothes and horses. "Shame about the missing princess, isn't it?"

"I don't know anything about that," Valenden said.

The man shifted from one foot to another, never taking his eyes off Bryn. "Lady Bryn Lindane. Captured by Baer princes. They say all three brothers take their turns with her."

Bryn couldn't help but flinch, and the man gave a darkly satisfied smile.

Valenden shoved his boot against the man's chest, causing him to stumble away. "Don't speak ill of ladies," he said, "*or* Baer princes. I hear the middle one likes to cut the lips off stray men in the street who slander him."

The man held up his hands, cackling slightly as he backed up, then turned and ran.

"You practically gave yourself away," Bryn hissed. "And me."

"That's the point, darling. We want rumors to spread, and that vagrant will do the job for us nicely."

Just the same, it made Bryn anxious.

They continued to ride, and now she was more aware of the looks from travelers and vendors. She saw vendors whispering to one another then throwing her stares. She could only imagine what they were saying.

That's the captive princess.

She's with the middle Baer prince.

Once they reached the Grand Market, she was sweating and flushed from nerves. Valenden dismounted, tied their horses to hitching posts, and then helped her down.

As she slid into his arms, she hung onto him for an extra moment and admitted in a whisper, "I can't say I'm not afraid, Val. For the both of us."

Valenden wrapped a hand around her waist as he glanced around the Grand Market square. "I recognize a few of Duke Dryden's bandits in the crowd. They're at the vendor stall with all the bird cages. And a few more at the alehouse across the street."

He gave a slight nod to the disguised bandits.

Bryn hunted through the crowd to find the men. Though she didn't recognize them without their masks, they gave her and Valenden a slight nod.

"So what now?" Bryn asked.

"We make a scene, but not until some Mir soldiers are around to witness it."

"And until then?"

Valenden shrugged slyly. "Well, that alehouse *is* a convenient place to wait. It would be irresponsible not to go where we have allies. We'll have a few pints to blend in."

She rolled her eyes—of course, he'd choose a place where he could drink. "Fine. Lead the way."

They crossed the square beneath the fluttering pennants. Bryn would have been utterly fascinated by the Grand Market with its canvas roofing and hundreds of trading stalls if she wasn't so afraid for her life.

They took seats in an outdoor seating area of the Hound's Hunt pub. After the waitress served them, another woman brushed into them. She was dressed scantly with her hair loose, and she gave them a lurid smile.

"Take care, lovebirds," she purred. "I have my eye on you. And so do my *friends*." She glanced back pointedly at the duke's men, who were disguised as traders, along with another female bandit dressed as a prostitute. Then the woman dropped her voice. "We'll be ready at your signal."

Valenden nodded and tossed her a few coins as though their transaction was over. Bryn sipped her beer slowly, watching him polish off three pints. They pretended to talk about the weather as they watched street performers out of the corner of their eyes. Eventually, Valenden placed his hand over hers.

"Look. There, at the gate."

A team of men was passing through the town gate. They were dressed in the unmistakable Mir army's golden armor with feather plumes. It wasn't a large contingent—only five men.

"Probably a scouting team," Valenden said quietly. "Sent here to protect some Mir oligarch who came for trading...or other vices."

The soldiers milled around the Grand Market, purchasing roasted chicken legs.

"This is it," Valenden said. "Are you ready?"

Bryn swallowed down another long sip of beer. "No. But let's do it anyway."

On the way out of the tavern, Valenden gave the bandit woman dressed as a prostitute a firm squeeze on her backside right in public where anyone could see. The woman yelled and stormed out of the tavern after them with disguised bandit men following.

"You blackguard!" the woman yelled loud enough to turn a few heads in the town square.

Valenden held up his hands innocently. "You're mistaken, madam."

"I saw it!" One of the duke's men accused, which turned a few more heads—everyone was interested in a bar brawl. "Don't think we don't know who you are. You're that middle Baer prince! Valenden Barendur!"

"The Baer prince?" One of the nearby vendors perked up at this, causing even more commotion. She whispered to her companion, who whispered back.

"*Mir princess . . . blonde hair . . .* " Whispers began to spread in the crowd as more people paid attention. Even the Mir soldiers turned their heads, watching and listening.

Valenden grabbed Bryn's arm, tugging her roughly toward their horses. "Come on. We're leaving."

Bryn dug in her heels and acted like she didn't want to go with him. "No!"

One of the duke's bandits said loudly, "Hold on

there, sir. Doesn't look like your woman wants to go with you. What's going on here?"

One of the vendors, who had doubtlessly heard the spreading rumors, cried out, "It's the missing Mir princess! Lady Bryn Lindane! That blackguard stole her!"

At this, the duke's men grabbed Valenden, who made a show of trying to fight them off. He slipped Bryn a wink as she pulled out of his grasp.

The entire crowd had turned their attention now to the scene. Rumors spread that this was the Baer prince who had stolen a Mir princess, and the promise of drama pulled everyone in closer.

"Come back here!" Valenden yelled at Bryn, swiping at her, but one of the duke's undercover men held him off.

Bryn stumbled back, trying to appear frazzled, which wasn't that difficult. She made her unsteady way through the crowd, flinching whenever someone called her name. The Mir soldiers had moved to attention and were watching closely. She made a show of spotting them across the square and gave a relieved gasp.

"Help!" She raced toward them. "I need help!" She practically threw herself into one of the soldier's arms.

He looked down from his helmet in confusion. "What is the matter, miss?"

"She's the princess," one of the other soldiers hissed. "Are you daft, Gunther? That's *Lady Bryn!*"

The soldier holding Bryn stiffened, his face going pale, but he quickly regained his composure. He drew his sword, which prompted the others to as well.

"It's him!" a shopkeeper cried, pointing to Valenden. "That's the Baer prince that abducted her!"

Two of the Mir soldiers remained with Bryn with swords drawn while the other three crossed toward Valenden. He struggled against the duke's men, who let him slip away while still making it look like a fight.

For a second, Valenden's eyes met Bryn's. His were on alert like a wild animal's. *He can't let himself get caught*, she thought. Rangar was already in the Castle Mir dungeon; if Valenden were there too, there would be no one to go back to the Baersladen for help.

Valenden saw the soldiers approaching and tore away from the duke's men, plunging into the thick of the crowd. The duke's men yelled and pretended to chase after him. The soldiers attempted to pursue him, but after a few minutes, they returned sweating and red-faced, claiming he'd vanished.

Thank the Saints, Bryn thought with relief. Valenden had gotten away—but now she was on her own.

Feeling sick to her stomach, she turned to face the Mir soldiers.

These men were loyal to Captain Carr. A man who had stolen her kingdom, threatened to rape and murder her, and had killed her parents. And now she had to convince them everything they'd just witnessed was the truth and that she was utterly without guile, a poor princess stolen by heathen princes.

The soldiers seemed uncertain what to do with her, suspicion still lingering in their eyes, so Bryn did all she could think to do: She fell at their feet, burying her face in her hands, and forced out tears.

"Thank the Saints, you found me! I've been living a nightmare. Is it over now? You'll take me home, won't you? Back to Castle Mir?"

Exchanging a wary look, the lead soldier—a sergeant by his emblem—turned away and muttered lowly with the others. Bryn heard one of them say, "I recognize her. With Mars gone, she's the *heir* now."

Bryn added for emphasis, "Captain Carr will be so pleased you rescued me from that rogue who dared to call himself a prince! I'm sure you'll be well rewarded for bringing me back home. I'll be sure to tell the captain of your bravery."

The sergeant's demeanor shifted. He knelt on one knee, touching his forehead to the hilt of his sword. "Lady Bryn. Or should I say, our future queen? I'm Sergeant Preston. It's our honor to have rescued you and return you to your rightful home."

He stood and extended his hand down to her. She let him pretend to be a hero when he was nothing of the sort. She let *herself* pretend to be a helpless woman when she was anything but.

And as the soldiers led her to the safety of their rooms at the inn where they stayed, all she could think about was Valenden's risk and, most of all, Rangar.

I'm coming, she whispered to the air, hoping the spirit of her words would reach him. *I swear I will find a way to see you soon.*

CHAPTER 24

RETURN TO CASTLE MIR . . . think like a queen . . . a map of hidden passages . . . her enemy's weakness

Castle Mir was a day's ride from Ardmoor, and Bryn spent the entire time alone in a carriage the soldiers had commandeered for her, planning what she would do as soon as she saw the castle that until a few months ago, she'd called home.

Her stomach roiled the entire ride. She couldn't keep down any of the pears or smoked fish the soldiers offered her. Thoughts ran through her mind on a repeating cycle, and she feared she would go mad until she forced herself to think like a queen.

First, I must ensure my own safety.

That meant continuing this dangerous charade of posing as Valenden's captive. She had to be able to look Captain Carr in the eye and swear she would never have left the Mirien of her own accord. Her life depended on him believing her loyalty.

Second, I must locate Rangar.

She'd never had any reason to visit the Castle Mir dungeon, so she wasn't certain how to get in. Castle Mir was far larger than Barendur Hold, with a network of subterranean passages that included not only the dungeon but extensive soldiers' barracks, the kitchens and storerooms, laundry facilities, and a portion of the stables. She'd have to either find a map or quietly ask around for directions without raising suspicion, which would be a challenge. She had no idea how she'd arrange to secretly speak to Rangar.

Third, I must discover Carr's weaknesses.

Once Valenden returned with reinforcements from the Baersladen, they would need to figure out exactly how to dethrone Captain Carr and instate Bryn as queen while convincing the common folk that she'd been on their side the entire time.

The weight of what rested ahead was daunting, but Bryn refused to let fear get the best of her. She'd learned how harsh life could be in the Baersladen and had long ago left behind self-pity. There were much larger concerns than her personal safety or happiness: a kingdom was at stake.

"My lady," one of the soldiers called through the open carriage window, riding alongside her. "I thought you'd like to know we're entering the gates of Mir Town. We'll be at Castle Mir within the hour."

She forced a grateful smile. "I shall ensure you're rewarded well for safely delivering me home."

She noted that there were only four soldiers now, which meant one had likely ridden ahead to inform Captain Carr of her impending arrival. Bryn chewed on her lip, wondering how the captain would take this news.

Would he be shrewd enough to see through her plan?

She continued to gaze out the window as they entered the urban area surrounding Castle Mir. The capital town of the Mirien, known as Mir Town, was protected by two sets of walls. The outer wall had once been an important defense, but the town had grown so much that houses and shops and workhouses now congested both sides of the wall. Passing through the city gate was merely a formality. The inner gate, however, was far more important. It separated Mir Town from the walled castle grounds, which encompassed not only the castle and servants' quarters, but most of Saint's Forest.

Bryn watched anxiously as they rolled through the first gate of Mir Town. Was this really the same place she'd left behind? She saw everything with fresh eyes now.

When Bryn had been a girl, Nan had occasionally taken her into Mir Town on errands or to watch the street performers. Bryn had delighted in the bustle of the city, but now she saw it very differently. The common folk weren't the happy peasants she'd been made to believe. There was nothing romantic about their poverty. They'd been exploited for decades by her parents, taxed out of a full larder, and what signs of happiness she did see didn't have anything to do with the Lindane royal family's leadership: it was quips among friends, shared pastries between street children. It was commoners helping one another because they'd been utterly failed by those who were supposed to care for them.

A shadow fell over the carriage as they reached the inner gate, where the posted soldiers flagged them to a stop. They stared intently at her while they exchanged words with her soldiers. She ducked back from the windows, breathing hard.

Saints, this is going to be hard.

She peeked back out and saw Sergeant Preston returning on foot from the castle. He said a few words to the gate guards and then addressed Bryn.

"Captain Carr is overwhelmed with relief to hear of your safe return, Lady Bryn," he announced. "He would like to speak with you immediately, assuming you are prepared for such a meeting."

As much as Bryn wanted to bathe and collect her thoughts before facing him, Bryn knew it would be better to appear before Captain Carr travel-worn with dirt streaking her face to make her look even more like the captive she claimed to be.

"Of course," she said. "I'm eager to see him."

The gate guards motioned them through, and the carriage rolled into the courtyard. Bryn gazed up at the stone edifice as though remembering a dream. There was her bedroom window overlooking the front lawn. She'd once stood there with Rangar's knife in her hand, watching the beginning of the siege.

Her body began to shake. *Good,* she thought. It would make her appear more helpless.

When the carriage rolled to a stop, a soldier opened the door and helped her out. She tried to make herself look small as she stepped through the castle's large oak doors.

Once inside, she froze.

The castle foyer had been stripped of its beautiful tapestries, velvet-lined benches, and woven wool rugs. It was now nothing but bare stone. Scorch marks revealed a terrible truth: the former decoration must have burned in the siege. What remained couldn't be salvaged.

It reminded Bryn that she was entering a very different place from the one she'd left.

"Captain Carr awaits you in the council chambers," Sergeant Preston said, motioning to the stairs.

She followed him up the winding stairs, trying not to appear too shocked by the changes to her childhood home. Most of the glass windowpanes were broken and hadn't yet been replaced. Soldiers were stationed at nearly every room.

This is no longer a home, but a fortress.

When they reached the council chambers, Bryn

found Captain Carr and two advisors, Lord Tarry and Lord Gerbert, waiting around the Little Table. She paused, overtaken by a moment of revulsion. She'd never much liked the advisors, but it was Carr himself that made her stomach turn. He had always been a formidable man, considered handsome by many; but now he appeared even more gray-haired and world-weary. The mark across his neck from where he'd been garroted as a young soldier gave him a permanent angry red scar.

He locked eyes with her, taking in her dirty face and wrinkled clothes, and then made a big show of bowing.

"Lady Bryn." His voice was as hoarse as she remembered, a result of his garroting. "Or should I say, Queen Bryn. What a terrible ordeal you must have suffered."

Bryn gave an equally deep bow. "Captain Carr. Please, don't call me queen. I'm not queen yet, and I don't even know if I ever can be. I never thought such a heavy duty would fall on my shoulders. I'm just so grateful your soldiers rescued me in Ardmoor!"

Captain Carr and his advisors continued to watch her closely, and she had the uncanny sense they were looking for signs of duplicity. She knew that if she didn't play this game correctly, they would soon realize her story was a lie and likely kill her as they had Mars.

She wiped her eyes. "Word reached me about Mars. I can't believe my brother is gone. Did you see him in his final moments? Did he suffer greatly? Oh, I hope not."

Captain Carr's face was incapable of displaying authentic sympathy, but he painted it on the best he could. "It was a terrible accident, but I can assure you it happened quickly. He didn't suffer."

Not an accident at all, Bryn thought with a stab of rage. *Murder, and at your hand.*

She sniffled, and one of the advisors pulled out a handkerchief, which she accepted gratefully. "I can't believe I'm home. I thought I'd be a captive of that barbaric family forever."

Captain Carr raised an eyebrow. "So it's true that the Barendur family captured you on the night of the siege and took you to Barendur Hold? I ask because your brother received several letters from them stating that you had come of your own volition."

Bryn gaped. "Of course, they would deny it! They're rogues! Why in the name of the Saints would I leave my home willingly? You know as well as anyone that the youngest prince, Rangar, has always believed that I belonged to him. He took advantage of the chaos in the siege to abduct me. I was alone; I couldn't defend myself against him."

Captain Carr said carefully, "Of course not, my lady. No one blames you for getting captured. However, I must ask: Rumors reached us that you and Rangar Barendur were romantically involved."

Bryn bristled. Of course, Captain Carr's spies in Barendur Hold must have reported back to him on

Bryn's activities. Had it been Broderick? She wondered what had happened to the traitor who'd killed Trei and captured Rangar. She had to stick close to the truth to echo the spy's report.

She looked away as though ashamed and whispered, "Captain, surely you do not want the lurid details of what that man made me do."

One of the advisors made a small noise in his throat as though he was very much interested in lurid details, which made Bryn's stomach turn even more.

"So the rumors *aren't* true?" Carr rasped.

Bryn kept her eyes on the floor. "Rangar Barendur is known for his violent temper. I saw him break his own brother's nose. I dared not cross his wishes. I feared for my safety, so I had to . . . please him." She placed her hands over her face as she muttered, "I'm deeply ashamed of the things they made me do: Keep Rangar company. Sleep on the floor with livestock. Tend to sheep like a commoner."

Captain Carr glanced back at the advisors as if to take stock of what they thought of Bryn's report. Her heart was galloping in her chest. They'd kill her if there was even a chance that she was lying. After all, killing her would be one way for Captain Carr to take the Mir throne, though not the simplest.

The simplest is for him to marry me.

Before they could make up their minds with their secretive looks, Bryn cleared her throat and stated, "Of course, once we found out about Mars's death and I became the crown heir, everything changed. King Aleth made me marry his eldest son."

"Trei Barendur," Captain Carr said in his hoarse voice. "Yes, we heard of his violent passing."

Because one of your spies killed him, Bryn thought angrily.

She temporarily went speechless as the memory of seeing Trei's body flashed before her eyes, and the terrible aftermath: Rangar arrested, Saraj's grief, a family torn apart.

She closed her eyes briefly, pained by the lie she had to speak. "Naturally, I was relieved Prince Trei was killed. I hadn't agreed to the marriage. The Barendur family only ever saw me as a political pawn."

Captain Carr folded his arms across his chest. "King Aleth has always been a harsh ruler."

He's nothing of the sort, Bryn thought. *His manner might be brusque, but he's twice the man you'd ever be.*

Captain Carr's demeanor shifted again. He dropped his hands and gave what was supposed to be a smile but came out as a grimace. "You're in safe hands now. Neither I nor my soldiers would ever hurt you or use you for political gain as the Barendurs did."

Anger screamed in Bryn's ears. She'd overheard Carr's very soldiers talking about how he'd wanted to force her and Elysander into bed.

The man before her was nothing less than a monster.

"I have no doubt." She gave him a soft, weak smile. "I recall you always being so loyal to my parents." She paused, frowning slightly. "Though I did hear alarming rumors after the siege that you had something to do with the uprising. Only rumors, I'm sure . . ."

The smile fell off his face as she turned the tables on him. The best way to cast off suspicion was to place it on the person you were trying to win the game against. Captain Carr stiffened as he said, "False rumors. Entirely false, spread by the leaders of the uprising. I helped your brother retake the castle from the treasonous common folk. I've been nothing but loyal to your family."

Her body started shaking from anger, and she didn't try to hide it. Let him think she was shaking from relief or exhaustion. She gave a nod. "That is what I assumed, naturally."

He turned away briskly. "You must be exhausted. I've given the orders for servants to prepare your former bedroom for you, and I've had them carry up a tub filled with hot water. Take some time to wash away the weariness of your travels. I can have food sent up as well." He paused. "Unless you'd like to join me for supper?"

There was an undeniable effort to make his words appear attractive. As she'd suspected, he was very aware that the fastest way to the throne was to marry her. With his advanced age, she couldn't imagine he would believe himself to be an attractive prospect to her, but then again, men seemed to delude themselves into all kinds of thinking.

Fighting back bile, she said, "Perhaps tomorrow. I would love to dine with you, but I fear I will fall asleep as soon as I step out of the bath."

Captain Carr gave a curt nod. "Of course. Tomorrow. Once more, let me welcome you home, Lady Bryn. Your return is one of the few bright occurrences during a dark time for this kingdom."

She bowed, all too anxious to be anywhere but in his presence.

Following the soldiers to her room, she glanced at the alcoves that she knew hid secret passages. These were the only ones whose tapestries had been replaced, clearly to hide the entryways.

She touched Elysander's key around her neck and wondered when she would get a chance to search the passages for a way to the dungeon.

To Rangar.

CHAPTER 25

PASSAGES . . . the man in the dungeon . . . the captain upstairs . . . a scratched map . . . a new spell

As soon as Bryn stepped into her former bedroom, she dismissed the servants and shut the door.

Nothing about the room felt familiar. Scorch marks on the walls reminded her of the terrible night when she'd left. All the bedding, rugs, and curtains had been changed, likely due to smoke damage. She threw open the door to her closet, which to her surprise, still contained her old gowns.

She held the silken sleeve of one up to her nose, recoiling at the trace of smoke, though it looked to have been washed multiple times. She sifted through the gowns with mixed emotions. A part of her missed her old life: there had been joy there, true love for her parents and her siblings, and happiness sneaking sugared treats from Mam Delice in the kitchen. But these dresses felt so flimsy and insubstantial compared to her clothes from the Baersladen. She couldn't imagine wearing lace again.

She peeled off her clothes and eased herself into the copper tub filled with steaming water that servants had prepared. The warm water unlocked her tight muscles, and she leaned her head back against the tub's rim, closing her eyes. Her hand drifted to the scars across her ribs, trailing along them lightly.

Rangar is somewhere in this castle.

It ached to know he was close and yet she couldn't go to him. Her heart constricted to think of everything he must have gone through: The terrible accusations that he'd murdered his own brother, trading out the Barendur Hold dungeon for the Castle Mir one. At least in the Baersladen, he'd been treated well while incarcerated. Here, he was nothing but an enemy. There was no telling what Captain Carr's men had done to torture him.

She ran a bar of scented soap over her skin, wishing it was Rangar's hands instead. When she'd agreed to marry Trei, she'd thought everything between her and Rangar would be lost. And she would do nearly anything to have saved Trei's life, but the hard truth was that he was gone and nothing now stopped her and Rangar from being together.

Except bars.

She closed her eyes again, wetting her lips. Memories filled her head of the times she'd been with Rangar. Though they hadn't made love, they'd come tantalizingly close. Thinking of his broad hands on her thighs made her heartbeat pick up. She dipped the soap over her thighs, sighing. Then memory turned to fantasy, and she imagined what they would do when they were finally reunited. There would come a time when they were safe—at least for a night—and nothing would hold them back. They were soulbound, each having saved the others' life, and it meant something.

That night, she tossed and turned, frustrated to only have Rangar's imaginary hands on her instead of his real ones. It was a cruel joke to wake in the morning alone, in her childhood bed, now under the roof of a castle her enemy controlled, having to pretend she wasn't in love with the prisoner in the dungeon.

"Ah, Lady Bryn. I hope you don't mind I already began eating. I wasn't sure if you were coming." Captain Carr stood as she entered the dining hall.

He sat alone at a table set for two. She'd slept through breakfast, so it was a midday meal of mutton and roasted vegetables. Mam Delice, the head chef, had fled to the Baersladen, so Bryn wondered who was now running the kitchen.

She forced a smile and took her seat. "I'm quite famished. I feel so much better being home, sleeping in my own bed, knowing I'm finally safe." She paused. "All because of you."

His eyes traced down her gown in a way that made her skin crawl. She'd wanted to wear one of her plainer dresses but had reluctantly chosen a low-cut one that would keep him distracted. A servant moved forward to ladle out some vegetables.

"Oh, please, I can do it," Bryn said in a rush, slightly horrified to think of someone doing something for her that she could so easily do for herself.

The servant froze, and Bryn remembered that she was supposed to be playing the part of a helpless, spoiled princess.

She cleared her throat and said to Captain Carr, "I, ah, was made to do everything for myself in the Baersladen. I suppose I got used to it. It feels strange to be waited on."

He gave her a placating smile and said in his raspy voice, "You need not attend to such trivialities here."

She picked at her food, skin crawling to be back in this castle that should feel like home but didn't. The smoke stains on the ceiling hadn't been painted over yet. She briefly wondered if her father's bloodstains were still in the throne room and promptly lost her appetite.

Setting down her fork, she said carefully, "I was told your men captured Rangar Barendur."

He raised an eyebrow, then finished eating and

wiped his mouth. "I didn't think word had gotten out about that. My men are usually more close-lipped."

"Gossip travels fast on the road. Valenden Barendur put out feelers for word on his brother." She paused before asking, "What did you do to Rangar? Naturally, I hope he hasn't been too comfortable."

Captain Carr set down his napkin and was about to speak when a soldier came in and spoke quietly in his ear.

He nodded and stood. "My lady, I'm afraid I'm needed elsewhere. As it happens, it has to do with the very rogue we speak of. I'll be sure to let him know you are safe now and no longer a prisoner of his family."

He was going to speak with Rangar? Her heart racing, she gave a tight smile. "Yes, please let him know how pleased I am he's behind bars. He deserves it after everything he did to me."

The captain left, and Bryn forced down some food, knowing she wouldn't be very useful if she were starving. The meal was under-spiced, and she missed Mam Delice fiercely. If only she could be back in the Baersladen, sitting at one of the long communal dining tables in the great hall, listening to the musicians play while the fires crackled in the hearths...

If only she could be home...

She nearly dropped a chunk of bread as she realized she'd thought of Barendur Hold as *home*, but it was true. That remote, windswept castle was where her heart and soul felt most at rest.

She told the soldiers she wanted to see how the

castle had changed after the siege and was allowed to walk around with a guard. She made note aloud of all the repairs that would need to be done to bring it back to working order, though in her head she was carefully making mental notes of where every soldier was stationed. She tried to gauge which ones looked lazy, which looked like they could be bribed. She made a point of walking by each entrance to the secret passageways, noting if they were hidden behind tapestries or blocked by armoires.

That night, back in the safety of her bedroom, she scratched a map into the underside of a dresser drawer along with notes from her observations. She squeezed Elysander's key on the chain around her neck.

She only had to await her opportunity.

After a few days, Bryn still hadn't settled back into Castle Mir. It was the home of a different, previous version of herself. Everywhere she looked, all she could think of was how everything had been paid for by exploiting the commoners her parents were supposed to have led. She still flinched whenever a servant catered to her. When Captain Carr wasn't around, she made a point of doing as much as she could for herself.

She spent as much time as possible observing the soldiers' activities under the ruse of planning repairs to the castle. Though it appeared that Captain Carr believed her story, he still insisted guards accompany her everywhere. She might not be in a dungeon, but she was just as much a prisoner as Rangar was.

One night, alone in her room, she slid off her shoes and pressed her ear to the door.

She had determined that the guards outside her room changed at midnight and that the one who arrived to relieve the first one would often disappear for a few minutes to the latrine at the end of the hall as soon as he'd relieved his partner.

She waited until she heard his approaching footsteps.

"Boggins," said the first guard.

"Caldus," the other soldier remarked. "Nothing to report. Lady Bryn retired around nine. Lights went off by ten."

"Right. Guarding a future queen isn't such a bad job, eh?"

The first lowered his voice. "You know what Carr is planning . . . "

"Hardly a secret. Wouldn't you do the same?"

Bryn shuddered to think of what they were referring to: It was most likely his plan to marry her to become king, but it could easily be something viler.

The first soldier departed, and Bryn held her breath, waiting to see if the second one would take his usual trip to the latrine. Sure enough, as soon as he was alone and thought no one was watching, his footsteps ambled down the hall.

She eased her door open, peeking through the

crack. As soon as he closed the door to the latrines, she darted out of her room, closed the door, and raced around the corner. Her bare feet kept her steps silent, though her heartbeat felt loud enough to wake the entire castle. She darted down the next hall past her parents' former bedroom and into an alcove with a statue of Saint Albin. Dropping to her knees, she swung open a small doorway hidden behind the statue's base.

Inside, the passage was pitch black. A musty odor came from within, and she knew there must be all kinds of spiderwebs and vermin in there. She crawled in and closed the door behind her.

She hadn't brought a lantern, knowing that if she were caught in the hallways with one, she'd be instantly under suspicion. But she outstretched her palm now, traced a hexmark in the air, and whispered the spark spell Valenden had taught her while on the road.

"Kora yoquin."

A small flame danced to life an inch from her palm. She'd seen Rangar perform this spell countless times to light his *statua* pipe, and villagers in the Baersladen to get a bonfire going. She had no candle to light to keep the flame going, so it died after only a moment. But it had given her enough light to see which direction to go.

Feeling along one wall, she tried to remember the map of the passages. When she reached the end of the wall, she recited the spell again and summoned a new flame.

It flickered just long enough for her to see that the passage had run into another perpendicular passage. She knew the right turn would take her to the hall outside of the council chamber, so she turned left. After a few feet, her hand brushed something that clattered, and she summoned another flame.

The dim light of the fire in her hand revealed a china plate on the floor. There was a crust of bread and cheese rind that vermin hadn't yet gotten to, so it couldn't be more than a few hours old.

Someone else has been in here. Recently.

It was probably a servant who'd worked in the castle long enough to know about the passages. But it made Bryn uneasy. Now, afraid she might run into someone, she continued to make her slow way crawling in the dark, pausing at every turn to summon a flame and find her way as she moved down halls and sets of stairs so perilous she feared she'd fall to her death.

The musty smell grew stronger the further down she went. The passage walls were no longer the smooth limestone bricks of the upper portion of the castle; now they were roughly hewn boulders slick with condensation. She heard the scurrying sound of mice. Her heartbeat sped up, still thinking about that plate she'd found and knowing that other people knew about these passages.

If Captain Carr caught her here, he'd know imme-diately that her whole act was a ruse.

She descended another set of stairs and splashed into a puddle.

"Kora yoquin."

The fire lit up, revealing a more spacious passage-way. Finally, she could stand to her full height. The walls had been blasted out of pure bedrock and still bore the marks of explosives. She heard voices not far away. She quickly doused her flame.

Pressing her back to the wall, she listened.

"No, the inspection isn't until Tuesday," a male voice said.

"You're wrong. Roquin said Monday."

As the two men argued, Bryn stepped silently down the length of the hall. A light flickered at the end, drawing her attention. When she dared to peek around the corner, she spotted the dungeon's main guard station. Lit lanterns flickered on the walls next to a wooden table where the two men sat with their backs to her. They were facing a larger staircase which must have been the primary dungeon entrance; the old, narrow stair passage she'd descended probably wasn't used enough to be worth guarding.

Her bare feet were freezing on the cold stone floor. She sucked in a breath, watching the backs of the soldiers' heads, and then took the risk of darting the few feet to the cell block.

Her body was trembling both from the cold and from fear that if any prisoners saw her, they would likely call the guards. But the first cells were empty, and the few prisoners she did see were asleep, as it was well after midnight.

The cells were spaced far apart from one another due to the rock's thickness. She squinted into the dark cells, searching the sleeping bodies for a tousled-haired man with scars on his face.

Finally, in a cell set off by itself, she identified the outline of a man sleeping propped against the bars. The shape of his shoulders was familiar. It stirred memories of running her hands over them.

Holding her breath, not daring to get her hopes up, she moved aside so that the closest hanging lantern would spill its light onto the man's face.

Four scars carved over his otherwise handsome features.

I found him, she thought with a rush of relief, pressing a hand to her mouth.

CHAPTER 26

ANOTHER DUNGEON . . . the unexpected visitor . . . in the name of the gods . . . kisses between bars

*I*t *was really him.*

After so many hardships, Bryn was finally looking at Rangar. She was almost afraid to believe it was true at first, as though she was trapped in a dream. But the faint lantern light coming from the guard station around the corner shone on features that she knew by heart. She'd kissed those lips. Run her fingers along those scars. Raked her nails through that tangled hair.

Glancing in the direction of the guards, she dropped to her knees.

We don't have much time.

She hadn't planned on this exact situation. She'd

hoped to find Rangar, and she had—but he was asleep. She had to find a way to wake him without having him make any noise.

After some consideration, she reached carefully through the bars he was reclined against and pressed her hands over his mouth.

His eyes shot open immediately.

He tried to sit fully up, but her grip over his mouth kept him against the bars. He started to make a garbled noise, but she leaned in a whispered fiercely, "Stay quiet. It's me."

Rangar's body remained rigid, but he went silent. His head turned in her direction. They locked eyes through the cell bars.

For a moment, neither spoke. Her hand was still pressed tightly over his lips, and she felt his jaw slacken. He looked much worse than he had in the Barendur Hold dungeon. He'd lost weight, had bruises darkening one side of his face, and blood crusting along one ear.

Slowly, he removed her hand from his mouth.

"Bryn?" His voice was hoarse with disuse.

She now had to press her hand against her own mouth to muffle her sob. "It's me, Rangar."

He twisted around to face her, reaching through the bars to grab her wrists, squeezing a little too hard like he had to verify she was real. His eyes scanned every inch of her, looking for signs she'd been hurt or simply lapping up every detail about her face. He licked his cracked lips and said, "I thought Carr was lying when he said you were in the castle. How did you get into the dungeon?"

"I took the secret passages from the residential floor," she whispered. "There's a rear entrance to the dungeon no one uses. My sister gave me the key."

"Your sister . . . ?" He rested a hand on his head. "Wait. First, I need to know: What in the name of the gods are you doing in Castle Mir? You're supposed to be with Valenden in the Wollin!"

"Shh. Keep your voice down. The guards are just around the corner."

His eyes seared into her, demanding answers.

She explained, "Val and I were on our way to the Wollin when we ran into bandits. It was my sister and her husband, Duke Dryden, in disguise."

His eyes widened. "It was Duke Dryden's men who got me out of Barendur Hold."

She nodded. "They came back and told us you'd been captured by Captain Carr's men and brought here. So, Val and I came up with a new plan."

Rangar stared at her in incomprehension. His hands around her wrists tightened. Even after weeks of starvation, he was still impossibly strong.

"You came *willingly* to the castle that your enemy overtook?"

There was an edge in his voice. The temper she knew all too well was returning, but she only narrowed her eyes right back at him.

"If you thought we were going to let you rot down here, you were mistaken. I had to do whatever I could to save you. Was it Broderick who helped you get captured by Carr's men? He's the one who killed Trei, Rangar. I'm sure of it."

He released her wrists and sat back on his heels, running a hand through his tangled hair. "How do you know?"

She told him about smelling Broderick's citrus liquor in the newlywed chamber.

"By the gods. Yes, I realized Broderick was our spy when he led Carr's men to intercept me, but I had no idea just how traitorous that man was. I'll kill him for what he's done." He briefly pinched the bridge of his nose before saying, "You should have continued to the Wollin. You aren't safe here."

"Captain Carr thinks I'm loyal to him," she explained. "Val and I, with the help of Duke Dryden's men, staged an escape in Ardmoor. We made it appear that I was Val's captive. Mir soldiers brought me back here, and I convinced Captain Carr I was an unwilling prisoner in the Baersladen."

"Carr visited me a few days ago," Rangar said darkly. "He claimed he plans on marrying you and becoming king."

She swallowed, feeling sick all over again. "Yes, I know. He hasn't brought it up to me yet, but everyone in the castle knows that's his intention." She added softly, "It's okay—I can draw out an engagement for the time it will take us to get you out of here. There's no way I'm actually marrying him, of course. I'd die before I'd let him be king."

"And Val?"

"He returned to the Baersladen to enlist help. He's going to bring soldiers and falconers and mages. But we need you to lead the uprising. You're the only one with the military training to determine how to take down Captain Carr and those loyal to him."

"Get me out of this cell," Rangar promised, clutching her hand tightly. "And I'll handle the rest. It would help to have a map of the castle and the names of any rebels in Mir Town who haven't yet been thrown in jail."

She bit her lip. "I'll see what I can do. Captain Carr has a tight rein on me."

Rangar flinched at the imagery her words evoked. He reached through the gap to cup her cheek.

"It makes my blood harden to think of that man's hold over you."

"Carr needs me alive," she assured him. "He won't hurt me as long as he thinks he can use me to become the legitimate king."

Her forehead and shoulders pressed against the bars, wanting to be as close to him as she could. She touched his face gently where the scars began near his hairline and then ran the pads of her fingertips lightly over his eyes.

His eyelids sank closed. A moan slipped out of his throat.

"I should have brought you water," she whispered. "And food."

"I'm fine."

"I'll come back with something for you to eat."

Eyes still closed, he leaned his head into her palm. "This is all I need."

A delicious shudder ran through her. For so long she'd denied that the *fralen* bond was what bound them together. She'd insisted to herself and anyone who would listen that their love didn't have anything to do with who saved who's life. Now, however, the tugging sensation within her made her second-guess herself. She'd never felt this way around anyone. Being away from Rangar had felt like a stitch had come loose in her heart, steadily leaking blood into her body, poisoning her other organs.

But now that she was back with Rangar, the stitch was healed. She practically trembled with feeling whole, feeling *right*.

"You feel it too, don't you?" he whispered, opening his eyes to study hers.

Her lips were shaking as she said, "The bond?"

"I don't care what you call it. Just that you feel it. For *me*, not for anyone else. Not for that usurper Captain Carr. Not for my brothers. For me."

His hand folded around her waist, pulling her as close as the bars would allow. The cold metal pressed into her thighs and against her chest like it was taunting her. She wanted to be flush with Rangar, not bars.

"Just you," she whispered.

He combed his other hand through her hair at the back of her head, his eyes simmering. "Good. I've had to endure you being married to one brother who's gone now. Then posing as the wife of the other. Bryn Lindane, when are you going to be *mine*?"

Her fingers twisted in the dirty fabric of his shirt. The faint lamp light from around the corner gave everything a midnight air, reminding her how dangerous it was to be here.

She stood on tiptoes to whisper a hair from his lips, "I'm already yours."

He claimed her lips with more passion than his weakened condition suggested possible. Even after imprisonment and starvation, he was still all hard muscle. Hands cupping her chin, he broke the kiss so that his lips could glide over her cheeks, her jawline, her neck.

An ache flooded her body. She arched her back, pressing her breasts against the bars. They had to contort themselves for his lips to reach all the places he wanted them to visit.

Her breath rushed in and out. He dragged his hand down her arm and then cupped her waist, giving her a squeeze as though to see how much meat she still had on her bones. A flush of warmth radiated out from everywhere his hand explored. Her own lips were aching with a need to touch and taste.

She found his lips again, pouring all of her frustration over the last few weeks into the kiss. He matched her emotion, nipping and grazing at her bottom lip.

She slipped a leg through the bars, wrapping it around Rangar's calf muscle. He dropped a hand to grab her by the thigh, lifting her leg higher. The cell bar rubbed between her legs, and she gasped as a sudden throbbing stirred to life.

Rangar pulled her skirt up over her knee, digging his fingers into the bare skin of her thigh.

Eyes hooded, he whispered, "I had every intention of bedding you the proper way after we're married, but I'm seriously tempted to take you right here in the dungeon."

Her heartbeat pounded harder. They would have to contort a little, but it could be done. Her leg was already around his hips, her groin pressed close to his.

She could feel the space between her legs grow wet at his words. *Saints.* Should she let him take her here like some prisoner's whore? She sucked in a breath, meeting his eyes.

Then, something fell around the corner. It sounded like a clatter of a plate or book.

They both froze.

Eyes widening in fear, Bryn went silent. Rangar pressed a finger to his lips. His hand holding her thigh slowly lowered it back to the ground. With his attention aimed in the direction of the guard station, he whispered, "You should go."

She gripped the bars hard. "I'll come back."

"No—don't. It's too much of a risk. Tell Carr instead that you want to see me in chains for yourself. He'll oblige if you lean on his pride. Make him feel powerful for having caught me."

Her breath came stilted. "I don't want to leave you."

His hands wrapped around hers on the bars. "We're under the same roof, Bryn. Our souls know it. It's only a matter of time before we're together."

He settled his lips over hers in a final kiss. She broke away reluctantly at the sound of another clatter coming from the guard's station.

"I love you," she whispered.

He touched her chin softly. "Love doesn't begin to describe how I feel about you."

He pushed her gently away from the bars, urging her back toward the secret passage stairs. One of the hardest things Bryn had ever done was to turn away and leave him there.

CHAPTER 27

A BOTCHED PROPOSAL . . . orange biscuits and roses . . . the water shrine . . . a ruined woman . . . arrows

In the morning, Bryn was awoken by one of the guards rapping on her door.

"Lady Bryn? Are you well?"

She sat up groggily, squinting at the window. Bright sunlight streamed in. She must have overslept after staying up well past midnight to abscond down to the dungeon.

"Yes—one minute!" she called.

She took a moment to sink back into the pillows, letting her eyes fall closed as she breathed in, hoping to catch a trace of Rangar's smell still on her skin.

Seeing him again felt like taking a long drink of water after a grueling hike.

Yet he'd looked so haggard.

I have to get him out of that dungeon.

She slipped on a dressing coat and stuck her head out the door. "I'm still recovering from my captivity. I have much sleep to catch up on."

The guard said in a clipped tone, "Captain Carr wishes to speak with you before he leaves for a military exercise."

Bryn's stomach revolted at the idea of playing nice with Carr, but she smiled tightly. "I'll need a few moments to get dressed. You may tell the captain I'll be down shortly."

The guard nodded curtly as she closed the door.

Once she'd begrudgingly dressed and dabbed rust on her cheeks, she came downstairs expecting to find Captain Carr waiting for her at the dining table, as was the rhythm they'd fallen into.

But the instant she walked into the dining hall, she froze.

A silver tray of orange-glazed biscuits rested at her place at the table.

Orange biscuits.

She immediately recalled last year's Low Sun Gathering, when she'd ridden in a carriage with Elysander and Baron Marmose with a tray of orange biscuits balanced in her lap. Elysander had been the one to explain to Bryn that orange biscuits were a symbol that a man intended to court a woman.

"Lady Bryn. You look lovely as a dawnsong angel." Captain Carr's rasping voice behind her broke the silence.

She still felt numb, staring at the biscuits. But she snapped to her senses and turned slowly. Her stomach plummeted to find the captain holding an extravagantly large bouquet of red roses. He clutched them as artlessly as though they were like a pile of kindling.

"I thought we might take a ride through Saint's Forest to Saint Rennard's shrine. The gardeners tell me the snowdrops are still blooming."

The sour feeling in her stomach intensified.

So the courtship has begun.

She took a pair of steadying breaths. This had been the plan—to get him to propose as a means of saving her from the gallows. She'd heard the whispers among servants and knew the proposal was coming. But now that she was faced with the prospect of the captain actually courting her, she wished to be anywhere but here.

He was her father's age, with gray hair in his beard. The scar across his neck was still red and angry after all these decades. His body might have retained a powerful build from his days spent soldiering, but she found nothing attractive about him in the slightest.

"Oh." It was a chore not to gag. "What a . . . thoughtful gesture. You must have read my mind to know how much I've missed Saint's Forest. Saint Rennard's shrine was always among my favorites."

A flat smile cut across his face. He was as bad at

courting as Bryn was at being courted. "Yes. I remembered, Lady Bryn."

He practically shoved the roses at her. She accepted them with a smile she suspected looked more like a grimace. She flinched as a thorn scratched her forearm.

He stared at her, expectantly.

"Oh, you mean touring the shrine right now?" she asked in dismay.

He nodded curtly. "If it suits you. I must travel to Tureen this evening on state business."

Bryn fought the urge to roll her eyes. How *generous* of him to squeeze courting her in between his duties. The captain's ego was truly inflated if he thought a man his age could charm a future queen so easily.

"Of course," she said through a clenched jaw. "I'd like nothing better."

Captain Carr gestured to one of the guards. "You. Bring the biscuits. The carriage is waiting in the courtyard."

He started to stride out of the dining hall but then stopped and turned back to Bryn, extending his hand as an afterthought. "You first, my lady."

Clearly, chivalry was as foreign to Captain Carr as loyalty.

The open-topped carriage that waited for them in the courtyard, pulled by two prancing white mares, was the same one she'd taken for Baron Marmose's courting during the Low Sun Gathering. As Captain Carr helped her settle onto the rear bench, she wished more than anything that Elysander was here with her. Elysander had known exactly what to say in these situations. Frankly, Bryn would have been happy with *anyone* as a buffer between her and Carr.

She settled into the seat and, to her revulsion, Carr sat next to her instead of across. She adjusted the bouquet of roses in her lap with the hopes that if he got too close, a thorn would scratch him.

"To Saint Rennard's glen," Captain Carr ordered the driver.

It was a cloudy day, and Bryn hoped it would rain to cut short this excursion, but the sky remained dry. Captain Carr offered her an orange biscuit, but she declined, blaming an upset stomach.

As the carriage rumbled over the courtyard cobblestones toward the mulched paths of Saint's Forest, Bryn felt an unexpected nostalgia. Her childhood at Castle Mir had been highly sheltered, so wandering Saint's Forest on her own had been the only time she'd felt free. No wonder she'd come to love the Baersladen with its ancient forests and windswept mountains. Saint's Forest was lovely, but it was like everything else in the Mirien: carefully controlled.

Captain Carr cleared his throat awkwardly. "I had hoped to take this opportunity to discuss your future prospects, Lady Bryn."

Dread rose in her throat, but she swallowed it down. She asked, "Oh?"

"If you'll forgive me for being blunt, many now consider you to be a ruined woman after what you underwent in the Baersladen. I refer to the violations that occurred at the hands of the Barendur princes."

She couldn't keep her anger from reddening her cheeks. "I was married to Prince Trei—I would hardly consider myself ruined for having relations with my husband."

He conceded this with a nod. "I was thinking more of Prince Rangar's . . . *attention*."

Bryn turned sharply to look out at the trees, unable to look Captain Carr in the eyes. Hands squeezed tightly in her lap, she said in a guarded voice, "It's true that Prince Rangar made me do unladylike acts, but I can assure you, I was a virgin on my wedding day."

Captain Carr's eyes dragged their way down her body, shamelessly inspecting every curve. "Perhaps, but there are those who say a woman ravished by a Baer prince is ruined whether her purity remains intact or not."

She folded her arms tightly, unable to keep the anger off her face.

He leaned forward, resting his arm behind her back. "Look at you blushing. I didn't intend to humiliate you, Lady Bryn, only to state a hard reality. You're no longer a virgin. You've been improperly touched by more than one Baer savage. There are not many men of standing who would, in good conscience, marry you now."

The captain's argument was utterly ludicrous, and she marveled at his gall. She was the future queen. Her husband would be king of the wealthiest kingdom in the Eyrie. She could have spread her legs on the Little Table before the kingdom's top advisors and still had princes clamoring for her hand.

"I'm grateful for your honest appraisal," she said between a clenched jaw. "You can imagine how much I value honesty after all I've been through. It's timely for you to bring up Prince Rangar. I've been troubled by the fact that my captor is under the same roof, even if he is in the dungeon. I've been having these nightmares, you see, that he gets loose. I thought if I could see him locked up, it might give me some peace of mind . . ."

Captain Carr placed his calloused hand on her knee and rasped, "You can trust me, Lady Bryn. The prisoner is secure."

"Still—"

"Seeing that rogue would only upset your delicate constitution."

The carriage rumbled over the paths, skirting the stream that babbled through Saint's Forest. They had almost reached the water shrine.

Just a few more minutes, Bryn assured herself. *And I can get out of this damnable carriage.*

Captain Carr plucked an orange biscuit from the silver tray and held it up to her mouth in what she assumed was supposed to be a seductive gesture.

"I have always had your best interest at heart." His breath smelled strongly of *statua* pipe herb. "I assured your parents that if anything should ever happen to them, I would see to your well-being. And since your marriage prospects are so low, I believe it is my duty—and my honor, of course—to offer you my hand—"

No sooner had he begun the proposal than an arrow shot straight into the carriage door.

Bryn jumped, letting out a shriek.

The driver immediately reined the horses to a halt.

Bryn's heart cranked up. She ducked low, though there was little cover in the open-topped carriage. A year ago, she would have screamed and thrown herself to the bottom of the carriage. Now, she knew better how to protect herself.

Instantly on guard, Captain Carr leaned over the carriage side to wrench the arrow out of the splintered wood. He held it up, noting the bushcraft make of the arrow, and snapped into military mode.

"This isn't a Mir army arrow." He snapped at the driver, "Go. Back to Castle Mir. *Now.*"

The driver tried to steer the panicking horses into a turn, though the path was too narrow, and they had to veer into the woods.

Another arrow zinged through the air just over Bryn's head.

She gasped, keeping low, and then immediately traced its trajectory to a trio of maple trees each as wide around as a pony. A face peered out from behind one of the trees, already taking aim for another shot. And there were more, too: at least four rebels taking shelter behind the trees.

Captain Carr shoved a hand against her shoulder to keep her low. "Stay down, Lady Bryn. Wils, get the damn horses turned around! And pass me your crossbow!"

As the driver struggled to redirect the horses toward the castle, Bryn kept her sights on the trees. Her heart stampeded in her chest.

This was an attack on Carr—but it was also one on her. The rebels had no way of knowing she was on their side.

She grabbed the silver tray, throwing the biscuits on the carriage floor, and used it as a shield. Captain Carr notched the soldier's crossbow with an arrow and aimed it at the rebels. He let loose the shot.

It sank into the exposed knee of one of the rebels. The man cried out and slumped back against the tree.

As Captain Carr notched another arrow, the driver finally got the horses free of the forest underbrush. He snapped the whip, and the steeds took off in a gallop.

Another arrow slammed into the rear corner of the carriage an inch from Bryn's hand. Before the carriage thundered away, she caught sight of the man who'd shot it.

I know him.

It was a woodcutter from the village—he was the son of her beloved old seamstress, Mam Nelle.

"Get down, Lady Bryn!" Captain Carr shoved her out of range of the rebel's arrows, smashing her chest to the carriage floor with the crumbly biscuits, as he fired one last time at their attackers.

CHAPTER 28

THE SECRET STRANGER . . . a wounded man . . . if the rumors are true . . . a crown in jeopardy . . . rosemary

For the days following the rebel attack in Saint's Forest, Captain Carr posted extra security around Castle Mir. The number of soldiers was doubled while the servant force was slashed in half to only the most trusted and essential individuals. For all his failings, Carr wasn't an idiot. He knew the rebels had support among the common folk and it would be highly likely that many of the castle staff were sympathetic to their cause.

He restricted Bryn to the residence floor—her room, the hallways, and the latrine. Whenever she tried to argue that she needed to fetch something from the rest of the castle, he had it brought to her instead.

She had plenty of time to mull over the rebel attack. It was no surprise that such an attack would happen given the general hatred of Captain Carr among the common folk, but it deeply troubled her that she'd been as much a target as him. It was going to take much work to convince the common folk that she had returned to Castle Mir under false pretenses. They hadn't believed Elysander when she'd sworn she was on their side. If it hadn't been for a few soldiers who knew her sister's position, Elysander would be dead.

Bryn's only chance was to get a message to the rebels, and soon. Before another attack.

Christof Joster.

It had taken Bryn days of scouring her memory to recall the name of Mam Nelle's son, the woodcutter she'd recognized in Saint's Forest. Mam Nelle was among the servants who'd been removed from the castle for security, so there was no hope in getting a message to him through her. Bryn would have to find someone else to carry the message.

One night, when the guards posted at her door changed shifts, she snuck out of her room and into the secret passages. She'd been avoiding the passages ever since discovering evidence that someone else was using them, as it could very well be rebels who had infiltrated the castle, but now she had no choice.

"Kora yoquin."

Using the spark spell to light her way, she crawled in a direction she hadn't gone since she was a girl, sneaking down to the kitchen for a midnight treat when the cooks were asleep.

Back then, this passage had been rarely used, and her nightgown had come out black after crawling through dust and grime. But now, as she whispered the spark spell and traced the hex shape in the air, she was disturbed to find that the ground was clean.

Someone has been using this passage recently.

She closed her fist to douse the spark out of caution, listening in the pitch-black darkness. There were the usual creaks and groans of the castle, some vermin squeaking, and the thumping of her own heart.

She needed the cover of darkness, and yet without light, how could she find her way to the kitchen?

She closed her eyes and touched the hexmark on her shoulder.

"Jin jan en veera."

The finding spell was notoriously tricky. It had led her astray plenty of times before when her mind wandered from the object she wished to find. But now she focused on the big iron stove in the kitchen, letting all other thoughts fall away.

Gradually, she detected a change in the air to her left. She crawled in the direction of the spell's tug. It was frightening to move in complete blackness, not knowing who else might be down there. She had to move slowly, feeling ahead with her hands. Eventually, she reached a narrow staircase and scaled down it carefully. If her memory was correct, she was only a few passageways from the kitchen—

Her hand collided with a metal bar.

She cursed. She'd forgotten about the locked passageway gates. This one had always been unlocked before, but now the gate was firmly fastened.

Then, she recalled Elysander's key.

Whispering a prayer of gratitude, she fished the chain out from under her collar. The three rings from Rangar, Valenden, and Trei clattered softly, and she held her breath, hoping the sound hadn't given her away to anyone else who might be down here.

After a few moments, she muffled the rings in her palm and twisted the gate's lock.

The hinges groaned. She cringed, her heart pounding.

Did something scrape behind her—someone's boot?

She froze, breath going still.

She could almost feel the presence of someone else, but after a few heart-pounding moments, no one made any more noise.

She scrambled through the gate, hurrying toward the kitchen, praying that the sound she'd heard had only been a mouse. The finding spell's tug led her down a passageway where a faint light shone from the end. She crawled to a wooden vent with slats that allowed her to peer down into the kitchen.

Judging by the lack of dust around this vent,

someone else knew it was an entrance to the tunnels, too.

A handful of late-night scullery maids were seated around the kitchen worktable, kneading bread for the morning. They were all older women except for one who looked just a few years older than Bryn. She was pretty, with raven hair and a darker complexion than most Mir common folk. She kept to herself while the older women gossiped about someone's ailing health.

Bryn listened for some time, hoping to overhear some indication that they were sympathetic to the rebels and could take a message to them on Bryn's behalf, but they never mentioned the attack in Saint's Forest.

Reluctantly, she turned back and started crawling through the tunnels again. She didn't dare risk being away from her room for much longer in case the guards came to check on her. She'd have to return another night and try to find—

Another scrape sounded just up ahead.

Bryn went still.

This time, it was clearly too loud to have been caused by a mouse. Her eyes scoured the darkness, but it was impossible to see more than a few inches in front of her face. She thought she heard someone breathing, but it could have been her fears distorting her senses.

Since she couldn't go forward, she backtracked down another passage.

The breathing followed her.

She crawled faster. She didn't dare use the spark spell now. Even whispering the finding spell would make too much noise. She had a vague idea of where she was in the castle's network of secret passages. She hadn't climbed stairs, so she was likely still on the lower level. There was an opening to the stables somewhere, but her sense of direction was too impaired to know if she was headed in the right direction.

She heard a scrape of someone's boot, louder and bolder this time, behind her.

Bryn gave up trying to remain silent as she scrambled faster. What could she use as a weapon? *I should have brought a knife.* She felt along the passageway floor until her hand brushed a loose brick. She clutched it in her palm, spinning around, pressing her back to the passageway wall.

Her pursuer wasn't far behind. Their movements echoed in the narrow passage. She tried to silence her breath as she raised the brick, listening for their approach—

When she heard the floorboards groan only a foot away from where she crouched, she brought down the brick through the air.

Someone caught her wrist mid-swing before it could connect.

A strong grip clutched her arm, squeezing so hard that she cried out and dropped the brick.

She gasped, "Let me go. I'm the queen!"

A chuckle came out of the darkness. It was masculine and strained but not in the way Captain Carr's voice rasped.

"You aren't queen yet, mouse."

That voice.

Bryn sucked in a gasp. There was only one person who ever called her "mouse."

Her jaw fell open as a chill passed over her body like she'd walked through a ghost—or was facing one.

In a trembling whisper, she said, "Mars?"

Her brother released her hand. He coughed a few times, sounding weak, before saying, "Why in the Saints' names did you come back here, mouse?"

Bryn grabbed the air until she found his shoulders. She needed to verify that he was flesh and bone, not a spirit. Her breath came so fast she thought she might pass out.

"Is it really you?"

That chuckle again. "It's me."

"I was told you were dead!"

"Not all rumors are true."

She squeezed his shoulders tight. "I don't understand. How..."

"Captain Carr plotted to assassinate me, but the soldier he paid to kill me in a military practice drill was one of my closest childhood friends. Finley *did* have to wound me to make it look convincing, and unfortunately, the wounds were more severe than either of us intended. Afterward, he managed to sneak me here to the passages where a handful of loyal servants have been helping me recover."

That explained all the frequently used passages free of dust and cobwebs.

"You mean you've been hiding out in these passages for *months*? Alone? In the dark?"

Her brother was strangely silent. Eventually, he said, "The dark has no impact on me." Before she could ask what he meant, he found her hand and raised it to his face, where her fingers brushed against the familiar jaw and nose before discovering a cloth tied around his eyes. "Finley's wounds left me blind."

Her heart faltered as she silenced a gasp. "But you knew it was me. And you caught the brick."

"Using sound, not sight."

She pressed a hand to her mouth. "Oh, Mars."

He released her hand. "That isn't the worst of it, I'm afraid. The wounds were severe; I almost died when an infection set it. I've only recently been able to move around on my own. If it wasn't for Illiana—"

"Who's Illiana?"

Mars hesitated. "A kitchen maid. She oversees the herb garden—she has a way with healing plants. She's been bringing me medicine, food, news from the outside. At great risk to herself, I may add."

"She's sympathetic to the rebels?" Bryn asked.

"She is."

If that is so, then she could get a message to Christof Joster, Bryn realized.

Mars broke into another coughing fit, and Bryn frowned. "It can't be good for you to have spent so much time down here. You need fresh air and sunlight."

"And reveal to Carr that I'm alive? No. Not until I'm healed enough to confront him properly."

Bryn held back the fears that tiptoed into her head. Mars' lost sight wouldn't heal even if the rest of his body did; how could he go up against Captain Carr impaired?

"And this Illiana, did she tell you that I had returned?"

Mars's voice darkened. "She did. That's how I knew it was you down here. She says the whole castle is speculating that Carr intends to marry you."

A shudder ran through Bryn as she recalled Captain Carr's advances. "I have no loyalty to that usurper, I can assure you. You can ask Illiana to convey to the rebels that I'm sympathetic to their cause. I didn't return here under the pretenses everyone believes. The throne isn't my aim. I'm only here because—"

She stopped before speaking Rangar's name.

Mars pressed at her silence. "Why did you come back if not for the throne?"

It struck Bryn that if Mars was alive, then the crown was no longer hers. It was his by right, and yet there was a reason the refugees in the Baersladen had been relieved that it had fallen to Bryn, not Mars.

"Brother," she started hesitantly. "I also heard rumors about you. They say that before your apparent death, you ruled the Mirien with as much severity as our parents."

She hoped that her brother would deny the accusation—perhaps the rumors had been as false as the ones of his death. She waited to hear him fervently deny that he'd been anything like their despotic parents.

But Mars was quiet.

Eventually, he said slowly, "I wish I could say that wasn't true."

She recoiled, rattled. "But why? You knew how cruel our parents' reign was to the Mir people!"

His clothing rustled as though he was sagging back against the wall. "Mouse, there's so much you don't know. After the siege, it was chaos here. Mother and Father were dead. You and Elysander were both missing. It was impossible for me to know which of our advisors to trust. Captain Carr led the uprising, so I thought I could put my faith in him. It was my sincere belief that he and I wanted the same things for the kingdom. He urged me that it was essential to maintain a strong hand to prevent any attacks from outside forces who might see instability as a weakness to exploit."

"There's a difference between a strong hand and oppression," she said tightly.

Mars let out a long sigh. "Yes. I see that now, whether you believe me or not. My grip on the kingdom was slipping. I sided with the rebels, but their demands were getting out of control. They would have bankrupted the entire kingdom. I didn't know what else to do but fall back on my political training. I only meant to reassert my leadership, but it got out of hand."

Bryn listened closely, not yet convinced.

Mars emphasized, "I was wrong. I know that now. Illiana—she was the one who explained to me just how wrong I was. I credit her with showing me the correct way forward."

Ah, there it was—the note of truth in his voice she'd been waiting for.

"I believe you," Bryn whispered.

His hand closed over hers. For a moment, they remained like that, their shared strength flowing from one to another. Then, Mars sighed again.

"Now I just have to convince the entire kingdom to believe me."

A groan of hinges came from the end of the corridor. Bryn sucked in a breath, reaching automatically for the brick, but Mars stilled her hand.

"It's all right," he calmed her.

In another few moments, someone shuffled toward them. Bryn smelled a trace of rosemary.

Mars's voice was velvety with affection when he said, "Bryn, this is Illiana."

CHAPTER 29

**THE HERB MISTRESS . . . one key and three rings . .
. spark of new love . . . reinforcements . . . a
new plan**

A light flickered in the dark passageway. Illiana struck a match and lit the gas lamp she'd brought with her, holding it up to her face.

It was one of the maids Bryn had seen in the kitchen. The raven-haired young woman kneading dough with the older kitchen workers. Up close, she was even more beautiful than Bryn had first thought. Lush lips and dark, velvet-brown eyes. The way Mars looked at her made it clear their relationship wasn't limited to an herb mistress risking her life to help a disgraced prince.

He loves her, Bryn realized.

Bryn studied her brother closer now that there was some light. A strip of black linen covered his eyes. He looked shockingly gaunt, a shell of his former self. But there was resolve in the way he held himself—this wasn't a man about to give up.

"Illiana," Mars said. "I'd like for you to meet my sister. We have nothing to fear from her. Bryn is on our side."

Illiana regarded Bryn with clear suspicion, though unless Bryn was mistaken, there was also a touch of empathy. "Lady Bryn," the woman said softly. "If you'll excuse my boldness, I was under the impression you'd returned to Castle Mir to take your parents' place."

"If I'd returned under any other pretense," Bryn said, "Captain Carr would have slit my throat."

Illiana lifted her eyebrows in acknowledgment of this fact, but then cocked her head. "Why even return at all?"

Bryn glanced at Mars out of the corner of her eye. Once upon a time, he had been fiercely protective of his little sister's honor. How many times had he warned her away from the "savage" Baer princes?

What would he say if he knew she'd become embroiled with all three?

"I returned for Rangar Barendur," she said quietly.

Sure enough, as she had feared, Mars's nostrils flared with outrage. "That bastard prince from the Outlands who stole you away?"

"I went with him willingly." Bryn kept her head high and her voice firm. "He saved my life that day."

Mars scoffed, a ghost of his arrogant former self coming out. "He's in the dungeon for a reason. In fact, the only joyful news I've heard in months was that he was captured."

Bryn shook her head slowly, though she knew her brother couldn't see it. "You're mistaken about the Barendur family. They did right by me. Trei married me in an effort to save the Mirien. He *died* for it. Valenden risked his life to get me here. And Rangar . . . "

"The rumors were true, weren't they?" Mars spat the words like a curse. "You two were *romantic*."

Speaking evenly so as not to back down from his harsh tone, she said, "I came here to free Rangar from the dungeon. He and I had a plan for how to take the Mirien from Captain Carr: We were going to lean on the Hytooth family in the Wollin for aid. But when Rangar was captured, I had to change strategies. If you think I wished to risk my life by coming back here, you're wrong. But I refuse to abandon Rangar after all he's done for me."

"What exactly has he done for you?" Mars asked hotly.

Illiana rested a cautioning hand on his arm. He tensed initially, but then his shoulders eased.

He sighed. "I apologize for my temper, mouse. I spent years keeping you safe from that prince, so to hear now that you've ended up in his arms is a hard dram to down."

"People were wrong about us," Bryn pointed out. "All of us: you, me, Elysander. The common folk believed we were in league with our parents when that wasn't true. You and Elysander knew of their cruelty the whole time. As soon as I learned the truth, I sided with the rebels. If people were wrong about us, why can't you admit you might have been wrong about Rangar and his brothers?"

Mars scratched at his chin, considering this. "How do you know that about Elysander? Have you been to Dresel?"

Bryn told him about meeting the Forest King in the woods outside of Othwall and showed him the key Elysander had given her, sliding the chain off her neck and pressing it into his palm so he could feel it.

"It's true. This is her key." Mars examined the shape of the key, then cupped the three wedding bands also strung on the chain. They clattered together in his palm. "And these?"

Bryn quickly took the necklace back and replaced it around her neck. "Don't worry about those. Just trinkets."

Mars cocked his head, listening closely. "Rings. I can guess who from. You wear them next to your heart. Is that where your heart lies, Bryn? In the Baersladen?"

She pressed her hand over the rings dangling between her breasts. She'd been prepared to assume the Mir crown in the name of duty. It was the least she could do to attempt to right her parents' wrongs.

But now that Mars was alive, maybe she was absolved of that duty.

Maybe I could return to the Outlands.

"It is," she verified.

Mars didn't seem entirely pleased by this revelation, but to his credit, he didn't shout or order her around as he might have when they were younger.

Had he truly changed, she wondered?

Illiana rested her hand on Mars's knee. "This is good news, Mars," she urged. "Your sister is on our side—not to mention the fact that she has Captain Carr's ear."

Bryn piped up, "Yes, and speaking of the captain, the day our carriage was attacked in Saint's Forest, Captain Carr was on the verge of proposing marriage." She briefly tasted orange biscuits in the back of her throat, which turned her stomach. "Which means he'll probably attempt to propose again soon."

"Put him off," Mars said firmly. "Tell him you need time to heal after your captivity."

"No," Illiana cut in. "Accept his proposal. Make him think you're perfectly willing to marry him. If he trusts you—even better if he thinks you're nothing but a pawn for him to manipulate—he'll lower his guard around you."

Bryn looked at the herb gardener a little more closely, wondering if perhaps Illiana was playing the part of a pawn as well. Did *she* have greater ambitions? Was her interest in Mars political? Romantic? Was Bryn making a mistake in trusting her too quickly?

Bryn rested a hand on Mars's wrist to get his attention. "The fact that you're alive changes everything. Valenden Barendur is returning to the Mirien any day now with Baer reinforcements."

Mars's hand fell away from his chin as his face grew serious. "The Baer army is coming?"

"Not the entire army, but some troops, yes, and a few falconers, and hopefully some . . . " She stopped herself, wondering if it was prudent to mention mages. She didn't know how her brother felt about magic. She finally said, "Some mages."

Mars's jaw tightened. He tilted his head in Illiana's direction as though asking a silent question. Illiana squeezed his knee.

"That is welcome news," Mars stated.

Bryn blinked in surprise. "You don't fear the mages?"

He rested his hand over Illiana's hand on his knee. "It was our parents who spurned magic, not me. With Baer support, we could move against Carr sooner than planned."

"Do you think the rebels will side with us?" Bryn asked, fiddling anxiously with the chain around her neck. "When they attacked our carriage in Saint's Forest, I recognized Mam Nelle's son among them. Christof Joster, I believe his name is. I've been searching for a way to get a message to him."

Mars's hand tightened over Illiana's. He said quietly, "Christof is Illiana's brother."

Bryn turned on the herb mistress with renewed hope. "Then you can take him the message."

Illiana looked hesitant, however. "After the siege, Christof ran away to the woods. He's been hiding out in Saint's Forest with a handful of other rebels who would be shot on sight if they returned to Mir Town. I haven't dared meet with him in person out of fear of exposing him."

"We need the rebels on our side," Bryn insisted.

Illiana interlaced her fingers with Mars's. "I'll see what I can do. It won't be easy with the castle's increased security. And my brother is not a trusting person—it would help if we had a token of your sincerity. Some indication that they can rely on you in the thick of it."

Bryn touched the chain around her neck, the only object of value she owned, yet she doubted rebels would see Outland rings as anything more than baubles. "Isn't Mars's word enough to vouch for my intentions?"

Mars let out a dark chuckle. "Illiana barely convinced the rebels that *I'm* to be trusted."

Bryn thought for a time, running over the possible ways she could demonstrate her sincerity. "The Feast of Saint Amice's Day begins tomorrow night. Tell the rebels I'll produce a sign there."

Mars's brow furrowed above the cloth covering his eyes. "What do you have in mind?"

Bryn toyed more with her necklace. "Something to prove I'm a valuable ally and I'm not afraid to risk my life to help them."

Illiana's lantern flickered, the oil running low, and Bryn realized how long they'd been in the passages.

"I should return before the guards note my absence," she said, then reached out to squeeze Mars's shoulder. "Though it pains me to leave you down here."

"Illiana has taken good care of me."

His hand rubbed gently over the herb mistress's arm with a softness Bryn had rarely seen her brother display. Mars had always been rakish, taking a different girl to bed every night, barely knowing their names. But now, the way he tilted his head toward the quiet, beautiful girl, Bryn was inclined to believe he'd changed.

"I'm so glad to have found you," Bryn said to him. "That you're alive."

Mars pulled her into an embrace, pressing a kiss to the top of her head like he'd done when she'd been a child. His mouth hitched in a grin. "You too, mouse."

Crawling back to her bedroom, Bryn felt flushed with a dewy sense of hope. Was it possible that their fortunes had turned? After the siege, all three Lindane children had suffered greatly, but now it seemed Bryn and her siblings might be made of stronger stuff than anyone believed—even themselves.

She returned to her bedroom, but sleep didn't come. All night, her mind raced with possibilities for the future. Mars was alive, which meant he was the rightful heir. Maybe she wouldn't have to sit on the Mir throne after all—maybe she could return to the place that made her heart sing, the wild land whose whipping winds and salt-laden air wrapped around her like a blanket.

With the man who held her heart—and always would.

But first, they needed to remove the usurper, Captain Carr, from his designs on the throne. The first step was proving to the rebels that they could trust Bryn.

She pulled back her nightgown's sleeve, tracing the small purge hex carved into her right wrist.

Using magic openly in the Mirien was forbidden, so she would have to take exceptional care that no one loyal to Captain Carr saw—or else face the same gallows that had ended her mother.

CHAPTER 30

**SAINT AMICE'S DAY . . . first fire . . . a dress too fine
. . . ambush at the banquet . . . a dangerous request**

As a little girl, Saint Amice's Day had always
been one of Bryn's favorite holidays. It coin-
cided with the coming of winter, which
whispered promises of spiced honey buns, warm apple
cider, and lighting cozy fires in each of the castle's fire-
places. Mir winters were mild compared to what she'd
experienced in the Baersladen, but when she woke in
the morning, a chill was already creeping down her
room's chimney.

A servant had laid wood for a fire the day before
in anticipation of the day's traditions. Bryn slid out
from under the bedcovers and padded over to the
fireplace.

"*Kora yoquin,*" she whispered, tracing the hex in the air.

The kindling sparked, caught flame, and in another minute, the fire was crackling.

A knock came at the door. She tightened her robe around her.

"Enter."

Lisbeth, a quiet servant girl who couldn't be older than eight, peeked in. Since the attack, Captain Carr had replaced most of the older servants with young ones that weren't as much of a threat.

Lisbeth's eyes widened to see the roaring fire. "Good morning, my lady. I came to light the Saint Amice's Day fire, but—"

Bryn smiled. "I already took care of it, Lisbeth. Thank you."

The servant girl twisted the doorknob anxiously as though she had more to say. "Captain Carr asked me to help you prepare yourself for the midday feast."

Bryn brushed a few flecks of ash off her robe. "Oh, that's all right. I can manage on my own."

Saint Amice's Day wasn't one of the grander holidays in the Mirien. The first fires of the season were lit in castle and cottage hearths alike throughout the kingdom, and spiced dough balls were baked over the fires at the end of roasting sticks and dipped in mulled wine. It was an occasion for families to reflect on the upcoming quieter months of winter, not a time for grand banquets or dances.

Lisbeth's small fingers tightened on the doorknob.

"He insisted I braid your hair and dress you in a formal gown."

A vein of suspicion ran through Bryn's mind. Why did she need to wear a formal gown to roast dough balls over a fire?

Still, she could hardly turn Lisbeth away, which might get the girl in trouble.

"Very well. Shall I sit on the bed?"

Lisbeth looked relieved when Bryn perched on the foot of the bed. The little girl used Bryn's silver combs to brush her hair and divide it into sections, then braided them into intricate knots that circled her head with two thick braids draping down her shoulders. Lisbeth dusted powdered rust from a tin over Bryn's cheeks and neckline. Bryn sat patiently, trying to hide how she picked at her fingers in her lap. It had been a long time since she'd gone through the painstakingly long process of dressing as a proper Mir lady. Before, she'd been young enough that she'd escaped the worst of it, but she had vivid memories of her mother spending the better part of a day in her chambers preparing for an evening feast.

Another knock came as Lisbeth was putting the finishing touches on Bryn's styling.

"Enter," Bryn called.

A teenage servant girl came in with a gown draped over her arms. "Your gown for Saint Amice's Day, my lady."

Bryn recognized the gown immediately. It was a

shimmering gold color with white satin ribbons over the bodice and lace sleeves.

My mother's gown.

"That gown is intended for the winter solstice," Bryn said. "It's too formal for this occasion. I shall wear a simple velvet one from my closet."

The older servant girl exchanged a worried look with Lisbeth. "Captain Carr wishes for you to wear it today."

Now, it was evident that Captain Carr had something else in mind besides roasted dough balls and mulled wine. Bryn clamped her jaw shut, looking at the dress in dread. There was only one reason he'd want her looking so formal.

"Set it there." Bryn motioned to a chair near her dressing mirror.

Once Lisbeth had finished with her hair, Bryn let the two girls tie her up in her mother's golden gown. The stiff bodice squeezed her waist uncomfortably, leaving her only able to take shallow breaths. As the girls tugged harder at the stays, Bryn glimpsed a future she dreaded: being caged in uncomfortable clothes, hardly able to sit down or even breathe. How had her mother endured this?

By the time they'd finished, the morning was gone, and Bryn's stomach growled. Yet the idea of doughy balls was far less appealing now.

She made her way down the stairs with dread pooling in her stomach. Chatter came from the direction of the great hall, but it didn't carry the joviality of

Saint Amice's Days of the past with servants mixing with nobility and children chasing each other with their roasting sticks. Today, there was a heavy seriousness to the chatter.

As soon as she entered the great hall, she realized why.

The hall was decorated as though for a formal banquet. Holly garlands spanned the walls. Bouquets of white roses graced the table along with opulent dishes of roast pig, pheasant, and figs drizzled with Mir honey. Instead of the simple dough balls, enormous spiced cakes sat at either end.

Every Mir noble, along with the remaining servants who hadn't been dismissed, was gathered and dressed in clothes far too formal for the occasion. Lord Tarry and Lord Gerbert smiled sharply at her.

Bryn's face burned.

Was this an ambush? *If it is, I think I'd rather be ambushed by bandits than nobles.*

Captain Carr stepped out from the crowd. He wore his usual military uniform, though it had been freshly pressed, and a formal silk mantel draped over his shoulders.

"Lady Bryn. We've been awaiting your appearance. You look even more radiant than your beautiful mother, may the Saints keep her soul."

He took his time painting his gaze down her body. Her stomach lurched as he extended his hand to her. As much as she didn't want to take it, she knew what she had to do.

She forced an innocent smile. "What is this extravagance, Captain? Surely tradition has not changed this much in the time I was away."

He gave a thin chuckle. "New traditions for a new Mirien."

Her stomach tightened more. She pressed a hand to the stiff bodice. It was getting harder to breathe with all the eyes on her.

He led her toward the banquet table, where two places had been decorated at the table's head with holly garlands. A tray overflowing with orange biscuits rested at her place.

"We have much to celebrate this Saint Amice's Day," he said in his rasp.

Bryn's face burned. She felt everyone's eyes on her. Did they all know that this was Captain Carr's plan? Were they in on this ridiculously opulent charade?

She couldn't look up to meet their eyes. These nobles and advisors who'd only kept their heads by betraying her family. And the servants who probably hated her for the sins of her parents, thinking her no better.

I can't breathe.

She was starting to feel dizzy. The dress was too tight. The fires in the great hall were too strong, too warm . . .

Captain Carr raised her hand to his lips, echoing the knightly pose that graced the wall tapestries, though there was nothing noble about him in the least.

A hush fell over the room.

All eyes were on her. Waiting excitedly for the next words as much as she dreaded them.

"Lady Bryn Lindane," Captain Carr pronounced. "On this auspicious occasion of Saint Amice's Day, I do indeed wish to start a new tradition for a new Mirien. This shall be a kingdom governed by rulers who exhibit strength and charity toward their people. I wish to banish the old ways, usher in an era of even greater prosperity. As you are crown heir, the Mirien goes to the man you take as husband, so long as he has royal blood. I would humbly request that you consider me as that man. Though I am a mere servant of the people, I do have royal blood through a distant relation to your father."

He produced a gold ring from his pocket. It was ornate. Dotted with diamonds.

It was her *dead mother's* ring.

Bryn went numb. As far as proposals, this one couldn't be more stiff, even macabre. *So much for a new Mirien.* Captain Carr was demonstrating that he was exactly the same as her parents. He didn't care for the betterment of the common folk—only for a crown atop his own head.

A few excited gasps came from the audience. They irritated Bryn like buzzing flies.

"Though your parents were disgraced," Captain Carr continued, his speech clearly intended for the audience, not her, "I have nothing but compassion for you. You were too young at the time to be party to their tyranny, and I would humbly request that the kingdom spare you from its judgment and trust that under my guidance, you will grow to be the merciful queen that your mother never was."

It might be true that Bryn had little compassion for her deceased mother, but it infuriated her to hear Captain Carr suggest that *he* had the power to shape Bryn into a suitable ruler. The threat was clear—if she didn't marry him, he would turn her over to the fury of the common folk, who would string her up on the galleys.

She opened her mouth, but he wasn't done.

Talking over her, he said, "Had Prince Mars survived until his coronation, I would have served him as his chief advisor. Urging him to be a suitable king, not following in his parents' footsteps. I believe Prince Mars, despite his shortcomings, had the potential to be a good ruler. He would have wanted this—a union between his sister and his most trusted advisor."

Bryn nearly gasped aloud at his audacity.

The last thing Mars wants is for me to marry this traitor!

The rust dusted over her face and shoulders left a metallic taste in her mouth. She'd suspected this proposal was coming, and yet there had been no preparing for the bile that rose in her throat at the prospect of pretending to care for this man.

Captain Carr stared at her expectantly, her fingers still clutched in his hand, her mother's ring in his other.

He was old enough to be her father. He'd once bragged to his soldiers about his desire to have her and Elysander on their backs for him. Every ounce of hatred in her heart belonged to him.

I will see you ruined, she promised in her head.

She smiled tightly and said aloud, "I will happily take both your hand and your guidance, Captain."

The applause from the crowd sounded sincere enough, but Bryn noted the strongest supporters came from the nobility. Though the servants politely clapped, no joy touched their expressions.

Satisfaction simmered in Captain Carr's eyes as he slid the ring on her finger. He pressed his lips to her knuckles. The kiss was as dry and rasping as his voice.

She swallowed her revulsion as various nobles approached to offer their congratulations. Everyone spoke of what a blessing it would be for the kingdom to have new leadership on the throne, though there was nothing new about Captain Carr in the slightest. He'd been at her parents' side throughout their entire despotic reign.

But he could make himself useful to the nobles, and so they pretended to believe his claims.

"Let us celebrate the new tradition," Captain Carr announced to the crowd. "May Saint Amice grace us with her warmth and bounty. Everyone, enjoy the feast!"

Captain Carr started to lead Bryn to the decorated banquet table, but she didn't budge.

She lifted her voice to speak over the buzzing

crowd. "Wait, Captain. I'd humbly like to request that not *all* traditions be left behind."

He raised an eyebrow, clearly not liking her challenge but with all the watching eyes, he could hardly chastise her.

"What tradition is that, my bride?"

"The engagement gifts, of course."

It was tradition upon any engagement that the future bride be gifted three presents by her groom. For the common folk, those gifts were often simple tokens: a jug of brandy, a sack of apples. But in the case of the royals, it could be horses or even a new castle.

Captain Carr didn't bother to hide his derisive snort. "Ah, of course. You're still a young girl even as crown heir. And what girl doesn't want her engagement gifts? What shall it be then, my bride? Jewels? Was the ring not enough?"

The crowd tittered at the suggestion that Bryn was only after treasures.

She gave a guilty laugh, pretending to blush. "It's true that I have my heart set on presents, but not jewels. For my first engagement gift, I'd like to see with my own eyes the traitor, Rangar Barendur, in chains."

CHAPTER 31

FIRST GIFT . . . unwanted congratulations . . . new traditions . . . the man in chains . . . secrets in a ring box

The condescending smile melted off Captain Carr's face.

The crowd hushed.

Bryn kept her chin high, enjoying this brief moment of triumph at having rendered Captain Carr speechless. He'd reveled in insulting her under the guise of proposing marriage, suggesting she was a silly girl who only craved shiny baubles. Well, she would play into his farce.

"The traitor, my lady?" His rasping voice was dangerously low.

She clasped her hands together, playing the part of

the spoiled princess. "Rangar Barendur kept me captive for months in a savage kingdom. There is nothing that would please me more than to see *him* now in chains at the mercy of my future husband."

The crowd murmured at this, but Bryn kept her head steady, closing her ears to it. Let them think she was that petty—they would discover her true sentiments once she'd defeated Carr.

Captain Carr seemed to be experiencing a rare moment of uncertainty. He'd orchestrated this banquet to ensure she would agree to his proposal, but he clearly hadn't been expecting her to make such an unusual request.

"I'm not certain that's a good idea, my lady," he said.

She gave an exaggerated pout. "Surely you aren't afraid of the traitor, Captain? Am I to wed a man who can't protect me against a simple prisoner in the dungeon, weakened and shackled?"

The captain's face burned red from the scar across his neck and spreading upward. Bryn was thankful for the audience now—he wouldn't dare rebuke her in public.

"Let's see the traitor in chains!" someone called from the crowd.

Captain Carr looked furious, but he gave a signal to two of his soldiers. "Very well. Bring up the Baer prince. Ensure he's shackled at wrists and ankles." He gave Bryn a hard look. "Whatever my bride wants, she gets."

His anger was clear, but Bryn pretended to ignore it.

As his soldiers left, the captain motioned to the banquet, though his mood had soured. "Please, everyone. Eat. Enjoy the banquet. This is indeed a *happy* day for the Mirien."

The nobles took great interest in filling their bellies with the offerings. Bryn couldn't help but notice that the servants weren't invited to partake in the feast, going against the Saint Amice's Day tradition of mingling ranks.

She grabbed a napkin and used it to smear the rust on her cheeks when no one was looking.

She turned to Captain Carr with an apologetic blush. "I'm afraid I've ruined my makeup. Would your guards escort me to my room so Lisbeth can repair the damage? I'd hate not to look perfect on my engagement day."

Carr was talking to Lord Gerbert and barely seemed to have heard her. He motioned to the guards who'd been assigned to follow her.

"Go with her," he told the guards. "Hurry back, Lady Bryn. You don't want to miss the gift you so insisted upon."

"Oh, trust me, I wouldn't miss it for the world."

She was all too relieved to get away from the crowd, though her pulse pounded too urgently for her to enjoy the moment of calm that followed. As soon as she was back in her room, Lisbeth jumped up from where she'd been sweeping ashes from the fireplace.

"My lady, I heard the good news!"

The little girl was too young to understand there was nothing joyous about the engagement—all she'd heard were the cheers from the crowd downstairs.

Bryn motioned distractedly toward the hall while she scanned the room for a scrap of paper. "I've made a mess of the rust you dusted me with—can you fix it? There are towels in the armoire outside."

"Of course, my lady."

While Lisbeth scampered to the hall armoire, Bryn took advantage of the brief privacy to rip a page out of one of her books. She snatched up a quill. Though Mage Marna's magic had granted her the ability to speak and understand Baer, her written ability with the language was not nearly as fluent. But she didn't dare write in Mir, which could easily be apprehended and read.

Trust me, she wrote in broken Baer. *Val comes soon. You will live to return to the Baersladen. I promise.*

She tucked the paper into the bottom of a ring box that she pulled out from her upper drawer just as Lisbeth returned.

Once her adornments were back in order, Bryn steeled herself to return to the banquet. There was still no sign of the usual roasting sticks and dough balls; everything she loved about the holiday had been plowed over by Carr's proposal and "new tradition" of yet another decadent feast for the nobility.

Carr himself was speaking with several senior military members. The excitement that danced in his small eyes had little to do with Bryn, she knew. Now that he had secured the future throne for himself, he was anxious to assert his power over the realm and demonstrate his strength to their allies and enemies alike.

Servants poured mulled wine for her, which she sipped carefully, wanting to keep her wits about her. Nobles lined up to fawn over her with congratulations, and Bryn made a show of accepting each of their good tidings, but her attention remained on the servants, not the nobles. They were the ones whose audience she wanted.

Only they could get a message to the rebels.

"You look refreshed, my lady," Captain Carr noted when he eventually joined her at the table. His nose was red, revealing how much wine he'd consumed. Bryn had never known Captain Carr to overindulge in alcohol, but the promise of being king must have loosened his inhibitions.

He saw the ring box at her side and looked momentarily confused since his engagement ring graced her finger. "What have you there?"

She rested a hand on the box. "A token to shame the traitor. Rangar Barendur humiliated me, and I wish to humiliate him in return."

Captain Carr nodded along, though he watched her carefully. "I must say I'm surprised by your degree of hatred for the Baer prince, given the rumors we heard."

"It's precisely those false rumors I wish to crush."

The banquet stretched on interminably, and Bryn couldn't stand the line of nobles offering their blessings to her and prattling on about the good of the Mirien. She ended up drinking more wine than she'd intended just to get through it.

The afternoon sun was sinking by the time a line of soldiers entered the great hall.

The crowd quieted except for a few murmurs of speculation. Bryn sat straighter in her chair, the prattling lord at her side talking to her about gourd harvests forgotten.

She pressed a hand to her tight dress, feeling breathless.

A clatter of iron chains echoed as the soldiers led in Rangar. He was shackled at the wrists and ankles, as Carr had commanded. Half a dozen soldiers surrounded him, one hand already on their swords. Rangar's clothes were so filthy it was hard to tell what color they'd once been. His hair was caked in dirt and sweat, a messy tangle that shadowed his face.

But when he lifted his chin, his brown eyes burned bright.

Bryn felt the breath slip from her lips. Her heart twisted like a knife at the sight of him. In the dark dungeon, she hadn't seen the deep bruises covering one side of his face, nor fully observed how gaunt he'd become.

Their eyes met over the crowd.

Bryn held his gaze, wishing more than anything

she could touch that bruised face, wipe away the grime.

"The prisoner, Prince Rangar Barendur of the Baersladen," the dungeon master announced.

The crowd broke into heated chatter. Bryn could only imagine the salacious rumors being bandied about. Here he was, a rival kingdom's prince who had once dared to believe a Mir princess belonged to him, chained now like a dog.

She closed the ring box in her palm has her pulse raced.

"Here he is," Captain Carr said, rising to his feet. A mean streak marred his face, brought on by too much wine. "The first of your three engagement presents."

Rangar must have heard Captain Carr's pronouncement, but he showed no reaction to the news of Bryn's supposed engagement. His shoulders were bowed, hands clasped by iron, but his head remained lifted.

Bryn recalled mere weeks ago when he'd stormed into Barendur Hold and punched Trei in the jaw for daring to offer Bryn an engagement. Little did all these gossiping nobles realize how true the rumors were: She did belong to Rangar. And he belonged to her. Not for the reason anyone thought, but for the look that ran between them now.

Captain Carr pointed a long finger in Rangar's direction. "Did you hear that, prince? You may have wanted her for yourself, but Lady Bryn has agreed to wed me. She knows the Mirien will always be her home. Not some hovel where she's defiled by a savage."

Bryn flinched at the harsh words. Captain Carr must seriously be deep in his cups to speak so plainly. The whispers grew bolder among the crowd.

"That is how you speak of your future bride?" Rangar said in an even voice.

Bryn cut him a hard look. Of all the times to lose his temper, this wasn't it. Rangar saw her look and clamped his mouth shut, though rage still churned deep in his eyes.

Captain Carr barked a laugh. "Says the man who treated a princess like a common whore."

Bryn stepped forward, feeling the situation was getting too heated. Now it was her own temper she was worried about; there was only so long she could take Captain Carr's insults.

"What this prince says about me bears no merit," she announced, keeping her eyes fixed on Rangar. "He is just as brutish as everyone says. It gives me nothing but pleasure to see him now in chains."

Rangar remained silent as she approached, narrowing her eyes at him as she paced slowly in front of him.

"Calling him a savage is too kind," she insisted. "The land he comes from is untamed, yes. The barren soil, the wild animals. But the nature of his home does not turn one's heart black enough to imprison a princess and call her his own, make her sleep on the floors with animals."

Bryn was the only one close enough to see the small flicker of amusement dance in Rangar's eyes. She'd come to like sleeping with the goats in the great hall, and he knew it.

"He's a rogue," she pressed. "And I thank the Saints that our places are now reversed. I have something to give you back, prince. The ring you forced on me. I have no need for it now that I have a new one."

She shoved the ring box in Rangar's hand with a look of disgust, then held up her hand to show off Captain Carr's glittering diamond.

For good show, she drew her hand back and slapped it across Rangar's face.

Bryn's performance delighted the crowd, who erupted in jaunts at Rangar's expense. For his part, Rangar kept his head lowered from the slap. He quietly slid the ring box into his pocket with his shackled hands, and only then lifted his head again.

Their eyes met.

Bryn gave a nod so slight only he could notice it.

She spun back toward the banquet table, her heart thundering. She'd never been much of an actress, but fortunately, everyone was too drunk to notice her poor ability.

Captain Carr's eyes were on fire as they swept over Bryn, as though he liked this violent streak in her.

He raised a glass. "To my bride, the jewel of the Mirien!"

"The jewel of the Mirien!" the crowd repeated.

Bryn kept her eyes on Rangar, who silently bore

the humiliation, though she knew his temper must be urging him to rush at Captain Carr with chained fists raised.

He has the ring box, she told herself. *He'll get my note.*

The small surge of triumph she felt was ambushed when Captain Carr suddenly let his arm fall around her waist. Her attention shot to him in alarm.

He wore a lustful look, sloppy with wine.

Bryn sucked in a tight breath.

Captain Carr, the man who'd betrayed her family, attempted to assassinate her brother, and had once threatened unspeakable things against her, leaned in for a kiss.

CHAPTER 32

ANOTHER SPELL . . . the thwarted kiss . . . servants and royals . . . lavender . . . "could be a great king"

Considering his age and the scar across his neck, Captain Carr could be considered a handsome man, but the prospect of kissing him—a traitor, no less—made Bryn's braised pork threaten to rise back up her throat.

Think swiftly, she thought as his dry mouth came toward hers.

His hand tightened around her waist to pull her closer, and she placed a hand on his shoulder as though welcoming the embrace. Meanwhile, behind his back, she traced the shape of a hex in the air.

Under her breath, she whispered, "*En videl.*"

It was risky to cast a spell in public in a

kingdom that forbade magic. But the whole Saint Amice's Day charade had painted her as merely a pawn, so she suspected that no one would ever expect her to perform magic. Fortunately, the din from the crowd drowned out her whispered words.

Captain Carr's lips were a breath away. She cringed to think of what it would feel like to kiss him—his skin was as rough as corn husks, and she didn't like that lustful look in his eye.

A second before he touched his mouth to hers, he suddenly stopped.

He pulled away, pressing a hand to his stomach.

Bryn scrambled out of his grasp, breathing hard. Her eyes were wide as she watched pain contort his facial features. He pressed a hand to his mouth, then suddenly pivoted toward the banquet table. Leaning over, he heaved a few times before vomiting all over the floor.

Gasps rang out among the crowd.

Bryn didn't attempt to hide her disgust. Soldiers rushed in to help Captain Carr, whose face had gone clammy.

"He was poisoned," one of the soldiers hypothe-sized, grabbing the wine glass and sniffing it.

"It isn't poison, you idiot," Captain Carr growled at him, swiping a cloth over his mouth. He held onto the table for balance, still looking weak. "We all drank the same wine."

Bryn cleared her throat. "Perhaps you

overindulged, Captain? It was quite an extravagant feast."

Pale-faced, he gave a shaky nod. "Yes, I believe the princess is right."

Still, he extended Rangar a suspicious look as though the prince had somehow cursed him even chained and all the way across the room.

A flicker of amusement danced in Rangar's eyes.

"Take the prisoner back to the dungeon," Captain Carr snapped, motioning toward Rangar. The sharp movement made him double over again.

"Captain, you must rest," Bryn said with false concern. She turned to the guards. "Be so good as to take him to his room. I fear the feast is too much for a man of his *advanced* age."

She knew it was dangerous to barb her words, but she couldn't resist. Fortunately, Captain Carr was too distracted to pick up on the insult.

He swatted away the guards' hands, grumbling, but nodded. "My lady, if you'll excuse me . . ."

"Of course. Oh, and thank you for my engagement gift. It's exactly what I wanted."

She smiled tightly.

As soon as Captain Carr was gone, Bryn took her time looking over the crowd still gathered for Saint Amice's Day festivities and all the plentiful food on the banquet table. Her eyes fell on a basket of roasting sticks shoved in a corner that a servant must have brought before Captain Carr decided to change the day's traditions.

"Lords and ladies," she announced. "Let us not forget the spirit of the day. Saint Amice's Day is the time we put aside rank and join together as Mir people. I invite the servants to partake in this feast."

None of the servants made a move toward the table. They all shuffled anxiously, passing each other uncomfortable glances.

"I insist," Bryn urged. "We are all citizens of the Mirien, and I would not have only those with a noble title celebrate my engagement."

The nobles had gone quiet, clearly disgruntled at this news. Most of the servants still made no move join in until Bryn picked up the tray of orange biscuits and circled the hall, passing them out to the common folk.

She was quite sure her mother had never served a maid a biscuit even on Saint Amice's Day. The shock of a princess distributing offerings broke some of the tension, and the younger maids nibbled on their biscuits with smiles. The older servants hesitantly puttered around the table, picking at grapes and figs.

The nobles didn't seem pleased, but they went back to socializing amongst themselves, unwilling to publicly question a queen's actions.

After she handed out the biscuits, Bryn returned to her place at the head of the table, wondering when Rangar would be able to safely read her note, when a young man came to clear away Captain Carr's plates.

In a low voice, the servant muttered, "Illiana said to look for a sign—she didn't say it would be a *hex*."

Bryn looked up in surprise to find herself facing

Christof Joster, Illiana's brother, the rebel who had shot an arrow at her in the Saint's Forest. He was disguised as a servant, and she'd had no idea how he'd managed to get inside the castle's well-guarded perimeter.

Bryn whispered, "I wasn't about to let that wrinkled old goat kiss me."

Christof hid a quick smile. He glanced surreptitiously at the crowd. "I never would have believed the daughter of King Deothanial and Queen Helena would bring magic into Castle Mir."

"It was a risk," she admitted. "But I see that it had a positive result. Do you believe me now that I have no loyalty to the old ways?"

Christof maintained his skepticism. "Illiana claims your brother has changed his ways, so I accept it's possible you might have as well, but that production of yours with the chained prince—"

"I had to get close enough to Rangar to slip him a message."

"The slap seemed very convincing."

"Good. Then I'm a decent actress after all." She raised a wry eyebrow. "Trust me, I've wanted to slap Rangar a time or two, but that time was only for show."

Christof eyed her closely, trying to gauge if she was to be trusted. He finally whispered, "Meet Illiana in the herb garden tonight."

Bryn nodded.

Christof carried the plates away, leaving her alone

with her heart thrashing. Before she had known that Captain Carr planned a proposal for Saint Amice's Day, she had intended to quietly use magic to light a dough ball on fire when only the servants were around as the "sign" of her loyalty to the rebels. But the purge spell had served the dual purpose of keeping Captain Carr far away from her.

She wouldn't always be able to keep him away, however. Which was why she had to act fast.

That night, it was easy to get past the guards and go to the herb garden. The engagement news—along with the plentiful leftover food and wine—had lulled the entire castle into a festive, relaxed spirit. Fortunately, this included the guards. Bryn had simply told them that she needed some fresh lavender to scent her bath and wanted to pick it herself. The guards who accompanied her waited in the warmth of the vestibule, swapping gossip about the day's events.

Bryn hadn't spent much time in the castle's herb garden in her youth. The garden was in an interior courtyard off a stairwell that was mostly used by servants. Her mother had encouraged her to take fresh air in the formal rose garden, a more suitable place for a young princess.

The moon was out overhead, casting cool, bluish light over the small garden. The plants had been left to bolt and reseed for the winter, and the place had a wild feel. For a moment, Bryn felt as though she was back in the Baersladen with its beautiful wilderness.

"That was quite the show you put on at the feast."

Bryn turned at the sound of Illiana's voice in the shadows. The herb mistress was crouched low with a wicker basket, gathering the last of the season's mint.

Bryn settled near her, filling her basket with lavender sprigs. "You were there?"

Illiana nodded. "On and off. We were busy in the kitchen. Captain Carr wanted the banquet table buried under dishes. He hoped to dazzle you into accepting his proposal, I think. Why do men think all women want is a show of wealth?"

"It isn't even *his* wealth," Bryn said wryly. "It's my family's."

Illiana's mouth turned up in a half-smile. "I nearly dropped a pitcher of mulled wine when Captain Carr vomited on the floor. Everyone thought he'd just had too much to drink, but I saw you trace the purge hex in the air."

"You told your brother about it, didn't you? That's how he knew."

Illiana nodded. "Lucky for you, there weren't many of us at the right angle to see you make the hex. And I was the only one who knew what it meant."

Bryn glanced over her shoulder toward the doorway where the guards were talking amongst themselves. "Magic is forbidden here. How did you recognize a purge hex?"

Illiana was silent for a few moments. She finally

held up a spring of mint, tracing a shape in the air with a mysterious glimmer in her eyes. "Just because it's forbidden doesn't mean it isn't practiced."

It was clear that Illiana didn't want to say more. Whether she herself could cast spells or merely was knowledgeable about them, Bryn didn't want to press. Not when the punishment for witchcraft could be death.

"Regardless, I'm grateful you told Christof I could be trusted."

Illiana gave a small nod. "My brother had to leave the castle before the guards changed shifts, so he asked me to meet with you in his place. He wants you to know that visitors have arrived in Mir Town."

Bryn clutched the lavender hard. "Visitors?"

The smell of crushed lavender rose to her nose.

"From the north," Illiana whispered. "Prince Valenden, and he's brought with him two dozen Baer soldiers. A few falconers and at least one mage are among them. Some of the Mir refugees who fled to the Baersladen returned with them and made the introduction to Christof. The rebels are currently hiding them in various houses in the town and nearby villages."

Bryn wrestled with all the emotions that surfaced: Relief that Valenden had survived the incident in Ardmoor and gotten safely back to Barendur Hold. Anxiousness that he was close, just a little way beyond the castle walls. Hope that for once, fortune might be turning in her favor.

"I must speak with Prince Valenden as soon as possible," Bryn said.

"That will be hard to arrange. We don't dare try to smuggle him into the castle. Christof had a guard paid off, but the man was caught."

Bryn looked up at the moon in the starless sky. "Then I'll have to leave the castle."

"Without guards? How?"

"I'll tell Captain Carr I want to go to the Sunday market to look at the fabric vendors for a wedding gown. Can you get a message to Valenden to meet me there?"

Illiana nodded. "My mother has run a seamstress stall there ever since Captain Carr dismissed her from the castle. She can provide a safe place for you to meet with the prince. We'll say you need privacy to try on dresses. That will keep the guards away."

"Mam Nelle?" Bryn said, remembering her old dressmaker. "She used to make all my gowns. Yes, that will serve us—Carr will understand why I'd want her to make a wedding dress."

Illiana nodded. "Good. Sunday, then. I'll have it ready."

The herb mistress started to vanish back toward the kitchen steps, but Bryn whispered, "Wait."

Illiana paused, half-standing in the shadows. Moonlight lit up the other half of her face.

"About Mars," Bryn whispered. "He's really . . . changed?"

A corner of Illiana's lips curled in a wry smile. "He

was still a smug bastard when I met him, but it's a wonder what almost dying will do to change a person's perspective."

Bryn countered, "I think his changed perspective has less to do with his near death and more to do with the beautiful rebel who nursed him to health."

Illiana was too reserved to blush, but she turned her face away from the moonlight.

Bryn pressed, "Am I wrong in seeing a connection between the two of you?"

Illiana adjusted her herb basket to buy time before answering, "There are plenty of commoners who never saw your brother's positive traits. I'll admit that before I met him, I always thought him handsome but arrogant. I'm glad I gave him the chance to prove he was more than that. He could be a great king."

Her words were measured but spoke volumes. It was plain to see she cared for Mars as much as he was taken with her.

Bryn returned to her room, and that night, lying awake and gazing at the night sky through her window, she wondered how much longer it would be before Rangar could look at the same moon.

Sunday, she told herself. *Everything will change.*

CHAPTER 33

**A NECK FOR THE GALLOWS . . . second
engagement gift . . . the Sunday Market . . . old
friends**

Sunday mornings were typically a day of reflection for the Mir people, when citizens would read from the great scientific and historical texts, go to the Mir Town square to listen to philosophers spouting wisdom, or tidy their homes for the coming week. Within the walls of Castle Mir, however, there was nothing peaceful about the following Sunday.

As soon as Bryn woke, she felt a blade of tension running throughout the entire castle's population. When Lisbeth came with cinnamon tea, the girl was uncharacteristically quiet. The guards posted at Bryn's door murmured amongst themselves but grew silent when Bryn stepped out of her room to use the latrine. As she made her way downstairs for breakfast, she noted most of the servants keeping their heads low.

Striding into the great hall where Captain Carr was flipping through parchment letters, she noted, "Everyone seems rather sullen this morning."

He barely glanced up from his letters. "A soldier was recently caught accepting bribes. When pressed, he revealed that the rebel plot is more organized than we suspected."

Bryn sat down slowly, reaching for a piece of toast. Now, the uncomfortable energy throughout the castle made sense. One of their own had been captured and likely tortured, and they were doubtless afraid of what Captain Carr would do to the rest of them.

"Goodness," she exclaimed with careful blandness. "What information did he reveal?"

It had to be the soldier that Illiana had mentioned in the herb garden who had been caught helping Christof sneak out of the castle. She silently prayed that the captured man hadn't revealed Christof and Illiana's names.

"Very little, unfortunately." Captain Carr took an angry sip of his coffee.

Bryn's shoulders sank in relief. While buttering her toast, she cleared her throat. "I had hoped to go to the Sunday Market in Mir Town today to pick out fabric for a wedding dress. My former seamstress has a stall there, I believe."

Carr flipped through the letters, shaking his head. "It isn't the best time for you to leave the castle, even with guards."

She leaned forward, batting her eyes. "That's wise of you, and yet I want to have a pretty gown for our wedding. I think it's important that the common folk see this union as a fresh start for the kingdom, don't you?"

She'd captured his attention by leaning forward so that her low-cut neckline was on display. He set down his letters and let his gaze linger on her chest.

"Hmm. Yes, of course, we want it to be a grand affair as a show of future prosperity. I suppose it will be acceptable if you take a unit of guards."

She beamed. "Of course."

Now that she had his attention, he moved his letters aside and folded his hands on the table. "Speaking of the rebels, I must say that I was impressed with your animosity toward the traitor prince."

She scoffed. "Rangar Barendur? A rogue through and through. It delighted me to see him in chains."

Captain Carr smiled thinly. "In that case, I think you'll be extremely pleased by my second engagement gift."

Bryn wiped the crumbs from her lips with her napkin. "Oh? Something to further humiliate him, I hope?"

"Indeed," he replied evenly. "I'm going to string him up at the gallows in Mir Town square."

Bryn nearly choked on the bite of toast. She coughed a few times before managing to swallow it down. "A . . . *hanging?*"

"As you said, the common folk need to know our union is a fresh start for the kingdom. A public execution of one of our enemies will rally the people even more behind us."

A chill crept over Bryn's skin. She tried hard to keep her expression under control, though her heart was racing.

"Is that really the tone we want to set?" she asked carefully. "A death right before our wedding? Better to keep him in chains, I think. Let him rot in the dungeon."

Captain Carr chuckled, his gaze still hovering around Bryn's breasts. "You underestimate how much the common folk love a hanging. Besides, a hint of violence before the wedding is exactly what we need to threaten the rebels, should they get any ideas."

Bryn's mind whirled. "Yes, but . . . "

Captain Carr cocked his head, eyes narrowing. "You *do* want to see your former captor dead, do you not?"

She pressed her lips together tightly and whispered, "Of course."

His smile returned. "Good. Then it's decided. One week from now, Rangar Barendur will hang."

⁓

Bryn couldn't get out of the castle walls fast enough. It was torture to sit through the rest of breakfast and then have to wait for the soldiers to prepare a carriage to take her into Mir Town. Now, as she finally sat in the carriage, blessedly alone with the curtains drawn, she could finally think.

I can't let Rangar hang.

Though Captain Carr didn't think much of women's intellect, he wasn't a stupid man, either. There was a good chance he suspected Bryn of pretending to detest Rangar, and this was a test of her real sentiments. She didn't dare beg for Rangar's life without giving away the truth.

She shoved back a window curtain to watch Mir Town roll by outside. The town, like the castle, felt oppressive today. Heavy gray clouds hung overhead, threatening rain. Common folk trudged through the dirt streets with slow steps as they went about their end-of-week chores. A young boy tugged on a stubborn donkey's lead, trying to urge the creature forward. A farmer carried a basket full of wormy squashes toward the market. A pair of girls huddled near the gutter, cleaning out chamber pots with grimaces.

It was only once they neared the market that the mood shifted. Bryn had occasionally been allowed to come to the Sunday Market as a child, and she had adored the towering stacks of pumpkins for sale, the spice vendors' colorful barrels, the children laughing in the street with their honeyed nuts. It was a busy day at the market, which was good. That would keep her guards distracted.

The driver stopped the carriage near the market's fabric section and opened the door.

"Lady Bryn. Please take care. I don't have to remind you that the rebels could be anywhere."

"Yes, thank you, Sergeant Preston."

She took the sergeant's hand and stepped down. A unit of six guards had accompanied the carriage and now surrounded her as she made her way down the aisle flanked with stalls selling bolts of silk, reams of yarn, and yards of fabric of every shade and pattern imaginable.

She pretended to admire the lace while she kept a close look for Mam Nelle's stall. At last, she saw the old woman accepting some coins from a noblewoman's maid.

Bryn smiled widely as she approached the stall. "Mam Nelle. What a pleasure to see you again after all this time."

The old seamstress was all smiles as she pressed her hands to her chest. "Lady Bryn! What a blessing!"

"I was surprised to find you were no longer working in the castle."

"Oh, it was high time I gave over that job to a younger seamstress with better eyesight."

Mam Nelle's tone was light and cheerful, though Bryn knew very well Captain Carr had forced Mam Nelle to leave the castle's service along with most of the other senior staff who knew too much about what had really gone on under his leadership.

The seamstress glanced sidelong at Bryn's guards. "What wonderful news about your upcoming wedding. This kind of joyous occasion is exactly what the kingdom needs after so many difficult years."

"Yes, that's why I came to see you. It's my hope you'll sew my wedding gown."

"Ah! You honor me, my lady. Let's see if any of my fabrics are worthy of such a gown." She ushered Bryn toward the reams of silks and lace, and the two women made a show of discussing various styles of gowns.

"I think the Ruma lace is an excellent choice," Mam Nelle said. "It will complement your complexion. All I'll need now are your measurements. You can just step into the tent here."

The guards looked bored as they stood around the seamstress's stall, watching the market goers with dull interest.

Bryn raised her voice casually. "I'll just be a moment, Sergeant Preston."

The sergeant took a moment to walk around the perimeter of the canvas tent to check for security concerns. He gave a small nod for Bryn to proceed.

Mam Nelle gathered up the bolts of lace and lifted the tent door for Bryn. Inside, a worktable laden with fabric and seamstress tools flanked one side, and a stool rested in the corner.

Valenden Barendur sat on the stool, sipping from a flask.

"Val!" Bryn rushed to throw her arms around him, nearly knocking him over as he rose from the stool.

"Whoa, take care, princess. You nearly made me spill my brandy."

Bryn squeezed him harder, burying her face in his chest. He smelled like the Baersladen; like horses and smoke and their long days together on the road. She felt the prickle of tears at her eyes.

She pulled back, gazing up at him. "Lords and ladies, I'm glad to see your face."

"Afraid it wouldn't be attached to my neck any longer?"

She grinned. "I knew you'd make it out of Ardmoor. This is Mam Nelle." Bryn motioned to the seamstress. "We can trust her, as well as her son and daughter."

Mam Nelle gave Valenden a wink as she pretended to busy herself with the lace.

"Yes, Christof smuggled me in here rolled up in a length of velvet," Valenden explained. "All in all, not an uncomfortable way to travel."

Bryn grinned up at him. He smoothed a tender hand over her hair. "You're all right?"

She nodded. "Carr believed my story—or at least he's acting like he does. I'm sure word has reached you of the engagement." She paused. "There's only one problem."

"Let me guess, it involves my brother?"

She swallowed, not wanting to speak the next words. "Carr wants to hang Rangar as my second engagement gift."

Mam Nelle, listening in, sucked in a breath as she measured lengths of lace.

Valenden muttered under his breath as he tipped his flask back for another long sip. "By the gods."

Bryn glanced toward the tent flap, knowing the guards would be suspicious if they took too long. She whispered, "Have you heard that my brother is alive?"

"Christof told me, yes. I'm happy for you, princess, that your brother still lives. But are you certain he can be trusted?"

"He was led astray by Captain Carr, but he sides with the rebels now."

Valenden's eyes filled with a healthy amount of skepticism, but he slowly nodded. "If that is truly the case, then Mars is the rightful crown heir."

"I've told him I'll support his claim to the throne."

"You'd give up your own claim so easily?"

She knit her fingers together, thinking of the bustling market outside. Though it was familiar, it didn't feel like where she belonged. "This isn't my home. The Baersladen is."

Valenden studied her face. "Have you seen Rangar?"

She nodded, though she couldn't hide her worry. "He's as well as one could be who's traded one dungeon for another. We need only to free him, and he'll lead the uprising."

Valenden's head pitched up toward the tent ceiling as he thought. "Christof says Captain Carr's turned the castle into a fortress, protected by those loyal to him. There's little chance of us smuggling Rangar out . . ." He stroked his chin. "So, maybe we let Carr do it for us."

"What do you mean?"

"Carr has to let Rangar out of the dungeon to take him to the gallows, doesn't he?"

Bryn rested her hands on her hips. "There's a slight problem with that plan."

Valenden waved his hand dismissively in the air. "Rangar will hang? Yes, and yet your sister told us in the forest outside of Othwall how she evaded the gallows. There's no reason we can't do the same for Rangar."

"Elysander was able to fake her death only with the help of loyal soldiers. We don't have them anymore."

"There are other ways to fake a death."

Bryn didn't like the glimmer of mischief in Valenden's eyes. She had a feeling that Rangar's fate might not be any safer in Valenden's hands than in Captain Carr's.

"What other ways?" she asked cautiously.

CHAPTER 34

SILK AND LACE . . . the death slumber . . . whispers of witches . . . an empty castle . . . an unwanted kiss

With a smirk on his lips, Valenden stepped close enough to Bryn that she flashed him a warning look. Despite the weeks they'd posed as newlyweds, there had never been anything romantic between them, but Bryn also knew Valenden delighted in teasing her.

He said, "How close can you get to Rangar at the hanging?"

"A few feet, I'd wager," she answered cautiously. "I'm certain I can convince Captain Carr to let me stand on the dais with him and the hangman."

"Excellent." Valenden loosened his shirt from his

trousers and started to tug it up over the sleek muscles of his abdomen.

Bryn gasped and tugged his shirt back down. "What in the Saints' names are you doing?"

She looked over her shoulder at Mam Nelle, who was pretending to be riveted by a basket of buttons. Valenden's smirk grew as he wrestled back control of his shirt and tugged it over his head. His collection of hex marks scarred his sinewy bare chest.

"Relax, princess," he purred. "If I intended to seduce you, I'd do it without the seamstress present."

Mam Nelle snorted while busying herself with the buttons.

Valenden tapped a spiral-shaped hex mark on his left pectoral muscle. "This is the death slumber hex. It's normally used to put soldiers in a comatose state if they've been badly wounded in battle; it gives their bodies a chance to heal. It also has the effect of making a person look an awful lot like a cadaver."

Bryn traced the spiraling scarred mark with her eyes. "You could put Rangar in a death slumber?"

"No," Valenden countered, "*I* can't. There's no way I could get close enough to him to cast the spell; it requires tactile contact. The caster must mark the subject with ash. But if you can get on the hangman's dais, you might be able to. The spell suppresses the body's activities so that breath is not required but every ten minutes or so. As long as the noose doesn't snap Rangar's neck when he hangs, it won't matter if the rope suffocates his breathing as long as he's cut down within a few minutes."

It sounded like an extremely dangerous plan to Bryn—but nothing they'd done had been without risk.

"I'd have to get the hex," she said. "Is it within my skill?"

Valenden wavered. "It's an advanced spell, but with some practice, I believe you could master it. You learned quite a bit on our trek together."

Every time Bryn thought of doing magic, a thrill sizzled through her. The type of hex Valenden spoke of wasn't just inducing nausea or sparking a flame—this was major magic. If she cast the spell wrong, it had the potential to kill Rangar instead of rendering him comatose.

She folded her arms. "Put your shirt back on."

Valenden smirked as he drew the fabric back over his neck. "Too distracting, eh?"

She didn't even bother to roll her eyes. "Did Mage Marna come with you? She's the only one I'd trust to carve a hex that dangerous into my skin."

As he tucked his shirt back in, he said, "Only Calista could come. My father is ill, and my aunt and Ren had to stay with him in Barendur Hold."

Bryn found this news troubling on more than one front. If word got out that King Aleth was ill, their enemies could see it as an opportunity to attack the Baersladen, especially with Valenden, Saraj, and so many of their soldiers currently in the Mirien.

But also, though Calista had successfully carved

the finding hex into Bryn's shoulder, it had been a simpler one. Calista was only an apprentice, still learning the ways of magic herself.

Mam Nelle cleared her throat. "Illiana could do it, my lady."

Both Bryn and Valenden turned toward the seamstress, who had abandoned the pretense that she was merely sorting buttons and not listening in.

Bryn felt another curious tingle. Illiana had all but admitted that she dabbled in magic, but Bryn had assumed her knowledge was limited to a few herbal potions. "Illiana is a mage?"

"We call it other things here," Mam Nelle said quietly. She pressed her lips tightly together as she whispered, "A witch."

Magic had been forbidden in the Mirien as long as Bryn could remember, but she'd always been aware that it existed, practiced by mages and apprentices in the Outlands. As far as witches—women who used magic within the Mirien borders—she'd dismissed their existence as mere legends.

But like so many things, she'd been wrong about that, too.

"And she can carve hexes?" Bryn asked.

Mam Nelle answered by rolling up her shirt sleeve to her shoulder socket, where a hexmark so small it could be mistaken for a normal scar rested. She immediately hid it again.

"You didn't think I could sew that fast without magic, did you?" she whispered with a wink.

It took Bryn a moment to process the information that her dear elderly dressmaker had been criminally dabbling in magic her whole childhood, spurred on by her witch daughter.

She sputtered, "Do all the servants have—"

"Goodness, no," Mam Nelle said quickly. "Hexmarks are still rare in the Mirien. You won't find them but on a few of us in Mir Town, and on even fewer in the further villages. Illiana's the only witch in all of Mir Town."

Bryn turned back to Valenden. "This plan could work. It isn't difficult for me to meet up with Illiana in the castle's secret passages where Mars is hiding. She could perform the hexmark ritual there, and I'd have some days to practice the spell before the hanging."

"You'll need to find a willing victim to practice it on," Valenden pointed out.

"Mars faked his own death once," Bryn said. "I'd wager that he'd be willing to do it again, assuming Illiana is present in case anything goes wrong. All that's left would be to ensure someone on our side is able to get Rangar's body immediately after the hanging."

"Christof can find a few trustworthy lads," Mam Nelle promised. "The undertaker is always looking for boys willing to work with the dead. They could get your prince's body into the castle morgue, and from there, the passages."

"And then Rangar can hide out with Mars until we're ready for the uprising," Bryn added.

Valenden snorted.

"What?" Bryn asked.

"For a decade, your brother threatened to kill Rangar if he so much as set foot in the Mirien with his sights on you. And now you want the two of them crammed in a dark passageway together?"

Bryn frowned as she muttered, "I'm sure they can put the past behind them."

At least, she hoped they could. Mars might have changed his sentiments, but his temper had always rivaled Rangar's. He had looked ready to hang Rangar himself when Bryn had told him they were romantically involved.

"They don't have a choice," she concluded at last. "They'll have to tolerate each other."

Let them bicker and throw a few swings, she thought. She felt fairly certain they wouldn't *permanently* maim each other.

"Lady Bryn?" It was Sergeant Preston's voice coming from outside the tent. "Everything all right in there? You've been getting fitted for the dress for quite a while."

Valenden fell silent as his hand rested on the hilt of his sword.

"Yes," Bryn called. "We're just finishing now."

She hurried to adjust her dress so that it looked like she'd taken it off to be fitted for the wedding gown.

Mam Nelle whispered, "And of the real dress, my lady? Shall I make it to your old measurements?"

"With luck, I won't need a wedding gown at all," she muttered. "I certainly have no intention of ever marrying Captain Carr. But you'd better make one in case he gets suspicious."

"Consider it done. I'll tell Illiana to meet you tonight in the passages."

Bryn nodded.

Valenden rested a hand on her arm. "I'll let Saraj and the others from the Baersladen know what we've discussed. We'll be at the hanging, disguised as Mir common folk, with weapons at the ready should anything not go according to plan."

"Thanks, Val." She squeezed his hand, then nudged him toward the stall's rolls of fabric. "You'd best go wrap yourself up in velvet and hide again."

As Bryn and Mam Nelle left the tent, pretending to chatter excitedly about the wedding dress, Sergeant Preston seemed annoyed.

"We should head back to the castle, my lady. Captain Carr didn't want you gone this long."

"Of course. We mustn't keep the captain waiting."

She bid farewell to Mam Nelle, slipping her hand a squeeze, before climbing into her carriage.

As they returned to Castle Mir, Bryn watched out the window for a glimpse of Mir Town square. When they passed it, she tried to imagine what it would look like in another week with a gallows constructed. Was their plan a foolish one? Risking Rangar's life with dangerous magic? Was she even truly capable of performing a death slumber hex?

Tonight, she would find out—if her brother was a willing victim.

The rest of the day was heavy with tension. Captain Carr was in a foul mood after learning the soldier who'd accepted the rebels' bribe had died during interrogation before revealing the rebels' names. It made for a sullen supper between the two of them. Bryn tried to prattle on about the wedding dress, but Captain Carr only grunted in response.

If he was truly ever my husband, Bryn thought to herself, *I think I'd hang* myself.

She finished her meal as quickly as she could.

Captain Carr raised his eyebrow as she stood. "Retiring so soon? One would almost think you didn't wish to spend time with your fiancé."

She hesitated. "I'm sure you'll want to spend the evening with your advisors. I'd hate to be a distraction from all this nasty business with the rebels."

He leveled her a dark look over his wine glass. "Perhaps a distraction is exactly what I'm in need of."

Bryn's stomach tightened. Captain Carr had never requested to spend time with her after supper before, so she'd assumed it was safe to sneak off to the secret passages to meet with Mars and Illiana.

"Oh. Well, I thought I would have Lisbeth wash my hair this evening, and it does take a while to bring up heated bath water . . . "

"Nonsense. Your hair is fine." He stood up, draining his wine. "Come walk with me in the courtyard."

Bryn knew she couldn't decline without raising his suspicions. What if Sergeant Preston had told him about the abnormally long time she'd spent in the seamstress's tent?

He extended his hand. She swallowed hard before taking it. She forced a smile. "I'd be delighted."

Two soldiers trailed behind them as they made their way through the castle hallways. Bryn shivered, though it wasn't yet cold enough to need a cloak. The castle felt empty and lifeless since she'd returned. With most of the staff dismissed and replaced by soldiers, she felt more like she was living in an army barracks than a home that used to be filled with laughter, warm chatter, and delicious smells.

They crossed the ballroom toward the balcony that led to the remembrance garden. It wasn't but months ago that she'd been here on the First Night of the Low Sun Gathering, shocked to find that Rangar Barendur and his brothers had dared to return to the Mirien. She and Rangar had conspired together there, behind that tapestry. They had danced next to that now-cold hearth. He had first spoken Mir to her on this balcony .

. .

Captain Carr held the door open for her, and she stepped out, clutching her arms across her chest as she shivered.

"Shall I lend you my jacket?" he asked.

Bryn flinched.

Tonight, it is cold. Take my coat. It was like Rangar's ghost was here, offering her his bearskin cloak as he had that First Night.

"No, thank you," she answered now.

They descended the stairs to the remembrance garden, with its rosebushes that had become over-grown since most of the gardening staff was dismissed.

Bryn cleared her throat, wondering how soon she could acceptably take her leave. "I was thinking, for the wedding, we could have maiden roses on the—"

"Maiden roses? Bah. Weeds. That's the kind of rubbish they'd do in the Outlands. No, you, my lady, will have proper roses befitting a queen."

"Oh." She smiled tightly. "Good."

He asked in his rasp, "Did you have maiden roses at your wedding to Trei Barendur?"

She thought over her words carefully as she sensed a possible trap. "I did. As you said, they're hardly more than weeds, but in the Baersladen, it was the best flowers they had."

Captain Carr rubbed a hand over his rough chin. "Forgive the insensitive question, but the consummation of your previous wedding . . . I can only imagine what that savage prince thought he could do to you in the bedroom. Trei had a better reputation than his two younger brothers, but not by much."

Bryn felt her face burning both from embarrassment and rage. Was she really going to have to discuss sex with this old man?

She said curtly, "Ah. Yes, as you've pointed out, all the Barendur princes are . . . savage. Trei was no different."

Captain Carr stopped Bryn with a hand on her arm. Alarm shot through her. The guards had hung back on the balcony, she realized. She was entirely alone with him.

"I assure you, my lady, the bedroom can be as pleasurable as it was doubtlessly painful for you previously. Our wedding night is something I look forward to with great relish. You'll find me to be a gentleman in every way that your previous husband was not."

It was almost laughable, and hard for Bryn to keep a straight face instead of balking in fury. Captain Carr had once said vile things about her and her sister to his soldiers, things anyone would deem "savage."

He was the brute here, not Trei. Trei had demonstrated true nobility in every way. He'd struggled to walk the line between duty and love for another just as she had. He hadn't so much as touched her without the utmost respect.

"I have no doubt about that, Captain." Her stomach turned at the same time she painted on a smile.

Captain Carr touched a rough finger to her chin, tipping it up toward the moonlight. Bryn's heart thundered in her chest. She knew there was a gardener's entrance nearby—but if she dared make a run for it, Captain Carr would doubt everything about her.

"You're a very pleasing woman to look at, Lady Bryn," he rasped. "I'll soon be the envy of every man in the kingdom to have you beneath me."

Bryn suppressed a gag. Did the captain possibly think this talk was seductive?

She let her gaze fall as though in modesty, though in reality, she couldn't stand to look at him another second.

But he chuckled and ran a hand down her jawline, taking his time as though examining some new weapon in the arsenal. Finally, he brushed the calloused pad of his thumb against her bottom lip.

"You'll forgive me for wanting a taste."

She braced herself as he leaned in for a kiss. The words of the purge spell were on her lips, but she knew better than to use it again. It had been risky enough to perform magic once; the same spell twice would raise his suspicions.

And then it was too late.

His lips were on her. Captain Carr had the experience that came with age, and the kiss was surprisingly confident, yet there was nothing tender in it. This was the kiss of a man used to taking what he wanted, not sparing a thought for his partner's pleasure. His hand clutched her skull, trapping her in place.

Bryn closed her eyes and tried to think of something else. *Just get through it . . .*

His other hand clutched her waist, fingers digging

into her skin painfully. His body might be powerful even at his age, but it was an unyielding, cruel kind of strength. A touch that promised pain despite what he'd promised.

She turned her head to break the kiss as soon as she thought it safe to do so. Her whole body was trembling in disgust.

For a moment, Captain Carr kept his hand around her skull, not releasing her, as though debating whether he wanted to take more from her that night. But then he let go.

Bryn fought to catch her breath, trying hard to maintain composure.

Captain Carr raked his gaze over her. "Soon, Lady Bryn, I'll rule this kingdom as king with you by my side. I'm not such an old man that I can't sire an heir on you." He leaned in to rasp, "Believe me, I'm going to enjoy every minute of it."

CHAPTER 35

THE DEATH SLUMBER HEX . . . mead and herbs . . . a sharp knife . . . the beautiful new falconer . . . a hanging

Bryn's stomach churned as she crawled through the dark passageway. She still felt Captain Carr's lips all over her. His revulsive words about their upcoming wedding night echoed in her head.

Rangar will slit his throat, she assured herself with dark satisfaction. *If I don't do it myself first.*

She'd become familiar enough with the passages that she no longer needed light to find her way to the ground level where Mars had set up his camp in an old, unused coal storage area. The glow from a lantern shone like a beacon ahead.

"Bryn?" Mars's head turned toward her at the sound of her movement.

"It's me, Mars."

"We've been waiting all night. We feared you'd been caught by Carr."

Mars and Illiana sat on Mars's makeshift bed of blankets with several half-burned candles around them. Illiana's wicker gardening basket rested near her feet.

Bryn dusted off her hands on her dress as she grimaced. "I *was* with Carr. I couldn't get away. He thought he'd try to seduce me in the courtyard."

Mars frowned, and Illiana shuddered.

"That man acts noble enough when he has an audience," Illiana said, "but he's known to frequent the pleasure dens in Mir Town. The prostitutes whisper that he has vile predilections."

Mars let out a growl. "As though I needed another reason to hate that man, I now get to picture his hands all over my little sister. Are you all right, mouse?"

It meant something that Mars was concerned for her—she knew he'd always loved her, but he'd also been so duty-bound that a few years ago, he wouldn't have balked at the idea of an older man with a known cruel streak marrying his sister if it benefited their family's reign. He'd have told her to accept her duty and not complain.

Bryn shook off the remnants of the experience. "He's the kind of man who takes what he wants. I don't know how long I'll be able to put off the wedding."

Illiana started unpacking her wicker basket. Usually, it was filled with herb snip scissors and trowels, but today she unrolled a set of knives.

Bryn watched their blades gleam in the lantern light.

"Then let's not dally any longer," Illiana said lowly. "The death slumber hex is finicky. The carving must be precise—one small nick in the wrong place and it won't work. It's intricate, so it will take me a while. You must remain calm while I cut. Here. This will help."

She took a small glass bottle out of her basket filled with a chalky dark powder.

Bryn took it, holding it up to the light.

"Valerian root powder mixed with sedative herbs," Illiana explained. "It won't stop the pain, but it will make it more bearable. Rub it under your tongue."

Mars felt around his few belongings and produced a bottle of mead that he thrust in her direction. "I suggest you take a few swigs of this, too. An old army trick before a soldier gets surgery on the battlefield."

Bryn twisted open the bottle and rubbed the powder under her tongue. It tasted of ash and bitter herbs, and she was all too happy to wash it down with Mars's mead.

"You'll have to remove your blouse," Illiana said.

Bryn undid the buttons, sliding it off her shoulders, relieved that the bandages around Mars's eyes meant she didn't have to worry about her brother seeing her bare skin. She laid down on the makeshift bed. Illiana draped a cloth across her chest, then moved the candles to have the best light.

"It's ideal to carve a hex beneath bare moonlight," Illiana explained as she traced her finger over Bryn's shoulder, searching for the correct spot for the hex. "But we work with what we have."

She motioned to the old coal shoot, a narrow brick tunnel that led to the second-floor servants' balcony. A small beam of moonlight filtered through.

"Mars, I'll need you to hold her down. She can't move, or I could cut the mark wrong."

"Sorry about this, mouse," Mars said as he felt his way over and gripped her wrists above her head.

Bryn filled her lungs with steady, well-paced breaths. *I've done this before.* Because she'd already gotten hexes, however, she also knew how painful they could be. But she was no stranger to pain now.

If Rangar can withstand torture down in the dungeon, I can take a few cuts.

Illiana selected a knife. "Ready?"

Bryn gave a tight nod.

The valerian root powder and mead had unwound her fears a little. Her mind felt dulled, her muscles slack. When Illiana touched the blade to the place where her shoulder met her chest just above and to the side of her breast, she braced herself.

Illiana began muttering magical words as she pierced Bryn's skin. Bryn squeezed her eyes closed and grunted against the pain. Mars kept her wrists pressed steadily against the bedroll, making sure she didn't flinch.

Pain shrieked through her shoulder. A trickle of blood ran down her skin. She didn't dare open her eyes, as it was only in the darkness behind her eyelids that she could find the strength to stay perfectly still.

Rangar needs me. I can save his life.

During the weeks on the road with Valenden, she had practiced what little magic she knew, and he had shown her more of the possibilities of what hexes could accomplish. She knew in her heart that magic was the path forward for the Mirien. It was the great equalizer that would give power to the common folk. It would take time to change the Mir people's ideas about hexes, but with trustworthy people like Illiana and Mam Nelle, real change could happen.

And it starts with me, here.

Bryn kept her thoughts on Rangar to get through the pain. She imagined her success during the hanging. She'd come here after to revive Rangar and tend to him as Illiana had once done for Mars. She'd have Rangar in her arms again soon, and this time, they wouldn't let anything drive them apart.

Bryn's mind spun from the pain, the herbs, and the mead. She lost track of time as Illiana carved the spiral into her skin, then rubbed in ash to ensure it would scar.

Finally, the witch sat up, wiping her brow. Despite the cold, sweat beaded on her face.

"It's done. Don't move. Let me stop the bleeding."

Mars squeezed Bryn's wrists. "Nicely done, mouse. I don't know many trained soldiers who could take the pain without flinching."

Illiana cleaned the wound and changed the blood-stained bedroll linens, then pressed a clean bandage over Bryn's cut. "Because of where the hexmark is, I can't properly wrap a bandage. So you'll have to keep this compress on until the bleeding stops. Take care to keep it covered so no one sees it—your dresses should hide it unless the neckline is especially low."

With Mars's help, Bryn sat up slowly, holding the compress to the hexmark. She spared a brief glance down at it.

The mark was just above her breast, near her armpit. Illiana was skilled with the blade; it looked as cleanly carved as even Mage Marna's hex on her inner ear.

Bryn tested out tracing the shape in the air.

"Now," Illiana said. "All that's left is to learn the spell. *Ana somna mortinya.*"

"*Ana somna mortinya,*" Bryn repeated, whispering it until it was committed to memory. Then she turned to Mars, biting her lip. "There's one more thing, actually. I need to practice it on a real person."

Mars's face fell beneath his blindfold. "The things I must do for my kingdom. Very well. Put me in a death slumber, sister."

∽

Over the following days, Bryn spent her days going through the motions of planning a wedding that she had no intention of going through with. Each night, she snuck into the secret passages to practice the death slumber hex on Mars. The first time she'd tried it, black bile had bubbled up from his throat until Illiana had quickly whispered a spell to calm his stomach. The next night, Bryn had managed to induce a comatose state, but it only lasted a few seconds before Mars gasped for breath again. But by the fifth evening, when the hexmark was settling into the permanent scar, Bryn managed to put Mars into a death slumber for a full seven minutes.

The day before Rangar's hanging, Bryn convinced Captain Carr to allow her to return to Mam Nelle's seamstress stall in the market for another gown fitting. Valenden was waiting for her there, this time with Saraj and another falconer.

"Saraj!" Bryn threw her arms around her friend's neck, squeezing tightly. "I've missed you with all my heart."

"It's good to see you, Bryn." Saraj looked better than when Bryn had last seen her. That had been only a short time after Trei's death, and Saraj had been broken-hearted, looking like a shell of her former self. But now there was more color in the head falconer's cheeks, and her thin body had filled back out.

"Where is Zephyr?" Bryn asked of Saraj's falcon, who was usually perched on her arm.

"At our camp in Saint's Forest." Saraj motioned to

the other falconer, a beautiful dark-haired woman around Bryn's age. "This is Aya. She's been posing as a traveling acrobatics performer so that she can do reconnaissance around Mir Town."

Bryn recognized Aya, though they hadn't spoken before in the Baersladen. She'd kept a distance from Aya for a good reason: before Bryn had arrived, Aya and Rangar had been romantically involved with one another. Rangar had assured her Aya was merely a friend who'd occasionally warm his bed on a cold winter night, but it didn't stop Bryn from feeling a pang of jealousy to see the lithe, beautiful falconer now.

"I'm grateful you came all this way," Bryn said to Aya.

Aya held her head proudly, not the type to bow to a princess. "I'd do anything for Prince Rangar."

Bryn gave a tight smile she hoped didn't look nervous. "Wonderful."

Valenden laughed and clapped her on the shoulder. "Now, princess, we've been making our preparations for the hanging. Everything is as ready as it can be. Two of the rebels are working with the undertaker. You'll be ready to revive Rangar?"

"Yes. Mars and Illiana will be waiting to get him from the castle surgeon's chamber and smuggle him into the passages."

Valenden held up a finger. "One final thing. Has anyone actually informed Rangar that we don't intend for his hanging to succeed?"

Bryn hesitated. "There's no way for me to get a message to him in the dungeon, but I slipped him a note hidden in a ring box assuring him that we'd devise a plan to keep him alive."

Valenden scoffed. "If I were Rangar, a vague note wouldn't be much reassurance as the noose tightened around my neck."

"It's the best we can do," Bryn said. "He'll just have to trust us. To trust *me*."

Valenden drew in a breath like the world tried his patience. "Well, let's hope my brother doesn't stand on the gallows tomorrow with his Saved at his side, thinking she's happily sending him back to the gods."

CHAPTER 36

A PUBLIC EXECUTION . . . bloodlust . . . ashes and gloves . . . a forbidden touch . . . eternal trust

On the day Rangar Barendur was scheduled to hang, heavy clouds rolled in to blanket Mir Town. The promise of a storm crackled in the air, matching the dark excitement that coursed throughout the population.

Everyone is hungry for violence, Bryn thought.

Tensions had been high in the Mirien ever since the uprising that had killed her parents and left a question mark on the throne. Rebels anxious to see Captain Carr's head on a spike had sewn discontent among the servants and commoners who had come to suspect the captain's political aims were just as bad as his predecessors.

But if the populace couldn't get Captain Carr's head on a spike to quench their rage, it seemed they would settle for anyone's, include a rival prince's.

Bryn dismissed her maid, Lisbeth, for the day and dressed herself in a somber green dress, not wanting to risk the chance that her maid might see her fresh hexmark. Her hands shook as she tried to braid her own hair. She was confident in her ability to perform the death slumber spell—poor Mars had certainly undergone enough practice as a cadaver—but she didn't yet know how she would get close enough to Rangar to convey the plan to him. She couldn't let him see her standing between the hangman and Captain Carr and think *she* wanted him dead, too.

Besides, the death slumber spell required that the subject be marked with ash, which would require touching him.

She knelt next to her cold hearth, carefully dragging her index finger through the ashes. Then, she pulled on gloves.

When it was time to climb in the carriage to ride to Mir Town square, her nerves were on fire. Settling on the bench seat next to her, Captain Carr rested a hand on her knee.

"You look beautiful, my lady. I daresay everyone will be looking at you instead of the criminal."

She gave a quick, distracted smile.

His hand tightened on her knee in a threatening way. "You seem anxious."

She stilled her gloved hands in her lap. "Oh—I

suppose the idea of the gallows makes me jumpy. It reminds me of what happened to my mother. To my sister . . . "

"It's fortunate that Lady Elysander escaped the noose. As for your mother, though it is a sad fate, she had to pay for her crimes."

Crimes you're equally guilty of, Bryn thought with simmering anger.

"Well," she said in a clipped tone, "At least we know that the common folk will never want *our* necks in the hangman's noose once we're married. I'm sure you'll be a magnanimous king."

He didn't seem to pick up on her sarcasm as he squeezed her leg again, this time higher up her thigh.

As much as she wanted to shove his hand off her, she called on her patience and gave him a practiced smile. "I'd hoped to exchange a few words to the prisoner before the executioner does his job."

"What could you possibly have to say to Rangar Barendur?"

She leaned in conspiratorially toward Captain Carr, making sure he got a good view down her neckline to distract him. She purred, "I want Rangar to know that we won't stop at his death. That your guards will soon hunt down his traitor brother, Valenden, and make sure he joins Rangar and Trei in death, so all the Baer princes' lines will end."

Captain Carr barely seemed to hear her with his attention on her neckline. He cleared his throat. "You have a vicious streak, my lady."

"Only for those who have wronged me. And who have wronged *you*."

The carriage entered the town square, and Bryn glanced out the window. The square was packed with common folk from all over the Mirien who had traveled there to witness the hanging. Food vendors even walked around selling roasted meat on sticks as though Rangar's death was a carnival.

Overhead, the clouds rumbled with thunder.

Bryn's stomach roiled as they descended the carriage and made their way toward the hangman's dais. She squeezed her gloved hands, reassuring herself that her finger was marked with ash. Captain Carr had commanded most of the Mir army to be on hand, a precaution in case the rebels might use the occasion to attempt another uprising.

A line of soldiers led to the gallows, holding back the crowd.

Bryn's heart pounded as she lifted her skirt to climb the wooden steps. The executioner was already there in his black mask, as well as Sergeant Preston and Lord Tarry. Her eyes latched onto the noose dangling from a wooden brace.

Where was Rangar?

The crowd roared as Captain Carr and Bryn took the stage to join the others. Captain Carr exchanged a few words with his advisor, and then lifted his hands to address the crowd.

"People of Mir," his rasping voice rang out. "Today my bride receives her second engagement gift, which in keeping with tradition, is actually a gift for the entire kingdom. Today, an enemy of the Mirien hangs!"

The crowd cheered. Bryn watched them eating their roasted meats and felt sick all over again, though she knew the common folk couldn't be blamed for their bloodlust. They'd been told that Rangar was a villain, and she herself had attested to it.

She searched the crowd closely, hoping to spot a familiar face. Valenden, or Saraj, or Calista, or any of the Baer soldiers she'd known from her time in the Outlands. But the crowd was too tightly packed. Everyone wore cloaks against the coming storm with raised hoods hiding their faces.

She had to trust she wasn't alone. Somewhere, Valenden and the others were out there.

Captain Carr wrapped his arm around her shoulders, and she snapped back to attention. He announced, "By marrying the crown heir to the Mir throne, I shall soon have the blessing of serving as your king. Lady Bryn and I both vow we will not lead this kingdom down the same dark path as the previous rulers. Together, we will usher in a new era of strength and prosperity. Let this execution today be the symbol of the Mirien's new future!"

The crowd cheered. Bryn couldn't help but wonder if the crowd believed Captain Carr's speech or if they were merely playing along. She hoped they would embrace Mars as their king as readily as they seemed to embrace Captain Carr. It was true that Mars had failed them once, but she trusted that if given a second chance, he would repair the damage done.

"Bring out the prisoner," Captain Carr ordered Sergeant Preston.

All other thoughts evaporated from Bryn's head.

She turned toward the soldier's station within the city wall. Two soldiers emerged, pulling along Rangar between them. His hands were bound with rope. His hair was mussed and caked in dirt.

Fury laced Bryn's breath. They hadn't even let him bathe before his execution. She would make sure that Captain Carr would pay dearly for what he'd done to Rangar.

As the soldiers started up the dais with Rangar, Bryn couldn't keep her hands from shaking no matter how hard she clasped them. He stepped onto the platform, and their eyes met. Bryn's breath stilled. How badly she wanted to wash the dirt off his face, kiss each of his scars. She dared to raise an eyebrow in a hint of a question.

He gave the barest nod.

He got my note in the ring box, she reassured herself.

Was that the reason no fear showed on his face—because her note had assured him Valenden was back and they had a plan? Or was it simply Rangar's bottomless courage?

He met Captain Carr's eyes boldly, and the captain stiffened.

"Prince Rangar Barendur of the Baersladen is an enemy of the Mir people!" The captain yelled in his rasping voice. "He absconded with the Lady Bryn, a daughter of the Mirien, and conspired with his brothers to take the Mir crown for his own family. His blood will fall on Mir soil!"

Bryn ignored the din of the crowd. She glanced at Sergeant Preston and the executioner as she plotted when would be the right time to approach Rangar. She tugged off her gloves, tucking them into her dress's sash. A streak of ash still clung to her index finger.

She leaned toward Captain Carr. "Let me say my piece to the prisoner, Captain."

But Captain Carr dismissed her with a condescending hand pressed to the small of her back. "I shall handle it myself, my lady."

He addressed the crowd again and said, "Rangar Barendur's blood is not the only Baer blood that shall soon fall. I vow to you today that his brother, Prince Valenden, will also pay for his crimes with his life!"

Bryn tried to hide the panic that crossed her face. No, no, no. *She* was supposed to have said this directly to Rangar as an excuse to get close to him. She passed a worried look to Rangar, then leaned closer to the captain, careful to keep her index finger from wiping off the ash. "I wanted to tell him myself—"

"Nonsense. You have no business going near that filthy prisoner." His hand tightened around her waist possessively.

She felt sick all over again. This was wrong, all wrong. If she couldn't get close enough to Rangar to perform the hex, he'd hang for real . . .

"I'm not feeling well," she gasped, knowing her pale face would look convincing. "I fear I need to sit . . . "

She stumbled away from Captain Carr toward the stairs back to the carriage but then made a show of tripping. She made sure she fell near Rangar.

Even with his hands bound, Rangar immediately moved to break her fall. She grabbed his shoulder with one hand, pretending to steady herself as the crowd gasped to see their princess touch a dirty prisoner.

"Trust me," she whispered urgently, searching Rangar's eyes. "I promise you won't die."

His brown eyes burned into her with the same intensity of the building storm overhead. And then Captain Carr's soldiers grabbed her away from Rangar, rushing to get her to safety. Bryn swiped her bare index finger against the scar that ran across his cheek a second before they led her away. The trace of ash from her fireplace left a mark against his skin.

She felt her breath coming fast. It had been a risk to touch Rangar publicly, but she had to mark him for the spell to work. It was fortunate the ash blended in with the dirt already streaking his face.

Captain Carr strode over with angry steps. "Lady Bryn. Are you all right? He didn't hurt you?"

"I'm fine," she said breathlessly, raising a hand to her head. "I was just dizzy . . . I was headed for the carriage to sit, and I stumbled."

The captain narrowed his eyes. Perhaps the pretend fall could be overlooked as clumsiness, but he had seen her tenderly touch Rangar's face with her bare hand.

There was no explaining that away.

Suspicion was clearly written on his face. Captain Carr hadn't fully trusted her since she'd returned; if he hadn't needed her as much as he did, she doubted he would have believed a word of her story about being imprisoned against her will in the Baersladen.

Now, she had to hope that he believed she'd touched Rangar's face because of secret affection—it was a dangerous truth, but it was better than him guessing that it had to do with magic.

His jaw tightened as he stepped toward Bryn. His whole energy had shifted; the undercurrent of threat that he usually masked with composure reared up now, fully aimed at her. He leaned in close enough so only she'd hear while he pretended to straighten her skirt out of concern.

"I don't know what existed between you and that Baer prince, but it doesn't matter now. He's going to die whether you love him or not. So I hope you said your goodbye."

He drew back, motioning sharply to a soldier. "She isn't feeling well. Take her to the carriage. Keep a close eye on her."

The soldiers forcibly led her off stage under the guise of helping a woman who'd apparently taken ill. The crowd was awash in murmurs. Some of the gossip reached Bryn's ears as the soldiers led her through the throngs.

"*. . . such a delicate constitution . . .*"

"*. . . too much for a lady to take, she shouldn't have been so close to the noose . . .*"

"*. . . It shows she's not bloodthirsty like the old king and queen . . .*"

At least the crowd didn't seem suspicious of her—they'd been too far away to see how she'd touched Rangar's face.

As the soldiers thrust her into the carriage and closed the door sharply, she heard Captain Carr address the crowd again. Bryn pressed her hands against the carriage window, locking eyes with the stage. The soldiers had led Rangar to the trap door beneath the noose. The executioner lowered the rope around his neck.

"Rangar Barendur, for your crimes, the kingdom of the Mirien sentences you to hang!"

Alone in the carriage, no one watched when Bryn raised her hand and traced the spiraling death slumber hexmark shape in the air.

She'd have to time the spell perfectly. Too soon, and Rangar would pass out before the hanging, and it would be clear that someone was interfering with magic. Too late, and the noose would do its job.

Please don't let it snap his neck . . .

She had to trust that Rangar believed her message that they wouldn't let him die. If he took care to fall at an angle, swinging rather than dropping directly down, there was a much greater chance his neck wouldn't break.

The executioner gripped the trap door's lever.

"For the Mirien!" Captain Carr yelled.

The executioner pulled the lever. The trap door fell. Rangar plunged downward. Bryn gripped the carriage door handle with white knuckles—

The rope went taut, but Rangar's body convulsed —he was choking, but he hadn't snapped his neck.

"*Ana somna mortinya,*" she whispered quickly.

His body stilled at once.

It all happened fast. He hung at the end of the rope, looking for all the world like a cadaver, red-faced and utterly without breath.

The crowd cheered.

Bryn buried her face in her hands, unable to look at the boy swinging at the rope's end, terrified her hex might not have worked—and Rangar Barendur was dead.

CHAPTER 37

THE POWER OF MAGIC . . . a long awaited reunion . . . two ghosts . . . "when are you going to be mine?"

"Where is he?" Bryn couldn't move fast enough through the hidden passage into the old coal room. "Where's Rangar? Is he alive?"

After her stunt during the hanging, Captain Carr had posted extra guards at her door, which had meant that to escape, she'd had to climb out her window and into Elysander's old room. She'd cut her hand on one of the rooftop's iron nails. Blood stained her sleeve, but she could hardly focus on anything other than ensuring her spell had worked.

Mars and Illiana crouched over a bedroll lit by

candles and lanterns. Bryn spotted Rangar's bare feet, cold and still. As panic flooded her, she shoved her way between her brother and the witch.

"Rangar!" she cried.

He lay on the bedroll looking pale. A rope burn circled his neck, but his eyes were open.

Bryn collapsed next to him, stroking his matted hair. "Thank the Saints—I can't believe it. You're alive!"

Rangar reached a hand to cup her jaw, brushing his thumb over the same place on her cheek where she had marked him with ash. "You said to trust you. I did. I always have."

She threw her arms around him, then immediately thought better of it, and pulled back. She patted her hands over his body to ensure nothing was broken. "And you're well? Are you weak?"

"From my time in the dungeon, yes," he admitted. "But nothing a few days of ample food and rest won't mend. I'm afraid I might sound like your fiancé for a while, though."

He touched his hand to the rope burn around his throat. His voice was slightly hoarse but nothing like Captain Carr's heavy rasp.

Rangar suddenly grabbed her wrist. "Bryn, you're bleeding."

"It's nothing," she said dismissively. "I had to climb onto the roof to get out of my bedroom."

Rangar sat up, reaching for a rag they'd stuffed in a

pillowcase as a makeshift pillow. He ripped it into a long shred and started wrapping it around her palm.

"Here, let me," Illiana offered. "You should rest."

Rangar seemed reluctant to turn over Bryn's care to anyone else, but Illiana was already pulling herbs out of her basket. She set to cleaning Bryn's hand and rubbing in an herbed salve.

"I'm glad you're here," Illiana said to Bryn, then gave a slight wink. "It hasn't been easy being a buffer between these two." She nodded between Mars and Rangar.

Bryn had been so concerned with Rangar's state that she hadn't noticed the tension between him and Mars. Her brother leaned against the wall, toying with a knife. He must have dedicated a good deal of time practicing with it, because even blind, he wielded it with the swift grace of a street performer.

Bryn rested her hands on her hips. "Mars, are you being beastly to Rangar? After he nearly died?"

Her brother scowled. "I know he matters to you, Bryn, but I'll never understand why. I spent years protecting you from him, and you ran straight into his arms."

Rangar raked the hair off his face, his scars flashing in the lantern light as he turned toward Mars. "I saved her life while you drank and chased girls in the ballroom."

Mars's hand tightened on the knife hilt. "You're a guest in *my* kingdom, savage. If you wish to still be welcome once I'm back on the throne, you'll watch your words."

Bryn could tell that a barbed response was posed on Rangar's tongue, but she held out her hands as though separating feral dogs.

"Stop it, both of you. I won't have you two fighting. For what it's worth, Mars, I saved Rangar's life, as well. The *fralen* bond goes both ways now. If he ever owned my soul, then I own his now, too."

This had the effect of quieting the two princes, though the tension was still palpable.

Illiana chuckled. "Lady Bryn is right. If the two of you must trade barbs, do so after we've retaken the throne, eh? Can we agree on a truce for now?"

Rangar wiped a cloth over his face, giving a tight nod.

Mars sighed. "Very well. But we shall discuss this further at a later date, savage."

"After I help you retake your throne?" Rangar threw out. "You'd best not make threats when you're too weak to fight. You couldn't even see danger coming. You need this 'savage' to do the fighting for you—"

"Enough!" Bryn grabbed the cloth from Rangar, dipped it into a water bucket, and rang it out. "Rangar makes a good point, Mars. He, Val, and two dozen Baer fighters have traveled across the Eyrie to help you retake the Mirien. The least you could do is show some manners."

Mars grumbled but acquiesced. "I'll admit that the savage has come up with a decent plan, at least."

Bryn dabbed the damp cloth against Rangar's face, washing off some of the dirt. "Tell me."

In his hoarse voice, he explained, "As I understand it, Mir tradition allows for three engagement gifts. You used the first to slap me. The second you used to hang me—"

"But I—" Her jaw fell open, ready to protest, but he cocked a grin.

"I know, I know—you did what you had to. I don't hold it against you, my love. In any case, you have one gift remaining."

Her brow wrinkled. "That may be true, but I doubt Captain Carr will be inclined to honor any more gifts. When I touched your face at the hanging, he surmised that we'd been lovers. He's suspicious of me now. He's posted extra guards at my door."

"He won't refuse a third gift," Rangar stated, pausing to clear his sore throat. "Not if you make the request publicly. Otherwise, he would have to explain why he refused, and he won't be inclined to admit that his fiancé had an affair with a rival prince."

She raised an eyebrow. "So what do I ask for?"

"To visit Saint Serrel's water shrine with him before the wedding." Rangar motioned toward Mars. "Your brother says it's a common place lovers go before their union to drink from the sacred waters and receive a blessing. Make it sound like you're trying to get back in Captain Carr's good graces. To prove you're sincere about the wedding, and that I was only a passing affair. His ego will force him to believe it. He thinks I'm dead, anyway. Hardly a rival for your hand now."

Saint Serrel's shrine in Saint's Forest was the place Bryn had snuck off to ten years ago to see the rumored black fawn whose presence predicted war throughout the Eyrie. She touched her ribcage, thinking of the scars there and the matching ones that marred Rangar's face.

When she met his gaze, she knew he was recalling the same night.

"And assuming he agrees?" she asked.

"Then Valenden and our Baer soldiers will be lying in wait to attack."

"And Christof and the rebels will be with them," Illiana added.

A chill seemed to grow in the air. Bryn could already foresee the battle that would most likely happen at the water shrine: blood mixing in the sacred water, arrows piercing the aspens. It was a risky plan. Captain Carr wouldn't go anywhere without a fleet of well-trained, well-armed soldiers. Would the rebels and a few Baer fighters be enough to defeat them?

"All we need is to dispatch Carr," Mars explained. "Once word gets out that he's dead, I'll storm the throne room with the rebels. The kingdom's advisors will have no choice but to accept my claim as legitimate king."

Bryn hugged her arms, staying quiet as she

thought through the plan. Rangar brushed his thumb over her cheek. His dark eyes searched hers, asking a question.

Quietly, she confessed, "I almost lost you today. We didn't survive the wolf attack at the water shrine all those years ago just to go back there and have it be *our* carcasses staining the water this time."

Rangar stroked her long hair. "We've defied death before. We will again."

Bryn leaned into his palm, letting her eyes sink closed.

Illiana cleared her throat. "Mars, I think we should leave these two to reconnect. I need to get back to the kitchen before the night cook notices I'm gone, anyway. Come with me. I can hide you in the pantry. This late, there's only a few nearsighted old maids awake. It'll be good for you to get some fresh air outside of these passages."

Illiana took his hand, guiding him to his feet. Mars paused and jabbed a finger in the air in Rangar's general direction. "Watch your hands, savage. That is still my sister, and she is still not yours to do with as you wish."

Rangar's answer was the ghost of a smirk. "Isn't she?"

Mars reached for his knife, but Illiana grabbed his wrist with a roll of her eyes and led him down the passage toward the kitchen.

In the lantern light, Bryn studied Rangar. He was still filthy from his time in the dungeon and weakened from the hanging, but a fire blazed in his dark eyes.

She picked up the cloth and then dipped it into the water bucket. "Let me help you bathe—it looks like you haven't seen soap in weeks."

"I haven't," he admitted.

His gaze explored as he watched her wring out the cloth. She brushed his tangled hair back from his face, dabbing the cloth against his temples.

Goosebumps ran up and down her arms to be this close to him again. She wiped the cloth along the contours of his face, then rinsed it and repeated until the water turned black. When she reached his neck, dusted with several days' worth of beard, she toyed with his shirt's top button.

"I'd like to throw these filthy clothes in the fire. I see Illiana brought you fresh ones."

His lips hitched in a smirk as he lifted his chin, giving her better access to his buttons. "By all means, princess. If there's one thing I'd love most in this world, it's to have your hands on me instead of these soiled clothes."

A fluttery sensation beat in her chest as she slowly undid his shirt buttons and then smoothed the disheveled fabric off his shoulders. He'd grown leaner in his time in the dungeons of both Barendur Hold and Castle Mir. His muscles were wiry, taut. She traced the cloth over the hexmark scars carved into his flesh, pausing at his own death slumber hex near his underarm.

"Illiana gave me this hex," she said softly as she dabbed the cloth over his mark. "Did you know there were witches in the Mirien?"

"I'd heard rumors. I suspected magic was practiced here on some level."

"It bodes well for introducing magic to the kingdom in the future. If it's already quietly practiced, the populace will be more likely to accept it." She rung out the cloth again, satisfied she'd gotten the worse of the grime off him.

"Have you discussed bringing magic to the Mirien with your brother?"

"Not yet, but Mars knows Illiana's abilities. I'm confident he'll see it as the best way forward."

Rangar brought a hand up to run his palm over her sleeve, squeezing her shoulder. "Speaking of your brother, what do you make of his command not to touch you?"

Bryn boldly met his eyes. "Mars isn't my king yet."

Rangar's hand moved to her neck. He guided her toward him until his lips scorched their way across her cheek, settling on her lips.

Bryn threw herself into the kiss. Her arms slid over his bare shoulders, hands locking behind his neck. She crushed her lips to his, wanting to taste all the familiar parts of him she'd been craving.

He vocalized a moan as his hand raked down her back. "By the gods, Bryn. I've wanted you in my hands every cursed day."

She answered by trailing kisses along his cheeks,

his forehead, his scars, wanting to cover every inch of him with her lips. She pulled her skirt around her knees so she could straddle the place where he reclined against the wall with his legs extended.

He gave a slight hiss as her weight settled on him.

She gasped. "Is this too much for you? You're still weak—"

He gave a husky laugh. "It isn't too much. Gods, it isn't even close to being enough. Come here."

He gripped her around the hips and secured her position against his lap. A flood of desire rushed up through Bryn as she pressed her hands over his scarred chest.

She closed the distance between them. Her lips possessed his, and he answered by dragging his teeth across her lower lip. She gasped as she locked her hands on the hard edge of his shoulder muscles, holding on to keep herself steady.

His muscles tightened beneath her palms. Her own body flushed with warmth and a desire to feel him touching every inch of her. His grip around her waist grew more intense. He kneaded the fabric like he wanted to tear it off.

Then, he broke the kiss, one hand cradling the back of her head as he pressed his forehead to hers.

She wasn't sure which one of them was breathing harder.

"Bryn Lindane," he said in his hoarse voice. "I asked you to marry me once. I've endured seeing you married to one brother and posing as the wife of the other. Now you're wearing the engagement ring of my enemy. When are you going to be mine?"

"Now," she whispered breathlessly. "And forever."

"I want it official. I want my ring on your finger. I want to call you wife."

She nodded against his forehead, her gaze locked to his. "I'll marry you, Rangar Barendur."

He kissed her with a passion matched only by her own as their hands drifted and caressed and squeezed, and Bryn felt the premonition that tonight might be her last as a maiden.

CHAPTER 38

THE THIRD GIFT . . . jealous of those who came before . . . a trip to the water shrine . . . fire and ash

Alone in the secret passages, lantern light flickered over Bryn and Rangar's bodies entangled together.

"Your wedding night with Trei . . ." Rangar started gruffly.

Bryn shook her head quickly. "We didn't consummate the marriage. Trei could think only of Saraj, and I . . ." She wet her lips, chest rising and falling fast. "I couldn't bear to be touched by anyone but you."

His eyes simmered with desire. "And the nights on the road with Valenden? Do you know how it tortured me to think of you sharing beds in roadside inns with him?" His hips shifted under her with urgency.

"Believe it or not, Val kept his hands to himself."

"He knew I'd murder him if he touched you."

She leaned back, taking him in, and gently brushed her finger over his lips.

Rangar gripped her by the back of the neck, and thoughts of his brothers vanished from her mind. His body's desire for her was becoming more and more obvious as she straddled his waist, their hips pressed together.

She brushed her lips close to his ear. "I'm innocent if that's what you're asking. No man has taken my virginity by force, and I haven't given it to anyone."

"Virginity isn't prized in the Baersladen." His voice was guttural. "It's backward to demand women not enjoy themselves when men are free to."

She raised an eyebrow. "I take it you're quite experienced, then?"

Her words were flirtatious, but in truth, her heart was pounding. She knew Rangar was hardly a virgin. Trei and Valenden had both told her of Rangar's sexual prowess. She couldn't stop thinking of Aya, the falconer. Such a strong, beautiful girl—how many times had she been in Rangar's bed?

"One of us should be." His voice was low as he stroked a curl off her face. "Does it bother you?"

She tried to banish the thought of Rangar and Aya from her mind, but it lodged there like a stubborn thorn. "No. Yes. I don't know—I suppose I'm jealous of the girls who came before."

A wicked smile crossed his face as he adjusted her

in his lap. "Every one of them knew my heart belonged to the youngest Mir princess. I've been ridiculed for a decade for being in love with a girl I barely knew. I've endured it enough. I want you, Bryn."

There was a question in his words, and she felt an overwhelming wave of nerves. She licked her lips again, then met his eyes.

She nodded.

He took her lips in a slow, stirring kiss. He tasted of salt and bitter herbs, and her stomach rumbled. He slid his arms around her waist in a claiming gesture, his fingers pulling at her dress's fabric.

"The buttons," she whispered, feeling breathless. "They're in the back."

He helped her turn around on his lap and then bent her down as he went at the buttons. Though she could feel his urgent desire in the tightness of his muscles, he took his time. He freed her from the cloth, then drew it down over her back.

She tugged the sleeves down her arms, wriggling free of the garment. She raised her hips to let him slide it over her curves.

As soon as she was free of the dress, left in only a scrap of a chemise that barely covered her hips, she tried to turn around to face him again, but his fingers splayed over her backside, thumbs pushing up the chemise's hem.

"I've fantasized about this," he said low. "About driving into you. Sinking deep. Filling you up with my seed."

A shock of energy jolted through her, making her jaw slacken.

His hands wrapped around her hips, fingers digging into her hip bones. She tipped her head back as he gently palmed her breast through the chemise, teasing her nipple.

"You gave me back my ring." His voice was a gentle chastisement.

"I had to," she panted, pressing her breast harder into his grip. "It was the only way I could get you the message—"

"I want it back on your finger." His lips grazed her ear. "I want it to stay there this time."

She moved in for a kiss, but he captured her wrists, sitting up. He guided her back against the bedroll. Balling her chemise in one hand, he raised it over her head, then set it aside.

Leaning over her, he took the time to let his gaze inspect every inch of her bare skin before reaching for his belt.

"By the gods, Bryn. You're the most beautiful creature I've seen in this world or shall ever see in the next."

Breathless, Bryn relaxed back against the bedroll as she watched him shed his trousers. There was nothing between them now, not a stitch of clothing. She'd never seen him completely bare. The hexmarks scarring his chest and arms were like a map to unlock secrets she'd only wondered about.

She wanted to touch each of them. To kiss them, to feel his magic.

He took his place on top of her, holding himself up with one hand. His cock was positioned between her legs. She eased her legs open to grant him access, but he didn't take advantage.

"What are you waiting for?" she whispered.

"I want your first time to feel exquisite," he said. "There's no rush." He dragged his hand from her neck down to the hollow between her legs, his finger stroking and probing. Her lips parted as invisible flames sprang to life at her core. Rangar was rarely gentle like this, and she was torn between wanting to savor his tenderness and begging him to take her in a rush of passion.

He watched her steadily as his fingers continued to stoke the fire between her legs until she was letting out little moans of pleasure. Finally, he lifted an eyebrow in a question.

"Please," she whispered. "Take me."

His hand wrapped around his cock, pressing the tip against her swollen heat. She spread her legs, wriggling to get the pressure she craved.

With a slow thrust, he entered her.

Her eyes sank closed as she let out a soft cry. There were a few moments of pain as he stretched her with slow thrusts, holding himself back from the heady abandon she knew he wanted.

As the sting subsided, she opened her eyes.

Locking eye contact with him, she angled her hips

to nudge him in deeper. He needed no more encouragement than that. He sank all the way into her with one hard thrust. She cried out, and he fell on her with his lips, taking her mouth in a kiss. He drove into her again. Bryn arched her back, twisting the bedroll in her fists, feeling the need to hold onto something.

They rocked together to meet his thrusts. Her nerves burned with pleasure. A flush of warmth was building in her groin, urging her to grind harder against him.

He suddenly grabbed her shoulder, pinning her down as he pressed into her with a final thrust. A moment of pleasure shuddered across his face, and then she felt an equal sweep of release.

He sagged against her, sweaty. The candles flickered low, almost burned out. Bryn's body trembled from the aftermath of their coupling. Her thoughts felt floaty. Her vision blurred.

Rangar took a moment with the rag to clean up his seed on her and the spot of blood.

She reached for her chemise, but he shook his head. He drew her to him on the bedroll, holding her naked body flush to his, burying his face in her hair.

"Stay with me tonight, princess."

It was risky. The guards could discover she wasn't in her room. But if anything was worth the risk, it was this.

~

"Lady Bryn. You're late to breakfast."

Captain Carr looked up from his correspondence as Bryn entered the dining hall in the morning, sitting down to cold eggs and tea. She felt the heat of his scrutiny.

He continued, "The guards said Lisbeth arrived at dawn to lay a fire in the fireplace. She knocked, but you didn't answer. The door was locked."

Bryn picked up her knife and fork, trying to play it off with a casual shrug.

I still smell of Rangar.

"I was utterly exhausted," she explained. "I didn't even hear them knocking. I suppose yesterday's excitement was too much for me."

Captain Carr watched her in a straight-forward way that didn't try to hide his suspicion. "The crowd enjoyed watching Rangar Barendur die."

She took a bite of cold toast. "Indeed they did."

He angled his head. "You didn't appear quite so amused, I noted. In fact, there were whispers that your faintness came from seeing your paramour in a noose."

The dry bread felt like sand in her mouth. She swallowed it down with cold tea. "I'm a lady, Captain Carr. My faintness came from the proximity to violence, nothing more. As for the rumors, those are nothing new. The Barendur brothers intentionally spread lies that Rangar and I were romantically involved in an attempt to mask their crimes. I told you when I arrived that there was nothing to the rumors."

She went on eating as though nothing was amiss, though her heart was racing. Was he going to press her about the moment when she'd touched Rangar's face? Or had he tortured her enough for one morning?

He folded his hands slowly, calloused thumbs rubbing together. "I suppose it doesn't matter. Not anymore. Whether he was your lover or not, he's supper for the worms now."

She paused, then took another sip of tea. She had to be careful now. Between the guards and the servants, there were at least ten other people in the room—enough of an audience.

She softened her expression. "I can tell the rumors trouble you, as they would any man. It would please me if there was something I could do to put your mind at ease."

She set aside her napkin, then stood and took a few slow steps to his end of the table. He straightened to give her his attention, though it was still laced with suspicion.

"I was thinking of ways I might show my affection." She trailed her hand along the tablecloth. "I still have one engagement gift remaining. The first two were all about exacting revenge on Rangar Barendur, but I'd like the third one to be about you. About us."

Her fingers reached his hand, and she skated her fingertips over his skin.

He studied her hand on his and then asked, "What did you have in mind?"

"Saint Serrel's shrine. It's where my parents went

to receive a blessing before their union. We can take a procession. For protection in these uncertain times, of course, but also to make a statement. We'll pass through Mir Town and the villages along the forest's border so that everyone may whisper new rumors about the devotion of the princess to her future king."

She squeezed his hand and said, "I want so badly to prove my devotion."

Captain Carr slowly placed his other hand on top of hers. His skin was rough like sandpaper. His touch was too hard.

He slowly lifted her hand to his lips. "As you wish, princess."

She offered him an adoring smile despite how her stomach roiled. Her body recalled all too well his awful embrace in the remembrance garden.

He pressed his lips to her hand. A cold kiss. Utterly unmoving. If Rangar's kiss was the hottest part of a fire, Captain Carr's was the cold ashes left behind.

"It will take a few days to organize security for such an excursion. On the eve of the next full moon, we'll depart." He tugged her closer, bending her ear toward his lips. "And afterwards, in my chambers, you'll show me more of that devotion you speak of."

Her skin crawled. She wanted nothing more than to jerk her hand out of his grasp and use it to slap him.

Still, as she had no intention of him continuing to live after the moonlit procession, it was easy for her to smile. "It will be my pleasure, Captain."

CHAPTER 39

THE MOONLIT PROCESSION . . . feigned illness . . . arrows . . . not true love . . . the ultimate rogue

It was fortunate that the next full moon wasn't for almost a fortnight, as Rangar needed the time to heal. Once he had regained most of his strength, Illiana helped smuggle him out of the castle to Mir Town, where he was able to rendezvous with Valenden in Mam Nelle's seamstress stall and, from there, abscond to Saint's Forest, where the rebels were preparing for their attack.

Bryn heard of all these developments secondhand from Mars on the few occasions she dared venture into the secret passages. They went over the plan's details again and again to ensure they'd be prepared for any surprises.

Bryn feigned more faintness as an excuse to stay away from Captain Carr. On the occasions when he came to visit her in her room, she made sure Lisbeth remained present and coughed so voraciously that she hoped she'd seem unappealing. Still, it didn't stop the captain from making every excuse to touch her: feeling her forehead for a fever, adjusting a wrinkle in her blouse over her breast, brushing a crumb off her lips.

Every time he touched her, she burned with fury.

On the night of the full moon, her nerves were frayed when the procession to Saint Serrel's shrine was ready to leave. Besides their carriage, Captain Carr had assured her that most of Castle Mir's soldiers would accompany them in front and behind for protection. She dressed in a simple, dark green gown with no train, reasoning that it would be easier to flee into the woods in such a gown if anything were to go wrong. Though she wore Captain Carr's ring on her finger, she dared to drape her chain with Valenden and Trei's rings between her breasts.

Soon, she would add Rangar's to it again.

In the courtyard, soldiers on foot and horseback were already in formation as they waited for the carriage to drive up. Captain Carr dropped a hand around her waist. He gave a possessive squeeze. "Feeling better, I hope?"

"A bit, yes. The prospect of the procession has cheered me."

She shifted, trying to move away from his hand, but at that moment, Sergeant Preston appeared steering the carriage. It was the close-topped carriage they had used for her trips into Mir Town.

Oh no, she thought in dread. Rangar and the rebels had made their attack plans anticipating an open-top carriage.

Bryn's spine went rigid. "I, ah, I'd hoped for an open carriage to see the moon on our drive."

Captain Carr waved away her concern. "It's safer this way, my lady. We don't want another incident with the arrows."

She pressed her lips together tightly. That was *exactly* what she wanted.

"Besides," he added off-hand, "It looks like it will rain."

It was true that dark clouds were rolling in from the south, but for now, only broken clouds shaded the moon.

The carriage stopped in the courtyard's center, and Captain Carr helped Bryn into it. She settled onto the center of the bench seat, hoping the captain would sit opposite her, but he stared at her hard until she scooted aside to make room for him.

His weight settled next to hers, the bench seat groaning.

"Go," he called to the driver outside. She heard the soldiers ahead of and behind them call commands to one another, and the procession began.

The windows were open, and Bryn could feel the fresh night air on her face. She watched the forest roll by outside, its trails and glens so familiar to her, though at night everything looked different. With the bright moon shining down, the forest details were strangely illuminated. She found herself looking twice at every shadow, wondering if she saw the shape of a person hiding in it.

Her hand went to the chain around her neck, toying with the links, not daring to touch the rings hanging from it.

"I didn't realize you were so interested in Mir tradition," Captain Carr observed. "The moonlit procession is an old practice. I don't believe I've heard of anyone doing it in decades."

"My mother used to tell me about it," Bryn explained. "The moment she drank the water was the instant she fell in love with my father. Theirs had been a strictly political union until then."

He gave a harsh laugh. "Your parents were never in love."

She'd carefully prepared to act her way through the entire evening, but she couldn't hide how this genuinely flustered her. "Pardon?"

As far as Bryn knew, her parents had been in love. In every speech, her father professed his devotion to her mother. She used to overhear her mother brag to the other royal women about her father's romantic nature. But now that she thought about it, she realized she'd only ever heard them vocalize their affection for one another in public. She'd never once seen them embrace while alone.

"Your parents shared a political goal," the captain

said. "An ambition. That was all. They didn't spend a moment with each other they didn't have to. They each had, if you'll excuse me for speaking ill of the dead, paramours."

Bryn didn't think she could still be disappointed by her previous naiveté, but now she found herself feeling lied to all over again.

Captain Carr pursed his lips as though pitying her, though it held a twinge of mockery. "My lady, you didn't really believe they were in love, did you? Ah, you are such a young, pure-hearted thing. Taking the world at face value." He lowered his voice. "No wonder you fell for that savage prince. Don't try to deny it—I saw the way you looked at him. But I don't blame you. Men like him know how to lead a simpleminded thing like yourself astray."

He reached for her cheek, but she turned her face away sharply. Then, she realized what a dangerous mistake that could be and, thinking better of it, placated him with a smile.

"Yes, I suppose I'm fortunate to have you to guide me. Your keen sight sees the truth in everyone. You saw Rangar for what he really was—a brute."

He smiled. "The Baer prince is a threat no longer. I know that his death must likely still be painful for you, but in time, you'll understand he was using you for your crown." His eyes dropped to her chest. "I'm sure your body was a pleasing bonus for him."

The way he regarded her made her skin go clammy. The carriage felt too small and stifling. She wanted desperately to throw open the door and run out into the woods to put distance between them.

Soon, she told herself. *It will all be over. By the night's end, he'll be dead.*

The carriage bumped over a root, and Captain Carr grabbed her knee to steady her. When the path evened out, he left his hand there.

"I will make you forget about that wild prince," he promised in his rasping voice. "He might be younger than me but certainly not more appealing to the eye. Not with those scars."

Bryn couldn't believe the man's arrogance to think he, at his advanced age, could be any physical rival to Rangar Barendur.

He cocked his head at her silence. "Ah. Maybe you liked the scars, is that it? You surprise me, my lady. Well, then I should definitely please you."

He traced a finger along the red line that crossed his neck. Bryn was grateful for the low light, hoping it hid the contempt she couldn't keep off her face.

He leaned forward, this time succeeding in capturing her jaw. "Kiss me, Lady Bryn."

She stuttered a nervous, "Later tonight, Captain. After the moonlit procession. That's what we had discussed, was it not?"

His fingers were rough on her cheek. "What's the difference between a few hours?"

She tried for a laugh that didn't bring any lightness to the situation. "I'm thinking of the Saint Serrel waters . . . the tradition."

He dragged his thumb over her bottom lip as though he wanted to snare it between his teeth. "Ah, I see. You were hoping that once we'd sipped from the waters, you'd fall in love with me like your mother claims she did with your father. You'd be less repulsed by an old man you have no choice but to marry."

"That isn't it at all," Bryn whispered insistently.

"Let go of those childish notions," he growled, his voice even raspier than ever. "It's time you became a woman, Bryn. I watched you grow from a tiny thing into a girl every man in the castle had his eye on. And now it's my bed you're going to warm after our wedding. But we needn't wait until then."

He lunged at her for a kiss. The carriage was so tight that when she recoiled, her shoulder hit the opposite door. There was nowhere to go.

Had he planned for this? Was this why he wanted a closed carriage, so he could ravish her here?

Undeterred, his hand tightened on her knee, squeezing its way up her thigh. His other hand clutched her jaw like testing a ripe peach for freshness.

His lips found hers.

This can't be happening, she thought. She had felt safe putting off his romantic advances until later that evening, knowing that Rangar and Valenden were lying in wait just ahead to slit his throat.

She wrapped her hand around his wrist, trying to free her face from his grasp, but he was too strong for her. His lips were unrelenting as they drank deeply from her. His tongue forced its way between her teeth.

I should bite it off, she thought angrily. But she had to play along with the ruse until they reached the water shrine.

"Captain, please." She managed to twist her head away, fighting for breath. "This is hardly the place. Let your advances wait until after we're out of this carriage."

He answered by groping her upper thigh, fingers digging into the folds of clothing between her legs. He chuckled darkly. "I've let you have your way for long enough, Bryn. I've been patient. Someone has to take charge now."

She fought off his hands with as much vigor as she dared.

"You're no virgin," he sneered. "Trei Barendur already had his cock between your legs. So don't play the part of a modest bride now. Fortunately for you, I don't mind a tainted woman as long as she's still young enough to be tight for me."

Alarm shot through Bryn. Glancing outside the carriage, she recognized a pair of towering oaks. They were halfway to the saint's glen, but it would still take at least ten minutes to get there.

Enough time for Captain Carr to force himself on her.

Struggling against him, she dropped the pretense. "So, your true nature comes out. You speak to your future bride like she's a common whore."

He sneered in derision as he gripped her hips,

pulling her toward him. "You're the one who came to me begging for a place at the castle again."

"It's my castle! I'm the crown heir!"

"A woman can't lead the Mirien. You need me to marry you so your claim is valid. So if I were you, I'd lay back, spread your legs, and be grateful for my charity."

She nearly choked on her disbelief that he would speak to her like this. It was no surprise that this was how he truly felt, as she'd overheard his soldiers repeat similar vile things he'd say previously, but she didn't think he'd dare speak so bluntly directly to her.

He dug his hands into her thighs, trying to force her legs apart. She scooted as far back as she could on the bench seat, lifting a foot to try to kick him. But her skirt got in the way, and he captured her leg, dragging it up over his lap.

His other hand gripped her wrist to pull her in for another kiss.

She shrieked and fought against him. The driver must have heard her distress, but he didn't stop the carriage, loyal to Captain Carr even when he was performing a crime.

She flashed a glance outside, trying to place where they were. She recognized a group of boulders flanking the path.

We're getting close. I just have to hold him off a few more minutes . . .

He grabbed her by the back of the head, pulling her skull back so he could slide his tongue between her lips. She bucked her hips, but this only seemed to excite him.

She slapped at his shoulder, trying to push away. Her fingers twisted in his shirt, and she heard the fabric rip at the shoulder seam.

As she struggled, she glimpsed his bare shoulder in the moonlight through his torn shirt.

A hexmark was scarred into his skin.

She sucked in a breath and held it, frozen. "You have magic," she finally gasped in accusation.

He leveled her with a cold smile.

Captain Carr, along with her parents and the other advisors, had been the staunchest critics of the Outland kingdoms for their use of magic. They'd called magic sinful. They'd derided it as nothing more than parlor tricks. They said it was backward, against science.

Fresh rage curdled in her chest. She made a fist and pounded it against his arm. "You have magic! Such hypocrisy from what you preach!"

He caught her wrists, giving her a dangerous look. Clearly, he'd never wanted her nor anyone to find out about this. Now it made sense why he always wore such heavy shirts even in summer.

"You'd do better to keep your mouth shut and your legs open, Lady Bryn. I'm growing impatient with it being the other way around."

He lunged for her again.

CHAPTER 40

THE BATTLE OF SAINT SERREL . . . a parent's lies . . . a spark and fire . . . brothers at war . . . fallen friends

Of all the hypocritical, disgraceful sins that Bryn knew Captain Carr to be guilty of, it had never once entered her mind that he might have magic.

It was one thing for a witch like Illiana to work for the Mir common folk, but for someone as high ranking as Captain Carr to be fully versed in hexes was inconceivable. Did *all* the Mirien's advisors have the ability to cast spells, she wondered?

"My parents?" she murmured.

Captain Carr gave a snide laugh, her wrists still trapped in his fists.

"They both cast magic. A mage from Ruma came once a year to the High Sun Gathering to train them in new spells and carve fresh hexmarks."

Now, everything began to make sense. This was how her parents were able to stay in power for so long despite their poor leadership, why their trade deals with the other kingdoms always worked in their favor, how Mir crops were always so prosperous, and the army nearly undefeated.

My parents had magic.

Shock gave way to anger. Her whole life, Bryn's mother and father had preached the benefits of science, hard work, and innovation to the common folk, discouraging magic as backward. They rooted out any evidence of magic, making an example of anyone caught using hexes by imprisoning them in a pillory in Mir Town square. And all of that, Bryn realized now, was to cover their own use of magic. If the common folk had magic, then they'd have more control over their own lives—as Bryn had witnessed in the Baersladen—and less need for a king and queen.

Captain Carr's hands tightened on her wrists. "Had we more time, I wouldn't mind your struggles. The look of fear in a woman's eyes can be exciting, in fact. But I want you now, before we reach Saint Serrel's shrine. You've seen that I have hexmarks—I won't hesitate to use them to fill your body with pain unless you make it easy for me. It's up to you."

The carriage was slowing. They were close to the shrine—it was just around the next bend.

She had no ash, so even if her hands were free, she couldn't mark Captain Carr to perform the death slumber spell on him to incapacitate him. Still, there were other spells that didn't require ash, though they *did* require use of her hands.

She lunged forward, closing her teeth around the captain's ear. He cried out, shocked. Blood poured down his face, and he instinctively clapped his hand over the wound.

As soon as he'd released her wrist, she traced the purge hex shape in the air.

"*En videl*," she whispered.

He immediately clutched his stomach with his free hand. The blood drained out of his face. His eyes locked onto her, filled with rage.

"You duplicitous little whore! You accuse *me* of magic when *you*—"

He stopped short, pressing his lips together against the bile rising in his throat. He turned sharply away, bracing a hand on the side of the carriage.

Bryn scrambled as far away from him as she could. The saint's glen was just ahead. She could already hear the burble of the stream running alongside the path. She'd risk throwing herself out of a moving carriage if she had to . . .

She reached for the door handle, but Captain Carr grabbed her foot to pull her away from it.

He snarled, "I should have known those Baer savages would tempt you with magic. It was you the night of the engagement, wasn't it? *You* made me vomit. What hexmarks do you have? Let me see your arms . . . ”

He was sweating now as he fought against the purge spell's effects. He tore at her shirt, trying to rip it off her chest and shoulders to see her hexmarks. She shrieked as she fought him off, still attempting to reach the door.

He ripped her dress's neckline, tugging the fabric roughly off her and down over her bare shoulder.

The death slumber hex flashed in the moonlight.

He froze.

“I know this mark . . . ” And then his jaw tightened. “It feigns death. Rangar Barendur—he isn't dead, isn't he? You *whore* . . . ”

He doubled over suddenly as the purge spell seized control of his stomach, making him vacate his stomach onto the carriage floor. While he heaved, Bryn threw herself at the door.

She tugged the latch open—

Just as the carriage pulled to a stop.

“We've arrived, Captain,” Sergeant Preston called from the driver's seat outside. “Shall I . . . give you a moment?”

He'd heard their struggles and her shrieks, Bryn realized, and he wanted to let the captain finish the job of ravishing her.

Still vomiting onto the carriage floor, Captain Carr wasn't able to answer.

Bryn gave him one more hateful look before throwing open the door. She was about to hurtle outside when an arrow suddenly slammed into the carriage's side.

Another arrow shot out of the forest to strike Sergeant Preston in the neck. The driver screamed and fell out of his seat, slamming to the ground as blood poured from the wound.

Bryn tossed a look toward the dark forest, searching for a sign of the rebels. Her heart pounded frantically.

"Come back here, you bitch . . . " Captain Carr, wiping his mouth, reached for her through the open door.

She picked up her torn skirt and stumbled toward the glen. It was a sin to step in the spring's water, but she didn't have much choice. She had to keep out of the way of the arrows and plunging underwater was her best option.

More arrows zinged through the air, aimed at the Mir soldiers that were on foot and on horseback behind the carriage. The soldiers immediately drew their swords.

Captain Carr cursed, lunged for her, and dragged her back inside the carriage. He slammed the door closed, barricading them inside.

"You warned the rebels," he seethed. "You set up an ambush!"

Battle cries rang out in the forest as rebels and Baer fighters descended on the procession. The clank of colliding swords echoed among the trees along with the sound of arrows.

"You're right about my hex," Bryn spat at him. "Rangar is alive. He's leading the ambush."

Captain Carr sneered, "You think he'll save your life again?"

She grabbed a bottle of liquor that the captain had packed as an offering to the saint's shrine. He held up a hand to protect his face, but she smashed it against the side of the carriage, not him.

"I don't need Rangar to save me."

The alcohol's sticky-sweet smell permeated the tight space as it soaked into the walls and seats. She traced a shape in the air, then whispered, "*Kora yoquin.*"

A flame ignited in her palm. She thrust it toward the dripping liquor, which caught fire immediately. An entire wall of the carriage erupted in flames.

Captain Carr coughed against the smoke. He drew his sword with one hand and gripped Bryn's arm tightly with the other, refusing to let her go.

She clawed and kicked at him. The flames spread, singing her hair. Outside, battle cries rang out along with the clink of steel blades. Through the window, she glimpsed cloaked rebels engaged in combat with Captain Carr's golden-armored soldiers.

"Let me go!" she shrieked.

Captain Carr dragged her away from the flaming wall toward the opposite door—

But the door was suddenly flung open.

Rangar stood in the opening with a sword at his side.

He took one look at Captain Carr and then Bryn's ripped gown. With a growl, he grabbed the captain's shoulder and pulled him out of the carriage.

Captain Carr fell onto the ground amid the battling soldiers and rebels. He drew his sword, but Rangar slammed a fist into his face before he could strike. Rangar dug his boot against the captain's torso, pinning him to the ground, while he held out a hand for Bryn.

"Hurry," he barked.

She was all too eager to be out of the flaming carriage. She fell into Rangar's embrace, fingers latching onto his shirt as their eyes met.

"By the saints. Rangar . . ."

Sparks shot out from the carriage, and Rangar shielded Bryn as he moved them back toward the trees. Now freed, Captain Carr lifted himself onto his hands, coughing. Smoke poured out of the carriage, blinding Bryn and Rangar.

The captain shoved to his feet, swinging back his sword—

"Rangar—watch out!"

Before Rangar could move away, a falcon shot out of the smoke, clawing at the captain's eyes.

Captain Carr growled and swung a hand at the falcon. It flapped away, but a second falcon immediately launching itself at the blood seeping from his ear wound where Bryn had bit him.

The captain cried out in pain.

"Zephyr!" Bryn gasped, whirling toward the forest.

Saraj and Aya stood at the edge of the trees, dressed in forest-brown cloaks, commanding their falcons with hand gestures. Saraj's falcon's talons dug into the captain's cheek. Aya's falcon went for his eye, but the captain was too fast. He ducked it just in time.

Saraj whistled loudly and made a gesture. Zephyr swooped down on the carriage that was now engulfed in flames. The falcon plunged into the carriage, and then burst out moments later with a piece of burning wood in its talons. It dropped it into the center of the fighting soldiers, who scrambled back from the sparks.

The Mir soldiers tried to fall back into the northern woods, away from the fire and the rebels, but Calista was waiting for them at the edge of the shrine. She had her hands raised in the air and was focused on the soldiers who were scrambling out of the way of the flames. She traced a hex symbol in the air, and the babbling water from Saint Serrel's shrine rose as though swept up by a great wind, forming a shield of water to keep Christof's rebels safe from the fire.

"Bryn, get somewhere safe!" Saraj shouted.

"Come on," Rangar commanded, tugging her toward the forest. She glanced back over her shoulder at Captain Carr, who was bleeding badly from his wounds but still standing. Aya's falcon, Hurricane, was circling him for another dive-attack. On the other side of the clearing, Bryn spotted Christof leading a group of rebels, protected by Calista's wall of water, to push the soldiers toward the fire.

As Bryn and Rangar took cover among the trees, a

figure in a hooded cloak materialized out of the shadows.

"Valenden!" Bryn cried.

He thrust back his hood over his tangled hair, giving her a quick nod. "Now who's saved whose life, eh?"

But his joking tone ended swiftly as his attention returned to the battle. "It looks like Christof's rebels and our Baer fighters have the soldiers blocked off to the east. Saraj and Aya are preventing any escape to the west with their falcons, and Calista has the northern woods closed off. If the three of us can keep Carr and his soldiers pinned from the south, we'll have them."

Rangar drew his sword. "We can hold them."

Bryn's heart lurched into her throat. She'd finally caught her breath—easier said than done when one was panting and chugging like a runaway horse—and had turned around to face the enemy forces. The Mir soldiers were drenched with sweat, huffing and puffing under their heavy armor so close to the fire, and wielding their swords like men possessed.

"Bryn, stay back," Rangar warned as the soldiers took the only open path available—south—which directed them straight at Rangar and Valenden.

Battle cries rang out as the soldiers clashed swords with Valenden and Rangar. But the Mir soldiers' heavy golden armor weighed down their movements. Dressed in lightweight breeches and cloaks, Rangar and Valenden had more freedom of movement. Their Baer military tactics mimicked nature—swift like the wind, fluid like water—giving them the upper hand against the Mir soldiers' more formal training.

"Aim for their sides!" Bryn yelled to Rangar. "Their armor is weakest there!"

As the Baer princes fought against the soldiers, a caw caught Bryn's attention. Captain Carr had managed to grab Aya's falcon's wing. Though Hurricane beat his other wing hard against the captain's face, he hurled the bird to the ground and slammed his sword into its chest.

Bryn could only watch in horror as the bird died.

"No!" Aya cried out from the forest's edge, rage contorting her face.

Captain Carr, dripping with blood, pulled the dead falcon off his blade and swung around, breathing hard, until his gaze fell on Rangar, who was locked in swordplay with a hulking Mir soldier. Rangar's back was turned to Carr.

Carr raised his sword again—he had a clear shot at Rangar's back.

Bryn didn't think; she just reacted.

She swiped a finger against the burning carriage, coming away with a streak of black ash. Bunching her muscles, she rushed toward Captain Carr and smeared the ash on his bloody cheek.

"*Ana somna mortinya,*" she hissed, tracing the death slumber hexmark in the air.

Captain Carr's attention shifted from Rangar to

Bryn. He clapped a hand on the ash mark. "What did you do?"

"The death slumber hex."

The captain watched her in disbelief for a moment, then his eyes glazed over, and his sword dropped from his fingers. He collapsed like a marionette whose strings had been cut.

Rangar whirled toward Bryn, his eyes wide, his sword still raised. The giant Mir soldier lay slain at his feet.

"Bryn, are you all right?" Rangar demanded as he stepped protectively between Bryn and the fallen captain. "I told you to take cover!"

"He's still alive," she said between breaths, dismissing Rangar's worry. "It's the death slumber. He'll wake in a few minutes."

"No, he won't." Rangar drew a knife from his side and offered it to Bryn. "Do you want to slit his throat or shall I?"

Bryn's eyes widened, but then she accepted the knife from Rangar's hand. "I'll do it," she said grimly.

Rangar nodded. "Don't let anyone tell you that a princess cannot also be a savage."

Bryn knelt beside the captain. She didn't want to be responsible for anyone's death, but if she and Rangar were to escape, she had no choice.

I'm not like him, she told herself, willing her hands not to shake. *I'm not like Carr. I'm not like my parents, either.*

She straddled the captain's comatose body,

pressing the blade against his neck where his red scar already mapped out the cut mark.

"You will *never* be king," she said.

She thrust the knife into his jugular, hacking her way through his neck. Blood poured out. The spell kept him comatose as his life drained away.

A Mir soldier suddenly broke away from a fight with Valenden and rushed toward them, but Rangar easily fought him back, stabbing his sword through the man's chest.

Valenden staggered over, breathing hard, and took one look at Carr's body. He gave a grim nod. "Bryn, you must hurry back to Castle Mir. Christof's rebels and our fighters will finish off the soldiers here. You must get word that Carr is dead."

Rangar pressed a hand on the small of Bryn's back, urging her toward one of the horses, who stood wild-eyed in the middle of the creek. He splashed into the water, capturing the horse's reins, and guided it over to a stump on the stream bank.

"After you, princess."

Rangar helped her climb on the horse, and then swung up behind her. Wrapping a steadying arm around her waist, he squeezed his heels.

As the horse took off, the remainder of the battle raged around them. Fallen rebels lay on the ground, but the dead were mostly made up of Mir soldiers in their golden armor, which was now caked in blood and ash. The fire had fully engulfed the carriage, sending sparks up into the night.

Calista maintained the wall of water, continuing to shield the rebels from the flames. But a shape moved in the stream behind her. A Mir soldier had submerged himself and was now rising from the water with a knife raised—

"No!" Bryn shouted, but it was too late.

The soldier thrust his blade into Calista's back. The apprentice gasped, her body going stiff. The wall of water instantly collapsed, splashing over the entire battle.

With her dying energy, Calista spun toward the soldier. She made another hex symbol in the air, and bright blue light engulfed him. Grabbing his throat as though he was choking, he collapsed.

A second later, Calista fell beside him.

"No!" Bryn shouted again.

Rangar tightened his arm around her waist and whispered fiercely in her ear, "There's nothing we can do for her now."

He kicked the horse into a faster gallop. Saint's Forest was a blur around them as the stead's hooves tore up the mulched path, fleeing from the smoke and screams.

Back to Castle Mir, she thought.

Back to Mars.

Time to put the correct family on the throne, now and forever.

CHAPTER 41

BACK FROM THE DEAD . . . the rightful heir . . . a surprise announcement . . . "make me your wife"

I lliana was waiting for them in Castle Mir's courtyard, pacing anxiously with a lantern raised against the dark clouds overhead. She rushed over as soon as Bryn and Rangar's horse galloped to a stop.

"It's done?" Her voice was breathless.

Rangar swung down from the horse, then reached up to help Bryn dismount. Even when her feet were safely on the ground, he locked a hand around her waist, unwilling to be parted from her.

"Carr is dead," Bryn reported. "The battle is still going on, but the rebels are winning. They need only dispatch the final few Mir soldiers. It won't be long now."

"And my brother?"

"Christof was alive and well when last I saw him," Bryn reassured her. "He's a strong fighter."

Illiana whispered a prayer of gratitude under her breath. Then she raised the lantern and ushered them toward the door she had propped open.

"Bryn, your brother is outside the throne room, hidden on the balcony. He's ready to take the throne and declare his rightful rule. We need only gather the advisors as witnesses."

"I'll get them," Bryn said confidently. "They still believe me to be the crown heir. They'll listen to me even if they don't wish to. Rangar, help Illiana get Mars into the throne room. Once they realize he's blind, they might question his ability to lead. We need him to appear as kingly as possible."

Rather than answering, Rangar's hand tightened on her back. He took a moment to brush her tangled hair off her face. "You're all right, Bryn?"

She hadn't realized until that moment how tightly wound she was. She flinched as she thought of Captain Carr's attack in the carriage, his harsh words, and his even more violent hands as he'd torn her dress. Though it had been no pleasure to thrust the knife into his neck, she was glad he was dead.

"I'm all right," she reassured Rangar. "Or at least I will be once Mars is on the throne."

"Be careful," Rangar urged. "I only now have you back—I can't lose you again."

She brushed the pads of her fingers over the scars on his face. Maybe it had been fate that the battle had taken place at the location where their lives had first collided. Months ago, she would have scoffed at the idea of fate, but now she was becoming a believer.

"You won't lose me," she promised. "Not ever."

She tore herself away from Rangar, lifting her tattered skirt to hurry up the stairs to the ballroom.

Most of the Mirien's soldiers had been commandeered to accompany the moonlit procession, so only a handful remained to guard the castle. As Bryn raced up to the two guards stationed outside the ballroom, they drew their swords in alarm to see her disheveled.

"My lady . . ." One started.

"Captain Carr is dead," she cut him off firmly. "Wake Lord Tarry and Lord Gerbert. As crown heir, I'm ordering all the kingdom's advisors to the throne room immediately."

The soldiers looked uncertain but did as she commanded, heading to the apartments in the east of the castle where the advisors slept.

She found two more guards beside the stairs to the royal apartments and sent them to wake the remaining advisors and senior military staff.

Before heading back to the throne room, she glanced briefly up the stairs toward her old bedroom. She was covered in blood, ash, and mud, and her dress was torn scandalously over her chest. It was no kind of way to appear as her brother was named king—and even more importantly, the death slumber hexmark was visible on the bare skin that showed through the tear. If the advisors saw it, they would know of her use of magic—and yet she couldn't afford the time to change.

So be it, she thought. *They think me merely a pawn. Let them see me as I truly am.*

She strode down the hall to the throne room. Several servants in thrown-together clothes were scurrying around the halls, lighting the lanterns. They gave her messy appearance startled looks.

"Mars!" Bryn cried in relief as she entered the throne room and caught sight of Rangar and Illiana leading Mars toward the pair of thrones. Her brother wore a crisp black band around his eyes as well as fresh clothes and their father's silk mantel. He looked every bit a king.

"Bryn. My dear sister." Mars held out his hand, and when she slipped hers into his palm, he squeezed it. "You made this happen. You and the Baer princes." He angled himself toward Rangar's direction and said loudly, "I am in your debt, Prince Rangar."

They were interrupted by the sounds of footsteps in the hall. Lord Tarry, wearing hastily donned clothes, his gray hair still messy from sleep, strode in.

"What is the meaning of this?" Lord Tarry froze when he spotted Mars. His face went as pale as if he'd seen a ghost—which he perhaps thought was precisely what he was seeing. "Prince Mars? You're . . . you're alive!"

Lord Gerbert entered behind him and drifted to a stop with equal shock on his face. A few soldiers came in behind them along with some servants. Whispers began to run wild throughout the gathering crowd about the prince who'd returned from the dead.

"Illiana," Mars stated. "Lead me to the throne."

Illiana helped him make his way there, where he sank into the bronze chair with a straight back. With his chin high, he announced, "Yes, Lord Tarry, as you noted, I am indeed alive. Which is more than I can say for the usurper, Captain Carr. His lies led me astray when I took the throne after my parents' death—and I shall generously assume that he lied to you as well, unless you wish to be associated with a traitor, but now I know my proper place."

His fingers curled firmly over the throne's armrests.

Despite the late hour, the throne room quickly filled with the remainder of the shocked advisors, servants, and common folk who'd heard the rumors and rushed to see the truth with their own eyes.

A few minutes later, Christof appeared at the throne room entrance.

Bryn sucked in a relieved breath.

The battle must be over.

Blood streaked Christof's arm, but he appeared to be otherwise unhurt. As the crowd parted for him, he strode directly to the throne and leaned close to Mars.

"My king, the battle is won." Christof reported. "Baer fighters, along with our own rebel forces, are surrounding the castle as we speak. Any Mir soldiers remaining here will be given the choice between swearing loyalty to you, or death."

Mars gave a decisive nod.

Christof straightened and moved back to stand next to his sister, who pressed her face against his shoulder in relief. Bryn felt a swell of disbelief—she never dreamed she'd actually be standing in Castle Mir again with her brother on his throne.

Mars announced to the gathering crowd, "Thanks to our Baer allies, my sister Lady Bryn and I have restored our family to its rightful place. Lady Bryn has agreed to willingly surrender the title of crown heir back to me, and I am grateful for her loyal service. The Mirien owes a great debt to her."

Bryn kept her chin high, though her body was shaking. For a second, she wondered if she was doing the right thing by giving up the crown. But she had to admit to herself that she'd never had any real aspirations to lead the Mirien. Her heart's true desire was outside of this throne room, far away in a windswept, seaside kingdom.

She took Rangar's hand, squeezing it. His eyes rested on the curves of her face, memorizing the way she looked in the early-morning light.

"However," Mars continued in a loud voice, drawing Bryn's attention back to the present, "Though the Lindane family belongs on this throne, the

Lindane legacy does not. For too many decades, the previous king and queen, our parents, exploited this kingdom and its people for their own gain. Their tactics were dishonest, duplicitous, and despotic. Under my reign, prosperity will reach all Mir citizens: royals and common folk alike."

Louder chatter spread throughout the crowd in the throne room. *An uprising doesn't happen every day*, Bryn thought to herself. *And they're witnesses to history.* Several servants ran off to spread word of what was happening throughout Mir Town. The advisors stood stony-faced, looking utterly shocked by Mars's proclamation.

Mars held out his hand, palm-up. "Illiana Joster, please come here."

The herb mistress looked surprised to hear herself summoned, and quietly moved to take Mars's hand. He closed his fingers over hers, then stood.

"As a symbol of the new direction of this kingdom, and a testament to my promise, I wish to make another vow. Illiana Joster is a Mir commoner that many of you know. She serves the castle as the herb mistress and is daughter to the realm's longtime dressmaker, Nelle Joster." He paused briefly, taking a deep breath, before facing Illiana instead of the crowd. "Illiana, would you do me the honor of accepting my hand in marriage?"

A shocked hush fell over the crowd. Witnesses of all ranks were too stunned by Mars's declaration to speak.

Illiana looked most speechless of all as she pressed her free hand to her lips.

Lord Tarry stepped forward, sputtering, "My lord, no king has ever taken a commoner to wife before. It breaks the kingdom's covenants."

"It breaks tradition," Mars agreed. "But I would argue that Mir tradition needs breaking. As for the covenants, you'll find there is an exception to be made if the king is married before his coronation."

"An exception? If there is, I've never heard of it," Lord Tarry countered.

"I take it Lord Gerbert is present, yes?" Mars asked. All eyes turned to the portly advisor with the bulbous nose. "Lord Gerbert instructed me in the political arts, including the covenants. Please, explain it to them, Lord Gerbert."

Lord Gerbert, uncomfortable being the center of attention, cleared his throat. "I believe Prince Mars is referring to the rule that a royal child who isn't the crown heir is allowed to marry a commoner. If that royal child, through a sibling's death or another unforeseen reason, were to become crown heir at a later date and was already wed, the commoner woman would be allowed as queen."

Lord Tarry was red-faced as he argued, "Prince Mars *is* already the crown heir."

"Not yet," Bryn piped up as she began to understand Mars's plan. "I haven't yet formally relinquished my claim on the crown. If Mars is married before I do, then he can marry a commoner and assume the crown afterwards. What my brother suggests might bend the rules but doesn't break them."

"Thank you, mouse," Mars said quietly to Bryn.

Illiana pressed one hand to her chest and squeezed Mars's hand with the other. She whispered, "Mars, are you sure about this?"

Bryn was close enough to hear her brother say, "I've never been surer of anything, Illiana. Not only do I want you by my side, but I need you. To be my eyes. To be my heart. To guide me where others have led me astray in the past."

Chatter was running wild throughout the throne room as more townspeople and servants flooded the castle to witness this historic occasion.

Illiana ducked her head with a slight grin tugging at her lips. "I accept, my king."

Mars held up their clasped hands in a gesture of triumph as he announced, "The new Mir queen comes from the common folk. Our marriage shall join royalty and commoners in union, just as this kingdom shall break the despotic divide from the past!"

Applause erupted among the crowd, led largely by the servants and common folk. The advisors clapped less enthusiastically, but it was clear they'd weighed their options and decided it was most prudent to support Mars's claim.

While all the attention was on the Mirien's new king and future queen, Rangar drew Bryn close to his side a few paces away from the throne, pressing a kiss to her temple. His voice was soft as he said, "It looks like you'll soon be relieved of your duty as crown heir."

She leaned into him, resting her head on his shoulder. "The kingdom will be in good hands with Mars and Illiana. They'll bring in a new era of change. Of greater equality. Maybe even of magic."

"And once you are free to live as you wish, where will you go?"

There was a rare playful note to his voice, and she grinned up at him knowingly. "I told Mars we would stay to help him with the transition. A few months, perhaps. Through the winter."

"And after that?"

She rested a hand on his chest. "You already know the answer to that, Rangar."

"Do I?"

She laid her fingers gently over the scars crossing his temples, thinking of her own matching ones across her ribcage. As a wide smile bloomed across her face, she said, "Take me home to the Baersladen and make me your wife."

Cheers continue to fill the throne room at the announcement of Mars and Illiana's wedding, but as Bryn pressed to her tiptoes to meet Rangar's lips in a kiss, she felt the thrill of a bold new future for her and Rangar, too.

Together at last. No dungeon bars between them. No other engagements. It was simple: She belonged to him, and he belonged to her.

The Eyrie might still be on the eve of war, but her heart was finally at peace.

CHAPTER 42

NEWS FROM HOME . . . a music box . . . clean sheets . . . an unwanted interruption . . . chaos

It felt strange to Bryn to have Rangar Barendur standing in her childhood bedroom.

She hung back in the doorway as she watched her prince move in a slow circle over the woven rug, examining the gilded decor that couldn't be more different from Barendur Hold's heavy oak furniture. In his bearskin cloak, with his back to her as he picked up her old music box from the dressing table, he looked every bit the shaggy bear she had once mistaken him for.

At eight years old, she'd misheard "princes of the *Baer*" as "princes of the *bear*" and thought the three untamed brothers in their bearskin cloaks were like

411

the creatures out of Nan's story, animals who turned human beneath the full moon.

I wasn't so wrong, she thought wryly to herself, watching him. Rangar, Valenden, and Trei all had possessed the qualities of a bear: strength, perseverance, and an uncultivated spirit she found intoxicating.

She strode into her room to join him, picking up the music box, an ingenious device that played a plinking tune and spun a mermaid carved of abalone shell.

"This was a gift to my parents on the occasion of my birth," she explained. "From the Hytooth family in the Wollin."

"The Hytooths didn't send my father anything so fine on my birth," he retorted. "Not even a basket of seashells: trinkets the ocean provides them for free."

She set back down the box, closing it, and the tune ended. "They didn't need to win your father's favor. You were already allies."

He slid open her dressing table drawer, looking over the silver combs and jewelry boxes.

Bryn felt herself blushing. "Such finery feels frivolous now."

He lifted a crystal bottle of perfume to his nose, breathing in it. "I like seeing this side of you. Where you came from. You have no idea how, as a boy, I hungered for any scraps of information about your life. I would have traded a finger to have seen this bedroom. Touched your things." He set back down the perfume and turned to her. "Laid down in the bed you spent every night in."

She glanced at her four-post bed. Lisbeth had made it fresh that morning with crisp white sheets and a brocade bedspread. It was almost laughable how different it was from the humble bedroll she'd gotten used to at Barendur Hold.

She leaned back against the dressing table, lifting an eyebrow. "Perhaps you'd like to lie in it now?"

His eyes darkened as he closed the small space between them, running his hands through the hair at the back of her scalp. He murmured, "Only if you'll join me."

Bryn bit her lip as a thrill raced through her.

A devilish look crossed Rangar's face, and before she knew it, he'd thrown her over his shoulder.

"Hey!" she cried, teasingly pounding her fists into his back.

He carted her over to the door, which he kicked closed with one foot, and then tossed her on the bedspread like she weighed nothing more than a load of clothes.

She lifted herself to her elbows, giggling.

He shed his bearskin cloak, letting it fall to the floor, and then climbed on top of her. She fell back down, her head supported by the soft mattress like she was lying in the clouds.

His weight pinned her to the bed, sinking her further into the soft covers.

"I've never made love in a bed so fancy as this," he said as his gaze worshipped her lying beneath him.

She relaxed under his weight, running a light hand across her décolleté, where Trei and Valenden's rings hung on the gold chain around her neck—Rangar's engagement ring now permanently graced her finger.

"And I've never been ravished in one," she said.

He settled his mouth over hers, pushing his lips against hers in a soft stroke. Her body hummed with a wave of desire. She squirmed beneath him as her skin grew hot, and he responded by deepening the kiss.

She ran her hands up to his shirt collar, fumbling with the buttons. She'd gotten one taste of coupling with him in the secret passages, and she hadn't been able to think of much else since then but having him inside her again.

He chuckled as he pulled back, sitting up to tug his shirt over his head. "You're eager."

She painted her fingers across his chest's hexmark scars, wanting to trace every one of them. She anchored her hands on his hips, grinding her own upward.

"Is it so wrong I want you to take me on clean sheets for once?"

He reached for his belt with shadowed lust in his eyes. "You didn't like it when I kissed you senselessly on the forest floor? In the barn? In the dungeon?"

She tugged at his pants, anxious for him to shed his clothing. "Oh, I liked those, too. I'd like you to take me anywhere, Rangar Barendur."

He kicked off his pants, and then they were both fumbling with her buttons and laces, ready to feel one another's touch on bare skin. He shoved her clothes onto the floor, then dragged her down over the sheets to meet his hips.

She sucked in a breath. The space between her legs throbbed.

He leaned over her, supporting his weight with one arm while he ran his other hand down her soft inner thigh.

"You have no idea how many nights I dreamed of this." His voice was a growl. "Of you, naked and willing beneath me. Looking up at me with that same look you have now."

She bit her lip again. "And now you have me."

He fell on her with a moan, thrusting inside her wet heat. His eyes sank closed as his breath came ragged. He pulled out only to push into her even deeper.

Bryn's hands twisted in the sheets as her head fell back. Coupling with Rangar was like nothing she'd ever felt before. Both their scars were bared to each other. Their hexmarks. Their souls on full display, meeting in this feverish union.

He took her mouth in a heated kiss as his thrusts found a rhythm. Her hands cupped the swollen muscles of his shoulders, holding on as he rode her. His teeth nipped at her jaw. She clutched her fingers around his back, dragging her fingernails down his skin.

Rangar instinctively grabbed at her hips as his control was lost, pushing her harder into the mattress as his muscles shuddered.

A moan slipped out of Bryn's throat. Her fingernails carved deeper lines into his back. She was on the edge of losing control as well.

"I want to come inside you," Rangar breathed in her ear.

She knew the risks of such behavior. She could end up with his child in her, but his ring was already on her finger. They'd soon be married. The possibility of him impregnating her was hardly as scandalous as it once might have been.

"Do it."

He closed his eyes, fingers gripping her hips harder—

The door swung open.

Valenden stood there, the momentary shock on his face quickly giving way to a devilish smirk. "By the gods, Rangar, lock the door next time."

Rangar's muscles went rigid as he tossed his brother a scowl. "Get out, Val!"

Valenden had the grace to turn his head away, but he didn't leave. "I'm afraid it's urgent. You're needed immediately at the Little Table in the council chambers. Both of you."

Bryn was still breathless as she pulled the sheet up over them. Valenden might have little civility, but he wouldn't insist on interrupting them at such a delicate moment if it wasn't truly as important as he claimed.

Rangar looked down at her with a jaw hard with regret. "I'm going to throttle him. Can I throttle him?"

"You can't throttle your brother," she pointed out.

Valenden piped up, "I'm just the messenger, Rangar. Pull out your cock and come on." He finally closed the door, giving them a small amount of privacy.

Though Rangar was still hard, the romance had dissipated. A troubled look crossed his face as he broke away from her and started tugging back on his clothes.

Bryn sat up, readjusting her dress. "What do you think has happened that's so urgent?"

"Besides my brother ruining our pleasure?" He tossed her a frustrated look. "I don't know."

They finished dressing and quickly went out into the hall, heading for the council chambers. Rangar touched a hand to her back, leaning in to say quietly, "Don't get too relaxed, Bryn. I'm not finished with you. I fully intend on having you in that gilded bed, and then on that woven rug, and the hearth, and everywhere in this castle I can spread your legs."

Heat rushed to her face as they entered the council chambers.

Mars and Illiana stood near the head of the Little Table. Saraj waited by the window with Zephyr on her arm. Valenden sat at the table, smoking anxiously on a pipe. A letter rested in front of him.

Bryn swallowed, dreading what news they might have. So much tragedy had befallen her loved ones in the past few days. Aya had lost her falcon in the battle.

Calista, the mage apprentice, had died along with a dozen rebels and a half dozen Baer fighters. The Battle of Saint Serrel's shrine had been a bittersweet victory.

"Sit," Valenden said, motioning to the other chairs.

Bryn took a seat, but Rangar hovered behind her, his hands on the chair's back.

"It's a letter from home," Valenden explained. "Our father's illness has taken a turn for the worst. Mage Marna fears he might not have many days left. She urges us to return to the Baersladen immediately. Our return can't wait until after winter."

Bryn rested her hands on the Little Table, trying to steady her thoughts. "We made an oath to Mars and Illiana that we'd stay here to help with the transition. It's a dangerous time. There are plenty within the Mirien who still do not accept Mars as the crown prince. His upcoming wedding and coronation will be a turbulent time."

"Go to the Baersladen," Illiana insisted. "Christof and his rebel forces have the region under control. We are making headway convincing the common folk of Mars's devotion to them."

"But I can't give up my claim on the crown until after you wed," Bryn pointed out.

"We'll figure something out," Mars said.

Bryn twisted in her seat to peer up at Rangar. "It's your father. It's your decision."

"It's about more than my father," Rangar said gravely. "It's about the future of the Baersladen. You know as well as anyone that there are those who will see a monarch's illness as a sign of weakness. And we have our enemies both within and outside of the Baersladen. Broderick, the spy who killed Trei, is still on the loose. Anyone of us is in danger while he lives."

Rangar looked at his brother and Saraj. "What say you?"

Saraj informed them, "Aya and most of the other Baer people have already returned to the Baersladen. The few Baer fighters who remain in the Mirien wish to return immediately to guard the Hold."

Valenden nodded, stroking his chin. "We came to the aid of the Mirien, but now it is our own land that needs our attention."

Rangar rested a heavy hand on Bryn's shoulder. She covered his with her own, looking up at him.

"Agreed," Rangar said.

"I'm sorry," she whispered. "For your father's health."

King Aleth had been a powerful ruler. No one had dared to attempt to take the Baer crown from him in his lifetime. And no one had questioned that Trei would become a great ruler after him, but since Trei's death, there was only more opportunity for chaos.

Rangar stroked her cheek gently. "Did you mean it when you said the Baersladen is your home now?"

She didn't hesitate. "I did."

"Then we should start to ready your things and the horses. I'm taking you home, though I fear what we might find there."

Now it was time for Bryn to cast a long look

around the room at her friends and family. It might be a long time before she returned to see her brother again. She'd expected her return to the Baersladen to be one of triumph and joy as she planned her wedding to Rangar—but now a toothy shadow darkened the prospect.

An ill king, a throne in jeopardy, enemies at the gate: their return would be a dangerous one.

"Let's go," she said firmly.

~

What secrets will Bryn and Rangar uncover when they return to the Baersladen? *Find out in Scarcrossed!*

~

To claim your Scarlight bonus scenes, join my author mailing list!

A NOTE FROM EVIE

Dear Reader,

Thank you for reading the second book in the Castles of the Eyrie series. I loved every minute of writing the forbidden romance between Bryn and Rangar, and I can't wait for you to discover what happens next.

Was this a 3, 4, or 5 star read for you? If you enjoyed this book, help fellow readers discover their next binge-worthy read by leaving a rating!

xo,
   Evie

About the Author

Evie Marceau writes fantasies to satisfy her nagging curiosity that there is more out there just beyond the veil. She is the author of romantic fantasies with a touch of darkness and hint of magic.

www.eviemarceau.com

Join Evie's FB Reader Group! https://www.facebook.com/groups/344599161310206

www.eviemarceau.com/newsletter
(PS: get exclusive bonus scenes when you join!)

www.ingramcontent.com/pod-product-compliance
Lightning Source LLC
Chambersburg PA
CBHW061046310726
48969CB00004B/1107